WALKING GREENBUSH

WALKING GREENBUSH

A Novel

Philip A. Fortnam

iUniverse, Inc.
New York Lincoln Shanghai

WALKING GREENBUSH

iUniverse books may be ordered through booksellers or by contacting:

iUniverse
2021 Pine Lake Road, Suite 100
Lincoln, NE 68512
www.iuniverse.com
1-800-Authors (1-800-288-4677)

Because of the dynamic nature of the Internet, any Web addresses or links contained in this book may have changed since publication and may no longer be valid.

This is a work of fiction. All of the characters, names, incidents, organizations, and dialogue in this novel are either the products of the author's imagination or are used fictitiously.

The author photo is credited to Bill Lax.

The cover design by Dave Woodruff.

ISBN: 978-0-595-42338-5 (pbk)
ISBN: 978-0-595-86677-9 (ebk)

Printed in the United States of America

This book is dedicated to my mother and father
with honor, appreciation, respect, and love.

I appreciate all the help and motivation that came from my family and friends, all of whom took the time to read the early first drafts and offer suggestions. In particular, the first editor, my wife Annie, my brothers Daniel, Michael, and James; friends Gary Lesser, Bill Lax, Gael Rene, Suki Edwards, Norm Bizon, and my sister-in-law Anne Torza. Thanks to Tim Gorey for explaining geological stuff to me, Dr. Kelly, D.M.D. and his staff for some character insight, Mark Harper for web help, and Vicky Campo for her careful and encouraging editing.

Thank you Nanci for helping me make my path easier to walk, therefore, this piece possible, and D.W.W., your influence on me was profound and greater than you'll ever know. Harold Loud, I am glad to have met you.

Lastly, my daughters Kelsey and Katie, and my pride and joy; Daddy-hood suits me well thanks to you two. God blessed me with you.

PROLOGUE

▼

AM RADIO

If I understood Spanish at all I could tell you where the Spanish language radio station at 820 AM originated. I thought I heard the announcer say San Luis and Yuma a couple times as I drove, but it was in the middle of a burst of cincos, quartos, and ochos, so I'm not sure. Regardless of the language, what I am sure of is, the selection and sequence of songs that night demanded acknowledgment of places, people, and feelings I thought I had buried more than twenty years ago when I fled Weymouth.

As the music played, it seemed as though I was invisible and had an omniscient overhead point of view. While the signal was strong and the music clear I felt vigorous, virile, and vibrant, easy dizzy, slightly drunk, and numb. Comfortably numb, like a high school junior who compounds the three nips of Jack Daniels he drank, plus the other four he shared with his girlfriend, with a Friday night joint reputed to be Columbian Gold.

Then, like waking up during a dream, when real sounds are absorbed into the nebulous world between dream, sleep, and awake, at the first beat of one particular song that may have come from my car radio or from the stereo playing in the fantasy, I saw the boy, his best guy friend, and his closet female friend run toward the living room where the stereo was. The girl got there first. She turned the music up louder. They threw their arms around each other's shoulders, and made an impenetrable circle. They danced in the circle and sang the song as loud as they could. Then, at the final refrain of, "Thank you for being a friend," they collapsed into each other, onto the pile of parkas, and cemented their adolescent bond.

The music in my car that night mysteriously spun me back to that familiar and slightly disconcerting place with vivid and precise memory, and tangible feelings.

That night was also the final episode in a series of events I only now recognize as destiny.

It was not as though I'd not heard those songs other times over the previous twenty years, but that late desert afternoon near Jacumba, California those songs resonated in a different lobe. The difference lay with the sequence, the drive, the place I stopped, and the specific memories each song dredged up. The memories were ones I usually keep out. Or perhaps better said, I keep in.

The DJ that night might have been advertising a hardware store in San Luis or the phone number for an immigration specialist attorney, but soon enough he stopped talking and played a fateful string of songs that unlocked a cerebral dungeon I didn't even know held me.

FM radio vanished into the desert air somewhere westbound between El Centro and Ocotillo. When I reached that point in the road where FM ended and the tire noise and the whistle made by the worn window weather stripping was not enough to cover the aloneness of a three times divorced, over employed, middle age man, I went AM. I couldn't even find the band select switch at first. It had been years since I listened to AM. The last time I went AM I found too many blathering, callous talk-show hosts, and way too many commercials. It was too conservative and had too much religious programming for my tastes.

The seek button on the radio looped the AM band 520 to 1710 three times before I let it set on 820. Those songs, released from some time capsule secreted in the strata over of Interstate 8 in California, sounded tinny like the transistor radio earplugs that preceded the Walkman. The DJ, too, in Spanish, sounded as though he was stuck around 1970 on WRKO 680 AM in Boston.

It was time travel. Who'd a thought it possible in a Nissan.

I sped off the interstate at the Jacumba exit, turned where it said Railroad Street, and sat on a rail listening to the radio and more of its poignant selection of songs as a late flash of sun burst through the clouds on its way to setting. The depot stood still, three old Southern Pacific coaches were up on blocks next to the tracks, and some old locked sheds next to the tracks held secrets I wanted to know. I spent hours there within a one hundred yard radius of the station. I walked the tracks only as far the sign that read, "Tracks Out Of Service." It was desolate enough that I heard the car radio the whole time I walked. The radio shoved the music into my head and unwillingly I thought more of the friends and bastards connected to those songs. I knew every word from the first beat of the music.

After midnight, I resumed my drive west, away from Jacumba. I held eighty miles an hour over most of the rest of Route 94. The road became slicker, more winding, and narrower. Not one set of headlights pounced on me there that night.

It was AM radio so there wasn't the fidelity or stability of an FM signal. The music crackled, faded, and surged. My car, at the time, was a Nissan Sentra. It didn't have fidelity or stability either. The tired shock absorbers made my car pitch and yaw over every crack in the concrete, but it stayed in the lane. It slid toward the shoulder on several of the curves and the rear end fishtailed on the gravel close to the guardrail. I never let up on the gas and it righted itself each time.

When the music ceased and the only sound was the transmitter noise, I stopped. The sign at the place I stopped read, "Dog Patch." The little dale I found myself in could have been anywhere in New England. The moisture broke smells out of the tall grass and soil, and somebody had set the boulders to form a stonewall. The sky cleared during the night. The stars remained out of touch. I stayed until dawn.

Throughout the night I didn't have one complete thought. Whatever dam broke sent the neurons and synapses of my memory tumbling uncontrollably.

The music that night might have been the result of one of the odd moments when a radio signal hits some cosmic disturbance and bounces out into space then hits another piece of cosmic debris and bounces back to earth years later. Whatever it was, its aggregate was more powerful than any remedy I'd previously tried; anti-depressants, alcohol, overwork, wealth, therapy or physical conquest. It was simply AM radio, in the car at the right time, late at night on the right stretch of highway with the right songs. It was a time machine powerful enough to stop a Nissan, send a grown man out under the stars, and drop him to the chilly March mountain floor with the realization he has unfinished business three thousand miles away, and acknowledgment that a murder witnessed and another murder left undone might be part of the unfinished work.

Alone is a familiar and safe place for me. I dodge fret and regret easily, but that night I was isolated and deeply feeling my friends, the verve, and the very earth of my life twenty-five years earlier. I was lonely, melancholy, and bewildered, but this time the path that got me to this point in my life lay, finally, open to inspection.

And then, there, for the first time ever I did know what to do with myself.

I had to walk Greenbush.

CHAPTER 1

▼

PAROXYSM

I hated Weymouth.

I hated everything about it, but if I was going to walk Greenbush I was going to have step foot in Weymouth, again. Something I had sworn I would never do.

Greenbush came back into my thoughts about two years earlier. An article in the paper reported about the problems the community was having agreeing to a plan to redevelop McClellan Air Force Base. The article listed other closed military bases around the country where there was a lack of community consensus for redevelopment plans, including Naval Air Station South Weymouth.

That article was the first time I had seen or heard any reference to Weymouth in years. I surfed the web looking for more information on NAS South Weymouth and stumbled across a link that took me to a page that said the MBTA was going to restore the Greenbush Branch of the Old Colony Division to passenger service. With a few more clicks I discovered the T had already restored passenger service on two of the other idle, south of Boston railroad lines that once belonged to the Old Colony Division of the New York, New Haven & Hartford Railroad.

I was surprised. I thought those lines were dead, the right of way acquired, and the subsequent development obliterated all indications of there ever having been railroad service on the South Shore.

My home was in San Francisco, three thousand miles away from where I grew up. I acknowledged very little memory of or connection to Weymouth since I left. I searched the web until three o'clock in the morning and discovered all kinds of change had indeed happened in Weymouth. What surprised me most was the fact that there had been change there at all. Its buildings, roads, and its geographical countenance had not changed, but another iteration of its suburban face had materialized. It rolled on with new players and different children in a very familiar setting.

Since I left Weymouth had changed its incorporation from a town to a city. One of its two high schools and two of its four junior high schools closed. East Junior High School changed it name to Abigail Adams Middle School and a new high school opened. Passenger rail service had already returned to the Plymouth Line that ran through South Weymouth. There were efforts to expand some parks and preserve the few undeveloped acres that remained in the city. I was sure the look and tenor of the town was the same as it was when I lived there, but maybe the tone of Weymouth had changed. I certainly had changed.

My life lay beyond Weymouth's boundaries. I knew that about myself young. I left as soon as I could. I tried college in Boston. After a year and half I knew it wasn't for me. A little more than two years after I graduated high school I left for the Navy. After my hitch in the Navy was over, I stayed away. I forced my connections to Weymouth to wilt and die.

Two of my three lingering thread-thin connections broke before I was thirty. The first when Kelli, my best female friend died. She saved my life and I regret not seeing her while she was sick. I made it to her funeral, though.

The second connection severed when Danny, my best guy friend growing up, got tired of his unreciprocated friendship efforts.

Danny and I maintained a slight connection while we were in college and when I left for the service, but that, too, ultimately wilted and died. I let it die. Danny tried to stay in touch in the most minimal way, Christmas cards, but after a few years of my not responding he included a note in his last card to me. He wrote, "Marty, friendship is a two way street." I meant to stop by a store and send him a funny card to let him know that I thought of him, but I never did.

The one meager, abstruse connection I kept to Weymouth laid with Harold Asher. Harold was an old, never-married, misanthrope living in the same house in which he was born. Beginning the year I left for the Navy and every year following I sent him a Christmas card. I never received one in return, but as long as the card didn't come back to me stamped, Undeliverable. Return to Sender, I assumed he was still alive.

Harold worked for the railroad in Weymouth on the Greenbush line. We met because my parents and most of our family friends knew I liked trains and, in particular, the Greenbush line. I had been brought home by the police several times for hopping trains and trespassing in the old, abandoned stations that remained along the line. A woman Danny's mother knew worked with a lady who lived near Harold. She described Harold as, "The crabby old man who lived in the house that was falling down." She knew he once worked for the railroad in Weymouth. I was curious to meet him so I volunteered to go to his house and mow his lawn. What I thought would be a one-shot gesture turned into three-and-a-half years of cutting his grass, shoveling snow from his walkway, and significant maintenance and repair work to his house.

Once I left, one thing lead to another, and the longer I stayed away the more certain I became that vigor, vibrancy, color, and light lay anywhere but in New England. I went to boot camp in Illinois and transferred to the West Coast with the Navy. Once there I stayed. After the Navy I worked as a photographer and completed my degree. When my time as a photographer ended, I took another job and was quickly immersed in one of the high tech, high-pressure computer companies on the West Coast. There, smugly ensconced in California, I disdained my middle of middle class East Coast upbringing deeply. I distanced myself from it as much as possible. I had left everything I could behind me, arrived in California, and remade myself. I went to a hair stylist instead of a barber. No more Levi dungarees, Calvin Klein jeans for me. I drank wine instead of beer and got my buzz from cocaine instead of pot. I thought if I acted Weymouth, I would remain Weymouth.

As far as I was concerned Weymouth couldn't evolve. The people there, unwilling to evolve. In my mind, Weymouth was as far from urbane as possible. I thought the Birches and Lake Street Projects were undoubtedly still scummy, East Weymouth typically and predictably suburban, North Weymouth dingy, South Weymouth boring, and Weymouth Landing inconsequential.

There was no question that over the years the whole town had gone the way of Wal-Mart; vulgar people with rotten teeth, rusty old cars, and sullen winters with dirty snow. Instead of eagles soaring in the skies over Weymouth, pigeons shit everywhere. In the summer, dandelions grew instead of flowers.

I didn't recall any one particular overwhelming reason to think that way, but I did.

Every once in a while the remnants of my Boston accent surfaced and I was asked where I grew up. I dismissed the question with a vague, bitter, contempt-filled reference to a dull, white, suburban town back East. There was so much venom in my response that no one ever pressed me for more detail.

After Greenbush reemerged in my life, I recalled the trains I hopped, what I saw along the line, and the adventures in the places near the tracks. I thought about Harold and the color and detail he added to what I knew about Greenbush. I found the old photos of Greenbush he had given me. There were shots of the stations, the trains, and the railroad men at work. I looked at them many times over those two pensive years. I started to wonder what parts of me were shaped by Greenbush, and the greater influence of Weymouth and the South Shore. Then, of all the unlikely things that could happen to me, the most unbelievable was – I got introspective.

I tried to talk with my new live-in girlfriend about my friends and experiences growing up there. She was too stressed out by work during the day and absorbed by television at night to listen to me. I stopped trying to talk with her about it.

When I sent Harold his Christmas card that year I put a little note with it saying how I read about the Greenbush restoration project and hoped he was well.

The Greenbush restoration project grew to be the only reason I could reconcile to myself to take a trip to Massachusetts. Its imminent resurrection triggered a longing to see Greenbush and its corridor through the South Shore, again, as I knew it. I wished there was a way I could do that without passing through East Weymouth, but that was impossible. The two were inextricably intertwined.

There was no way I could look at Greenbush and East Weymouth as an adult from behind a windshield; analyzing it's intersections, school systems, and property values. I needed to revisit it as an adult with the knowledge of a native, someone who knew its shortcuts and secrets, as someone who lived its complex character under its predictably suburban veneer. I wanted to see what it looked like. I wanted to feel what it felt like, again.

And I fought feeling all that. It was foolish sentimentality, I told myself. It seemed like a Southern or Mid-Western thing to do, walk abandoned railroad tracks. It was hardly a characteristic of dour, old New England and stuffy, bland, suburban Boston. Worse it seemed like a trendy, self-help therapy thing – closure. There would be nothing new for me to see in Weymouth, but a boring, white, middle-class suburb. I already knew all about that.

But, and in spite of my effort trying to force myself out of feeling anything about my upbringing, and after all the years of distancing myself from that place, I wondered the purpose of that place and why was I being drawn to it. I didn't like the connection I had to Weymouth. There were some rough experiences there. I forgot there were good experiences, too.

Five months after my fateful drive on California's Route 94 I acted on my decision to make a pilgrimage, of sorts, to East Weymouth, Greenbush, and the South Shore. Something compelled me to want to understand better how it shaped me and what I took from that place. I needed to authenticate the places, people, and events that connected me to the rocky soil of the South Shore. I would walk around East Weymouth and see the banal things that illustrated the postcards of my youth, then walk and photograph Greenbush end to end. I wanted to hop one more train, as it were, before the line was fenced, scheduled, and patrolled.

The last passenger train on Greenbush ran in 1959. The last freight train went to Hingham in 1985. By walking the tracks before its rebirth I was sure to be the last person to see the hidden spectacularness of Greenbush. The engineers and construction workers would see it as a paycheck and a project. The not-in-my-backyard protesters saw the idle line as a little more property they could grab and the active line as a threat to their property's value. The transportation planners looked at it as a way to get a few more cars off the roads. Everyone looked at it differently. Everyone had something to say about it, but no one saw it as I did. No one could speak about it as I could.

With the construction scheduled to begin in the spring of the following year I had a little time before it started. My girlfriend thought I was having a mid-life crisis in my late thirties. It was very much out of my character to spend the money, take the time off of work, and frivolously pursue something with no significance, purpose or connection to my career or the friends I had around California, but I was bound to do it.

The answer to the question that had disturbed my homeostasis for the last two years lingered in East Weymouth. That much I knew. Walking Greenbush might be the treatment for that imbalance.

I set my plans. I would go in October, bring a camera, a notebook, and walk. I'd start in East Weymouth, get up to Braintree then go the whole length of the line finishing up in the Greenbush section of Scituate at the North River. I'd travel three thousand miles to walk three miles around East Weymouth and seventeen miles of abandoned railroad tracks. I planned to do this over a long weekend; fly San Francisco to Boston on Friday, spend the night in Boston, walk all day Saturday, maneuver back to Logan Airport on Sunday morning, and be back in California Sunday night. Then, depending on how I felt, I'd go into work late on Monday morning.

I mapped my route to take advantage of public transportation. I confirmed the MBTA's bus route 222 still terminated in Jackson Square. I would begin there; I'd walk the sidewalks of East Weymouth. I'd go out to the Back River. I'd stand on the old East Weymouth station passenger-loading platform. I'd walk by the town hall, Legion Field, and along Gilbert Road. I'd pass the Vincent Gorman memorial at the intersection of Middle and Commercial Streets and wonder once again what happened that earned him a memorial intersection. I'd continue down King Oak Hill and out of East Weymouth into Weymouth Landing. Catch a bus back to Quincy and take the subway to Boston then walk through the woods and over the abandoned sidings, rusted tracks, and empty rail bed all the way down to Scituate. The walk would take me through twenty or so different villages; there would be ample opportunity for food and water, so I didn't need to carry that.

In October the trees would be turning color and the light pretty. The fallen gold, red, green and brown oak and maple leaves would soften my steps. I remembered the mosquitoes. If it were summer there would be plenty of them lurking in the swamps and drainage ditches along the tracks, but with the cooler temperature the bugs would be at a minimum.

I thought I'd blast through East Weymouth in an hour or two then have another hour of moving on public transportation to the beginning of Greenbush and the walk. I could probably do it all in one long day. It would be a push and tiring with the unnatural stride of short-stepping railroad tie to railroad tie or over stepping tie to second tie. I anticipated being in Cohasset by late Saturday afternoon. Since this was a personal pilgrimage of sorts, I decided that I shouldn't rush myself. I reserved a room in Cohasset for Saturday night; I'd finish the last few miles Sunday morning.

At one time, Greenbush extended past Scituate all the way down through Marshfield and Duxbury, it rejoined the Plymouth line in Kingston, but since before World War II it had terminated in Scituate. I'd stop there. I had my cell phone. I'd take a taxi back to Braintree, get on the subway, and connect back to Logan.

Every moment was full, scheduled tight. I made it so. That way I wouldn't have to face the crush of, "I should do this," and, "I ought to do that." If I stuck to my schedule, even in the aloneness of the trip, I could still keep myself busy. But as I concluded my plan and schedule one particular thought came to me. It came to me like a cold spring's plume grabs your attention as you swim in a pond, I should visit my mother's grave. I'd been there twice, the first time at her funeral and then several months later, January 30th, when I considered my first serious run-away-from-home plan. I promised her then I'd come back someday.

A promise to dead person was nonsense, I told myself, but I did want to pay my respects.

CHAPTER 2

▼

WHITE STEEPLES

My second to last trip to New England was fifteen years ago, with my second wife. We were a perfect match, until we got divorced. Neither of us had a strong connection to our families or the place of our origins. She was an Indian who wanted to get away from the bleak life, dismal employment prospects, and alcohol problems of reservation life. I too had moved on. I was done with Weymouth, the South Shore, Massachusetts, New England, and the whole East Coast.

Soon after we completed our civil service wedding with the judge, she took me on an obligatory trip to see the reservation were she grew up in New Mexico. She felt I should at least see what it was she left. It was a hard trip for her. The listlessness of the reservation made her cry most of trip. We ended our trip early. We didn't visit any of her relatives while we were there. On a business trip to Boston a few months later I took her to Weymouth, the South Shore, and around New England to show her what I left. We didn't visit anyone I knew, either.

I gave her a tourist's tour of New England, the post card stuff. I showed her the white steeples, old cemeteries, and apple orchards. Through the windshield she saw the stonewalls, foliage, trees, and fields, the stuff and sentiment of Robert Frost's New England. We spent a week racing through New England, hardly stepping out of the car except to eat and sleep. I showed her a piece of the Maine coast, the White Mountains of New Hampshire, Lake Champlain in Vermont; Boston; Cape Cod; Newport, Rhode Island, and Mystic, Connecticut. The only place she expressed curiosity about was Salem. She wanted to decide for herself if the witch burnings were real.

She saw lobster boats and tourist windjammers. She had fried clams in Provincetown and didn't like them. I drove her past the house I grew up in and my high school. I pointed out the only remotely interesting thing about Weymouth, Abigail Adams' birthplace. Like everyone else in North America, she thought New England was pretty and steeped in history, but we had made our life elsewhere and wanted to get back there.

As we drove around on that visit I saw Weymouth and the South Shore as dross, stagnant, and as old as I saw it when I left. I felt nauseous there. Compared to the vibrancy I felt on the West Coast, Weymouth was moribund. I affirmed that I had made the right decision when I long ago left Weymouth behind. If on that trip I had had a warm thought of Weymouth, there was too much poison in my hate-filled heart for it to survive.

She asked me during the trip, "Do you ever want to live back here again?"

"No, never," I said. "I have no reason to ever come here again, except, maybe, to bury my old man or a business trip." I buried my father a few months after I made that prophetic statement.

There was no sentimental, nostalgic draw to Weymouth. If she and I decided to have kids, and that was very unlikely, I didn't see a Cape Cod vacation or an East Coast college for my children. There was Disneyland, Stanford, and the whole Western United States to explore.

My last trip to Weymouth, to bury my father, lasted two weeks. Only one of my brothers and I buried our father. My other brother didn't bother showing up for the funeral. I relinquished my claim to any of my father's meager estate to my brother. He was in and out of rehab in Texas and needed the money more than I did.

Jeff, my youngest brother, told me there were three boxes in the cellar that had my name on them. He had them delivered to me at the motel. I didn't open them. Before I got in the taxi to go back to the airport, I found a dumpster and threw them away.

Good riddance Weymouth.

CHAPTER 3

▼

WEYMOUTH
HEIGHTS

After I set my plans, I started looking forward to my walk very much. Not only for the sentimental journey, but because of the one idiosyncrasy I allowed myself to take from Weymouth; I let myself enjoy idle and abandoned railroad tracks wherever I am. I'm not a goofy railfan; an FRN I've heard them described, fucking rail nut. I simply enjoy the solace and serendipity I find near abandoned, idle, and infrequently used railroad tracks.

Whether it's West LA; Detroit; Gulfport, Mississippi; Canova, South Dakota or Randolph, New Hampshire, urban, suburban or rural, inactive railroad tracks give me a kind of sanctuary that a corner park doesn't. Maybe it's the order of the ties or the precision of the distance between the rails. I like the level of quiet there. Weeds and brush along the bed muffle the sounds of cars and trucks, even alongside the busiest California freeway. I used to think the rusted rails and wooden ties longed to feel the roll of train traffic again. It was oddly exciting to think Greenbush would feel the weight of purpose again.

Since I was in the position to make it so, at one of my jobs, I very specifically sought office space that bordered a lightly used freight train line. It was an old warehouse. I had the interior modified into office space and the exterior restored. I bought three old boxcars for excess office and building equipment storage and had them parked on the old siding that ran to the building. I had the building maintenance people build me a stairway from my office down to the tracks. I tried to purchase an old caboose and old passenger car and justify it as a break or meeting room. I was overridden on that decision. So I bought my own caboose that sits on a siding in Canaan, Connecticut. Someday I'll figure out how to use it.

In the most difficult personal times or during stressful periods at work I can step onto the old rail bed and find instant calm. It's almost as though the rail bed makes a path out of that place I'm in.

Over all the years that I've wandered abandoned railroad tracks, I've only run into trouble a few times. I was mugged once. I walked along some tracks lost in my daydreams and ran into a fence the city had put up to keep the homeless from living in a tunnel that went under the freeway. I failed to pay attention to the fact that someone had been following me. I was trapped. I got my head smacked with a rock and my wallet stolen.

I didn't anticipate any kind of problem when I walked Greenbush. The only people I might encounter would be young boys exploring and walkers seeking an out-of-the-way place for their constitutionals and dogs. I could be there completely unnoticed.

I did however, contact Harold. I wrote him a note saying I was going to walk Greenbush and asked, when I passed by his house, would it be okay if I stopped in and said hello.

About a week before the trip I received a personal, first class letter. The return address wasn't legible, but the hand-cancelled postmark read, "WEYMOUTH 02188," and the date.

When I opened the letter, I could barley decipher the handwriting. After studying it for a few moments I realized it was from Harold. He told me to be at his house at ten o'clock in the morning on Saturday, October 12.

I had a pleasant feeling when I figured out the letter was from Harold. After I read it, the warm fuzzy feeling waned and a slight nervousness passed through me. It was the same old feeling I had when I worked for Harold. Even though I grew to understand him, I always got a little nervous as I approached his house. It was that feeling all over again. I'd be glad to see him and wondered what was in store for me.

When the day came I took a cab to the airport, then a non-stop flight, first class, all the way to Boston. We approached Logan Airport from the south. I easily spotted some landmarks that had not changed; the crane at the shutdown Quincy Shipyard, Weymouth Port Condominiums, the runway at the abandoned NAS South Weymouth, and the old warehouses at the Hingham Shipyard. The geographical landmarks were unaltered, too; the Back River, the Boston Harbor Islands, and Hull Gut were exactly the same as when I left. Even though I had never flown over the South Shore the entire time I lived there, it was easy to flip the ground level perspective I had to an aerial point of view.

I spent Friday night at the Four Seasons Hotel in Boston. Very early Saturday morning I embarked on the subways and buses and planned to terminate with Massachusetts Bay Transportation Authority's bus route 222 in Jackson Square; East Weymouth, Massachusetts. Instead, spontaneously, I got off the bus as close as I could to the Old North Cemetery in Weymouth.

The sun wasn't up, but the predawn gray was diluting. As I stepped off the bus and onto Weymouth's soil for the first time in years I hesitated. I had every right to be there, but my feet lagged behind my head. I nearly stumbled. It was as though some bramble snared my lower legs. I had to tug my feet to break the hold and then it was okay. I walked straight to my mother's grave. It was unkempt. The town mowed the grass, but there were no flowers there. The grass grew around the base of the headstone where the mower didn't cut close enough. It didn't seem right that a weed-whacker should be used to trim the grass there. I pulled them by hand. I spoke to my mother, silently at first. In my head I said, 'Hi, I'm sorry I haven't visited more often. I hope you can forgive me.' Then, out loud I said, "It hasn't been easy without you." I couldn't come up with anything else to say.

I usually have some thought, some situation, something running through my brain. Following numerous admonitions to chill out, I took some self-relaxation classes. However, in spite of the classes on how to meditate and clear my thoughts, I still am always busy in my head, but, there, I found the clearing-of-the-mind gurus seek. For many moments at my mother's grave my head was quiet for the first time in my life. Then it passed. Although cemeteries are usually quiet, even when they run up against busy streets, a dump truck with a busted muffler is quite capable of shattering even the most profound quiet.

"Well Mom. I'll get some flowers here," I said. I turned to leave. When I got to the end of the road I looked back and added, "I'll be back. I promise."

There was no point to waiting for the next bus to take me to Jackson Square. I could walk it in less than a half an hour. I could have detoured there and gone straight to Harold's, but I still wanted to begin my pilgrimage at Jackson Square as I had planned. I walked under the North Street railroad bridge. In a few hours I'd be on the bridge, walking Greenbush. I headed toward Commercial Street and up King Oak Hill.

My last thought, before my mind was run over by a memory, was wondering if the florist in Central Square was still in business. If it were, I'd have them bring flowers to her grave once a month. I certainly could afford it.

CHAPTER 4

▼

HAROLD ASHER

Harold worked as a crossing guard for the New York, New Haven & Hartford Railroad in Weymouth from 1939, cranking the crossing gates up and down until the railroad installed lights and automated the Tufts crossing in 1953. He started working for the railroad underage when his father got him the job. He retired in 1953 and had been collecting pension ever since. He lived next to the tracks up-hill from the Commercial Street crossing outside of Weymouth Landing. His house looked out over the tracks where it passed Rhines Lumber Company and bent into a cut through glacial moraine that littered Weymouth.

He had a great view of Braintree Bay near where the Town River emptied into the Fore River. I was fixing the railing on his front porch one day and turned around and saw the gorgeous view. He could see all the way across the basin and into the bay. He could see the freighter and tanker activity, shipyard activity, and pleasure boats on the water. His crummy little place had one of the best views in town and no one knew it. No one dared go close enough to him to see the view.

The first time I went to his house to cut the grass, it was about two feet high. As I stepped onto his front porch to ring the doorbell and some of the floorboards broke. It was probably the first time anyone had been on the front porch in twenty years.

"What?" he said as he opened the door.

I was taken back by his immediate brusqueness. I said, "I'm here to mow your grass, Sir."

"Back door," he said with flip of his arm toward the back of the house. He moved to close the door.

"Mr. Asher, the wood on the porch cracked when I stepped on it."

"Damn you," he said as came out the door, swearing more.

I thought he was going to hit me; self-preservation kicked in. I nearly fell backwards off the porch, pulling back, trying to get away from him quickly.

He looked at the cracked planking then rotated his head toward me.

"You fix the porch, boy," he said, glaring from under his overgrown mono-brow and rutted forehead.

"I'm sorry," I stammered. I was overwhelmed by his intensity. I felt as though I had destroyed his house and I had to rebuild it before he would forgive me.

He met me at the back of his house and showed me where he had some scrap wood. He gave me a dull saw, a hammer, and some nails that looked like they had been already used once, pulled out, and banged straight again.

As I replaced the floorboards I saw most of the rest of the planking on the porch and the beams supporting the porch were rotted, too. I went around back to tell him what I saw.

He said, "You can fix that later."

Later, I didn't know what he meant. All I wanted to do was cut the grass and get out of there.

Not knowing if Harold had a mower or not, I had pushed my father's mower all the way from my house to Harold's house. I went to the mower and pulled on the cord to start it. When it sputtered to life the back door swung open and Harold burst out and came at me swinging his cane as though he was going to hit me, again. I put the mower between Harold and me like it was a matador's cape.

"Shut that damn fool contraption off," Harold bellowed over the motor noise.

I did, but I kept the mower between the two of us.

"Don't use a power mower on grass this tall. You'll kill it," he said. "There's a scythe and a sickle and push mower in the garage. Use them." With that he turned and went back in the house. The door closed with a weak thud, but the deadbolt being set in place sounded very certain.

I went to the garage and looked around for something that said scythe and sickle. I didn't know what they looked like. Eventually I gave up and went and knocked on his door.

He didn't open the door. He pushed the tattered curtain to the side and stared at me through the grimy glass window.

"Mr. Asher, I don't know what a scythe and sickle look like."

From behind the locked door he mumbled something about me being a friggin' moron. He disappeared for several minutes then opened the door. He came out, locked it behind him, walked to the shed, and showed me the tools.

"If you're going to work for me, boy, you're not to go into the house. If you have to go the bathroom go before you get here or use the bushes. If you want water use the spigot." He left and locked himself back in the house.

He watched me from the windows. It wouldn't surprise me at all if he had a blunderbuss pointed at me the whole time I was there.

There were weeds, briars, bramble, wild raspberries and rhubarb, saplings, weeds, rocks, and a tiny patch of actual grass on his property. The blade on the sy was dull when I started and soon had deep pits on it from all the rocks I hit. I had to knock on his back door again. I told him about the dulled blade. He mumbled something and came outside. I noticed he locked the door to his house with a large worn skeleton key he kept tethered to himself. He took me into the garage and showed me a whetstone I was to use to sharpen the blade.

"Come here, boy."

I shuffled a couple feet closer to him.

"Take a good look at the blade." He held it up toward the window, closed one eye and tipped the blade to catch the light. He lowered it and ran his thumb down the honed edge then passed it me. "You see how it looks now."

I held it up toward the light, closed one eye, and looked down the cutting edge line. I really didn't see anything. I lowered the blade and ran my thumb along the edge then passed it back to him and said, "Sure is dull."

"You got some spit, boy?"

I didn't know what he was asking so I responded, "No thanks I'm not thirsty."

He looked at me and I knew I answered wrong. "Like this, boy." He dribbled a big glob of spit on to the stone; with a couple dozen quick strokes the blade was sharp. He held it up to the light again, ran his thumb with the angle of the cut, and passed it to me. "You sharpen the sickle."

I spit. I stroked. It worked quickly and easily on the blade. Until then I thought lawn mower blades, knives, scissors, saws, and the likes had to be taken to a specialist to be sharpened. Since that day with Harold, I have never paid to have a tool sharpened.

After I sharpened the blade and started cutting again he came outside a couple times and gave me homemade lemonade and, alternately, eggnog, then went back inside to monitor my progress. He'd make some comment about the poor job I was doing and lock himself back in the house. The drinks were really good.

My first time there I fixed the step and mowed the grass, and I was mad. I cussed the whole time I pushed his crappy old mower through the jungle that was his yard. I swore I was never going back to help the miserable old ingrate ever again. It was hot and humid. I was cut by thorns and stung regularly while he glowered at me from behind the kitchen window. I stirred up mosquitoes, disturbed a beehive, and ultimately got a terrible poison ivy rash around my ankles and calves.

When I was done, I put the tools away and left without saying anything. Screw getting paid, it wasn't worth it to have to deal with him a minute more. I wasn't going back. I got about halfway down the hill when he called out to me.

"Boy! Do you want your money!"

I turned back and stared at him. I waved him off.

"Come here!" he ordered. He gave me ten nineteenth century silver dollars, homemade cherry soda, and the old handle he used to crank the crossing gate up and down.

"Come back next week."

I did.

CHAPTER 5

▼

TERRA FIRMA

At first I'd tell Harold I'd show up on a certain day. He'd say ten o'clock and I say sure and show up whenever I wanted. That didn't work for Harold. He insisted on punctuality. It was almost as though he was cranking the gate for the trains again. After being lambasted a few times for not showing up when I said I would our ritual evolved. After that, when I opened the gate to his property, he would step through his doorway. He looked at his watch and nodded toward me as I greeted him. If I didn't show up on time I got a lecture on the necessity and courtesy of punctuality. His financial generosity failed on those days, but his lectures worked on me. To this day I am precise, anal, my friends, wives, and employees have said, about punctuality.

He took a lot of getting used to. He looked older than God. He wore wide suspenders that held up old gray woolen pants. His pants swelled at the waist. I wondered if he wrapped a towel around his groin for padding or the disgusting thought of absorption. He had pince-nez glasses, three variations of flannel shirts, and slippers. He had a powerful voice. When he spoke he yelled. He always sounded angry. His comments had the subtlety of a shark attack. His words came out like cannon shot. When he stood on his porch and surveyed his domain, he looked like a general or land baron planning his next maneuver. He showed more vigor and strength than most of the middle-age men I knew.

According to Harold, it was wrong for a woman to wear pants and it was almost a sin for a woman to drive a car. There were only two acceptable occupations for women, nursing and teaching. He was beside himself the day he saw a woman driving a MBTA bus wearing a pantsuit uniform. I expected him to be prejudiced and bigoted toward other races, but he wasn't. Some of his thinking was generational, meaning the different races kept to themselves, but he showed no bigotry, no hatred, and no scorn.

He insisted I work for three hours, stop for a fifteen-minute break then resume my task. He wasn't concerned about the volume or pace of work. He did, however, worship ritual; even our greeting was ritualized.

"What are you here to steal today, boy," he asked when I showed up.

"Whatever you didn't have under lock and key," I'd respond.

I teased him about being old and ugly, his body odor, the sounds that emanated from him, and having the vilest flatulence ever. He smirked, but rarely let out a laugh. Occasionally he would get a good dig in on me. He was very pleased with himself when he did that.

He was a belligerent, iconoclastic curmudgeon and I came to completely enjoy being around someone with that much personality. He called me boy and, at first, considered me a punk, a hoodlum, and there only to steal his stuff. I addressed him as an old fart and said he might look less like Grendel if he trimmed his nose hairs. He didn't know who Grendel was. I did. It made me feel superior.

Throughout the summer and into the fall I worked replacing the rest of the wood planking, studs, and railing on his porch. The next summer I chipped and painted his whole house. With him dogging me the whole time, I fixed his fence and reset the fallen rocks that made up the stonewall that bordered his property. I cleared weeds, turned soil, and reclaimed his garden from the jungle that was his yard. I put new shingles on the roof and fixed or replaced all of the stuck windows, broken glass, and torn screen.

His neighbors made comments to me as they went past; "Thanks for cleaning his place up," and, "What's he really like?" They remarked on his gruffness and surliness.

I shrugged at their comments and said, "Harold's okay, once you get to know him."

If I needed a particular item as I worked, he pulled all kinds of old tools and supplies out of the shed. He made me use all of the supplies and materials he had first, then, if we ran out of something like putty, he'd show me how to make it. If it still wasn't right or we didn't have enough, then I could go to the hardware store with silver dollars and buy more putty or whatever. To work on his place, absent all the power tools and conveniences, was a remarkable lesson in resourcefulness for me. Everything he had was rusty and dull, but he had all the tools and materials to make all of it sharp and shine again. When I broke a shovel handle, actually it disintegrated in my hands the first time I went to turn some dirt with it, he had me cut a branch from a tree and with some sandpaper, mineral oil, his knife, and the grindstone we made a new handle.

He paid me with late nineteenth and early twentieth century coins. It was cool to be paid with silver dollars, initially, but it got annoying quickly because I had a hard time spending them.

One day I asked, "Could you pay me with paper money instead of the silver dollars. I didn't want to spend them because they're rare and worth more than just a buck."

So he started giving me five, ten, and twenty-dollar silver certificates, currency that also was worth more than its face value.

I wondered how he got his food. He never asked me to shop for him and I hardly ever saw wrappers or cans or empty milk jars in the trash. He composted for the garden, but still there were few remnants of food packaging. I wondered if he might have stockpiled canned food during the A-bomb threat of the fifties and still be eating that stuff. One day in the garage, I came across a crate of canned peaches that must have been thirty years old. He asked me to bring the box onto the porch. When I dumped the grass clippings into the garbage the next week I saw some of the cans in the garbage bin. Eventually I learned that he walked to the bank each week to deposit his railroad pension check and he bought the exact same food stuff each week at the Capitol supermarket near the bank; bananas, eggs, dry milk, cube steak, canned peas, Saltine crackers, and Ovaltine.

He didn't own a television, just an ancient tube radio. When transistor radios surfaced, he anticipated the demise of tube radios. He sent me to buy as many of the various kinds of tubes his radio needed. With silver dollars I went and bought dozens of tubes.

Over the three and a half years we were acquainted we didn't spend a lot of idle time chatting. I was there to work. He directed. It was while I worked he talked. There wasn't much deep, bonding subject matter in our conversations.

I told him about my plan to go to college then, hopefully, join the Coast Guard and go through its OCS program. We talked about the weather and devised methods to accomplish repairs to his house. Occasionally he would tell me a story of the railroad. That's what I wanted to hear. From the trains I had hopped and from riding my mini-bike along Greenbush I saw many things along the line. I wanted to hear about those things, the empty sidings, old warehouses and wharves, and the spurs that ran off into the woods. But I learned not to push him for the stories or ask him to repeat a story he already told me.

When he first starting talking about Greenbush, no matter the topic, he spoke as though he were giving a report. As the story progressed he became more engaging. Good. I wanted to hear his thoughts on what he had witnessed, but he wouldn't be prodded. If I pushed too hard he stopped talking for that day and sometimes never resumed the story. There were only two ways I could get the rest of the story or more detail in a story. One was if he forgot he had already told me the story. The second, third, and even fourth telling filled with more detail each time. The second variable in his storytelling depended on what time of day I was there. The mornings were all work, no chatter irrelevant to the work at hand. However, if it was the afternoon or I worked there all day, as he sipped whatever it was he drank after lunchtime, Harold became a chatter-box, at least as much as Harold could. I learned to take what he was offering in the story and be happy with it.

He worked the line during the interesting era of World War Two. Greenbush served a shipyard, a Navy ammo depot, and its annex further down in Hingham. Because more steel, fuel, and shipbuilding supplies passed over his crossing, Harold had to be more precise.

Soldiers and sailors moved over the line regularly, also. Some were on patrol. Others were assigned duty at the various Coast Guard stations and Coastal Artillery Corp batteries that were established on the South Shore. Many of the men were sent to man the ships being built in Hingham.

The ships built at the Bethlehem Steel shipyard in Hingham passed up the Back River into Boston Harbor onto the Boston Naval Shipyard for commissioning and eventually duty. Harold never saw the ships out of Hingham sail up the harbor. All he saw was the material disappear southbound past his shack.

He did, however give me reports on the ships he saw from his front porch out on the Fore River as they left the Quincy Bethlehem Steel shipyard for the war. He saw the U.S.S. Massachusetts, U.S.S. Wasp, U.S.S. Lexington, and dozens of other cruisers and destroyers leave Quincy. He made notes on what he saw and read from his notebooks when he told me about the ships and activity he witnessed. It was tremendously exciting for me to hear about all this naval activity. I wanted to hear more about the war ships; every detail fascinated me, but he just relayed the facts from his notes. His comments about what he saw would be that he saw it come off the ways on a certain date at a specific time. His next entry was the time it took for the ship to be tugged to the pier, the date and time it left for sea trials, and its return. Then the date and time it disappeared forever.

He kept lists on everything. The time and length of the various trains that passed his house, police and fire department activity near his house, the cost of the food he bought each time he went to the market, how much rain and snow had fallen, and the temperature at various times throughout the day. He kept a list of all the shipping activity he saw over the years, not just the shipyard activity. When a ship was in the bay, he stood out on his porch and noted the ship's name, hull number, and what flag it was sailing under. He had plenty to talk about because of the years of lists he kept. The more he talked the more he would go and get his lists and refer to them as he spoke.

With his lists in hand, he told me of washouts on the line, derailments, the drunks that worked for the railroad, the accidents of the trains, and the collisions of trains and cars. He loved talking about the precision of railroad operation, the clock, the mechanized detail of a steam engine, the late night quiet of his shack, and the people who knocked on the door looking for information or a handout. He detailed every business that had a siding on Greenbush, every stationmaster's personality, the speed restrictions, and the general and operating rules of the Greenbush division.

Every day while I was working on his yard, we heard the distant train whistles' as they left the South Braintree yard. We heard the horn again as the train moved over the various tracks and we guessed if it was heading for the Greenbush or Plymouth or Middleboro lines.

Sometimes he'd give me a day off, of sorts. We'd hear the horn as the train left the yard then hear it again as it passed through East Braintree. We'd see it as it crept into view on the Quincy Avenue side of the Weymouth Landing station.

Harold would say something like, "I'm curious if the switch to the old engine house in Cohasset is still in place."

I looked at him and he looked back at me with an eyebrow raised.

I'd say, "I'll let you know tomorrow at nine when I come back to finish the lawn." With that I ran down the hill and hid in the bushes behind the lumber company's siding. The train crept closer, crossing Quincy Avenue and then Commercial Street. When the engine passed and bent into the woods near the siding, I hopped up onto the train. I crossed to the other side of the train and waved at Harold. Just before it disappeared into the woods, he waved back.

At the end of the first summer he gave me the signal lantern he swung at the crossing to stop traffic and signal the engineer. I still have it. If there were ever a fire in my house, it is what I would grab on my way out.

When school got underway, and during autumn I stopped by at least once a week. I even brought my friend Kelli with me a couple times. He liked her. They sat on the porch and talked while I raked leaves. During the winter I stopped in more regularly. If it had snowed the night before, I'd walk to his house first thing in the morning and shovel the snow from his walkway. He only lived about two miles from me. My father got annoyed with me because I'd leave our driveway unshoveled and walk to Harold's to shovel his. My father was full of it. He had our driveway plowed and had a snow-blower for the walkway.

It was winter when Harold finally let me into his house. During the summer and fall I sat on the porch when I took a break. Of course I had to repair the Adirondack chairs he had on the porch before I could use them to sit on for my breaks. I'd hear him moving around inside then he'd come out to the porch and sit with me. He always had a glass in his hand. I couldn't see into the house because of the shades and the remains of the moth-eaten curtains. If he was coming out to help me or show me something he locked the door behind him. Even if he was crossing the lawn to go the carriage house or shed he locked the door. I had a peek into the kitchen once, and all I saw was a potbelly stove and a really old refrigerator before he blocked my view. But one day, a very cold day when school was canceled because of snow, I walked to his house and shoveled him out. He finally invited me in.

Every time I shoveled his walkway he'd come out to supervise my work wearing an old ulster, woolen cap, leather boots, and a barvel. He'd bring me some hot chocolate while I shoveled. This one day was especially cold. The storm dropped snow all day the day before, then, during the night, the front shifted and it warmed enough to make it rain, but not for long and not enough to dissolve the snow. Rain mixed in with the snow, then the front shifted again and it got very cold. It snowed more and the rain froze to the snow. I was miserable. He saw it and said come in. I had to go to the front door. He came through the house and unlocked the door. I kicked my boots off and sat in the parlor on an old, rotted overstuffed davenport.

There were two old pictures in the living room; a stern looking woman and timid looking man sat on a table in a frame next to a bible in a little sanctuary-like setting. There were a couple candles nearby and a crucifix hovering over it all.

Cobwebs hung everywhere. I could see dead insect carcasses still wrapped in the webs. Everything was in a very deep green, purple or brown color. The wallpaper was stained, dirty, and curled back from its seams. There was a single overhead bulb that didn't work and push-button switches. If the building inspector got into Harold's house, he would be mortified. I think the house was built before electricity, because the wires that provided the juice ran on the outside of the baseboards and up the walls.

A stairway ran up from a corner of the hallway, but a heavy drape blocked my view of the stairwell and another heavy drape blocked my view of anything else in the house. There was a phonograph and a big box that was the radio.

Harold had started a fire in the fireplace and the room felt warm. As he pulled back the drape to come into the parlor, I saw cut wood in what I guessed was the dinning room. I knew he bought a cord of wood every fall. I stacked it on the porch I repaired. There was a table, roll top desk, and newspapers everywhere. I wondered if he had a bathroom.

The hot chocolate he gave had some kind of alcohol splashed in it. It was good. Two cups of that and my walk home was a breeze. He handed me a mug and sat down, heavily. He never seemed to sit, but rather fall backwards into a chair. That was when his age showed. In spite of his vigor, he was an old man.

We sat in total silence for fifteen minutes. The only sounds were the crackle of the insects' carapaces as the draft pushed its way around the parlor, and an occasional slurp. He refilled my mug, once.

"You must be warm enough by now," he said.

I was dismissed.

He gave me five regular dollar bills; a thermos filled with the spiked hot chocolate, and sent me on my way home.

I worked around his house a little each spring. Then every summer I resumed my routine of repair. The summer after I gave up on college and was waiting to leave for Navy boot camp, Harold paid me particularly well. I had a part time job pumping gas and with the money he gave me I left Weymouth money ahead.

The day before I left for Navy boot camp I cut his grass for the last time. I had spent so much time tending his lawn that it was now the best looking lawn in town. It could have been the lawn at one of the Newport mansions. I put the tools away and went to say good-bye.

Harold spoke very abruptly. "I appreciate all the work you've done." He handed me a large manila envelope.

I looked inside. I saw some cash and a series of photographs. I had seen the photos before; they were pictures of Greenbush he had taken over the years.

"Good luck, Martin." He extended his hand. When I gave mine back to him, he gave it one good shake, like it was a pump handle.

Before I could say anything he turned, went back in his house, and locked the door. I turned and walked away abruptly, also.

At the bottom of the hill I stopped and looked in the envelope. Harold had given me five, new, one-hundred dollar bills along with the photos. I looked back up at Harold's house. I was sure he was inside making note of the time I departed.

It seemed to me more should have been said.

I walked the tracks back to the Unicorn Avenue crossing, stepped off Greenbush, and spent my last night in Weymouth at my father's house. The next day I left Weymouth. I took the bus and subway to Boston, boarded Greyhound, and started sending Harold Christmas cards.

CHAPTER 6

▼

GREENBUSH

Right after I left the cemetery I heard a horn from either a ship in the harbor or a truck. I stopped and listened hard, in case it happened to be a train horn. I scolded my wishful thinking; hearing a train horn would have to have been either my imagination or the wind direction, temperature, and dew point would have to be perfect for me to hear it all the way from Braintree or across the bay in Quincy. But I stayed still and listened hard, again, just in case.

I passed under the railroad bridge at the base of Weymouth Heights and planned to go straight up and over King Oak Hill toward Jackson Square, instead I turned left at Green Street and walked forty yards to a grade crossing.

Greenbush.

The southbound railbed was completely obscured by overgrowth. The line didn't look to be in any better shape on the other side of the street either. If it weren't for a much-weathered crossing signal post, newcomers to Weymouth probably couldn't even tell there was a railroad crossing here.

In 1970 when the New Haven Railroad could no longer limp along in bankruptcy, the Penn Central Railroad took over operating the freight trains on Greenbush. The Penn Central debacle ebbed into the ConRail idea. Finally, ConRail spun Greenbush off to The Bay Colony Railroad as part of their acquisition of several small lines in Southeastern Massachusetts. In 1985 The Bay Colony gave up on Greenbush, too, when the last shipper, the GSA warehouse in the Hingham Shipyard, closed. Greenbush was abandoned.

Long before the abandonment, the years of neglect, under use, and indifference caused the small and infrequent freight trains to proceed slowly and, in places, to go so slow that the high school cross-country team could pass the trains. Because of the slow-moving trains, one place in particular, beyond the site of the former Weymouth Heights station and south of the Green Street crossing, the trains had to nearly stop because of a questionable switch to an abandoned siding.

It was the perfect place to hop the train. There were plenty of trees, bramble, and bushes for cover. A little curve in the tracks provided enough concealment so that, as the train curved, one side of it was completely concealed from the crew. No one from either the caboose or engine could see us hop the train.

Being out of sight from the train crew was paramount; there were rumors that the caboose crew would shoot anyone hopping the train with pepper shot. I didn't know what pepper shot was, but it sounded painful. One time someone from the train crew did see us hop on the train. They stopped the train, but because the bramble was dense and close to the tracks, the crew couldn't get us. We dove into the briars and got away, with cuts and slashes in our clothes and skin. It was a painful, but great escape.

During the school year, if my paper route was done or almost done and the train was running late in either direction, when I heard the horn, I hid the papers and my bike in the brush and hoped for an open boxcar door. If the train was going south, I could hop the train and ride to Hingham. If the train wasn't heading to Hingham until that late in the afternoon the crew wasn't going to waste anytime. They switched the cars they needed and sped, as much as possible, back to Braintree. I'd jump off back at the point where I dropped the bike and remaining newspapers. I always got the papers delivered and back home before the streetlights came on. If the train were northbound, I'd have to gauge where it was and scramble to finish delivering the papers. A ride to Braintree meant I had to either walk or hitchhike back home. I always had to come up with an excuse as to why missed I supper. I said I went for a ride. My parents made the assumption I was on my bike.

One time the train did not stop back in Braintree. It continued all the way to Attleboro. It was nearly ten at night before I got back home. Fortunately, my father had fallen asleep and my mother was relieved to see me, alive and intact. She kept the secret.

Most of the time I rode the train alone. If the conditions were right I would hear the engine's horn as it worked through the crossings and switched cars in East Braintree. I got so I could separate the engine's whistle out of all the background noise. If the horn was quiet for a few minutes then sounded the sequence for a grade crossing back to back, it meant it was moving through Weymouth Landing and therefore on its way south. I scrambled toward the tracks and took a ride.

On those trains the South Shore opened for me as I was sure it did for no one else.

In winter the train plowed the bed smooth. Snow clung to the branches that enveloped the tracks. The sun set early in the winter. In places, where the low side light shined through the trees, the light reflecting off the snow gave my entire vista a diffused warm glow. Even if it was raining or snowing, from the confines of the train, it was still beautiful, everything I knew so well was surrounded in the action of winter. I never got cold no matter how wet I was or how low the temperature dropped. On the tiny trains that traversed Greenbush, I was warm and safe.

Spring brought out the buds and mud. During summer the once-barren branches slapped the train with their leaves and branches. Then autumn.

Fall bought perfect weather, the leaves turning and dropping, revealing what had hidden behind the leaves. Weymouth and the South Shore became visible again. Everything was in place. Everything was as it should be, exactly as I last saw it the previous winter.

No matter what the season of the ride, hidden on the train, it was spectacular. Creeping out of Weymouth Heights I saw the backbone and backside of Weymouth and the South Shore: backdoors, backyards, back lit autumn leaves, back streets, the backwater of the Fore River, the backwash, the flotsam and jetsam of the tide and Boston Harbor, the Edison plant, and the General Dynamics shipyard. On Greenbush, wending on down to Scituate, I traveled the spine of the South Shore. There were lobster boats, mud flats, the abandoned Naval Ammunition Depot in Hingham, cemeteries, town squares, Hingham Bay, the alternating woods and marshes of Cohasset and Scituate until the end of the line at Greenbush near the North River between Scituate and Marshfield.

I knew the line so well, so intimately, that one time I reshaped my model train set to a replica of Greenbush.

It was easy to hop the train. Ride as fast as possible to the short cut at the bottom of King Oak Hill. I rode over the dirt road to the high-tension power lines maintenance road that paralleled the tracks. I'd dump the bike in the brush at the edge of the swamp and wait at the edge of the drainage ditch until I heard the whistle at Green Street. When I crouched down in the bushes at the edge of the woods, it was inevitable that the tips of my sneakers ended up in the swampy water. I'd look through the curve of the cars to spot an open door. If none of the doors were open, I'd spot which ladder I wanted jump up onto. The wheels of the engine passed two feet away from my face as I hid in the brush. I was usually so close to the train that it blocked out much of the sunlight. Once the engine passed, I stood up, tensed, and leapt. The bottom of the boxcar door opening was four feet off the ground. In my scramble alongside the car the branches slapped my face. The vines grabbed at my ankles. It was as though I was running along a cliff. When I got parallel to the car I wanted jump up into, I crashed my chest into the bottom of the opening as I swung my feet up and rolled into the open door. Splinters, grease, and metal shards in my palms were part of the escapade. I scrambled deep into the car, then crept forward again to see if anyone noticed me. Or, if I was with my friends, to see who else had made it.

One time in the winter I slipped on the ice frozen in the drainage ditch. I fell toward the undercarriage of the car. I rolled under the car through to the other side. I got through with a couple feet to spare before the wheels would have hit me.

Hanging onto the ladder required a lot of effort. It was much easier and safer to ride inside one of the cars. As the train went along Greenbush it lurched and shook at each decayed grade crossing and rotted tie. Branches and leaves slapped us constantly as we held on. Whether I was alone or with my friends I fatigued quickly, usually within a couple miles. If we had jumped onto the ladders we usually got off at the abandoned East Weymouth station and waited for the train to come back.

The East Weymouth station stop was a good place to hang out. The area around the East Weymouth siding and station was secluded. It offered plenty of adventure. Sometimes the train crew would drop off a car at the siding there. When they did that, we had to bail out early. That was okay; we knew all the hiding places.

The station itself was down the tracks another hundred yards from the siding. A padlock on the door to the station still hung from the useless hasp. The hasp was busted away from the frame and all the windows to the station were broken. The station platform crossed over the Herring Run. It was near the town dump, Great Esker Park, and end of the Back River. The area was rich with mud flats, old warehouses, tidal water, isolation, and the fringe of Jackson Square.

It was marvelous. Whether I was with all my friends and we'd just hopped off the train or just Danny or Kelli and I had walked there or if I was by myself it was splendid. Late summer was the best. A thunderstorm could roll up the river, blot out all the sun, burst, be gone, and have the sun shinning again within twenty minutes. If the tide was out I could sit in the concrete tunnels that punched through the embankment built up to support the tracks and watch the storm or find shelter in a stand of oak tress. Standing out in the middle of the storm was okay, too.

Few boats ever ventured that far up the river. The water was gentle there. There was current and tidal push and pull, but it was friendly. The water in the river was always welcoming and safe. Although one time I'm sure I saw a shark fin pierce the surface as I stood on the banks of the river at high tide one day. The shadow in the water told me it was big, but that summer everyone was seeing sharks everywhere there was water.

It was the summer Jaws was released. Danny and I had already been made to look foolish because of that movie. We had seen the movie on Tuesday and ridden our bikes to Nantasket Beach on Wednesday. Since the movie was the talk of the town we decide to demonstrate that we weren't scared of no stupid shark, so we swam out several hundred yards off the beach. When we stopped to rest we looked back at the beach and everyone was out of the water and waving their arms at us. The MDC police car was there and its blue light was flashing. We saw a fire truck rolling up the road toward the beach. I don't know if he said it first or if I did, but we screamed "SHARK" and nearly ran on top of the water back to the beach. When we got back to the beach the police took our names and told us we weren't supposed to be out that far. The hysteria of Jaws had made someone think they had seen something in the water that day. It was the first shark scare at Nantasket Beach in years.

The train usually ended at the Hingham shipyard and the crew got lunch there. An hour or so later it crept its way back north. If we had bailed out at East Weymouth, we reboarded there and rode back to our bikes.

There was no risk involved with hopping a train, as far as any of us knew. Our mothers hadn't cautioned us against hopping train like they had about riding a bicycle in traffic or crossing the street. Just hearing the horn as it approached Weymouth Landing sent us off to the tracks looking for a ride away from boredom.

Summer was when my friends usually came along.

One boring day, when a pickup baseball game never got quite got going, and the park summer recreation program was over for the morning. No one wanted to go for a bike ride. Wessegusett Beach was closed because of a jellyfish infestation in Boston Harbor, and because a tanker had spilled some oil into the Fore River. We stood on the basketball court and there was a break in the chatter. We all heard it—the whistle of the engine. We waited to hear the back-to-back whistles at Weymouth Landing. We had been faked out a couple times already that summer by the engine switching cars in East Braintree. But that day we heard the second and soon the third whistle as the train passed through Weymouth Landing and then where it crossed Commercial Street beyond the Landing on its way to Hingham. It was exactly the kind of activity we didn't know we had been hoping for.

If the train was going to drop a car off at the lumber company way down in Hingham, we could go to Hingham Beach. Hingham's beach was not affected by the oil spill and the jellyfish infestation there was minor. It had not been closed. Even if the train was switching off to the old shipyard, a ride on the train was still a diversion. We could stomp around the abandoned ways at the shipyard or the abandoned ammo dump until the train came back.

We had all made the ride before. Some of us still had something left from lunch. It was to have been a simple summer day.

Seven of us took off for Weymouth Heights. Down King Oak Hill, and into the woods behind Murleys' Sunoco garage. It was Kevin, Billy, Jason, Danny, Mike, Alex, and I scrambling into the brush. Jason pressed his ear to the track. He always did that and pretended to tell us exactly how far away the train was. By the time Jason said he could feel the tracks rumbling, we all could see the train crossing Green Street.

Danny took out a penny as he always did and set it on the tracks.

The train began its whistle ahead of the crossing, and then the lights started flashing. The crossing bell rang. Traffic stopped except one car, third in the line from the crossing. It cut out around the stopped cars and crossed just in front of the engine.

Kevin, Danny, Alex, and Mike hid in the bushes on the east side of the tracks. Jason, Billy, and I buried ourselves in the west side bushes. The train had only four boxcars, plus the engine and caboose. We couldn't spot an open door. Kevin and Jason jumped up onto the set of ladders between the first and second cars. Danny, Alex, and Mike jumped up to the second set of ladders. The train was moving so slow we hardly had to run at all. As long as the first person up moved inboard over the coupling there was plenty of room for everyone else. Billy moved to jump up onto the lower rung of the ladder. I was right behind him. Billy slipped. It wasn't unusual for one of us to miss on the first attempt. But this time Billy fell back and bounced off me. I fell backwards into the ditch and Billy's legs went under the train.

The first truck of the next boxcar severed both of his legs immediately. One leg was chopped off in the middle of the knee and the other leg suffered an above the knee amputation. Billy didn't scream.

From where I lay I had a perfect uninterrupted view of the amputation. The blood shot all over me. By the time the next set of the trucks approached Billy, he screamed. He was screaming because he couldn't move out of the way. He didn't realize he had lost his legs. The caboose crew heard his cry. They came out onto the rear platform and saw Billy as he came out from under their car. His torso was to the outside of the tracks and wheels so it looked like he had been cut in two.

The conductor was out on the back of the caboose platform when he looked down and saw Billy's lower legs atop the ties in the middle of the rail bed, about four feet from the rest of Billy.

He called the engineer on the radio. The train moved so slowly that it stopped quickly. The conductor was off the train instantly with a first aid kit.

I watched all of this. Kevin, Jason, Danny, Mike, and Alex dismounted the train. At first they ran into the woods as though they were going to bolt, but they realized what had happened and made their way back to Billy. The engineer ran to the back of the train. He was furious. He yelled at us, saying, "How stupid could you boys be? Don't you know how dangerous it is to hop trains?"

The conductor knelt beside Billy. He said, "I was a medic in the Army. I'm going to take care of you." He told the engineer he was going to try a tourniquet and he needed someone's belt. The engineer and the rest of the train crew worked to help Billy.

I saw Billy's eyes roll back into his head. He passed out. A police car stopped on the crossing and two cops were running down the tracks. My friends and I slid away from the commotion back to the edge of the woods. This was an issue for adults.

How could something so enjoyable as a slow train ride to the beach have resulted in this? We watched from the side of the hill. The police came up to us and took all of our names. They called each of our parents. One by one parents came and took us away.

An ambulance took Billy away.

My father told me to never hop the trains again. The police posted a patrol car at the crossing for a few weeks following the accident, and an editorial in The Patriot Ledger wondered if there wasn't a better way to prevent this kind of thing from happening again.

I was back on the train, breathing in the South Shore, within one month. All my friends stayed away from the tracks and never hopped another train.

Billy came back to school a year later, a double amputee. He walked with crutches and prosthetics. Danny, Kevin, Jason, Mike, Alex, and I refriended him, but it didn't last. Billy couldn't keep up.

I changed the layout of my train set from a replica of the Greenbush line to a figure eight.

CHAPTER 7

▼

MRS. GILBERT'S PORCH

I shook off the memory of Billy and resumed my trajectory up King Oak Hill toward to Jackson Square.

Six days a week I walked up King Oak Hill delivering the Patriot Ledger. The ritual was the same every day. The sky blue truck left a bundle of papers at the end of Gilbert Road. I'd sit down, lean against the telephone pole, and read the paper in a very specific order; Aquarius horoscope first, then Dear Abby, the headlines, local news, sports, and, saving the best for last, the comics. If it was raining or snowing I'd stop at my first customers' house and read the paper in their carport. They were never home, but every Thursday there was a dollar twenty five for the paper and a thirty five cents tip in an envelop waiting for me.

Routines happen, an efficient course evolved. It took about an hour to deliver forty papers. I knew every dog and cat on the route, every sidewalk crack, and every unfenced yard that provided a shortcut.

The course began winding its way through the woods and swamp at the bottom of Cornish Street. The outer reach of my route was the railroad tracks at the end of Meetinghouse Lane. I looped back through Weymouth Heights and it ended at the top of King Oak Hill. From there it was a short-cut through two backyards and I was home. I avoided heavy traffic by sticking to the residential roads. Commercial Street was the busiest road on the route. I had to cross it only a couple times as I plowed the route. However, the last leg of the route took me on Commercial Street up King Oak Hill.

There were lots of cars on Commercial Street. They all went fast.

Before the trek up King Oak I stopped and bought Yankee Doodles and chocolate milk at the pharmacy there. Rain or shine I sat on the railroad bridge with my feast. At that confluence of roads, traffic, infrequent pedestrians, occasional trains, and seasons an unknown but permanent verve for Weymouth etched in me. I was enveloped in the world, as I knew it, and I reveled in it.

On Wednesdays, the newspapers, fat with grocery store ads, were too big to fit on my bicycle's paper rack. If I overstuffed the rack, inevitably the papers slid out while I sped through a turn, and, invariably, slid into a puddle or the wind scattered the papers all over the street.

Danny usually helped me on Wednesdays. I'd give him a dollar and bought an extra package of Yankee Doodles.

The dogs, however, were the best part of my paper route.

There was a German Shepherd, an Irish Setter, a Beagle, a couple of Poodles and terriers: a Doberman, a Cocker Spaniel, Golden Retriever, and mutts and mongrels of every imaginable combination. In the summer every time I rang the doorbell to collect money for the paper, the dog came running. I'd hear its nails scrape and slide as it dug in for traction against the floorboards. They barked every time. When the door opened I put my hand out and they sniffed then everything was okay. Sometimes I'd have to catch the dog if it escaped as I stood there. Others times it would be just me and the dog while the owner went to get money for the bill. Even the threatening dogs became friendly. There was not a lot of turn over of the pets on the route. I knew them all by name. Sometimes they walked with me. I'd pat them. I'd throw a ball if they had one. I'd talk to them. They'd roll over and I'd scratch their stomachs.

The cats were okay. Some of them were friendly and had a personality I could identify. If they didn't run away I'd pick them up and pat them. But most were skittish and fickle.

I had had the paper-route a couple of years when a new dog showed up. School had just resumed. The afternoons were warm and the days still long enough to grill supper and eat it at the picnic table in the backyard. I turned the corner off Richard's Road, dropped down King Oak Hill two houses to deliver one paper before I began the final trudge up the hill to the finish. I dropped the paper in between the screen door and front door of the house at the bottom of the hill. I closed the door and turned to go back up the hill when the strange dog first appeared.

It was a puppy; white neck, gold fur, huge paws, and ears that began upright but then folded down halfway up the cartilage mast, unleashed and no collar, unaccompanied bouncing from yard to yard sniffing the grass, and fallen maple leaves. The pup ran down Richard's Road into the middle of a kickball game. He sniffed every hand and crotch he came in contact with.

Two houses further up the hill the puppy came through the hedges. He lowered his chest to the ground, his haunches up, and tail wagging so strongly that it knocked him off balance for a moment. His eyes were eager anticipating play. I made sure the door latched and turned to the puppy. I stepped toward him and he settled low to the ground, shot around the yard, stopping, starting, banking left and right then blasted back through the hedge into the next yard.

When I whistled he stopped and looked back as though it was the most interesting sound he had ever heard. He looked at me as I slapped my thighs and called him. The dog came sniffing and licking then took off through the bushes again.

He ran and played close by. At one point he turned into the street. A car had to brake suddenly to avoid hitting him.

I left that house and went uphill to the next house, Mrs. Gilbert. She owned the duplex and lived on the downhill side. The other side of the house was level to the hill but the ground on her side dropped off so much that the porch had to be elevated twenty feet by the time it got to her door. It was a long walk to the rear doorway to drop her newspaper. She tipped ten cents each week and two dollars at Christmas.

Everyday, simultaneously, I turned her door handle with my right hand and dropped the paper with my left. The door needed oil. On collection day I looked down at the doorjamb before I dropped the paper. It was relief if the money was there. If she didn't leave the money on the doorjamb it meant I had to knock on the door. Then I would have to go into her kitchen and wait while she got the money out of her purse.

I dreaded going to her house.

Mrs. Gilbert was so old I was afraid I would find her dead when I went to collect. One time I read in the paper about a paperboy finding the homeowner dead when he went to collect. The body had been there for a week. In the article, he said it smelled really bad.

Her house already had an odd smell, like macaroni boiled and burnt to the bottom of a pan and concealed by Lysol. How would I know the smell if she died and I was the one to find her?

If I didn't discover her smelling, decaying dead body I was certain she was going to die in front of me when I collected the money. She trembled and titled when she stood still. My walk across her wooden deck grew creepier every week. It felt as though I was walking a gangplank.

The money wasn't there that dog's day. I had to ring the bell. When I pushed the ringer five things happened simultaneously; the bell sounded its peculiar tinkle, tires screeched, a girl screamed, the puppy cried and there, walking the plank between those four sounds, the puppy died.

Screeching tires in Weymouth were an automatic head-turner. Everyone waited for the crash. When a crunch followed the screech, everyone in the area left his or her house to see what happened. To me it seemed as though a hushed, spectral stillness seemed to fill the air. Even if someone was at the wreck trying to help or talking to the driver the silence hung mysterious until the police and fire truck sirens broke the barrier.

There was no crash this time and Mrs. Gilbert didn't answer the door.

When no one answered the door I usually waited a minute and then knocked or rang the doorbell a couple more times before I left. That day I pushed Mrs. Gilbert's ringer again and again and again. I knocked on the window, on the door, on the side of the house, and on the windows that faced the porch. I looked through her lace curtains praying she was there. I had to get into her house while she sought her money.

Behind me I heard cars stop, doors open and close, and a second girl crying.

Mrs. Gilbert never answered the door.

There was no shortcut for me to take here. I couldn't get off the porch without turning around. I would have broken my leg if I jumped off the porch. I could not avoid the tragedy behind me. I had to turn around. I had three papers still to deliver. I had to leave the comfort of Mrs. Gilbert's porch. I had to witness a death I couldn't even imagine.

When I turned I looked everywhere other than where the dog lay. Across Commercial Street two girls were crying. A half a dozen cars had stopped on both sides of the street. One car near the top of the hill halted, crept forward, and stopped again. I saw the driver look back. Then it lurched and disappeared over the brink. It seemed as though the car carried a degree of disgrace with it.

The stopped cars blocked my view of the puppy. I couldn't see and I didn't look. I didn't want to look. The sidewalk cracks, the weeds, and the swath of grass between someone's lawn and the curb was the only world I wanted to see. But when I was parallel to the puppy a telescopic point-of-view opened between two stopped cars. I looked. My eyes adjusted their focus and concentration automatically from the close up view I had looking down at the sidewalk to accommodate the twenty feet from me to the puppy.

It was a visual eruption. I saw enough in those three seconds so that to this day I don't look at a dead dog in the road. Why would I ever look at a dead dog in the road again? I already know what one looks like.

One time, years later, I was driving through Utah. I sat at intersection in Salt Lake City waiting for the light to change. There was a dead dog lying in my left peripheral vision. I never leveled my look to it to confirm what it was laying there. I knew. A dog becomes ignoble when fallen to a vehicle. A car pulled into the frontage road where the dog lay; the woman left the passenger side, her hands reaching to the dog; her steps unstable. The man leapt from the driver side. He threw his hands up toward the sky. His head tipped back and his whole body gave one massive convulsion. They walked up to the dog together. Fortunately I couldn't see the dog anymore, their car hid it. They knelt and slid from view. I didn't wait for the light to turn green. I pulled a u-turn in the road and drove an extra twenty minutes out of my way to get away from that scene.

In Weymouth, that awful afternoon I pushed my point of view beyond the puppy at the walkway up to Emory's estate. I swung my stare past everything there, uphill then into the sky. In three seconds I suddenly saw the world's abruptness in a way I never even imagined. Lying across the double yellow line in the road, facing downhill, gravity pulling blood from its mouth halfway up King Oak Hill, the puppy lay there, terribly still.

I ran up the rest of the hill. I did my job. I rolled the papers and threw them on the doorsteps of my three remaining customers. My paperbag was empty. I ran over the crest of the hill and turned down the little side street, King Oak Terrace. I knew of a patch of trees and brush between two neighborhoods where I could hide. When I turned onto King Oak Terrace I looked back and saw a policeman dragging the carcass to the side of the road. He pulled the puppy by its rear leg. It was terrible. I thought the puppy might feel the concrete rubbing and scarring its face.

I hid in the patch of brush and trees. I put the delivery bag over my head. No one could see me. I couldn't see anything.

Before I started up King Oak Hill, the next day, I looked where its body had been set. It was gone. Dead animal pick up or the street sweeper had made it disappear, from the side of the street.

CHAPTER 8

▼

SPEED

More than 1,200 times I climbed King Oak Hill; four years of a paper-route, six days a week, and other ascents as part of my daily routine.

In spite of my physical maturity and the context of my pilgrimage to Weymouth, the ascent of King Oak Hill that day was no different than any other time I made it to the top of King Oak Hill. I looked backwards, with uneasiness, nothing lay in the street. Good. All I could see were the greens and reds and yellows of New England autumn. I had an unusually clear view to the horizon, the harbor, and Boston's skyline. Fifty steps later I looked over the Vincent Gorman memorial at the intersection of Middle and Commercial Streets, and Legion Field.

There, just below me at the intersection, was the howitzer with which I personally saved the town, state, and country from invasion numerous times. The gun's trajectory controls were disabled and spun freely. Its wheels were cement pedestals and the gun's azimuth was permanently fixed, but always I won the war there, shooting down the planes, which always approached over Legion Field at the perfect angle to be shot down. The pilot always eluded capture until I caught him in the baseball stands, and the bomb I defused, just in time to save the town, always landed in the tall tree I could climb. When combat ended I stood at the center of the traffic island, under the Vincent Gorman plaque and flag and modestly received my medal in front of my friends, family, and all the girls in my class. The prettiest ones always wanted to stand near me.

Vincent Gorman's name was also etched on the war memorial wall, near town hall, as one of Weymouth's World War One veterans, but that was all I knew. I made a note to finally find out who he was and what happened that earned him a memorial intersection.

I moved to the edge of the sidewalk when two boys rode up the small hill from Middle Street to the crest of King Oak Hill. I watched them as they dropped from sight on their plummet down the hill.

King Oak Hill was great for reckless bicycle riding, but it was the most dangerous of the three bicycle riding hills in the area.

I love riding my bike. I started riding when I was four years old and never stopped. Perpetual motion soothes me. Idleness disquiets me. The earth is spinning and moving constantly at 24,000 miles per hour, but I like more, swifter, faster. I like speed. I always have.

I spilled a lot of blood during boyhood, too.

In Weymouth, Gilbert Road dead-ends uphill on a steep incline. That meant an equally steep decline, worthy of my new green Schwinn Varsity ten speed bike. The hill was my rocket ship. Racing down that hill thirty years ago I was sure I was near the same speed as Apollo 11 on its re-entry. I had ten speeds, and that wasn't enough. I'd be shifting through eight on my way to ten before I even got off the plateau. Barely fifteen feet off the shoulder headed down the incline, any resistance from gear ten was gone. The following two hundred foot plummet was ten-year-old rapture.

It didn't matter that a merged family of bullies lived up there. The boys were almost always in detention, so school afternoons we were generally safe from harassment. Besides, for being as tough as they were reputed to be, they were scared of speed. Only once did two of them race down the hill with us. They both held the brake all the way down. Wimps. Eventually, one of them ended up in jail, and the other died in a car wreck driving drunk. He took a dad and a small child with him.

Our launch pad was in front of the Carpenters' house. Gravity seemed to give up its hold by the time we passed the Doyles' house. We approached maximum velocity at Spinellis' house. Between the Doyles' and Spinellis', Mr. Miscowski always yelled from his front door, "Slow down! You'll get killed." The house below the Spinellis was the point of no return. On my ten-speed rocket I was certain I neared the speed of light there. The houses, evergreens, sewer grates, curbs, and driveways were a blur.

That final house was also the last point we could brake and stop before the intersection at the bottom of the hill. I never knew what their name was, but they had a large piece of property on that street. Passing their house we could get a glimpse of the intersection below, but only in the winter and spring before the leaves came back to the trees. There, it was commitment or brakes. Only once did I hit the brakes. I saw our station wagon coming with my mother at the wheel and it was right after I had been forbidden to ride the hill ever again. I hit the brakes, spun out in the sand, and crashed my bike down on the cement. I threw my bike over the shrubs and finished by breaking the top off the topiary when I leapt over.

She stopped at the bottom of the hill and looked up, studying my friend's faces for a clue as to whether or not I was there. Slowly, almost eerily, she pulled away. My best friend, Danny, gave me the all clear. I emerged from the bushes and pushed my bike back up hill. From the top of the hill I could see the crest of the smaller hillock at the other end of Gilbert Road. As soon as our car curved out of sight I resumed my ride.

Hitting the coaster brake meant you were a pussy, fag, wimp, dork, wuss, and more. It was better to go on. The cars stopped in time every time, except once. It wasn't a blood sport. It was paramount, however, that none of us whimpered or cried no matter how much skin we embedded into the pavement. All of us would look out and look up when one of us shot past the Miscowski's. If a car was spotted at least a warning was sounded. Braking was a dilemma; if you hit the brakes you spun out on the sand the town plows put down in winter so cars could get up the hill. If you didn't hit the brakes there could be car and kid impact. Every concussion, scrape, abrasion, and stitch earned there, except one, was the consequence of braking on the slope.

The audible deceleration of the baseball card clothes-pinned to the forks slapping against the spokes and the tire chirping are peculiar and strangely reassuring sounds. And, if it was long enough, the patch of rubber that lined the cement was a badge of honor for that day. Richard and Robert, the twins, hit the brakes a lot, but they had a swimming pool, so it was okay. Even the girls didn't hit the brakes. But they wouldn't accelerate all the way downhill either. They would make one of us stand at the bottom of the hill and watch for cars and wave them on. The girls rode with us only once or twice then went and played however they played.

Sometimes the objective was to see who could coast the farthest before he had to pedal or put his foot down to keep from falling over. I still hold the record; from the Carpenter's house all the way to the LeClercs'.

The glacier that made that area, Weymouth Heights, and the subsequent paved roads that striated the hillocks, formed a kind of roller coaster. There were three roads running off two different hills that created that bicycle-born carnival around the Heights. The largest was King Oak Hill. Commercial Street ran up and over, near the top but not over the top of that hill. The crest of Commercial Street provided a nice diminishing-into-the-hazy-distance view across the harbor of Boston's southeast face. It was the tallest and longest ride of the trilogy, but it was the most dangerous because of the traffic signal and yield sign at the bottom of the hill. Drivers had to look downhill and away from us. Instinctively we knew that King Oak Hill, the volume of traffic, and its intersections with Richards Road, Hale Street, North Street, Green Street, left-turning Commercial Street, and Church Street were somehow potentially lethal.

It was a mess with traffic, side streets, cracked and buckled pavement, and, worst of all, storm drain grates that were turned the wrong way. The skinny front tires on some of our bicycles would get caught in the grates and the consequence was painful and expensive, even at slow speeds. We used the word rupture to describe the act and consequence of any boy who came down hard on the cross bar that distinguished a boy's bike from a girl's. There was something insidiously funny and equally alarming about somebody else crushing his nuts. Furthermore, and more importantly, the rim would always get destroyed, and to replace it could cost a whole month's allowance and profit from additional chores.

To ride the other side of Commercial Street down King Oak was too weird. It accessed the driveways that lead to the top of the hill where there was a replica of George Washington's Mount Vernon estate. The hill slope was still covered with trees and brush, but there was lots of busted glass on that side of the street. After a couple attempts to ride the hill, we gave up. It was on the outer edge of our neighborhood comfort zone. Besides, I had to ride up it six days a week as part of my paper-route. However, later, during the mid-teenager evolution, the King Oak Hill became synonymous with cooperative, eager female classmates, drinking beer and Tango, and smoking dope. That side of the hill took a whole different connotation of the meaning of speed.

Cornish Street ran off another slope of King Oak Hill. It was our sledding hill in the winter. If you shot a bulls-eye with your bike or sled you could pass between the boulders that marked the end of the road with an inch to spare off either side of the pedals. Lot of kids weren't that accurate. There was a dirt road on the other side of the boulders, but a car couldn't get through to it. Stepping off onto the dirt road into the woods and swamp at the bottom of Cornish Street created a whole different planet out of the neighborhood; tall trees, short cuts, dirt paths, skunk cabbage, frogs and toads and pollywogs in the swamp, briars and bramble in the swampy muck at the bottom of the hill.

We found a stripped mini-bike frame in the woods there once. We were sure we could wish it back into wholeness by pulling it out of the muck and cleaning it up. I took window cleaner from my house. Danny brought a scrub brush from his. Larry brought an oilcan. He said we'd need it when we got a motor, wheels, and a chain.

Somebody else had built a tree fort in the woods there and we discovered his Playboy. Miss April 1969 was (and remains) immortalized in the minds and, without doubt, elsewhere, of at least four ten year-old boys. Someone stole it from our hiding spot two nights after we stole it from the fort.

It was an amazing place until, inevitably, they drained the swamp, opened the road, and put houses in there.

The third hill of the trilogy was the hill at the dead end of Gilbert Road.

Kevin's fate lay with a navy blue 1968 Plymouth Belvedere station wagon. From the top of the dead-end we saw it pull onto Candia Street minutes earlier, then we never saw it again. There was a faint registration among us, car there, and then it slipped out of mind.

The driver was lost in the neighborhood trying to find her sister who had moved into the first phase of development at the bottom of Cornish Street. She had been told the landmark was a big hill. She had pulled over and stopped behind a tree that completely blocked our view of her and her view of us. Kevin was past maximum momentum when she went into gear. Kevin didn't look up past Miscowski's. No one saw it coming, he hit the top of the shoot, and she hit the gas. He was in a full crouch on the toe section of the hill. The incline lessened there. It acted as a shoot where you sped past Candia Street and further along on Gilbert Road. Neither Kevin nor she hit the brakes. No one stopped in time. We saw her hood belch into view, Kevin sit up, turn his body, and put his feet down. She looked into her rear view mirror as she pulled out onto the road and then saw Kevin. His launch and tumble was stupefying. We heard her scream above his all the way to the top of the dead end.

It was amazing to watch. It was like we were high up in a tall tree; hidden, safe, watching the events unfold below us. Kevin cartwheeled in the air two and a half times. The Carl Yastremski baseball card he had clothes-pinned to his forks, slapping against the spokes, broke free. The card floated easily in the updraft created by car, bike, and kid. The shadow area under the front of the car ate his bicycle. Like a little splash of tomato sauce on someone's cheek, the streamer from his left side handlebar landed on the hood. For the longest time he defied gravity. The angle that the car hit him sent him flying toward the built up curbing on the corner that was there to channel the water off the hill toward the storm drain. At the end of his last half spin the right side of his head went against the curbing then his shoulder impacted too. The collision spun his body around counterclockwise and his left hip, thigh, and then knee smashed into the cement. He stopped moving when his right arm finished whipping around his body and snapped like a whip onto the road. There wasn't even enough momentum left in his hand for a dead-cat bounce.

At the top of the hill, Richard and Robert took off like the chickens they were and hid in the woods figuring they would be in trouble. Danny and I didn't know exactly what to do. We thought we might be in a lot of trouble too. Our parents were going to be mad because we had been told to never ride the hill again. That much was certain.

The idea came to us that maybe Kevin was like a solider that had been shot. We imagined that if we went to get him he'd throw his arms around our necks and we would half carry his limping self along. I suppose we thought we would carry him like a wounded war buddy in the movies. But he didn't get up. He didn't even wake up long enough to say something like, "It's only a flesh wound."

It was Columbus Day, so we weren't in school. Mothers poured from the homes surrounding the intersection with their children on their heels. The din rose all the way up the hill to us. They all started looking up at us. Mr. Miscowski was hopping up and down yelling, "I knew it." We got on our bikes and carefully rode down the hill with steady pressure on the brakes.

One of the women yelled at us, "This was bound to happen with you boys racing down that hill all the time."

Another one of the mothers turned all the small kids away so they wouldn't see Kevin, the blood, and his compound fracture. The woman who drove the station wagon was leaning against her car. She had her hands to her face. She was crying and shaking. A couple of the other women stood near her undoubtedly saying something like, "It wasn't your fault. He'll be okay."

More people came out of their houses. Someone said, "Go get Ann. She's a nurse." One of them took off in quick waddle to get her.

Danny and I skulked back across the street and lurked next to the hedges that lined one yard and watched the whole thing. I said to him, "Why didn't you yell that there was a car."

He said, "Why didn't you."

We heard a siren off in the distance turn onto Academy Avenue. Now it started to get exciting. We knew we were in big trouble and Kevin was hurt, but then a police-car and fire truck pulled up. They put some bandages on Kevin and set him on the stretcher that was in the back of the police station wagon and took him away. It was so cool to watch them at work and look at their pistols and handcuffs and billyclubs and fire hoses and helmets.

Then one of the women pointed to us. The police sergeant turned his head toward us.

He spoke to one of the other policemen who also turned his head toward us. Then the sergeant walked over to us. He was so big with his boots and badge and stripes and gun belt and bullets and handcuffs. My mouth was so dry I couldn't speak. Danny shook.

"What happened?"

"We were just going down the hill," I cried.

"Where do you live?"

"At 9 Gilbert Road."

"23 Jaffrey Street," whimpered Danny.

"Let's go talk to your parents."

We were doomed.

He said, "Go get your bikes." He got in the cruiser and followed me to my house first. I was shaking and sniffling the whole way. I couldn't even ride up the tiny hill that led to my house. I let my bike fall onto the lawn and stood there sniffling, wiping the snot and tears from my face onto my sleeve. Danny waited. He didn't even come into the yard. Sergeant Burke had told him to wait and pointed to a spot. Danny stood trembling at the far edge of the driveway, certain of his demise.

The sound is exclusive and unique to police cars, its door closing in the driveway or in front of your house. The doors of identical cars or neighbor's vehicles, uncles, friends, new cars or old make nothing like the sound of a police-car door. My mother came out to the breezeway and took the instant look of concern that quickly defaults to frustration when any mother's son comes home intact, but with the police. Sergeant Burke quietly explained about Kevin and what we had been doing. Now I knew I was dead, because I had been told not to ride there after another time when I had wiped out and tore up the side of my calf and new school shoes. Then I got caught again and was grounded, again.

Never before or since in my life has such a masterful display of understatement, restrained frustration, and annoyed concern play so precisely on me. Nor has such a display ever made me feel so guilty.

My mother said, "Thank you, Sergeant. I will get a hold of Kevin's mother." Then never taking her eyes away from Sergeant Burke, she said, "Pick up your bicycle, put it in the garage, and go to your room."

I was afraid to look anyone in the eye, lest it be some kind of unspoken challenge, but out of the corner of my eye I saw Danny mount his bike and start his dismal ride home. The police car door closed again, the tires ground on the gravel, and the engine noise disappeared into the oppressive Indian Summer stalking Danny.

As I walked past her I tried to explain that I hadn't done anything, "I was just there. Watching."

Silence.

"But Mom."

"Go to your room and do not come out until your father is home."

"Ma!"

I went to my room and started building a plastic model of the USS Massachusetts. That wasn't going my way either. I had glue strings everywhere before I even got the hull together. I heard her talk on the phone to Kevin's mother and again, later, to find out how Kevin was. I also heard her talking to my aunt in hushed tones.

I went downstairs to make a sandwich. I was instructed to return to my room. I laid on my bed and felt very heavy on the mattress. I crawled under the bed and stared up through the coils to the bottom of the mattress. There I saw the picture I had cut out of one my older cousins' Playboy. I thought I better get rid of it. I was sure I was in lot of trouble already and I knew there was something about that picture that could get me in more trouble.

But I didn't understand why I was in trouble. I hadn't done anything really wrong. I hadn't even ridden down the hill that day. I was just there, so I hadn't really disobeyed my parents.

I knew the noise signature of Danny's family car. Every morning it went past my window as his mother took her husband to the subway station. When they got the new station wagon it only took me four days to know its signature. I heard it coming up the street that afternoon. It was way too early in the day for her to be picking him up. I looked out the window and saw Danny in the back seat. His younger sister was in the front seat, which meant he was in big trouble. He looked up at my window as they drove past and I looked at him. The weight of the phrase Dead Man Walking was equivalent to Danny Back-Seat Riding. The wagon returned without Danny an hour later.

Danny was adopted and always wondered if somehow some day his parents would return him.

Maybe they did. Maybe parents got rid of kids. Maybe orphans and adoptees were kids who were returned because they were bad.

Would my parents return me? If they did, would I get to keep my models and my bike at the orphanage? Would my new parents take my brothers and me to the mountains every summer? Would I have brothers? Did I, technically, still have these siblings even if I was returned and got new ones? Suddenly the life I knew was over. It was unimaginable that new parents could be like my parents. I didn't want to be returned. Like Danny, had I been exchanged when I was born, too?

What was happening? I was in trouble and I hadn't even ridden that day. Kevin disappeared into the back of the police car. Danny was in trouble. His little sister had taken the front seat. Danny, maybe, was gone forever and I had left my ice skates at his house last winter. Could I get them back or would his mother send them to me at the orphanage? My mother was mad at me, my father was sure to be really mad at me, and it was one of the rare times when I hadn't done anything bad. But it still felt like the time I jumped on the roof of my brother's underground fort in the backyard and it collapsed on him. He had to have twenty-three stitches in his head. I knew I wasn't supposed to jump on it, but he had this cool fort and he and his friends wouldn't let me in. I didn't know he was in it.

He was supposed to be at Farm League practice. He had ditched practice to go to his stupid fort. He didn't get in any trouble for not going to practice. I got in trouble. Lots. I had to fix his fort and clean up after the dog when it was his turn. He got all the Spaghetti O's and 7-Up he wanted. Sometimes he did get in trouble for me. One time he was grounded for two weeks after I had tried to start the wood-floor in our bedroom on fire. Another time my bike scraped the paint on our new car when I put it in the garage. I moved my bike away and put his bike next to the car. He had to rake the lawn all fall.

The prospects of my life were grim.

Into the darkest corner of my closet I went, as far away as possible from the door so no light came through the cracks. There I considered my life. I swore I would be a better kid. I liked my brothers—sometimes, but I could like them all the time. I could look out for them. I'd share my stuff with them and make sure they didn't go near the hill. I'd cut the grass and do my chores. I could clean the dog poop in the cellar when Hunter had an accident even when it wasn't my turn.

I would start liking my aunt who had the little rolls filled with tuna salad at Christmas time at her house and stop tormenting her stupid little yippy poodle.

Maybe I could help Dad. Work always seemed to be a vague angry place and then he had so many chores to do on the weekends. I'd never ask for anything ever again because there was never enough money for the things I thought I must have: a black light, a pocketknife. Maybe he wouldn't want to get rid of me if I did all those things like washing the car, cutting the grass, painting, raking, fixing the roof, unplugging the toilet, changing the oil. Maybe he could do the things he liked to, like, like … the things he used to do before he got married like going to Red Sox games and flying and sailing. He always seemed so disappointed in his children and all of his problems seemed to start right after he got married. He seemed to like my brothers and me, but that was in old photographs of when we were all little kids.

But Mom wasn't speaking to me.

Dad would decide if I was to go or not, but he wasn't around that much. He had to work to keep a roof over our heads. Often I'd hear him getting home at seven or eight or nine o'clock at night and I'd see him at his desk or at the kitchen table with his papers, facts, and figures laying about. Then he'd be gone again in the morning by the time we got up to go to school. Every summer it was almost as though we all had to get reacquainted with each other on the first three or four days of our family vacations in August. By the end of the two weeks I really enjoyed being with him. He wasn't around the house too much, but Mom was always there. Her influence might sway him one way or the other as to whether I would stay or be returned.

How could she let me go if Dad decided I should be returned? She was ever present. Even when she wasn't in my sight and I not in hers she would, quick as a flash, jump in and out of my mind. I'd think about her for a second. Sometimes when I thought of her I wouldn't do something I knew I wasn't supposed to do because I didn't want her mad at me. Like the time we were going to ambush the neighborhood girls with mud balls with the really smelly mud that came from the swamp. Sometimes when Danny, Kevin, and me were riding bikes and we'd pass my house and she was in the yard we'd start yelling and hollering and showing off, riding with no hands on the handlebar or popping wheelies as we drove past. She would look at me. Sometimes she seemed scared when we went past and other times she smiled.

Maybe she, too, would say, "He is too much. Let's get a different son. We have the other boys who don't seem to be as much aggravation and I wouldn't mind having a daughter."

I really liked talking to her about things I saw, stories I heard, and the events of my ten years. She listened and seemed really interested. She would make me a sandwich whenever I was hungry. Once in a while she would let me have a half a glass of Coke. Even when I did things that were really dumb and sometimes hurt my brothers I could tell she still liked me even though she was really mad.

Dad shaped me by taking me places, showing me things, and teaching me how to be responsible to my paper-route customers. Mom stabilized me. If I were a kite, Dad was the wind and Mom was the string. Now both of them may be gone.

It was grave. I was history from this family.

I fell asleep in the closet. I woke when I heard my brothers come in. They were hushed and told to go over to the neighbors. The phone rang. I heard my mother say, "He's in a bad way, I think he is hurting a lot. Okay I'll see you soon then we can decide what we need to do. Bye." Her footfalls were many, long, and loud as she walked up to my room. She said, "Your father will be home soon and then we all need to talk." She went back downstairs.

Mothers are not necessarily women to their sons. They are distinct from the women we date and marry, but all males squirm when a female says, "We need to talk."

When Dad got home, he and Mom talked quietly for a while. I hated those conversations they had downstairs. Their voices would be so quiet and restrained then one or the other would bust a word out loudly. I knew those syncopated words were when whoever was listening was astounded by the incredulity of whatever information was just relayed. It was usually Dad as Mom relayed another one of my escapades.

Then Dad came to the bottom of the stairs and said, "Martin, come down here."

I thought maybe if I didn't go down and face the news I wouldn't have to go away.

A couple moments later my father spoke again in the tone that said he had no patience. "Do not make me come up there and get you."

I had fallen asleep for the last hour and a half of my solitary confinement. The door to the closet and my room were closed. The sun had set. The streetlight outside my window illuminated my room enough to make shadows and still show some detail of my room; my models and the books and desk that I would never see again. The hallway light silhouetted the bedroom door. I must go through that door. I suddenly felt very old, as if I were like the old men I saw living alone at the Y when I went for swimming lessons. They were solitary creatures. The old women talked a lot among themselves, but the old men slipped easily into solitude.

I moved old and slowly. As I looked around my room I knew I was never to be here again. I saw a picture of my whole family when we were camping in New Hampshire two years earlier. It was a great picture at the Dolly Copp campground near the Peabody River with the Presidential Range in the background. I thought I might be frisked as I was lead away so I stepped through my door and into the bathroom. Quickly I pulled my boot off and put the picture inside my sock wrapped around my ankle so I could leave this place with something to remember it by. I went down the stairs and stood there with my hands jammed into my dungaree pockets. They were seated in the living room. My father gestured for me to come closer. I shuffled a couple feet.

"Pick your feet up and come here," Dad said.

"Kevin will by okay." He continued. "He has a broken leg, a broken arm, and he needed 100 stitches."

Big deal I thought. Kevin gets a life. All the kids at school will hear his story and see his cast and crutches. He'll get to take the elevator. He'll be the most popular guy for the next few months. He'll get to leave class a little earlier than the rest of us. Someone will carry his books. The girls will get the door for him, they'll ask to sign his cast then sign it with their frilly signatures, and offer to return his tray to the dishroom. Danny and me were going to have to be like Oliver Twist and sleep on the floor in a room with lots of other boys and eat gross food and pick pockets to live.

"What do you have to say?"

Mumbling I said, "Nothing."

"Your best friend gets hurt and you don't have anything to say."

"He's not my best friend. Both he and Danny are my best friends."

"Don't speak. What were you doing on that hill when you have been told never to race down that hill again."

I stared at him.

"Well?"

"You just told me not to speak."

"Don't get smart. Answer the question."

I could do no right. He told me not to speak then got mad when I didn't. "I wasn't. I was just there."

"Don't start that. You will not be riding your bike until school is out. If you're lucky we will get lots of snow this winter so you won't miss it. You will come home right after school and do your homework and we are going to give you some new chores. And on the weekends you can go out in the yard, but you will be staying close by."

"For how long?"

"We'll let you know." The response cracked like a wet towel being snapped.

I started to think that maybe I wasn't going to be returned. I was feeling better and asked, "Can I ride Jason's bike?" He had a paper-route too and had just bought a new Schwinn Continental.

"I'm going to pretend I didn't hear that. Finally, we know how much you like speed. Ever since you were a little boy in the baby carriage you would want your mother and me to push it faster and faster. Neither of us have ever seen a tricycle go faster than when you were on it. So from now until the end of the school year you will walk everywhere. The only time you will get to ride anything is if we are all going somewhere together. You will walk your paper-route, to school, to Grandma's house, to the store. As soon as Kevin gets home from the hospital you will walk to his house after you're done with your paper-route and see if Kevin or his mother needs anything. Do you understand?"

"Yeah." Dad was mad but he was not going to send me away, but Ma still hadn't spoken. I thought she didn't want me around. I started sniffling and crying like a baby, "I'm sorry. I'll be good. Don't send me away with Danny."

Finally Mom spoke, "Are you hungry?"

My relief was misery and complete. I was staying, but I couldn't stay under my terms. I started running track that year.

CHAPTER 9

▼

MY MISOGYNY

It surprised me that my thoughts during my trip to Weymouth stayed connected to Weymouth related topics.

My thoughts are usually all over the place. Different scenarios run through my head in an incessant, intense, chaotic way. One moment I can be pretending I was a war hero when I was in the Navy, then I imagine myself displaying masterful prowess in all things; sport, business, art, and women, then a moment later I play out how I will act in a given situation. If diagnoses were as sophisticated then as they are now, I undoubtedly would have diagnosed with ADHD and probably OCD thirty years ago at Academy Avenue Elementary School in Weymouth. Those conditions linger into my adulthood, although they seem to have mellowed and I can marshal them, sometimes.

Greenbush was around the hill to my left and the tennis courts of Legion Field to my right as I continued along Commercial Street. From the intersection of Commercial Street and Unicorn Avenue I looked down Unicorn Avenue to where Greenbush crossed the road and saw one of the crossing lights still stood there. What happened to the other one I wondered? Did rust finally break it and it fell? If that were the case why didn't they both fall? The same elements wore on it, too. Or, if the town took it down why didn't they take them both down at the same time. Maybe the missing one was lying in brush waiting for someone to notice it. Do people steal railroad-crossing lights? Maybe I could get the crossing light somehow and ship it to my caboose.

Commercial Street bent slightly uphill and away from Unicorn Avenue and as I walked Weymouth North High School came into view. It was no longer Weymouth North. The population explosion settled and now it was simply Weymouth High School, along with the vocational and technical school. Its days were numbered with the opening of a new high school in South Weymouth. Just as well. Two high schools in Weymouth in the seventies left both schools lacking any distinction. At one time the Weymouth football team made it to the state high school finals. When I was in high school the teams barely won at anything. High school was a blur; it wasn't my glory days, my best of times, nor was it misery. Dad didn't encourage sports or academics or music or, frankly, anything. Left to my own methods I drifted my way through the Weymouth Public School System. I would like to have been more involved, but, like when I tried out for basketball and after fouling everyone on the court, repeatedly, I gave up.

Open tryouts. Everyone invited to play, the poster read. Why not I thought. I was okay at baseball, football never really interested me, but basketball looked fun and not too complicated, so I went to the gym on Saturday morning. I knew a couple guys on the team, a little. I watched everyone very carefully and hustled out on the floor when the coach called for anyone wanting to try out, to come one out. He said we were to play a game against the junior team and not to worry about winning. He was watching to see who had potential. Seemed reasonable to me, I thought I had a chance and gave it my best. From the moment the game started they blew whistle often and vigorously on me. The coach and teammates yelled for me to stop fouling, but no one bothered to show me what I was doing wrong. Thus ended my foray into basketball. I would dearly liked to have known what I was doing wrong. I could have corrected the problem instantly. But being male means you have to arrive with knowledge, confidence, and skill. It's easier to walk away than to suffer the humiliation of not being confident, skillful, and knowledgeable. In my alter life in California I mastered volleyball, tennis, and golf with the briefest instruction.

Standing there looking at the school I felt glad to have gone there, but frustrated, too. It was good. I learned, made some good friends, and grew physically and socially like everyone is supposed to in high school. But, whatever it was that held me back made it all, ultimately, feel hollow.

Like sports, I didn't arrive with the skill, confidence or knowledge to enjoy the high school girls either. Girls were not completely absent from my youth, but they didn't have prominent role either.

In the hindsight of the long sequence of events that compelled me to visit Weymouth, Lisa Sands' role came into view. Lisa and I were in the same homeroom. We were classmates who went separate ways after graduation. At graduation I'm sure our communication went some like this, "Good luck." "Have a nice life." "Don't do anything I wouldn't do." I never gave her another thought until she spotted me in San Diego about two years ago.

My work had sent me to San Diego to leverage an inconsistent supplier to be more consistent. I have an ability to effuse an intense displeasure. I can make people very uncomfortable and hardly say a word.

Whether I am on the road or at home I am not one for bars and clubs. They are uncomfortable places for me. I don't like yelling over the music all the time and I did not have anywhere near the success meeting women as my friends appeared to have. There were a few times when I met someone, danced a little, and bought her a drink. A couple times I got a phone number. But usually I stood there watching everyone, alternately feeling superior then anxious. Even in my late teens and throughout my twenties out with my friends in bars and clubs, most of the time, I was restless. It showed. Usually I chose to go somewhere else, like a bookstore, and often ended up going alone.

My best success at meeting women was in bookstores and libraries, but even there it was marginal.

On the last night of my trip to San Diego I was in a bookstore. As I sat in one of the chairs sampling a book I felt as though someone was looking at me. I glanced up and finally caught a woman glancing at me. I nodded at her and attempted a warm smile.

She said, "Hi."

I pushed my forehead up, lifted my eyebrows, and said, "Hello." She was not a familiar face. I couldn't place her as anyone I knew.

"You're Martin Roberts, aren't you? You grew up back in Massachusetts, Weymouth, and graduated from Weymouth North. Right?" she said.

"Yes." I had a reference point now. The synapses were firing furiously. I started processing the faces of the girls I knew in high school. "You must be from Weymouth."

She said, "We were in homeroom together. Do you remember me? It's okay if you don't. It's been more than twenty years."

I have always been amazed with the people who watch television shows like America's Most Wanted and are able to make a connection from an old photograph or sketch to a neighbor in a trailer park somewhere. I miss family resemblance among siblings regularly. I started to remember her. She sat behind me. Her last name began with S.

At the same moment we both said, "Lisa Sands."

I followed with, "Wow. Sorry I didn't remember you at first."

There was a pause. I set the book aside and stood up. I put out my hand and said, "Wow," again. "Do you live in San Diego?"

"No. I still live in Mass. In Norwood."

We stood there for a minute nodding our heads toward each other. She asked, "You went in the service after we graduated, didn't you?"

"Yes. I went to Northeastern for a year or so then I went into the Navy. How about you? What do you do?"

"I went to nursing school at BU."

"Husband? Kids?"

"Both. I met my husband at BU. We got married a couple years after college and moved to Norwood. He's a policeman for Norwood. We have two kids, one of each. My oldest is fourteen and my baby is ten. How about you? I don't see a ring."

"Not married. No kids."

"Oh. You have anyone special?"

"Not at the moment. I was married, but it didn't work out." I didn't offer any clues about my other two failed marriages and the several live-in girlfriend disasters.

"What do you do for work? I remember you were quite a shutterbug in high school and I think I heard that you went into the service as a photographer."

"I did go in the Navy as a photographer and ended up here in San Diego. Now I'm the operations manager for an Internet company. I live up near San Francisco."

"Do you still take pictures?"

"No I worked as a photographer for a few years after I got out of the service, but I lost my interest in it."

"That's too bad. I remember your pictures in the yearbook were really good."

"Thanks. I never got much feedback on my pictures, good or bad."

Then came the dip in the conversation. I broke eye contact with her and we both glanced around the store. We were going past the palaver and the conversation was about to expand or crash. The lull dangled between us. I raised my eyebrows and got ready to say, 'It was nice to see you, but I've got to go.'

She asked, "Do you ever get back to Weymouth or the South Shore at all?"

"Seldom. No, really, it's more like never. I haven't been there in years. I imagine you get there once in while."

"Actually I get there at least weekly. My father died a few years ago, but my mother still lives there. My sisters all married and moved away so I'm the dutiful daughter and check on Mom regularly."

She told me she was in San Diego for a conference. She had been promoted to a nurse manager and was representing her hospital at a conference on how to get more reimbursement from the government and insurance companies. The conference had ended yesterday, but she had stayed on another day to poke around the area and enjoy a little California sun. She was flying back to Boston tomorrow morning.

I hadn't eaten and I was getting hungry. Lisa seemed like she knew how to keep a conversation from plunging and some human interaction outside the business sphere was appealing.

"I'm hungry. You want to get a bite to eat?" I asked.

"That sounds good. I could go for something. What do you have in mind?"

"When I stationed here I knew some good places. I remember a Mexican place near the freeway that was pretty good. I'll ask someone if the place still exists."

It did.

"Can we walk there, or should I go get my rental car?"

"It's close enough to walk."

"I want to change into something else. I'm staying at the Hyatt. It's just around the corner. Would you mind waiting a minute?"

"Not at all. I'm staying there too."

I had to pay for the book. I asked her if she had anything to buy. She grabbed three or four postcards.

The nights in San Diego are always pleasant; the mild temperatures, the ocean, and this part of the harbor was safe for tourists. We walked along the bay working a conversation about high school. Did she like a particular teacher? Did I know that this person had married that person? Where did I spend my senior skip day? Who did she go to the prom with? And so on.

She told me Tony Ruzzo, the guy all the girls went crazy over, died of AIDS. David Welsh opened a restaurant in Jackson Square. Heather McDunough died recently in car wreck. The only real mutual acquaintance we had, Ken, ended up a lawyer.

"How do you know so much if you don't live there?" I asked.

"My mother. She's lived in Weymouth all her life. She keeps me up-to-date. Every week she tells me something about someone from our class."

"Does this mean my name is suddenly going to surface on the Weymouth wire?"

"Oh, absolutely. It'll give the Weymouth wire, as you call it, a real buzz. And everyone will be pleased to hear that someone with a connection to Weymouth has surfaced. Then you'll be processed. They'll be speculation about your family. They'll remember your mother died. Then they'll wonder what kind of man you turned out to be because of that. Then someone will remember something else they heard about someone else and the conversation will spin. You'll be news for about a month."

That idea was pleasing and disturbing. I intentionally cut my connections to Weymouth when I left. I had no communication with either one of my brothers for years. After my father died, I had no reason to stay in touch with them. And I didn't want to, either. I hadn't responded to Danny's Christmas cards in years. I hadn't received one from him for several years.

But I was pleased at the idea of being a celebrity on the Weymouth wire.

Lisa said, "I was sorry to hear your friend Kelli died." She paused a moment, then she asked, "Did you and Kelli ever go out? It was obvious to everyone that you were great friends and went well together."

"No. It would have been too weird."

"Why? I mean most girls, women, would love to have had a guy friend who was that close."

"I don't know. Sometimes I wonder about it, but when I left Weymouth I left a lot behind. She was the only person I visited when I got back there."

"Sounds like things weren't so good for you."

"It wasn't bad. No one grows up unscathed, but I knew I had to get away. And since I left, it's all kinda' faded."

"What about your friend Danny?"

I shrugged my shoulders. I didn't want to talk about me and my broken links to Weymouth anymore. She got the hint.

"Did you know Mrs. Smith from your neighborhood died all alone?"

"No. What happened?"

"My mother knows someone on almost every street in town, and she knew her. Mrs. Smith had gotten sick. She had no one, you know, her husband died a long time ago."

"I knew she was a widow."

"Like I said, she had gotten sick, but she was getting better and left the nursing home and went back to her house. Well she had a massive stroke. No one had seen or heard from her in a few days. Someone called the police and they went to her house and found her.

"She wasn't dead dead, but there was barley a heartbeat and virtually no brain function. They took her to the hospital. The Weymouth wire was at it best then. She had no heir or caretaker or anything, but then someone remembered she had a son and within a few hours they found him. Did you know him?"

"A little. He was older and left for Vietnam. I don't think he ever came back after the war."

"Well they tracked him down in Georgia. He had to come up to Weymouth. He decided they should pull the plug. He put the house on the market a week later. It sold and had new people living there within a month."

"That's too bad. She was nice lady." Something odd tugged at me when she told me about Mrs. Smith. I wish I had known she was sick. It made me sad to hear she died in such oblivion. She was always good to me. We had a ritual. I waved at her house each day when I got home from school. If she was outside she waved back, if not one of the lights in the house blinked back at me.

I mowed her grass and shoveled her walk. I guess I felt she would always be there in that house. She was a nice lady.

I couldn't remember much about Lisa. I had no idea who she hung with, whether she was one of the jocks or in the drama and music circle or part of the crowd that got stoned everyday on the way to school.

"I saw you a couple times," she said, "hanging off the trains that used go through Weymouth."

"You're kidding."

"Nope. I remember it was in the winter and I saw you again in the summer."

"What was I doing?"

"Just sitting there in the door of one the cars, and the other time just holding on. I thought you were crazy, but your friend Danny told me you hopped the trains all the time."

"Those trains never went far or fast, just Braintree to Hingham, but I spent a fair amount of time on them."

"There's talk of restarting commuter trains on that line again."

"Really. I would have never guessed."

"You kept to yourself a lot in high school, didn't you." It was more of a statement than a question.

"I guess I did."

She remembered more about me than I did her. She said, "There were girls in school that liked you, but you were so quiet, and because of Kelli, they never let on."

"I wish I had known there were girls that were interested in me. I lacked for dates back then. For that matter, I lack for dates now."

"You'd be surprised at some of the girls who liked you." That statement may have been accompanied with a coy look, but in addition to my lack of boldness with women, I misinterpreted and missed subtleties like that regularly.

The conversation slowed. We walked Harbor Drive commenting on what we saw as we walked to the hotel. Across the harbor helicopters were landing at the Naval Air Station North Island. Two carriers were docked there. The Pacific does not smell like the Atlantic. The Pacific doesn't have a briny smell, and, to me, the Atlantic has a green look to it. The Pacific is bluer. The sun set behind us over Point Loma as we walked Harbor Drive to the hotel. The harbor bustles. It's lined with restaurants, the Star of India sailing ship, ferry boats, cruise ships, the Pacific Fleet, Lindbergh Field, the Coast Guard Air Station, pleasure boats, jet-skis, container ships. People everywhere.

I said, "It's not like Wessegusett Beach or the Fore River at all. Is it?"

"No, not at all. Funny, I was thinking the same thing."

We walked in silence a little farther then turned into the hotel. I wanted to go to my room for a minute. The elevator had a panel with floor buttons on both sides of the car. We pushed the same button.

"I'm in room fourteen twelve," she said. "When you're ready to go, knock on my door."

I turned left down the hallway and she went right. I grabbed a lightweight jacket, hung out a couple minutes to give her time to change, and went to her room.

She let me in then stepped into the bathroom to finish changing. "Open up the refrigerator and make us a drink."

I balked. I still struggled with some of my frugal New England upbringing. Even though money slips through my hands like trying to put butter on corn-on-the-cob, psychologically I struggle with paying for something so incredibly overpriced like the alcohol in hotel room refrigerators. I declined. "I'll wait until we get to the restaurant."

She stepped out of the bathroom. The change was dramatic. In about ten minutes she had altered her hair, put on a different dress, different shoes, make-up, and perfume. When we first said hello in the bookstore she had a borderline frumpy look. Suddenly she had an alluring pull to her. I felt a change toward her deep within myself. Her look set a new tone for me. Although I was still dining with an acquaintance and my relationship gauge indicated a brief, but benign friendship, now that friendship had a slight sexual tug, too.

A thousand times I have been in that spot, I'm attracted to a woman. I see her as sensual or sexy, and I think she is unattainable on every level because she is married or with someone, or only in my company because I'm a friend and my lack of sexual aggression makes me safe.

We left the hotel and resumed our conversation about Weymouth. She was a good conversationalist. She got me to talk about things I had seen in the Navy and what I had done with my life afterward. I told her about my stint as a medical and forensic photographer. Even though she worked in healthcare she had never given attention to medical photography. When I explained what the work involved, she said she was going to look at the photographer at her hospital with new appreciation. She talked about her kids. They were very different. One was a jock, the other a bookworm. But they liked each other. She didn't talk about her husband at all. Not even the customary husband bashing. I wondered if there was trouble there.

We found the restaurant. The bright colors and horn-saturated music pulled us right into the atmosphere. We had the first margarita while we waited for a seat. I don't know if it was the alcohol or our common background or her intelligence and sincerity, but she was the most interesting person I had enjoyed dinner with in years.

The tequila was showing. We both laughed out loud. I thought I was being clever and witty. She laughed at my jokes. I felt myself wanting to make a positive impression, like it was a date. However, I had a rule that I was generally good about obeying. The rule was, I tried to not view married women as sexual beings, particularly ones with children. I thought my compartmentalizing married women kept things uncomplicated and safe for everyone involved.

One time I fooled around with a married woman. She was in the middle of her divorce and there were no kids. We ended up living together; the outcome was another one of my relationship misadventures.

As Lisa talked, I listened much more closely than I thought I would have. I took it all in. High school and Weymouth were not her glory days either, but the difference between Lisa and I was she had enjoyed them.

When we left the restaurant I offered her my arm and she hooked her arm through mine. We walked back to the hotel. I asked her about her husband. Through our linked arms I felt her tense. She didn't respond right away so I interjected. "I'm guessing there's trouble there. I'm sorry for asking."

She nodded her head slightly, "Yes."

We kept walking, within ten minutes we were back at the hotel.

"Do you want to sit by the pool?" I asked.

"That'd be nice. I'd like to take a swim."

"I didn't bring a bathing suit."

"That's okay. Do you mind if I splash around?"

"Not at all."

I changed into a pair of shorts I had with me. I made it back to the pool first and ordered us a couple more drinks. I was sitting with my feet in the water when she returned. I watched her unwrap the towel from her waist and slide into the water. She wore a one-piece bathing suit.

The pool light silhouetted her body. When she surfaced, the water shimmered its odd blue-green coloring on her. I held up her drink. She did the water based sashay toward me then submerged and swam underwater to me. She looked like she was going to come up right between my legs, but at the last moment she balked and turned to her side and stopped to my right. She took the drink and finished it in one long swallow.

"Order me another." Then she swam away underwater.

I couldn't help but feel the sexual pull.

She swam back to me, splashing the water all over me. She climbed out of the pool and moved behind me toward our clothes. I should have known what was coming. She got very quiet. After a moment I turned to look back at her over my shoulder. She lunged and I was in the pool. I jumped back up at her and pulled her in. We swam around for a minute then our drinks arrived. At the pool's edge we stopped. I took a drink. She was right next to me. We were in physical contact. Her pelvis was against my hip. She didn't break away.

She said, "I went to a pool party back in Weymouth, in your neighborhood, once."

"Must have been Ken's. He was the only one in my area that had a pool."

"You and your friend Danny were there. Do you remember at all?"

"I remember Ken and the pool. Why?"

"Remember I said there were girls in high school who liked you. Why didn't you notice them? You said you didn't have many girlfriends."

"I'm just oblivious to those signals. I always have been. I'm sure there's deep-seated psychological reason for it. I've probably missed more opportunities with women than most men ever get."

She swam away again then left the pool, dried off, wrapped the towel around her waist, and pulled the chair close to the pool. "I'm glad we met here. I'm having a really nice time."

"Me too."

"Do you think we're friends?"

"Yes. Of course. I thought when we went to dinner this would be a passing, pleasant acquaintance, but I've really enjoyed spending the evening with you."

She leaned back in the chair. "It's so nice here." She rolled her head around looking over the pool area, "The lights, the night sky, it's a nice break from the kids and work and all."

I said I was going to the Jacuzzi. She followed me there. The water overheated me quickly and I sat on the edge. She stayed in the whirling water. She leaned her head toward me then rested it on my thigh.

The waitress came over. She was pretty and young. I had been watching her for the last couple minutes. She was arguing with the bartender. I couldn't hear anything, but her body language said they were definitely fighting.

She didn't look at us as she spoke. "The bar is closing soon. Do you want anything else?"

I always try and make eye contact with everyone I'm speaking to whether it's bank tellers, cashiers, waiters, my staff, everyone. I waited for her look at me.

Eventually, she looked at me. It was more of a glare.

"We'd like a couple more margaritas." Then I asked, "What's he done to make you so mad?"

I felt Lisa move her head off my thigh and look at her.

Her nametag said Renee. "He just told me he wants to be just friends. He met someone else and is not sure about us anymore."

"How long ago did he meet her?"

"Oh this has been going on for a few months."

"I'm really sorry to hear it."

"I thought things were going good." She took a deep breath. "You know what, if he thinks he can do better then the hell with him. Lot's of guys ask me out. I'm going to start saying yes since he wants to be just friends now." She turned and left.

When she left I looked at Lisa. I expected her to say something about her and her husband's troubles then. She laid her head back down on my thigh.

Renee came back she said, "Here you go. They're on the house. I'm sorry for venting on you. You seem like a nice couple."

Lisa looked at her. "Sometimes you meet someone really nice at the most unexpected time."

It was getting late. It was time to go. Everything had gone along well between Lisa and I, but there was a lull. I decided it was time to wrap up this evening. I said I was heading back to my room in a few minutes. She said she was tired too and had to pack and get ready for her flight.

As we walked back I said, "I'm really glad we ran into each other."

"Maybe we could stay in touch with email or something."

By now we at her room, I figured a hug was safe. It was. She went inside to get one of her business cards for me. Another hug. A restatement of the vague prom-ise to keep in touch, to look each other up if she was west or I was east. She moved her face close to mine. I thought it was the kiss-on-the-cheek adieu; I turned my face toward her cheek and kissed her. Then I turned and walked to my room.

There have been abundant moments in my life when I completely misread the situation with a woman. Annie, Jackie, Kathy, and so on, the list would be end-less. Once I was hiking with Annie. It was a third or fourth date. There had been no contact so far, we came down the hill and had half mile or so to go to get back to the car. She held out her hand. I took it and shook it and let it drop. I thought she was saying, via the handshake, thanks for a pleasant interaction. A couple hundred yards later she asked why I didn't want to hold her hand.

A classic Marty misinterpretation.

Kathy was another girl I missed the signals with. She was the sister of a friend. Whenever Glenn and I got together she always hung around talking to me, ask-ing me if there was anything I needed, sitting next to me, offering to pick me up and drop me off wherever while I was having car troubles. Finally another friend, a Brit, in that circle put it very bluntly, "Marty, what does she have to do before you get the hint. Take your willy and put it between her legs?"

I thought she was just being nice.

And Jackie. Jackie I met during my brief attempt at college. I suppose if my head hadn't been so far up my rear-end it might have been a very good relation-ship. To this day she is the only woman I regret never having asked out or acting on the hints even I noticed. And, to this day, she is the only woman I think of every day. If it didn't seem so pathetic and desperate I'd look her up.

That night in San Diego I locked myself in my room, pleased with the evening and having made a friend, and irritated with myself that I didn't know how to push for more of an interaction. Strangely, too, I was glad I didn't know how to push for more because it would complicate everything.

I brushed my teeth, settled into bed, and opened the Robert Lowell book of poems I bought that evening. After ten minutes the phone rang. I thought it might be my secretary. There was a problem brewing at the company and if it went a certain direction she was to call.

It was Lisa.

"Hi."

"Hi. What are you doing?"

"Reading that book of poetry I bought earlier."

"Oh."

"What are you doing?"

"Nothing. Can't sleep."

"I think I'll be asleep as soon as I put the book down."

"Oh. Well maybe I'll watch some TV."

"They've got a million channels here."

"Okay. Hey I am really glad we met tonight. You'll remind me of California. Do you think we'll stay friends? Stay in touch?"

"Sure we're friends. We'll stay in touch. I don't think we'll be going out for dinner every other weekend, but like we said earlier, if you get west again or when I make it east we'll hook up. Maybe we can meet for breakfast tomorrow."

"I'd like that. Call me when you get up. Enjoy your book. Good night."

"Good night."

I wondered if there was an unspoken message in that phone conversation. I decided there wasn't. I read one poem, turned out the light, and within moments headed into semi-awareness between wake and sleep. The phone rang again.

"I'm sorry. Did I wake you?"

"That's alright."

"I still can't sleep."

"Do you want some company?"

"Would you? That'd be nice. Will you come here or do you want me to come to your room?"

"Whatever."

"I'll be right there. Are you sure you don't mind?"

"No, not at all."

It took her ten minutes to get to my room. I was just about to call her when she knocked on my door. When I opened the door she smiled and said, "Package from Weymouth."

She came in and started apologizing immediately for interrupting my reading and waking me up. "No big deal," I said. I lay back down in bed. She sat in the chair. I reached for the remote control. She saw the book I bought and asked how it was. I offered to read her one of the poems. She nodded. She liked it and asked me to read her another one. She came over and sat on the edge of the bed.

"I don't know this guy's poetry very well. I haven't read enough to decide if this is another disturbed and dark poet or if he observes things and writes about what he feels. Good or bad."

"That's okay. I've never had anyone read me a poem before."

I read her a couple more poems.

She left her chair and lay down on the bed close to me.

She was wearing the hotel's robe. When she lay down, the rustle of the robe released her perfume into the room. The window was open, as always. An easy breeze came in off the bay, and her perfume gently mixed with the clean, Dove-soap like smell of the robe. It was bewitching. I rested the book on my chest and closed my eyes. The room rocked like a cradle. Traffic noise abated and I could hear the surf pulsing against the piers. I opened my eyes only halfway and through the softening filter effect of eyelashes the room was dim and the deep colors of the desk and trim were rich and soothing, indeed. I felt her chest rise and fall beside me. I opened my eyes further and looked at her. I could see her chest through the opening where the robe came together. She turned to her side and one of her breasts almost revealed itself.

I flipped through a few more pages and found another poem whose title and first line caught my eye.

She closed her eyes while I read. As she lay there I smelled perfume again. It was pleasant, but not mystifying like it was a few moments earlier. She had fresh make up on. When I lay back down on the bed, I put a pillow over my boxer shorts. I had an erection. Once again I was torn. Was she here because she trusted me and felt safe or was she here for another reason and was I supposed to do something about it?

I retreated to the belief that she was here because she felt safe and comfortable with me.

I read her one more poem then I set the book aside, turned out the light, and turned the TV on. She lay there. I read the TV menu for her. She didn't care. She seemed like she had suddenly gotten drowsy. I clicked on the History Channel. Some guy was analyzing Shakespeare's sonnets. Actors played the roles. Boring.

Lisa moved her leg over mine. Her pelvis pressed against my thigh. Even I picked up on this movement. I stroked her hair. She turned her face toward mine and we kissed. She stopped and rolled away. "I can't. I'm sorry." She rolled to edge of the bed and sat up. "I should leave."

"If you want to stay we don't have to do anything. We can watch Shakespeare's sonnets and next hour we can learn about wartime poetry."

She looked at the TV then looked back at me. "If I stay we will end up making love. I want to, but I shouldn't even be here now. I can't."

She kissed me and left. She almost ran to the door. The door to my room closed and a moment later I heard another door close down the hall.

I wasn't going back to sleep after that. Maybe A&E or Discovery had something interesting on. I could always pay for one of the adult movies and fantasize about what didn't happen with Lisa. I'd end up relieving my own tension and falling asleep. It would be almost as good as sex with another person. The phone rang.

"Hello."

"Hi. I'm sorry."

"There's nothing to be sorry about."

"I just found out about my husband's girlfriend, but I'm still married."

"I'm sorry to hear about it."

"This evening with you, it's been so easy, so uncomplicated. This is the first time in the three weeks that I haven't thought about it. I just need a friend right now."

"We are that."

"Thanks. I'll see you at breakfast."

I felt really bad for her. I didn't know her that well, but I guessed she put her heart into her family. For him to have had an affair must be killing her.

I've been where she is and it is a miserable place to be. My first wife had an affair. My second wife said she and her lover didn't have actual intercourse until after our divorce was final. She said it was just oral. I think she thought that my knowing they had not screwed each other would make me feel better. It didn't. I didn't feel anything but resignation.

My first wife, April, and I had an apartment. She wasn't working. One of our neighbors worked nights; a nice enough guy, Brian. We'd have him and his various girlfriends over for dinner occasionally, barbecue in the courtyard once in while. Then it was just he for dinner. Then he and April were spending time together during the day. I got suspicious and watched them one day. They were at the pool. She leaned over and kissed him. They held hands while they sat in the lounge chairs then, still holding hands they went in the building together.

I knew what was going on. As I sat in the car watching them I was alternately furious and hollow. I stifled my tears and my fury, and left the car. I quietly went into the apartment and saw more than I needed to. I can still see it.

With me she said she never liked mutual oral sex. She always wanted to enjoy the receiving without the distraction of giving at the same time. Yet there she was with Brian in the middle of mutual oral sex. A vibrator was lying on the nightstand, too. I never knew she had one much less included it in her sexual repertoire.

I stood there and watched for a moment and they sensed my presence. He jumped up and put on his bathing suit. She sat up and told me it wasn't what it looked like. She told me not to do anything stupid. She wanted the three of us to talk.

I turned and left. I couldn't think and wouldn't be able to do anything the rest of that day. There were some secluded railroad tracks near the apartment and I walked them all the way to mainline.

As I walked she kept trying to page me. I turned it off. I knew I'd eventually go back and listen to what she said.

That evening I went back to the apartment. I was not going to spend the night there, but I needed some clothes and a couple other things.

She said she was sorry for hurting me and not telling me. But she wasn't sorry for loving Brian. He was her soul mate. She just knew it. She couldn't give him up.

I didn't marry a very stable woman. I knew that going in. She poured affection and devotion on me while we dated. If I wasn't at work I was with her. Initially I liked the attention, but soon I felt smothered. She pushed to get married. She said maybe if she knew the stability of being married she wouldn't be so clingy. Made sense to me, so I went along with it and we got married.

That night she suggested that maybe we all could live together. She knew she could love both of us. She said Brian was okay with the idea. Was I okay with it?

I filed the papers for divorce the next day.

What I felt during my last twelve hours with April was what let me empathize with Lisa.

There was a knock at my door. It was Lisa. She came in, slipped off her robe and slid under the covers. I removed my boxers and pulled her close to me.

It was the third time in my life I had a Weymouth woman naked with me. Two of those three times we touched in sexual ways, but we didn't have sex.

I held her until she fell asleep. I stayed awake unsure of what I was supposed to be doing.

The next morning she was gone. I called her room. No answer.

I went and worked out, then to breakfast. I took a walk along the harbor-front again. Back at the hotel I asked the concierge for shuttle information to the airport. I had a few hours to kill. I went to pack and there in my suitcase was a note from Lisa.

Dear Marty,

Thank you for being a friend.

Thank you for a wonderful evening. Dinner, swimming, even spending the night with you was exactly what I needed. I'm sorry if I frustrated you.

Last night I wish you had tried to make love to me. This morning I wish we had made love. Also, this morning, I'm glad we didn't.

I'll treasure our friendship and our time in California forever.

See you in Weymouth someday.

With love

Your Weymouth friend,
Lisa

CHAPTER 10

▼

PROTOCOLS

I thought about giving Lisa a call while I was in Weymouth. Maybe we could have lunch, but then I thought she had been in a bad way that night in San Diego. If I called her I was sure to make her uncomfortable. I'm always uncomfortable around women with whom I've had some level of a sexual interaction with. I think, maybe, the indiscretions women have had with me haunt them like a nightmare. Maybe there's some modesty involved. Most of all I don't want to face them and see the embarrassment in their eyes when they realize it's me. It's pathetic to think this, I know, but when a number of the women I've known have said to me. "You're not the best and you're not the worst I've had. You're in the middle." Oh, I'm average. I don't want to see that contempt in their eyes, either. No I wasn't going to call Lisa or anyone.

It was my therapist who explained to me how I viewed myself, as far as women are concerned. She said in time I'll come to not believe that perception I have of myself with women. Ten years later I'm still waiting to believe something different.

I glanced at my watch. I was moving along okay. I'd make it to Harold's on time.

By then I was passing Pingree School and just outside of Jackson Square. Looking across the ball field there I saw the embankment that had been built up to let Greenbush's rail bed cross the Herring Run where it emptied into the Back River. In my mind's eye I saw a small train transiting the line and disappear into the trees. I shook my head and told myself it couldn't be. But I stopped and strained to hear the engine's horn at the East Weymouth station grade crossing. If there were indeed a train there I would have heard the horn within a minute or so. Nothing. I moved on toward Jackson Square.

Before I walked into the square, I noticed the Wilson's house. I had forgotten all about them and the escapades that originated with them. I wasn't always so pathetic with women.

Matt and Rob Wilson traveled from Belle Chase, Louisiana to Weymouth fastened to the back of their family car, rocking and rolling the whole way in a travel trailer. Every time Chief Petty Officer Wilson transferred that's how they moved. I think it was a noxious thrill for them.

It would have been for me.

My family did not have a travel trailer and no one I knew did, either. The closest thing to a travel trailer anyone in my family had was an uncle who had a pop-up camp trailer. To my pubescent way of thinking, having a trailer was like having a swimming pool. Cool. My family did not have anything that made me stand out in junior high school. I prayed for my father to get something that would have attracted envious attention to me; a travel trailer, a boat, a pool, a plane, a gun, anything. Without something, I was certain I was doomed to the captious isolation of junior high school.

Several months before the Wilson's arrived in Weymouth my mother had died. In an inexplicable way, I liked being the center of sad attention. But a new school year began, the disconnect of summer vacation had transpired, and life went on. I lacked distinction.

The Wilsons materialized in Weymouth because Chief Wilson transferred from Naval Air Station Belle Chase to Naval Air Station South Weymouth. My reprieve from the adolescent isolation I dreaded arrived with them and their travel trailer.

Housing for personnel and families stationed at NAS South Weymouth was in Quincy. The housing units were left over World War II dormitories in bad shape and full. The Wilson's did not want to live there; so all five of them lived in the trailer for their first couple of weeks at the base. They finally rented a house in East Weymouth at the edge of Jackson Square. They parked the trailer at the end of their driveway, put it up on stands, and let it be.

We were a couple of weeks into the new school year at East Junior High School when the Wilson brothers showed up. We all spotted the strangers immediately. Danny and I greeted them with the same disdain all teenagers show newcomers. We thought they were odd because of their accent and goofy military-issue glasses. Everyone was already edgy, in a strange situation because we were on double sessions at Central Junior High School. The actual school building for East Junior High had been set on fire a couple years earlier.

Further, throughout Greater Boston the fallout from forced integration via busing drove many adult white Bostonians to the surrounding white suburbs like Weymouth. They fled South Boston and Dorchester with their white children so their kids would not and could not play with the black kids from Roxbury and Mattapan.

In the middle of all that, Matt and Rob Wilson successfully integrated themselves into the white, middle-of-middle-class town of Weymouth.

Matt and Rob were fraternal twins. Matt was the one burdened with the dorky genes. Beyond that they were different from everyone else in school because they did not look like anyone else in school, but the Wilson brothers were okay. They moved around so much with the Navy that mixing themselves into a new school and making friends was easy. If any of that disdain or mono-chromatic shading of Weymouth bothered them, they never let on.

Matt remains the smartest and most generous person I have ever met. It was through his intelligence and kindness that he and his brother came into our circle. In science class one day he saw me struggling with some concept and offered to help me. I took him up on his offer. A few days later when we were in the library going over a chapter for a test in physical science I met Rob. Danny stopped by and I introduced them to him.

Over the next year and a half Matt helped me for hours with my homework. As mad or as insistent as I got at him, he held his ground and would not do my homework for me. But, because he was so smart and could grasp the concepts so easily, he was able to teach Danny, me, and anyone else the concepts of physical science, chemistry, algebra, and so on. He was such a good teacher and used such relevant analogies that to this day his teachings remain with me.

Rob was a creative type. He could draw amazingly well. He played the trumpet in band and taught himself the guitar. He rarely had a bad word to say about anyone. Over the year and a half we hung out together there was only one thing that ever bothered him, his older brother.

A week after we were all introduced in the library, Danny and I stopped by their house on our bikes and asked them if they wanted to go to the movies with us. They did and the friendship developed. Mrs. Wilson invited us to stay for dinner that evening. Over the next year I had my first sampling of grits, po-boys, gumbo, jambalaya, and the best fried chicken I've ever had. In the summer, if there was C-130 or P-3 flying into Weymouth from Belle Chase, Chief Wilson sometimes arranged for crawdads to be on the plane and we had a crawdad boil; corn on the cob, baby new potatoes, and the blues and energetic gospel music playing off their old record player. He gave us a taste of his mint julep.

I was regular at the dinner table in Danny's house. I think his parents pitied me because of my mother's death. Danny's parents gave Rob and Matt a standing invitation to dinner and their family cookouts. Danny, Rob, and Matt ate at my house only once. My father was a good cook, but he got drunk and threw a tantrum.

I'd bring lobsters I had trapped in the Back River and clams I had dug to Danny's and the Wilson's homes. In season I'd pick wild raspberries and give them to Danny's mother. She would make me jam. Homemade jam, that was another one of the things I missed after my mother died.

Matt and Rob went to chapel on the base twice a week, Sunday mornings and early Wednesday evenings. They didn't want to go, but they didn't have a choice. Mr. Wilson had Rob excused from Wednesday afternoon basketball or baseball or band practice. Matt had to forgo whatever club meeting he had on Wednesdays. Their parents took us all bowling on base every Tuesday night. Every Sunday night they went to the spaghetti dinner at the American Legion Post. They had their own version of reveille every morning; raise the flag and say a prayer. Taps and the striking of colors were optional. We all joined the Sea Cadets.

The twins were, however, allowed free use of the trailer. It was their space. It became our fort, clubhouse, hut, cave. It was as marvelous as it was junky.

Its interior was magnificent; three-inch thick foam-padded seat cushions wrapped in crunchy lima bean green-colored vinyl. The orange shag carpet, yellow Formica tabletop and countertop ringed with the brown paneling, and green seat cushions upset any logical or pleasing blend of color combinations.

The trailer was white on the outside with light green lines painted down the sides. It was molded into a perverted streamline shape to give it an appearance of, if not sleekness, at least reduced air resistance. It had crank-out windows, dual propane tanks, an American flag tattooed along side the back door, and a "Go Navy" bumper sticker. The dealer gave it pin-stripping all the way around. While standing still it looked like it might go fast.

It leaked. It was not sound proof. We heard every sound that emanated from Jackson Square. The neighbors heard our sounds, too. The police came by and told us to shut up. It was hot in the summer, cold in the winter, and we couldn't use the toilet. The bathroom was small, very small. I was the biggest of the group. I couldn't fit in there side to side in front of the bowl. And, because the dump tank had fallen off on a highway somewhere, we would have been excreting our bodily waste onto the Wilson's driveway. Instead of a portable toilet it was more like a portable outhouse. That wouldn't have bothered us in the least bit. We were already peeing all over each other's backyards because we were too indifferent to walk indoors to the bathroom.

We ran an extension cord out of the cellar window to get some electricity in there for light, Rob's electric guitar, and Matt's 8-track/record player/cassette/radio. We hooked a garden hose up to the trailer water tank. The water tank and pipes in the trailer froze and cracked the first winter the Wilson's were there.

All year long we spilled food and drink on the trailer floor and ground it into the carpet; potato chips, Yankee Doodles, Devil Dogs, Yoo-Hoo, Fanta Orange soda, and Dr. Pepper. Through sheer volume and osmosis our residual flatulence molecules were embedded into the very atomic structure of the plywood, vinyl, and linoleum. An unfixed, male cat got in there and marked it as his lair, too. Matt wanted to name him Fluffy. We named him Spike and he became our mascot. He claimed a spot on top of the cabinets and looked down on us. We watched him come and go through a hole in the screen, his tail straight up and his mono eye-like anus glaring at us as he walked away. One night he came limping in, bleeding, the fur on his head wet and matted, and his left eye cut, swollen, and closed. He could not leap up to the bed and on up to his perch. We put him up there. We couldn't tell if he had been in a fight or had failed to fully dodge a car. Two days later we checked on him and he was dead.

When summer heat and humidity wrapped the South Shore it was beyond rank and fetid. It was indescribable, but it was ours. It was our castle. From there we began living new dimensions of our lives.

We cleaned it when we were ordered to.

Being male, in the eighth grade, and not being an outstanding jock, it's hard to have any relevance; too young to work, too cool to do things with family, too unsure to admit to anything, and too stubborn to ask for help. All there was were friends in a similar situation. There was much unspoken empathy in that trailer regarding the fears and uncertainties of adolescence. Expressing those fears, however, brought about an outpouring of ridicule and scorn. That reassuring and uniquely male-bonding; ribbing that says, 'You'll be okay. There is no need to talk about it because we know you're okay and you'll be okay. Ride it out.' That adhesive held well because no one in that group was but two steps any side of whatever you were going through.

Over the course of the year-and-a-half Wilson tour in Weymouth, a life altering presence foisted itself on us. It was as energizing as it was mystifying. Girls.

They changed from silly, bothersome objects on the other half of the playground to subjects of immense allure, riddle, and intrigue.

Midway through eighth grade and only in the refuge of that trailer was the matter of females allowed in our conversations. Rod was the first to notice it and call it to our attention.

He wondered, "How come we talk about girls all of sudden?"

No one had an answer. The subject was new and, in a puzzling primal way, tremendously interesting.

Danny broke a particular barrier first when he brought a badly mauled, crumpled, and folded cutout from one of his older brother's *Playboy* magazines to the trailer. I had seen pictures of naked girls from magazines before, but suddenly I couldn't take my eyes off her. I also felt embarrassed to look below her neck. My eyes would dart below her neckline then quickly look back in her eyes. I was afraid she was going to catch me staring at her boobs.

The subsequent discussion centered around what visual media each of us had seen that had to do with nude females; a *Playboy* magazine some cousin had, a found nudie magazine, National Geographic, a deck of playing cards, etc. I had seen a steering wheel grip my father had that, when turned upside down, showed a naked lady in some 1940's elongated, full length, mostly lateral, but slightly twisted toward the camera, pose. These discussions were a lot of hype, mystery, uncertainty, bravado, and speculation as to what it was we were actually seeing.

Thirty-six, twenty-four, thirty-six seemed to mean something. I pretended to know what those numbers meant, but I had no clue. When Danny said his sister wore a D-cup bra, I was totally lost.

That trailer, wherever it is now or whatever its pieces were recycled into, undoubtedly has the pheromones of our glands embedded into its atomic composition and arouses whatever walks past it.

Following Danny's lead, I reigned supreme when I scored us a *Penthouse* magazine until the night a couple months later when Rob boasted about actually making it to second base.

I looked older than my age. One night, late, we walked to the Cumberland Farms store in the square. It was Matt, Rob, Danny, and I creeping around at 10:30 PM late in April on a Thursday. We must have been on vacation or having a day off for some reason for us to be staying at the trailer on what would normally be a school night. Neither the Wilson brothers nor Danny had any money. I had some because I still had my paper route. I went into the store to get some chips when I saw the rack and the words *Penthouse* peeking over the top. There was a green over-tone to the cover. The girl was wrapped in a green toga; the banner and typeface were green. It was a new and much discussed publication. The intrigue surrounding it had built to frenzy in the twelve-, thirteen-, and fourteen-year-old male circles. Clearly it had something to do with females being viewed by men, but, still, the question remained in my mind, what was it exactly that men looked at.

In an unfettered existential moment I spoke and asked for a copy of *Penthouse*. The clerk handed it to me like I was real person. I couldn't believe it. I almost ran from the store like I stole it. I had to get out of there before the clerk changed his mind or looked up and saw that I was only thirteen. When I showed Danny, Matt, and Rob what I had, I was venerated. It was similar to how valued I was when I brought my Honda Q50 mini-bike out for them to ride along the railroad tracks.

The trailer was charged with a mighty and slightly dangerous vigor that night.

The magazine disappeared two nights later. I think Matt took it and hid it in a private spot for his private use.

Talk about girls surfaced this way; one of us heard that someone was caught making out behind the bleachers. Someone else heard that someone else had made it to second base. Someone else heard that this girl liked that guy and she had French kissed with him and so on. Sadly, the late bloomer I was, I assumed that the bleachers story and second base were somehow connected in an athletic pursuit. And, if there was French kissing, did that mean there was American kissing too? If so, what was it? What was the difference between American and French kissing?

I had two other brothers and no sisters, but I had been raised with the influence of females, my mother, aunts, cousins, girls in the neighborhood, and so on. I had a female friend, Kelli, who I met through Danny that year. Kelli and I shared some of the same classes, sat together at lunch, and grew to be unbelievably close.

At one time my father talked to me very specifically about respecting women and how he expected me to treat women. He defined for me what respect was, no hitting them. I was to hold doors for all of them, young or old. He said it was a good way to check out their bottoms. No mean or threatening talk toward any woman, ever! He also told me something I came to understand later, that if one of them was being mean or rotten to me, leave her. Leave her and do not say anything to her. He said that action would make her more upset than if I hit or talked mean to her.

I liked Mary and Chris in the second grade. I thought they were pretty. Then there was Terry Kelton in the third grade. There was an allure to her that made her stand out. The other girls in class stood out too because they wore different clothes, went to a different bathroom, and played the same games we did during recess, but with different rules. I didn't mind the girls. I liked them. I just didn't want to have much to do with them. But Terry really stood out. I liked walking near her. I liked talking to her and I tried really hard to kick the ball extra good in gym class when she was on my side.

All this first base, second base, French kissing stuff confused me, like Cindy, a girl who lived in my neighborhood I had known since the second grade. She now confused me, too.

Cindy, or Cynthia, as she preferred to be called by the time we got to seventh grade, changed. I never saw it coming or when it happened, but all of a sudden she wasn't as much fun to hangout with. She hardly played kickball with us anymore. She wanted me to call her if I wanted to hangout with her instead of just going over to her house and going in. I had to knock on the door to see if she was home instead of yelling up at her window like I had always done. My first clue about her evolution was when Danny wondered one night if she stuffed because she wasn't a pirate's dream, she didn't have a sunken chest. I didn't know what he was talking about.

She, and all the other girls in class, seemed to be anticipating something from us twelve and thirteen-year-old boys, and we, or at least I, didn't know what they wanted. Maybe I had cut school or was sick or down in the principal's office the day they handed out the handbook, *The Guide to Understanding the Other Gender.*

So now, it was as equally ruinous to get caught alone beyond our turf by another gang from another neighborhood as it was to make a physical or verbal blunder in front of a girl. Or the girls I had grown up with, or worst of all, in front of all the girls in class. I was doomed. I needed to understand.

Other sex related stories found their way to the trailer. Matt one night said he had heard that the weird kid, Gary, had kissed another boy's hog. After a lengthy toxic pause Danny announced that he had to get going home. Rob and Matt said they had to go in the house to do some homework. I got on my bike and rode home.

The whole homosexual thing was never discussed.

After I figured out what homosexuality was, I didn't have any empathy for it, but I didn't despise it, either, like so many of my peers seemed to. Everyone had something to say about it. None of it was nice. I went along with the herd saying fag and queer and fudge-packer when it seemed to fit the situation.

The most personal sexual topic to surface in the trailer was the subject of masturbation. Eventually Rob, Danny, and I, by being able to tell Matt about it, *de facto* admitted to the fact that we did indeed choke the chicken.

Once enlightened, Matt reveled in the knowledge and application of it.

We were in the trailer one night. Danny again had taken a Playboy from his brother. We passed it around and while I was looking at it Danny said, "Don't get the pages all sticky. I got to get it back in my brother's pile before he comes home Sunday."

Rob added, "Yah Marty, I don't want to hear you over there polishing the rocket again."

"Drop dead. You're the only one jerking off in here."

"I heard you the other night."

I was embarrassed. "You did not. That was Danny and I've seen the trailer bouncing up and down when you're in here beating off."

"Eat shit," Danny replied, never lifting his eyes from another much-tattered magazine. "Besides Marty you beat it at the top of King Oak Hill."

"No I don't." Damn. He knew about the little wooded spot at the top of King Oak. I had been caught. "I think it was Matt." I said hoping to deflect the attention.

Matt had not said a word. When he finally spoke he said, "What are you guys talking about?" It dawned on all of us that Matt never chided anyone about masturbation. Wow, he didn't know what it was.

Danny spoke first, "Come on Matt, ya' know, it's, ah, when you got a boner, and you know ..." Danny looked toward me, his eyes said, 'Help me out here Marty.'

Matt said, "You mean like when you really have to piss really bad and you can't because you've got morning thickness and you can't point it down to pee in the toilet?"

"No," I said. "It's nothing like that. It's when you grab your dick and you kinda' move your hand up and down." That was as far as I was going to go describing it.

Matt embarrassed his brother; it wasn't the first time Matt showed his ignorance and Rob snapped at him. "Grab your dick and jerk it up and down until something happens."

"What happens?"

"Something."

"How will I know?"

Danny and I said together, "You'll know." And that was the end of that conversation.

When Matt finally figured out masturbation, he let us know and then he couldn't stop referring to it and probably polished his rocket at every chance he got. He never seemed to get real interested in girls. I don't think he was gay. I think he just never got interested in females. I wonder if he ever figured out that an orgasm with a woman is, usually, much more fun than a self-inflicted orgasm.

Rob got his first girlfriend in the spring of that year. Shelly was loud, trash-mouthed, talked as though she was wild, and pretty good-looking. Through the remainder of the school year he implied he was doing this, that, and the other with her. But one night, the weekend before school was to let out for the summer, Matt, Danny, and I had gone for a midnight swim in Whitman's Pond while Rob was over at her house. We met back at the trailer and Rob said, "I made it to second base."

"You lie."

"Really."

"Bullshit."

"We were in her bedroom listening to music. Her parents had gone to the movies and she was babysitting her little brother and sister.

"We were lying on the floor with her albums and 45's scattered around. She was on her back holding up an album jacket looking at the cover. I was close to her, looking at another album, when she set the record aside and slid her face right under mine.

"She had a weird look in her eyes."

Now I know this to be the come-hither look, then, I couldn't even imagine what kind of look he was referring to.

We started to believe him. They were making out pretty regularly. It was obnoxious. Their faces were forever locked together, jaws pumping up down, heavy breathing, and almost panting when they stopped to come up for air.

"We started making out. She squirmed under me a little and suddenly I saw my hand was right next to her boob. I could feel her bra under her shirt. I moved my hand a little bit and I felt it with the back of my hand."

Danny and I were rapt by the story. I was trying to imagine every detail so if I ever had the chance to feel someone up, I would remember what to do.

Rod continued, "So I slid my hand onto her tit."

There was an absolute silence in the trailer. I had the largest, most painful erection I had ever had, up to that point, in my life. I'm sure Danny did, too.

Matt? Who knew, who cared? One of us had finally arrived. It was the beginning of the score mentality for all of us.

He went on to say that he unbuttoned her blouse, unhooked her bra, and alleged that he got close to third base. I didn't believe any of that. To my way of thinking he was months away from getting anywhere near third base. How in the world could the progression be that quick? Besides, the way he described how he got close to third base lacked all the detail he described in getting to second base. But, regardless, he got to second.

My acquisition of the *Penthouse* magazine had been trumped.

Danny got an ugly girlfriend that summer, too. He was the only one of us to directly ask a girl out instead of asking one of us to ask her out for him. Sometimes I would go over to her house with him. That got real boring real fast. Just like Rob and Shelly, all they would do was make out; lip smacking, drooling, heavy nose-breathing all over again and nothing for me to do but watch Gunsmoke, the Brady Bunch or Cannon. Danny liked her and she seemed sweet to him, but by midway through ninth grade they went their separate ways. Unlike Rob and his boast, Danny told me in confidence that he did get to second base briefly with her, but she removed his hand after a few moments.

I was closest with Danny. We hung out throughout junior high school. For years we had swum in the pond together in the summer and ice-skated over it in the winter. We rode our bikes all over the South Shore, hopped freight trains, jumped off the bridge into the Back River, and so on. He found good places to explore and neat things to check out. Like a stolen car he found one day half buried in a swamp in the woods out in back of his house. He lead us back there. He knew how to get it started. I said I knew how to drive and we got it out of the water. Unfortunately the only time I had driven a car before was up at my grandparent's summerhouse in New Hampshire. That driving experience constituted thirty feet across an open field.

That day in Weymouth I crashed the car, low speed, into a tree. We left it there, rode our bikes to the police station and told them that a car had been stolen and was abandoned in the woods.

I was the one always looking to do something. Not necessarily mischievous or troublesome, I just didn't want to be idle. I was the one who proposed that we leave the trailer at three o'clock in the morning to see what past-midnight was all about. I suggested we drink beer because I wanted to know what everyone got so excited about.

Acquiring beer was another awakening experience.

Matt and Rob had an older brother, Brad, who drank and smoked dope. We caught him taking money out of his mother's purse one afternoon. He told us to get lost. We knew he was going to get beer so we stalked him and saw him go into a package store that night. When he came out we told him that if he didn't buy us beer, too, we would go back to the house and show his parents where he kept his bong. Being from a conservative, southern, military family, he knew it was big trouble if his parents found out he smoked pot. He bought us beer. He walked out of the packie with a case of Narragansett beer and right in the middle of Jackson Square in plain sight of anyone who happened to look he gave it to us. This potentially undermined our success and the leverage we had over Brad because of the fact that we were likely to get arrested.

The Weymouth police station was on the very edge of Jackson Square. For the police to patrol three of the four hamlets of the town they had to drive through the middle of the square. Brad forced us, underage drinkers, to either traverse the square carrying a case of beer or ditch it and recover it later it. We quickly hid the case in a trashcan in the alley next to the package store. Then we moved the beer through the square as though we were participating in an extreme cold-war espionage operation.

While I went home to get my paper route bag, Rob, Matt, and Danny watched the trash can to see if anyone would notice it and take the beer from us. When I got back I put the beer in the bag and moved it to the next drop point. Then Matt carried one beer at a time under his coat to the next drop point. Rob moved into place. He picked up the beer and moved to the next drop. Then Danny moved it. Once we were beyond the perimeter of the square we hid behind Pingree Elementary School to drink it. Danny had to be home by 10:00 PM therefore between nine and ten o'clock that evening each of us drank at least four warm beers before we boasted to have a buzz or began throwing-up.

It was dark and swampy outside lower Jackson Square. We drank it all on the path that ran along the side of the Herring Run, near the school. We were very cool, like this was an everyday occurrence for us.

Danny and I pushed Rob to see if we could get Brad to buy more liquor for us on Friday nights. But Rob hated Brad and Matt stood loyal with Rob. He wouldn't budge on asking Brad for more favors.

Brad upset the symmetry of our gang by dating a girl Rob liked. He was a senior in high school, but he was dating a girl in our grade. My father thought it was inappropriate for Brad to be dating a girl that much younger. He said maybe it was something they did down south.

Melanie, Brad's girlfriend liked Rob and they had gone out, but Brad somehow or another was the one now dating Melanie. It was all very murky and I never got the complete story.

One event of maturity followed another. Over the next few months we bought a nickel bag of Panamanian Red, ZigZag papers, and got stoned. It was more of a headache for me than anything else. We listened to Bachmann Turner Overdrive and Grand Funk Railroad. Shot BB's at pigeons from the roof of the trailer. We learned that the Wilsons were being transferred to California the following spring. And I stumbled into a boob-in-hand, transcendent sixteen seconds with Jenni.

Danny had asked Jenni out for me. Going out meant we hung out together and told people we were going out. Supposedly she liked Paul DeAngelo and had already gone to third base and skinny-dipped with him. But Paul broke up with her. Jenni was hanging out with Shelly, who was going out with Rob courtesy of Melanie, which is how I ended up going out with her. As a first girlfriend Jenni was anti-climatic.

Since Jenni was my first girlfriend she must have talked to Melanie about my lack of knowledge regarding dating things. Melanie took it upon herself to give me some instruction. One afternoon while Melanie and I were hanging out waiting for Shelly and Rob to get back from where ever they were, she suddenly said, "I want to see how you hug. Hug me." I did or at least what I thought was a hug, which was resting my hands on the outside of her shoulders. Immediately following my hug demonstration she led me out to the shed in her yard and proceeded to demonstrate to me how to French kiss and properly hug someone. For the longest time, years, I really thought it was instruction. Who knows, I might have been lead to second base months earlier if Shelly and Rob hadn't come back when they did.

Jenni and I went out, such as it was, for the summer. Near the end of summer Jenni announced that her family was moving to Hull in October and she would be starting school there after Labor Day. She wouldn't be in the ninth grade with us.

By now I had put enough of the puzzle together to know what getting to first, second, and third base meant. I hadn't deciphered exactly what a home run was yet. I followed the protocols, as I understood them and Jenni and I were stuck at first base. I was perplexed as to how to get to second base. I kept looking for a way to get my hand onto her boob, but there were no obvious opportunities. Was there supposed to be a signal of some type? Then Matt and Rob set the scene for me, and many others, to leave first base and get to second and even third base.

Matt and Rob had been asked to check on a house across the street from theirs while the owner went to the mountains for a month. It became late night party central. Kids from all across Weymouth snuck out of their homes late at night. Kids from Quincy and Hingham made it there too. I was one of the Knights of the Round Table there, because I was a member of the core; Danny, Rob, Matt, and I reigned supreme. There was deference to us. We made this place of drinking and making-out happen.

It was a place of fulfilling some foolish dares; how much could you drink? Could you get out of the house without getting caught? Could you get back in without being caught?

On a dare, we even streaked one night from the trailer across Commercial Street to the house. With fifteen or so people watching from the house, Danny, Matt, Rob, and I, wearing just our sneakers, socks, and ski masks bolted across the street. Rob stumbled and gave himself a road rash. A car came around the corner out of Jackson Square. He was sitting in the road when the headlights locked onto him. We heard the car decelerate then the tires screech as Rob jumped up and, with full frontal nudity, flashed the driver and finished his run across the street and into the house.

We ran naked in full view of anyone who wanted to watch, and yet we hid in the backyard behind the garage to put our clothes back on.

Lackluster Jenni finally agreed to come to the house with Shelly one night. Shelly was there often. In the mysterious hours before dawn, my left arm strung uncertainly across Jenni's shoulders and my left hand dangling precariously downward close to her breasts, my nearly lifeless left hand awkwardly cupped her left breast.

It was so late. We were all tired. Everyone who had a girlfriend or boyfriend had paired up and settled into a dark corner. Jenni and I sat on the love seat. She had probably fallen asleep. I know my hand and most of my arm were numb from a loss of circulation. I doubt if I actually felt anything due to the loss of nerve sensation and muscle function from my arm and hand being in the same position for hours.

Once I got my arm across her shoulders I had no idea what was supposed to follow, if anything. So there my arm rested, fractions of an inch away from her boob, growing more lifeless with every minute while my penis hardened and grew larger than I ever thought it could. It hurt pushing against my bunched-up dungarees.

When I finally learned what first, second, and third base were all about, I remember thinking that there was a progression, a protocol if you will, as to how it happened with girls. Begin, ask her out or have a friend ask her out for you. Hang out a couple times, hold her hand, put your arm around her waist or shoulders when you walk, put your arm around her shoulders when you sit. Kiss her, French kiss, and then pretend to be distracted and see if you can let your hand fall on her boob. Count how long she allows your hand to stay on there, then, across the course of months, assuming you don't have to start all over again to get to second base, move incrementally, sixteenths of an inch at a time, toward third base.

I nearly got lost in the angst of the process, but I followed the protocol as best I imagined it to be. My mission was, once I got my arm across her shoulders and near her breast I wasn't going to move it.

That night my arm grew lifeless and my hand doomed to permanent nerve damage, but I let it hang there for hours.

When it finally actually happened, I couldn't actually feel anything because of the physical torture I was suffering, but, there deep in the still of the night there was enough light scattering the room for me to see where my hand was. It was Xanadu, hallelujah, an epiphany, and serendipity.

I giggled. My hand was abruptly removed from her breast and my arm from her shoulder, but still she sat there with me until she and her friends had to get back to their homes before their parents woke.

For the first time during those providential, eternal sixteen seconds I made it to second base. I first felt a breast, albeit from the barrier of her polyester blouse.

I couldn't wait to tell Danny, Rob, and Matt about it, but Matt saw it happen and told Danny and Rob.

The strategy had worked; I snuck my hand onto her boob and stayed for full count of sixteen Mississippi's. It never dawned on me that maybe she wanted a hand on her breast as much as I did.

Briefly I wondered what her insecure protocols of that age were, if any. Was she supposed to allow the boy's arm go across her shoulders? Was she not to leave if the boy wanted to sit next her? Was she on her guard all the time? Did her mother warn her, watch out, because boys were certain to try and sneak their hands onto your chest, and that was unacceptable. Was it her protocol to thwart that? Or did she want that hand on her breast. Was it is all complicated by the notion good girls don't? Don't what?

Ninth grade began. I bicycled to Jenni's new house a few times. We actually went out to the movies once or twice. Matt and Rob moved away later that year. Once we knew that they would be moving we slowly separated. They distanced themselves from Danny and me. We saw the termination of that friendship coming and we let them distance themselves. We couldn't stay in the trailer as much because of school. One weekend they were gone.

The Saturday morning of my Greenbush walk, I stopped in front of the Wilson's old house. I wanted to take a good look around and solidify the feelings I had in my mind. And I wanted to see if our names were still etched at the base of the concrete wall Mr. Wilson built while they lived there. I stooped and retied my boots. Sure enough our names were still there. It felt really good to know I left a mark on Weymouth.

I stood up, repositioned my backpack and resumed my walk.

Women have told me their most significant sexual experience is their first intercourse. I don't think intercourse is the first significant sexual experience for men, I think it is the first time they make it to second base.

I have issues with female sexuality. I have issues with my own sexuality. My brain tells me I should probably avoid relationships with women because they all end in disaster. I try to blunt my testosterone and tell myself that my sexual interaction with women is probably over, but of the half a dozen women I've slept with the best moment is the first time my hand lands on her breast. I enjoy all the other aspects of her anatomy immensely too, but to this day I enjoy that moment best. I get a sublime feeling when my hand falls on her breasts.

Sometimes I still giggle, too.

CHAPTER 11

▼

BARNEY FELL

Thus far, on my walk, I hadn't taken one picture. I had bought a particular camera for the trip, a Canon F1. I hadn't opened it since I bought it in California three days earlier. It was the same kind of camera I had used in the Navy. It was a workhorse. Canon doesn't make it anymore, so I shopped around and eventually found a used one in good shape.

Photography had been my vocation and avocation. I got my first camera when I was in the fourth grade. At one time I had a large box full of negatives and prints of Greenbush, Weymouth, my Weymouth life, and the South Shore. There were tons of photos of friends and events, strangers and landmarks throughout the South Shore, and images from the perspective of someone who knew the paths, took the shortcuts, crawled through storm drains, and knew the geography better than the surveyors. I dragged that box from apartment to apartment and barracks to condo. Finally I decided it was foolish to drag them around anyone. In a disconnecting, purging mania, I had a ceremonial bonfire and burned almost everything I took with me from Weymouth, including the box of photos, and another box of my life after Weymouth.

I burned it all. Everything burned when I tossed my old address book, letters, all my photographs, little novelty crap people pick up (or receive) on their way in life; postcards, stuffed animals, bandanas, key-chains, hastily scribbles notes, "I can't wait to see you. Come by after work. I don't care how late. S.W.A.K. Heather," and so on. All that survived were the photos Harold gave me and a family picture taken in the White Mountains of New Hampshire. I saved two addresses, Danny and Harold's.

Now, with the Wilson's house behind me I looked at Jackson Square. It was largely unchanged. I took the camera out and put it in my hand for the first time. It felt good. How a camera fit into my hand was the ultimate selling point for me. No matter how hard a salesman tries to push a camera's features, I know anyone can take beautiful pictures with simplest of cameras. What sells me is how it feels. When I bought the F1, the saleswoman offered it to me to hold. I knew by looking at it was in good shape. There was no reason for me to test fit it. I told her to just put it in a box, with three lenses, power winder, a particular flash, and twenty rolls of film. I hadn't touched it until that moment in Jackson Square.

It felt good.

I wish I hadn't burned all the photos. I had a perspective on Weymouth no one else had. There was never going to be a gallery showing of my Weymouth photos, I'm not an artist. However, if I had some photos I might recall my life here more fondly.

The problem and beauty of photography is, it takes that place at that moment in time and magnifies it, whether you want it to or not, regardless of how beautiful and good or horrible and bad the subject.

I popped off two shots of Jackson Square, one portrait orientation and one landscape. Then the awful page of the photo album in my head opened.

Woller Dawkins dropped his Barney on the floor of the bus terminal. His young Mom said pick it up. Twice. Center frame, he stood alone in front of door seven. Bordered by the lines at door nine and four, he and Barney waited.

Greyhound, late Friday night, near the border. I watched and thought it would be a great black and white photograph. Lit by flickering overhead fluorescent lights, shadows would edge the misunderstood immigrants, and crisp soldiers and sailors fresh from basic training with harsh film grain giving it a gritty 1960's look. Too bad the cacophony of loudspeaker static, television drivel, and payphone conversations in Spanish, Slovak, and poor English, and children punching the buttons on broken video games and out-of-order vending machines couldn't carry over to the photo.

I watched the dust burst off farm worker boots as they moved into line. The air-conditioning was timid and merely moved the odor of the garbage cans and hot dogs on the roller in the snack bar around the terminal. The smells wallpapered the waiting area.

Resigned women splayed out on the vinyl cream colored benches, a baby crying, weary men propped-up against support columns, and dignity. The choice of those people in the bus depot not to be sterile and perfumed and swift made the place so very intriguing. There were college students with their See-America passes, an older couple just glad to be with each other, a mother and baby off to New York and family, all kinds of examples of the connecting texture of humanity. These tired, hungry people would prevail in the photo and give it the hardscrabble aura I like.

Then, Woller's father stepped out of the background and into focus. I saw him reach for his belt-buckle. Maybe he was cinching it up or loosening it for the ride. He stopped and pulled his jacket open. Supine Barney watched. Woller flinched and held his ground. In one accomplished move, Dad had the belt off, folded, and dangling threateningly. For the want of his own anger and tiredness and relief Woller stood there. The belt hit him. There was no wind up to it. There was too much of a crack for it to be a motivating swat only. All of us in the terminal left parental judgment to the parent.

Woller cried.

Dad went to his eye level and said, "Don't you cry."

Woller tried to choke back the next wail, but soon enough. The following strike landed harder. He stifled his crying.

I snapped the picture.

Photographs are more than documentation; moods can be bound in the silver halide and dyes of a photograph. And I knew what tools to use to bind moods in the hardcore science and chemistry of a photograph to nudge your response a certain way to make you feel what I saw.

Years ago, other boys in the cabin felt something from a photograph I took and developed during a summer camp program. From that moment there was no question about my vocation. I took photography classes in high school, pictures for the yearbook and school newspaper, and photographed all over Weymouth to see what I saw. Then I went in the Navy and learned at its outstanding Photo A school. After a couple years working in a photo lab on a carrier I was assigned to Combat Camera as a combat photographer.

In peacetime being combat photographer is a really good job. I trained with helicopters, ships, and missiles in exotic places like Japan and Turkey. I hung out the side of helicopters flying at one hundred and fifty miles an hour. Held in by a gunner's belt, fifty feet above the water, I photographed Iranian tanker ships while one of our destroyers waited five hundred yards away with its guns sighted on the ship, waiting for the crew to show the slightest bit of non-cooperation or aggression. I knew Navy divers were under the ship placing tracking devices on its hull.

Peacetime combat photography is nothing compared to what Alfred Eisenstaedt saw at Normandy or as brutal as the Marine photographers had it at Tarawa. Nor was it as disheartening as it was for the Army photographers who had to document the obscenity at Buchenwald, et al, in 1945, but it did have its grim moments. I had to photograph a sailor who blew his brains out in the barracks at the air station at Miramar in California. Another time I had to photograph the wreckage of a helicopter crash and the bodies of the dozen men who died in it. But the job is high profile and it's fun. When I was on leave and someone asked what I did for a living, being able to say, "I'm a combat photographer," grabbed his or her attention.

When I met a woman and told her what I did for a living, most often, just saying, "I'm a photographer," got things going. Most of them would pose for me, half the time the woman would take some of her clothes off, and other times she would give an entire performance in front of the camera. I got out of the Navy, took some art courses and developed an eye to create a technically perfect and profound picture, when I was so inclined.

I always took surprisingly inadequate vacation photos. I shot the occasional wedding. Working for a newspaper never interested me, but I loved what I did. I can tell you, a poor photographer has a lot more film damaged in processing than a good one does. I know how to trick a center weighted TTL meter so the subject's face isn't dark. I can eliminate the green and yellow cast of indoor photography and get the flash to work as it's supposed to. I haven't played with digital cameras at all, but I know having a digital camera doesn't make anyone a better photographer.

I worked as a medical photographer briefly. When I had to photograph in surgery, usually, I had the time to observe and I had the means to document what no one else in the hospital could. The point where science and technology ends and the humanity of healing begins. Like a nurse I watched one time, while the cardiac surgeon cut the man's chest, spread his ribs, and made the patient's heart stop for the by-pass surgery, beyond the sterile drape she gave the temporarily dead patient a foot rub.

I am astounded at how a body can be manhandled, rebuilt, saved, altered, and made disease free and whole again. Orthopedic surgery amazed me. I've stumbled and hit cement hard, with my limbs not at stress-absorbing angles and nothing happened. But once I fell, not hard, dislocating my elbow and shattering the radial head. Having had that experience, when I photographed knee replacement surgery and saw the hammers, chisels, drills, and saws used during surgery on a patient, then later saw the same patient move around as though nothing happened, I was astonished.

Medical photography is not as sanitized as it sounds. Horrible stories came into the ER. I photographed abused children, stillborn children, and murdered children; fools with guns and tempers, and drunks with cars. I stayed above it all. I had a safety net, of sorts, the viewfinder. I thought I couldn't be consumed by what I saw.

The camera was a tangible barrier, sometimes a physical barrier. Once I was leaning in to focus on a nasty growth in an abdomen when a vessel burst and blood splashed into the lens. It was a psychological barrier, too, that provided detachment so I could photograph the disease, pain, and discomfort. In the military or in the hospital, there was nothing I could do about the things I photographed that could make a difference. I could give someone a few bucks for a meal or tell the refugee camp doctor that someone over there seemed to be suffering, unusually so. But the pictures I took could generate interest and aid.

The jump from a medical photographer to a forensic photographer was a natural. The barrier of the viewfinder became a more significant buffer with which I did my job; focus, exposure, painting with flash, film speed, resolving power, all for documentation in the police record. The camera absorbed the blood, skin, colors, and indignity of a crime scene. Often I got angry, sometimes sad, and usually dumbfounded at the endless stupidity and meanness wreaked by one upon another. But, I had my barrier. Even with the barrier aside, helping the morgue techs, I swam crosscurrent in the whirlpool.

Even though I had experience photographing gruesome stuff, I was warned early on in the job that every forensic photographer has to go through it. Alone in bed with the cerebral snapshot of the man sitting in his chair with the hole through his neck where his wife shot him. Or, at the hospital photographing a woman after her boyfriend beat her. Even in the unglamorous photography I did I could see she was gorgeous and had perfect symmetry of eyes and lips. In spite of the best reconstructive surgery she'd never be pretty again. Five years of that, every day I saw how someone screwed someone else.

In the department, we rotated responsibilities. Pulling overnight darkroom and lab duty, I percolated science into an image of someone's misery. Processing and printing the film I could gauge the photographer's mental health, too. If he was not being affected, his work was intricate, detailed. As he began to be affected, he sought some distraction with the lens, a landscape shot or a flower blooming in the middle of a roll. It's as though the photographer had to take a breath before going back under the bloody surface. If there were more than a half dozen of those breaths on a roll, I knew he was having a problem. I'd offer to swap a few days of lab duty with him so he could take a little break.

I thought I was stronger, more able to deal with it all, the child abuse, arson, rape, and murder. I didn't need a break. I was so accurate, so professional, so detached—my work sent bad people to jail and gave good people a measure of justice. I could look past the suffering of a crime scene and only see the details I had to document.

The reasoning, the experience, the art, and the science, I couldn't grasp any of it when instead of the crime scene I saw Woller—dead. His mother was vapid and his father saying the boy wouldn't do as he was told.

The image I had in my head from more than a year earlier in the bus terminal, and the lethal mix of being tired and two years old, Barney on the floor, and his Dad's leather belt rushed back to me. It hit me hard; in front of me was the most devolving and discouraging tragedy of all, an adult empty of patience and compassion for children.

I didn't call Child Protective Services from the bus terminal or ever. The unwritten rule is you don't interfere with a parent's parenting. I thought then, what would become of that boy? How many of these experiences would it take to warp him? What kind of a man would he turn out to be?

I found out.

I stood there. I couldn't get the camera out. I couldn't turn away. I couldn't say that I couldn't photograph this crime scene. My sergeant told me later it was like I was a mannequin. At first, they all thought I was assessing what I needed to do. After several minutes of staring at the body, one of the deputies called for assistance for me. I don't remember getting home.

I had to go through a debrief. They gave me a couple days off and a chance to see the department's shrink. They said I had to stop taking pictures for a while.

The lens had cracked. The barrier broke.

A few weeks later, I eased back out to the field. It didn't last.

During my leave of absence there were a couple clues that my lifelong visceral vocation was over. After week or so of leave I took my camera and went out to photograph some of my favorite subjects. I used to like to shoot anything that had been abandoned, crumbling, and had a layer of rust on it like an old car in the woods or a dilapidated pier. I walked around the waterfront, amid a number of abandoned ships, and an old warehouse. I didn't take one shot.

I also had a favorite model friend. She liked having her picture taken and I liked taking her picture. We met when she was the nurse for a patient I had to photograph. She asked if I would help her develop a new portfolio. She modeled clothes, shoes, bras, and panties for one of the local department stores then and knew that as she got older her time for those kinds of shoots was running out.

She was smart and a terrific nurse. She had a sexy aura that gave terminally flagging urology patients an erection. I photographed her wedding and made her a print from my negatives after she burned all the pictures following their divorce. I knew eventually she would come to see he was an important milestone in her life, even though he was an asshole. Sometimes, when neither of us had a lover, we would go out and catch dinner and a movie. Occasionally we ended up having buddy sex.

We got together to take some pictures while I was on leave. I kept putting her into Woller's morbid pose and then asked her to step out of it. I did this to her over and over and over. She didn't understand why I kept asking her to do that. Then she asked what was wrong. I threw my camera against the wall and said, "I'm done."

I wish it had been cathartic, it wasn't. I sold all of my photography equipment and bought a simple point and shoot camera that, maybe, I used twice in three years time. With that auto-focus and auto-exposure camera, I took pleasing vacation photos.

CHAPTER 12

▼

DANNY'S SONG

"Marty!"

I thought I heard someone yell out my name, but I wasn't expecting to speak with anyone in Weymouth until I got to Harold. I glanced around then continued on in my void.

"Marty. Hold up."

A car shot out of traffic and whipped into a parking spot just behind me. The car door flew open and a large, fat man struggled out. "Marty fuckin' Roberts. Unbelievable."

"Is that you, Danny?"

"You bet your streaking ass it is."

I stuck my hand out to shake his and he grabbed me and immersed me in his corpulent mass. When the vigorous backslapping man-hug was done and I extricated myself I said, "My streaking ass? What about your poison ivy ridden ass?"

He laughed a hee-hee, mischievous-glee laugh and then with a twinkle in his eyes and boisterous slap on my back he said, "What the hell are you doing here?"

"I decided to take a trip back here and walk around."

He looked me up and down and then right into my eyes. With a nod and slight dip of one eyelid he asked, "Just walking around. Are you walking around a minefield, a graveyard or a playground?"

I paused and dropped my eyes to look at the concrete, "I don't know yet, Danny."

"Well hell, you need a lift somewhere?"

"No. Thanks, though. I'm heading down toward the old East Weymouth station then I'm going to walk by Kelli's old house."

"Well I got some time to kill. You want some company?"

I almost said no. If we went to get coffee or dilly-dallied reminiscing I'd get off schedule. In that disproportionately large microsecond I also thought, we don't have anything in common. Our lives went two completely separate paths. We'll run out of things to say by the time we get to the end of Commercial Street, like what I dreaded with Lisa in San Diego, I was sure more conversational awkwardness waited with Danny. It had been years and I was the one who let the friendship slip away.

I said, "Absolutely." He left the door open on his car, an old, beat-up, rusted mini van, and we headed to lower Jackson Square.

"I'd forgotten all about that poison ivy. How'd I do that?"

"You took a dump in the woods and used the poison ivy leaves to wipe your ass." I could feel one of those laughing fits building in me. What a nice feeling. It had been years since I felt comfortable enough around someone to laugh like that.

"Oh yeah. That sucked." He was starting to laugh, too.

"Yup. I lived it with you. But it's a great story to tell. You're famous across the country for that."

"Gee. Thanks."

"Your poor ass had a run of bad luck that year. Remember trying to put a roach out in your back pocket and burning a hole in your butt?"

"No." Between his laughing gasps he asked, "Please remind me."

"We were smoking a joint one day when you were helping me with my paper-route and your mother pulled up in her car. You stuck that roach in your back pocket and tried to slap it out." I had to stop walking I was laughing so hard. "You looked like a stripper the way you were slapping your backside."

Danny recreated the action with his three-foot wide butt, gray sans-a-belt cut-off shorts held up with suspenders, and a tee shirt that said 'World's Greatest Dad.' I can only imagine what some soccer mom must have thought if she drove by and saw two middle age men laughing uncontrollably, the fat one slapping his behind, and the other bent over from laughing.

I continued the story, "She didn't stay too long, but you burned a hole in your pants and your butt. It got infected and you had to go to the doctor. Did you ever tell her what caused the burn?"

"No, but wasn't that the same summer that the seat in that old go-cart Paul had gave way and my ass dragged on the cement for a couple hundred feet until the gas pedal got unstuck?"

"You were something else. It's a wonder either of us are alive after all the dumb-ass things we did."

"Yeah. You were a beauty yourself. You know, I've got a permanent image of you in my head, too."

"What?" By the way he was laughing I knew it was some bonehead thing I had done.

"That girl you liked that lived near Kelli. Heather, yeah that was her name. You wanted to impress her so you went and bought some black pants and a yellow sweater and you rode your bike to her house for that party we all were at."

"Yeah?"

"You looked like a giant bumble-bee." We both were laughing so hard that we had to sit on the curb. When we finally got the laughter under control Danny added, "What you didn't know was you had a big mud streak that had kicked off your back tire all the way up your back. You looked like a bumble-bee from the front and massive skunk from the back. I'm sure it was all Heather could do to keep from pouncing on you." And the laughing seizure took over again.

Finally I said, "I got to take a piss."

"Me too. Let's duck into the woods there. We can take a leak there."

The woods were a little buffer that lead up against the Herring Run. As we stood there Danny said, "You know, if we got caught when we were twelve pissing in the woods like this, it'd be no big deal. Now somebody might think we're a couple homos and call the cops. If we didn't get arrested, we'd at least get a ticket."

"Let's get moving."

We walked back out of the woods. I asked Danny, "Do you still live in Weymouth?"

"No. I'm here helping my mother with some errands. We live in Rockland."

"We? Married?"

"Yup. Carol. Do you remember me telling you about her?"

Something came back to me. In one of his last Christmas cards he told me that he had met a really nice girl named Carol at a cookout.

"Well we got married and we have nine kids."

"Nine kids! Holy shit Danny. That's unheard of these days."

"Yup. Love 'em all. How about you? Wife? Kids? Really Marty, what the fuck became of you."

I sighed as I spoke, "I tried marriage a couple times, but, I don't know, I may not be the marrying type. Fortunately no kids."

"Married or not Marty, kids are great. I tell you, marriage and kids changed everything for me."

"How so?"

"It's not hard to figure out." He stopped moving for minute. He seemed to breath in everything that was around him at that moment. I think he said a brief prayer of appreciation. He dipped his head then started talking and walking again. He looked at me and said, "It's good to talk to an old friend like you."

"Ditto Danny." I was struck by how quickly we started laughing so hard and how comfortable I felt around him. It was as though no time passed. We were the world's oldest eleven-year-olds at that moment.

"Anyway, to your question. You know I was adopted and, even though my parents were terrific, as a kid I think I thought I shouldn't do anything that might get me shipped off to another set of parents. So I wasn't a trouble-maker, except when we were together. I didn't do good in school, but I didn't do bad, either. I just was, but when I met Carol and we got married and when we had Ian, our first boy, I knew that now there was someone who was my blood and I would always be connected to. No one can take that from me.

"I wanted more kids and I decided I was going to show my kids that I was their father and that I would be at their side until the day I died. It's kinda' like that George Foreman thing; he didn't know his father so he named all his kids George so they would know who theirs was.

"My sons and me get along good and I adore my daughters. Karen's the oldest girl. She's a teenager and everything is an issue, but daughters dote on their fathers and I've got a way with her that my wife doesn't, so I'll have her and all my kids forever. And that, Marty, my long lost friend, is what changed. I got some form of closure," he choked on that trendy word. "When I got married and had the kids I found what my birth parents took from me, acceptance."

"I'm happy for you. Your parents were great. They never treated you any different that I could ever tell. And they were really good to me after my mother died."

"My parents were great and they didn't treat me any different, but I was the one that thought I was on a perpetual audition."

"How are your folks by the way?"

"Mom's doing fine. She's slowing down. It's a lot of house for one person to look after."

"What happened to your Dad?"

"You never heard, huh? He died several years ago."

"I'm sorry, Dan." Damn it. My selfishness, my contempt for all things Weymouth made it so I permanently lost touch with two really good people, Danny's father and Mrs. Smith. "Tell your mom I said hi."

"Sure. You know she filled me in on you a few years ago that you were in San Diego and ran into Lisa Sands."

"How'd she find out?"

"You know how all those old broads talk."

Of course, the Weymouth wire. It was alive and well and my name surfaced on it just like Lisa said it would.

Danny continued, "Around the same time Ian was born, I found my birth mother."

"Really. What was she like?"

"White trash."

"That's too bad."

"No, not all, Marty. I found her with the help of my mother and father. She wants nothing to do with me and I could care less about her. I know who my parents are. My kids know who their grandmother is. And it's not her."

"Where did you find her?"

"In a mobile home in North Carolina. It was so stereotypical; she chewed tobacco, she was all wrinkled and coughing all the time, and had half of one tooth left. At first she wouldn't even acknowledge me, then she admitted I was hers, and told me to never bother her again."

"That's terrible Dan."

"No. Like I said, that's not the case. I left and immersed myself in Carol and my kids."

"Did she tell you anything about your father?"

"Only as much as she remembered. She was living in some shack near Worcester at the time and got picked up in a bar. Lo and behold there was me nine months later."

He turned to look at me. He had a shit-eating grin stretched across his face as he said, "What I did learn about my father does explain two things about me."

"What's that?"

"My big dick and the fact that I can dance."

"You lost me."

"He was black." He started humming Jimmie Crack Corn and asked, "Do you want to hear me sing some Negro spiritual songs?"

"I'll pass."

He started singing Old Man River.

"You know, Danny, hearing that makes me wonder if maybe the guy who I thought was my father, wasn't. I've got a bigger dick than you."

"Do not."

"Do too."

"You want to have a dick-out right here?"

"Then we'll get arrested for sure."

"Alright." He looked over at me. He said it again, "It's good to see you."

"Good to see you, too, buddy."

We walked on. We talked on. It was less than a half-mile from where we met to the station. I noticed the Bowl-A-Wey was closed and the MBTA had taken it over for the Greenbush restoration project headquarters. I asked him if he followed the restoration at all. He hadn't. There were undoubtedly few who were as interested in it as I was and no one else, I'm sure, traveled across the country to visit it before its restoration. We cut behind the building and walked up the embankment to the edge of the passenger platform that once belonged to the East Weymouth railroad station. The view up the Herring Run toward Jackson Square and the opposite angle out over the Back River was unchanged. It was beautiful and as lush as I remembered.

"You always liked this area."

"Yup. Still do. These tracks are the reason that got me here."

"Because they're being restored?"

"That's half of it." I recounted the evolution I went through that got me to Weymouth that weekend.

"Where are you going from here?"

"I'm heading over to Braintree where I'll pick up the tracks and start walking all the way down to Scituate." We walked the platform to where the station had once stood. The lot was now over grown with weeds and saplings. An old telegraph pole still stood. But the platform was over grown too much to walk out to East Street. We turned back.

"What else are you going to do while you're in Weymouth?"

"I'm going to walk down to the river there, maybe out onto the marsh a little, then, I don't know. I'll walk up by Gilbert Road and maybe I'll go past the old homestead, then I head to the Landing, see that old guy, Harold, and then to Braintree and back to California."

"Why don't you come to dinner before you fly out? You can meet Carol and the kids."

"Thanks for the invite. I'll have to see what time I finish and if I can make my flight."

"Here's my number. Give me a call and I'll come and pick you up. Even if you can't come for dinner you still need a ride to Logan, give me a call."

We walked back down to the Herring Run and under the railroad bridge to the marsh that surrounded the Back River. We stood at the water's edge. It was low tide. After we stood still for a minute the crabs came up out of the mud and shadows, scurrying around the river bottom.

Danny broke the silence. "Marty, I love you to death, but I gotta' tell you, it was a shitty thing you did by not seeing Kelli when she got sick."

It surprised me that was what he thought was shitty. I thought he was going to say something about my blowing him off. I felt the need to defend myself, "I went to her funeral. I didn't see you there."

"I got my own Tiny Tim and he was having surgery that day. Look, I'm not trying to jump on your shit, but you should know that she loved you."

"I loved her, too. We were great friends."

"No. She loved you. All she wanted was for you to come for her. She would have gone with you anywhere. Whether you stayed here or took off to California she would have gone with you without asking a question."

"I never knew she felt like that. We did so much together that for me it was like that romantic relationship stuff was, well, it was like we moved beyond that somehow."

"Kelli and me talked. We were friends in high school, we were good friends, not like the two of you, but we were friends. And we stayed in touch after high school. I saw her when she was sick."

"She told me in a letter she talked with you sometimes."

"All she ever wanted was for you to ask her out, official like. She would have said yes. She would have said yes whether you asked her out or asked her to marry you and move to Peru."

"I didn't know." I knew I was wrong to not visit her when she was sick, but I never realized she felt any other way about me than I did about her. The closeness we had precluded marriage or at least for me it ended up feeling that way. "I've never been very good at asking girls out. It scares the shit out of me."

"Yeah you were always like that. I think I set you up for every date you ever had."

"Probably."

"I don't know much about them, women, but I know this, if you ask them out, young or old, married or single, and if the only thing they ever say to you is no, you've still bought a huge amount of good will."

"They all seem to complain to me how tired they are of men hitting on them. I kinda' figure I'm a nuisance to them."

"They get sick of it if you're a pig about it. And I know you're not a pig."

What Danny was saying made sense, and I knew on an intellectual level he was right, talking to a girl with the goal of asking her out was no big deal. But it was for me. A bump of anger rose in me toward Danny. He seemed happy, he had a wife that he hadn't complained about once in the time we were together, and he, when we were young always had a girl around that could be loosely defined as a girlfriend. And when they were no longer boyfriend/girlfriend they still seemed to be friends. For the briefest moment I wished I had what he had.

It had been quiet for a moment then an airplane on its approach to Logan broke the malcontented moment I was having.

"Enough of this. I don't want to rag on you and I'm not giving you *Danny's Guide To The Other Sex* it's just that you two were just so close that you not showing up to see her really surprised me." We walked back in from the marsh and back on Commercial Street toward Jackson Square.

My ill-willed moment had passed. "I know it was a shitty thing to do, Dan. I really don't have an excuse. My head has been so far up my ass for so many years that I wonder what is real about me and what mask I put on for whatever situation I was in. I'd like to think Kelli forgives me."

"She does. She was happy when she was with you."

"Kelli and I went through a lot together."

"She hinted at stuff. Like I said, I'm not raggin' on you and I want to stay in touch so don't let some bug crawl up inside your ass and die then fall off the planet again. Stay in touch." He looked at his watch, "I got to start heading back. I gotta' go to work."

"What do you do?"

"I sell used cars."

"Oh."

"I make enough to get by and I don't ever have to worry about being too busy to miss my kids at their sports or plays or whatever."

"You're lucky Dan."

"I am, but I look around and I wonder if I need to do more. I mean I'm fat, I don't take care of myself, I don't make any money, I don't know how I'll pay for

college if any of the kids wants to go to college. I'm under motivated and I probably drink too much."

"But you got your wife and kids."

"I do, and that makes life good, but that doesn't make the logistics of living
any easier." He shrugged his shoulders as though he was shaking something off.
"Enough of that depressing crap." He turned to me and said, "Weymouth's not
so bad. It's like everywhere else, some good stuff and some bad. Maybe the South
Shore isn't for you, but whatever you're running from is still right behind you."

I stood there, feeling slightly defensive and sheepish at the same time. Danny
grabbed me hugged me again. He said, "Sometimes I get on my high-horse and
try to pass advice on to people and it isn't my place to do that. I do it to my kids,
too." He let me out of the embrace and turned and hurried back to Commercial
Street. He yelled back at me, "If you don't stay in touch I'll find you, sit on you,
and fart." He slapped his ass and with that he disappeared around the corner.

I looked at my watch. I had time. I'd still make Harold's on time. I looked
back over my shoulder in the direction of Kelli's house. I couldn't go there. I
walked back to Jackson Square. This time I walked Broad Street away from Jackson Square.

CHAPTER 13

▼

KELLI

I loved Kelli from the day I was born. It was just a matter of meeting her. We met in eighth grade.

She trusted me and I didn't want to jeopardize that. Ever. She knew I respected her and she didn't want to dim that under any circumstance. She listened to me. She knew how to draw me out, how to listen at length, without judgment, and with patience. She knew things about me I barely knew about myself. She even hopped the Greenbush trains with me a couple times.

As unusual as it is to have a true friend across the gender divide it's more unusual to have a true and very close friend across the gender divide in high school, college, and early adulthood and not have some form of romance or sex entangle the friendship. No relationship haze ever clouded our friendship. So I thought until Danny informed me otherwise.

In spite of some unusual and potentially sex-having situations, Kelli and I never had sex. Somehow sexual tension passed through us without leaving an obvious mark.

The closest we came to having any kind of boyfriend/girlfriend contact was at a party in the tenth grade. Everyone there was drinking and making-out. We were the only two left standing. Literally. Over by the record player we were picking out albums. I wanted Cheap Trick and she wanted Bread. I knelt down and reached behind her legs while simultaneously she reached over me. She stepped back and fell. I tumbled and caught her to break her fall. We ended up wrapped around each other. I looked at her and she at me. If either one of us moved toward the other we would have been making out. For some reason that instance brought up a sexual nudge, a sexual whiff that had never been there in spite of occasional skinny-dips together, being together as we changed clothes, and falling asleep together. We looked at each other and started laughing.

A friend of mine saw us and later asked me why I didn't go for it with her. All of our friends knew what good friends Kelli and I were. They were amazed that we had never had any type of a relationship collision. They all thought we would be a terrific couple. He picked up on the sexual bump, too.

I said, "I don't know. It would be too weird."

She wasn't one the popular girls in school and didn't seek to be one. She wasn't real smart. She worked hard for the good grades she got. Some things befuddled her. She never understood the combination of front and rear derailers on a ten-speed bike well enough to use the full range of gears. She was pretty, but not stunning. She had dark hair, blue eyes, and straight teeth from two years of braces; smooth skin, a nice body, small breasts, and long legs. She was always self-conscious about her large hands and feet.

We did things together and hung out as teenagers do; trying to dodge our parents, making sure we had someone to hang out with on Friday nights, and hoping we had parties to go to on Saturday nights. But it wasn't as though we were inseparable. I had girlfriends and she had boyfriends. She had her friends and I had mine.

We met in Social Studies. Danny knew her and snapped her bra strap one day. She laughed about it then, later in that class, surreptitiously taped a piece of paper to his back saying, Kick Me. I thought that was the funniest and coolest thing I ever saw. Danny introduced us later that day in study hall. The kick me sign still taped to his back. I helped her with history and she helped me with algebra. We talked so easy from the start you'd have thought we were happily married and catching up after having been apart for a week. I've never talked so easy with anyone before or since.

As we grew closer I discovered she wasn't all grace and goodness. More than once I'd stop her in the hall and tell her she tucked her blouse into her underwear, again. Occasionally she'd ask me to retrieve something at her house that she had forgotten. I was in a cooperative work-study program through which I could leave school for a couple hours each day. Usually it was her homework, sometimes her lunch. One day she needed new underpants because of her sudden period. She told me about that mysterious female stuff.

Often I'd wait with her outside her house for her mother to get home because Kelli had forgotten her key. I showed her how to break into her own house, but she wouldn't do it and her parents weren't the kind to leave a key under the door-mat. Eventually her parents made an extra key for me. Her parents and my father wondered why we didn't go to dances together, together as dates. We did go to dances together and hung out, but never on an official date.

We had our disagreements too. I hated it when we quarreled.

It was always over something inane and usually something I did or said. One time, right after I got my driver's license, we were driving up King Oak Hill and a car pulled out in front of us. I hit the horn.

"Why'd you beep at him?" she asked.

"He cut us off."

"That car was way in front of us. You don't own the road."

"How would you know? You flunked your road test." I knew the moment I said it that I shouldn't have.

"Drop me off."

"Kelli, I didn't mean that the way it sounded."

"You can be such a jerk sometimes, Marty. Stop the car."

She slammed the door as she got out of the car and I spun the tires as I pulled away. I was mad at her for being mad at me.

It was petty and foolish and two days later there was a note tapped inside my school locker. She said she was sorry for yelling at me. I put a note back in her locker saying I was sorry too. The guy didn't cut us off.

Whenever we fought it was over something small and stupid and trivial and meaningless. I hated those times when we weren't speaking. She did too. All of my ex-wives asked me why it was that I could never say I'm sorry even when clearly after the fact I was wrong and my actions warranted an apology. I said I didn't know. It's a guy thing.

With Kelli, most of the time it was me walking up to her saying, "I'm sorry."

She got incensed over restrictions given to her as a teenager. She couldn't wear make up and certain types of clothing or have her ears pierced until she was sixteen. She kept make up in her locker and would change into the clothes she wanted to wear as soon as she left the house.

She would get passionately mad at a perceived injustice. She would hear one side of a story and get indignant over the unfairness. Like one time when a girl-friend of hers got dumped; the girlfriend cried to Kelli about what a jerk that guy was because all she had done was walk to school with another boy. He just up and dumped her according to this girlfriend. Kelli was irate. I showed up at her house just as Kelli was getting ready to call him and tell him what a rotten person he was for doing this to her friend. She was going to tell him about the problems he was going to have with women if he got all mad and jealous because another guy was around 'his woman.' I told her how her girlfriend was spotted a couple nights earlier in the back seat of a car at Great Hill with the same boy who walked her to school. It took some time, but she backed down.

She was fiercely loyal to her friends. I think she got so caught up in her friends' lives because she listened so well. I tempered her irrationality with doses of reality. She came to trust my observations and suggestions.

Her family mattered most to her. She sought family stability and wanted to have it in her house. Her parents were nice, but obviously out-of-love with each other. There was always a sense that they could split in a moments notice. Animals held a soft spot in her. She wasn't allowed to have any at home. She would pet every dog and cat she came in contact with and a dead animal in the road always upset her.

She kept me in line. I had a tendency to drift, to lose focus in school, grades, sports, friends, and so on. I'd start something and get bored with it as soon as I understood it then move on. Without her, because of my restlessness, I would have never gotten good at anything. She helped me stick with a few things long enough to get good at them. Wrestling and trumpet come to mind. We learned how to keep a baseball scorecard together.

She saved my life.

My father beat me when he felt the world was being unfair to him. Give him a couple drinks and let him see something on television or in the paper and he took it out on whoever was within striking distance, which was usually me. Nights like that I'd leave my house and wander the streets for a while, then end up at her house. She'd hear me come in. She'd check on me. I was always okay, except for a fat lip or sore cheek or a welt somewhere. I'd fall asleep on her couch and we'd walk to school together the next morning.

The first time I turned to Kelli was after my father had one of his tantrums. I left my house around ten o'clock at night. I walked straight to her house and tossed pebbles at her window until she looked out and saw me. She let me in through the cellar door. She was livid and ready to call the cops. It wasn't a perceived injustice. I was there with a bloody nose, a split lip, and forming a black eye. She brought me some food and let me stay in the cellar that night. After her parents left for work she made me some breakfast and we walked to school together. She couldn't understand how someone could do that his own son.

I said, "My father's not a bad man. He's actually kinda' funny. You have to get to know him. He just has a temper."

I always defended him.

Often it was just my father and I at the house we lived in. My brother Dennis left the house as soon as he could. My other brother Jeff was in reform school and he only visited on the weekends, sometimes. I had started fighting back when I was fourteen, and that infuriated him more. But he began to slowly back down. Sober, he was fine; drunk, he was brutal. I stayed at Kelli's on the drunken nights. Odd as it was, he adored Kelli. She was the only one of my friends that came to my house when my father was home more than one time. When she was at my house, whether he was drunk or not, she listened to him. She actually thought he was interesting.

If he was drinking and Kelli was there, he didn't raise a hand to me or have a mean thing to say. Usually with a couple drinks in him he always had a dig or mean comment about everyone except Kelli. In his own way he saw to her comfort when she was at the house. He was a good cook. If he knew she was coming he'd prepare good food for all of us to enjoy. They'd be laughter and stories and kitchen table philosophizing. She blocked my father simply with her presence. I guess she gave him some relief from his self-imposed misery.

My father grew to be an angry old-young man. According to him, everyone else had it better than him, made more money, and had children to boast about. He had no confidence about himself except maybe his work. He became convinced that the world had screwed him and would rip him off at every opportunity. Eventually, unless Kelli was over, he'd make himself a burger, sit down and watch the Red Sox, Bruins, Celtics or Patriots, and fall asleep in the Lazy Boy. The next morning it was a glass of juice, a cup of coffee, bowl of Corn Flakes, and off to work. After I left for the Navy she checked on him once in a while.

As I became more of a presence in Kelli's house and she in mine, our parents relaxed some of their rules for us. Eventually I stopped sleeping in her cellar. If it looked like a night I could get hit, I'd head to Kelli's house early. We'd do our homework until late in the evening. Inevitably her mother asked if I was going to stay. As long as I called my father and told him where I was it was okay for me to stay there. I'd pretend to dial and talk to the dial tone.

I'd sleep on the couch at her house and eventually she slept at mine. I'd go to the couch and she would get my room. Eventually I took an old couch out of our cellar and put it upstairs in my room. I'd sleep there while Kelli was in my bed. After a while her parents allowed us to study in her room as long as the door was open. I started falling asleep in a big chair she kept in her room. Our parents came to trust that we weren't doing anything they thought we were too young to be doing.

We weren't doing anything anyway.

We walked to school together most days and I'd look for her in the hallways between classes. She'd come to my wrestling matches and I went to her swim meets. Her boyfriends didn't like me and my girlfriends didn't like her. Whenever there was a new boyfriend or girlfriend on the scene we took our relationship underground for a while.

Strangely enough, we never got territorial about each other. It was no problem to see one another with a new date. The only time that line was crossed was when I heard someone disrespecting her because she didn't put out or whatever. I'd remind the speaker that she was my friend. Most of them shut up. A few wanted to fight me. I fought them. One of my wives told me that it was wrong of me to rescue her like that. I wasn't her hero and I shouldn't have thought of myself as her hero, her knight in shinning armor.

I wasn't much of a fighter and lost each battle, but I fought. Kelli never found out about the few fights I had over her.

She never thought any girl I dated was good enough for me.

Over the years, as we both got busy with school, jobs, sports, church, band, and so on, we talked on the phone everyday. We'd get together a couple times a week; sometimes for homework or we'd watch television or listen to a new album. If neither of us was working and we had a few unfilled hours over the weekend, we'd take the subway into Boston. Most often we went out on the river. We had a favorite place to go.

She lived on River Drive, a very short, dead-end, and rarely used dirt road near the end of the Back River. There's only a couple houses there and Kelli's house was one of them. We'd go out there and sit on the riverbank or walk along the marsh. We bought a used canoe together and paddled up and down the river. We could easily carry it to the river from her house. In the evening or on the weekends we'd paddle up the river past Great Esker Park and the closed Navy base out to the edge of Boston Harbor. Sometimes we'd see some of my friends jumping off the Route 3A bridge into the river. I'd join them. She hung out with us when Danny and me and whoever else were jumping off the bridge, but she never jumped. Must have been some inherent sensibility she had and we lacked.

We beat out our own path through the marsh to a spot we created as ours. I can't tell you what we talked about there, but we talked about everything: Boyfriends, girlfriends, sex, money, aspirations, college, friends, parents, God, siblings, tragedy, crime, fantasy. It was the most safe and perfect friendship possible.

I told her the real story about losing my virginity. It was heavy and awkward, heated and very quick, not at all like the story I let my friends assume. She knew the girl and didn't like her, but she was very curious about how it came about. What did the girl do? What did I want her to do? How did she act? How did she move? Did I think any differently about her afterwards? What did my friends think about her now? She wondered about losing her virginity. Her boyfriends pressured her for sex and she wanted to, but she wrestled with wanting to hold on to her virginity so she could wear white at her wedding. Besides, good girls didn't. She was convinced that her mother would be able to tell if she did it with someone.

She asked me if I would think of her differently if she did it. I said no. I already knew she had come close to doing it. She had been asked as a junior to go the senior prom. She was thrilled. She had a great time and late that night she almost made love with him. At the last minute she said no. I suspected she was thinking about losing it with her current boyfriend. He was a good guy and she adored him. She was already looking forward to the prom.

During the summer we'd swim in the river regularly. Between swimming and walking the length of the Back River we could make it all the way to the abandoned Nike missile site, and, if we had any energy left, swim over to Grape or Slate Island. There we'd rest, feast on berries, and watch the ship traffic go in and out of Boston. We'd see cargo and tanker ships, Navy ships bound for and sailing from the Boston Navy Yard, pleasure boats, and airplane traffic out of Logan. It was so busy, but the island was quiet. We had the place to ourselves. Clams shells everywhere, a couple disintegrating cottage foundations, the gulls, and the waves. We would have gone there more often, if it wasn't so much work to get there.

South Shore summer nights can be very hot and very muggy. We'd take our canoe and paddle out on the river late in the evening. Off shore there was always a little breeze that kept the mosquitoes away. One night we were out on the river in our canoe and I said I wanted to swim. We beached the canoe and something moved me to say I wanted to skinny dip. She said go ahead. We'd already changed clothes, dressing for school, in each other's presence. We'd turn our backs to each other and hurry up about it, so we were no strangers to each other's unclothed presence. I stood up and undressed, as young males will, with bravado and a presence that says look at me and my magnificent tool. Watch out! In the middle of the hollow we had flattened in the marsh grass, I dropped my clothes on the ground and strutted toward the water with my old sneakers on.

We each kept a pair of ratty old sneakers, shorts, and a T-shirt in the canoe. There were too many things that could bite, and sharp and gooey things in the river to go without footwear. I trapped lobster there. There were those unevolved horseshoe crabs, muscle and clams shells all over the place.

It was high tide. I turned and looked back at her after I was in. I was surprised to see her undress and follow me. She changed as a sober young woman does. She stepped to the edge of the reeds and turned her back. Her arms bent back to unsnap her bra and she carefully folded her clothes. She did the panty removal wiggle. As she put her sneakers on she kept her knees together, moving both legs in unison. She hurried to the water's edge with her arms across her chest and slid in the water. We didn't skinny dip every time we swam there. In fact, it was unusual. The only times we did was when she didn't have a boyfriend, but every time we did that's how she changed.

It was pleasing to see her naked, but a mental, sexual, relationship barrier got in the way.

She dared me to go in the water, naked, in January once. I did. I dared her to follow me. She said no. She wasn't that stupid. She was astonished at how much my package shriveled.

We followed the seasons of beautiful things on the marsh. Baby animal life and spring flowers, summer shooting stars, autumn hurricane high tides swallowing the old abandoned piers, gleeful fish, and small winter animals. We dug our own clams, trapped our own lobster, and caught our own fish. My father showed us how to cook it all. We picked wild grapes, berries, pears, and apples. We'd eat like royalty. It was the most beautiful place in the world. We weren't recluses from the rest of Weymouth's teenage society. There were plenty of picnics and parties. We'd bring the lobster and clams. We each brought other friends and lovers out to the river. We just held the one place at the edge of the trees, on the marsh, near the river as special for us. When we were there we sat close. Sometimes I'd lay back and watch the clouds. She rested her head on my chest and watched the clouds, too.

Occasionally out on the river a Coast Guard boat out of the Point Allerton station or Boston patrolled the Back River. I wanted to do that. She wanted to get married there, at dawn with just a few family members, friends and me.

One day, as we watched the sun set, she said, "If neither of us are married by the time we're thirty we should meet back here and get married."

I didn't think she was serious, but I said, "Sure."

"Really?"

"Why not. Everyone already thinks we're going to get married."

"Promise?"

"I promise."

Even though she was already married, we met again out on the river when we were twenty-five. After I got out of the service I moved to Seattle for a year. I wasn't going back to Weymouth or my father. She stayed on the South Shore. We stayed in touch with letters and it worked out that I would be in Boston on a business trip. I extended my stay and we met on the marsh in the spot we had created as ours. It was growing over, but we made it ours again. The wind, water, sun, and grass welcomed us back. We talked just briefly then I laid back and looked up at the sky and clouds. She laid back and rested her head on my body and looked up too. Four serene hours later we hugged, parted, and said see ya' later.

Now it seems high school went past so fast, then, it mercilessly dragged.

In the autumn of our senior year, one evening as we walked along the marsh, she told me how a coworker had grabbed her a couple days earlier.

Across the few months she worked there she thought this guy, Todd, was odd, but harmless; just another kid out of high school working for minimum wage. She had read *Of Mice and Men* in her American Literature class and thought Todd was like George in the story. Todd wasn't too bright and the store manager looked out for him. She wondered one time if Todd wasn't starting to like her. She had a boyfriend and made sure he came by work occasionally and picked her up after her shift.

One night Todd cornered her in the storeroom. He tried to kiss her and pawed at her breasts. At first she asked what was he doing. She tried to push him away. She told him no. He pressed harder against her. He kept pressing his lips against hers. He grabbed her breast so hard it hurt. Finally she hit him and said, "Get away from me." But when she fought back he handled her more roughly, pushing her down and hitting her. She didn't tell me this part directly, but from what she didn't say I think he got her down on the ground and ran his hand up under her skirt and tugged at her panties. She made her own escape. She kneed him in the nuts.

She told the manager and he fired her.

He said, "I've seen how you lead Todd on. It doesn't surprise me that he made a pass at you."

"I never lead him on. He didn't make a pass at me, he grabbed me and hit me." Kelli replied.

"If you hadn't teased that boy like you do, none of this would have happened," he said. "I can't have someone like you working for me. You're fired. Get out of here."

Kelli was in tears when she told me this.

"I'm going to kick the shit out of both of them," I said. I was as angry as I had ever been.

"No. Leave it alone. It's over and done."

"What's your boyfriend going to do about this?"

"I haven't told him."

"Why not? If he needs help I'll hold Todd while he hits him."

"Marty, what if I really had lead Todd on." She broke another tear at that moment and quickly wiped it away. "Maybe it was my fault. The manager said he saw me. I didn't mean to. How could I tell John?"

"No. You didn't do anything wrong." I knew how she was and Todd was the problem, not Kelli. "You know sometimes people misread you. You're just being friendly and guys always think you like them. Even girls. Remember that girl at that party, Elizabeth. You talked to her boyfriend while she went to the bathroom and when she came back she got all mad and said you were flirting. You weren't flirting, you were just being you."

"Yeah. She got pissed, didn't she?"

"And if Todd's kind of a retard to begin with he probably completely misunderstood that you were being friendly."

We talked for a long time and I think because I told her it wasn't her fault she got over it fairly quickly. But I know it left a mark on her.

Years later another woman I knew told me about a similar situation. She said the outcome did no physical harm, but it made her more cautious and less spontaneous around men.

A few nights later Danny and another friend, Ed, and I waited for Todd outside of his work. We kicked the shit out of him. We never said a word to anyone. When Kelli found out about it, she knew I was involved. She was both mad and flattered that we stood up for her. She said I shouldn't have meddled. She also said she was glad to have a friend who acted in a way that clearly said he stood by her.

I didn't say a word.

During the same difficult fall that she got fired, I got arrested for underage drinking and smoking dope. We both panicked about the prospects of our lives. She wanted to be a teacher and I was thinking about applying to the Coast Guard Academy. The arrest killed my chances for the Academy. She thought her teaching goal was in jeopardy because of having been fired. The firing didn't hurt the prospects for her future at all; the arrest killed mine.

My father's mother died late that same fall. She was widowed years earlier and moved to Florida. We went down there for two weeks for the funeral and to close out her house. I called Kelli when we got back and said I wanted to see her. She said she couldn't that evening, she had to work. She told me to come over after she was off work.

I fell asleep and slept all night at home. I called her the next morning and she wasn't there. I went to her work. She wasn't there. I went to her house. Her family said she had left early that morning. They thought she went to work. I had a motorcycle and on that cool November Sunday morning I rode all over the town looking for her.

I didn't find her. I started to worry. The strange thing was, I never worried about not finding her before. Before long I was racing around town looking for her. Unless there was oncoming traffic, I didn't stop at red streetlights. I cut across parking lots and took every path and short cut I knew. I scared many of our friends during my search for her because I doubled back to people and places hoping she had made contact with them. I never thought to look out on the marsh for her. We had never gone to our spot without each other. I never thought to look there until Sunday afternoon.

I was tearing down Commercial Street trying to get to a small horse stable she liked to visit. As I flew past Commercial Lane I stomped on the foot brake. I rode the path out as far as I could then dropped the bike. I couldn't get my motorcycle out to our spot on the marsh. I knew the texture of the marsh and the river in all seasons. If I was meeting Kelli at our spot I knew she was coming by the way the grass and the wind moved. Even as she stepped off Commercial Lane and onto the path through the marsh the presence of the river changed. It welcomed her. Today there was no clue about her presence. Nothing unusual moved the marsh. Nothing moved the marsh at all. I ran to our spot. She wasn't there. I turned back toward the river's end, bewildered.

Where was my friend? She vanished. As much as I needed her she needed me. We balanced each other. We both knew in the back of our hearts we would always be available to each even though our lives were preparing to send us separate ways. She couldn't slide out of my life so easily, so anonymously, so abruptly.

I walked back in from the marsh. I picked up my motorcycle and then I saw her. She was at the edge of the trees on a little spit of land that stuck out into the river from Great Esker Park. I think she had been watching me the whole time and chose to let me see her then. I had looked there before. I turned my motorcycle off and faced her. We stared. We saw right into each other souls. Something had broken her spirit.

The same thing was about to break mine.

She put her hands to her face and lowered herself to the earth. I ran. I ran as hard as I ever had. That goddamn river became a canyon. I tripped in the mud. I splashed through the cold water. I stumbled on every rock and piece of driftwood that crossed my path. I slid on the seaweed. I watched Kelli settle from her seated position to a fetal position on the ground. I could see her convulsing as she cried. Her arms wrapped around her waist. My clothes weighed me down. I sank in the river. I couldn't get to her. The current pushed me downstream away from her. Without moving she seemed to stay ten feet out of reach. I finally made it across the river and ran to her. I stopped in front of her. She had to allow me come to her. I sat down. We waited. I grew cold. My wet clothes and the cold air chilled me. I looked over our beautiful river and saw stillness. There is always a breeze on the river. The grass blows. The water ripples. There was always a bird singing or flying. There were always raccoons or crabs at the waters edge. Fish break the surface, jet's fly overhead in the flight path to Logan Airport. A siren or truck noise fills the background with noise. Not now. Now there was an unholy silence. I imagine it like the silence of Hiroshima right after the bomb. Only here it extended for minutes. She moved toward me. I hugged her and tried to send her every healing vibe I had.

Eventually she spoke. She said, "I hoped you'd come looking for me." She paused and looked out over the river to our spot. "As much as I wanted to I couldn't go there without you." She stood up and said, "Let's go there now."

We walked in silence. She walked in a very disturbing way, she limped, then she burst out to be in front of me then she stopped and waited until I passed her. Not once did we walk side-by-side, like we almost always did. We crossed the river on a little up-river, low-tide sand bar we knew. I was in front there. We got to our spot. I stood and waited for her to settle. She never did. She sat, stood, and paced while she talked.

She told me. She told me what happened. She gave me all the detail I didn't want.

I listened.

"Jennifer called from work yesterday and told me everyone was getting together after work and if I wanted to I could go with them. So I went back to Burke's to meet her. I waited in the parking lot. I left my car there and we rode to the party together. It was a quiet party and wrapped up early. Jennifer stayed because her boyfriend was there. Eileen gave me a ride back to my car. She waited until I got my car started and waved at her, then she took off. I put the car in gear and turned to back out of the parking spot, but then a station wagon came around the corner and cut me off. I waited for it to pass, but it stopped. I looked and saw Todd was driving. I could tell he was nervous. He was looking around and then out of nowhere the manager, Mr. Wertz, was next to my car door. He yanked the door open and grabbed me by my hair. He said, 'Turn the car off.' I did and then he pulled me out of the car and dragged me to the station wagon."

She never looked at me while she talked. She kept rubbing her fingertips across the tip of her thumb. She'd stop suddenly and look around; she still wouldn't look at me, though. Then she'd take a couple deep breaths and start talking again.

"The thing that stuck in my mind," she said, was, "As I was being dragged the gravel from the parking lot had gotten into my new shoes and it was uncomfortable." We both looked at her feet. She was wearing her river sneakers. She looked away across the river and continued, "Todd opened the station wagon door and the manager pushed me into the car. He said I was going to 'Ride bitch.' Whatever that meant. He told Todd to hit the gas. The tires spun and threw up some gravel. I could smell the rubber burning a little. The car took off and the tires squealed when we turned onto Washington Street. The manager yelled at Todd to take it easy.

"He kept grabbing and digging his fingers into the back of my neck."

I couldn't see her neck, but I imagined it bruised like my face was after my father landed a good shot on me. I knew what she was going to tell me and I was furious, but I couldn't show it then. My fury would only have made her nervous to be around me. I swore I would avenge Kelli. Mr. Wertz took some of Kelli away from me and I needed every drop.

She was spitting the whole time she talked. "I was so stupid. I didn't figure out what was happening. I knew Todd and Mr. Wertz were all mad and tense and nervous, but I couldn't imagine what they wanted. I thought if I apologized for kicking Todd maybe they'd bring me back to my car. I said I was sorry. I said I was sorry that you had beaten Todd up. The manager said, 'So it was your pussy friend that did that.' He spoke to Todd, 'I told you Todd. She was behind it.'"

"I'm so sorry I did that, Kelli."

"It wasn't your fault." At last she sat down. She still didn't sit close to me like she usually did. She stayed five feet away. I watched gray November storm clouds move up the harbor behind her.

"They drove up the dirt road at the end of the parking lot to the high-tension lines. Todd stopped the car at the base of one the towers. He wouldn't look at me. Mr. Wertz opened his door and grabbed my arm and pulled me out of the car. He told Todd to open the tailgate. He ripped my jacket then my blouse and my bra. He was so hard about it the fabric actually gave me a burn.

"That's when I figured out what was going to happen. I started crying and tried to apologize again. Todd just stood there. The manager dropped his pants.

She stopped talking for long time. "He put his thing in my mouth."

She told me the rest of the story.

I wish she had spared me the details.

"He made Todd put his thing in my mouth too. Then he made me take off my pants. It seemed like I was there for an hour. It hurt everywhere he touched me.

"I can't remember everything. I don't want to remember.

"He bit me. And he made Todd do all the same things."

She said, "It hurt so bad."

I wanted to hug her. I wanted draw all the poison out of her and take it into me. I held my arms open to her, but she didn't move or even look at me.

"I thought about you during it. I thought about our place here and, of all the weird things to think about, for some reason, I thought about some homework that's due tomorrow.

"After a while I couldn't think about anything in particular so I kinda' tuned into the surroundings. I heard the electricity moving through the power lines. I wondered where it was going and why it was I could hear it. But the grunting and scflulling and panting they were doing drowned out all the other noises. Every once in a while Mr. Wertz yelled at Todd.

"I felt the coolness in the air," she said. "But they stunk. I looked at the stars, so I only caught glimpses of them."

That's when she started crying, and now she let me hold her, what a pair, the two of us on the marsh, Kelli crying and me so very angry. Murder is all I thought. I wanted to cry too. I didn't. I thought it might upset her more.

"They told me not to say anything to anyone or they'd come after me again."

She looked at me and said, "Marty, you can't do anything about this."

She said they pulled her from the back of the car and let her fall to the ground and drive off like she was no different than a hamburger wrapper someone threw out a car window. She didn't stay there long. She gathered her clothes and put them back on. She walked back to her car. She said it surprised her that she was that close to her car the whole time. She thought she was a terrifically long way away from everything. She drove away. She stopped crying. When she got home her parents where already in bed. Her mother whispered from the bedroom, "How was the party honey?"

"Fine."

"You're home late."

"Jennifer and I talked for a while afterwards."

I asked her, "Why didn't you tell your parents?"

"I didn't want to think about it anymore.

"I took a shower, put my clothes in the wash, and went to bed. But I didn't sleep. I wanted you to call or come over."

I was asleep at my house in my own bed. Damn me.

She said she got out of bed before dawn and left. She'd been on the river for hours before I found her. She said she hadn't cried until she saw me. She watched me search the marsh. She saw my panic. She saw my concern. She made it so I would see her as I was leaving.

I asked her, "Is there anything I can do."

"No."

"Are you going to go to the police?"

Her answer came back very quickly, "No." Then she added, "I just want to go to college and forget all about this."

I can't imagine what she was feeling or what she would forever feel. As hard as it was for me to hear all that, what she knew, what she felt put whatever I felt to shame. I was angry. I was sad. I was as impotent to fix it as I was to stop it before it happened.

She stayed in her corner of our spot and I stayed in mine. She stood to leave. In spite of all the horror she described to me, all the rage I felt, and how hard my heart was crying, the hardest part for me was when I asked if she wanted me to walk her home. She said, "No."

She left. I followed a couple minutes later. I didn't let her out of my sight. I saw her go into her house. I stood at the edge of the marsh and watched the window to her room. I saw her. She parted the curtains and looked out over the river. The view of the river from her bedroom window was beautiful. In the mornings when I'd wake up in her room I'd look out the window. I could see all the way up to the bridge. In the fall with the leaves changing color and first light it was magnificent. She said she looked out the window every morning. If some developer found out about the beautiful view that existed in that rundown part of town, he would seize it.

Finally she looked at me. She waved then let the curtains drop back together and turned back into her room.

In my own selfish despair I didn't know what to do. I couldn't go home and talk to anyone about what I felt. Who would I talk to?

I picked up my motorcycle. I rode slowly to where Todd worked. I was going to tear Todd, the manager, and the place apart. I stopped outside the building and watched them, my passion turning to premeditation.

CHAPTER 14

▼

PROM NIGHT

Kelli didn't come to school the next week. She didn't want to see me either. She told her mother she wasn't feeling well. I was the only one who knew why. I cut school that week and stalked Mr. Wertz and Todd.

Todd was an idiot. He couldn't have an original thought if his life depended it. He didn't know his life depended on me. He and Mr. Wertz were roommates. Todd walked everywhere. He couldn't afford a car or maybe because he was so stupid the state wouldn't give him a license to drive.

Mr. Wertz became my target. He would die. I would kill him. Todd might live.

It was going to be easy. It was going to be bloody. If I was doomed to hell for what happened, so be it. I had no feelings. I'd have no remorse.

As I followed them around however, a sense of déjà vu grew in me. After I followed them home one night I could swear I had been in the house before or at least in that neighborhood. And, although I didn't know his name until Kelli told me it, I thought there was something uncomfortably familiar about him. Maybe he was someone I met or somebody I knew, knew him. Either way he was the bastard behind Kelli's pain.

Todd and the manager were two goofs. He thought he was so cool. He watched out for Todd. He also made Todd his manservant. Todd ran errands. Todd waxed his car. Mr. Wertz gave Todd approval and promised rewards for Todd's assistance. One time I heard him tell Todd that if he washed his car for him he'd take him to a strip club. Even though Todd was underage, the manager said he had a friend who worked there. They would sneak him in and make sure he got a beer. Todd made that car shine. The strip club never materialized. His friend no longer worked there so he couldn't get Todd in. The manager promised Todd he'd find something else for them to do.

The anonymity of only the four of us knowing about what happened made it safe for me. Kelli was never going to talk about it again. The manager and Todd probably didn't talk about it. If they did they only boasted to themselves. Because of the murder I was to commit I didn't say anything. My initial target was Todd. In his stupidity he could say something. The manager watched him closely.

On the outside by all appearances Kelli recovered, but I knew she hadn't. She broke up with her boyfriend. She told him she had to concentrate on getting into college. We resumed our connection, but it was in an altered state. She still trusted me, but she didn't trust men anymore. I was one of them so she couldn't trust me as much. She decided she wasn't going to her prom. In one of the few references she ever made to her rape she said there would be too much pressure on her after the prom. She didn't want to deal with that.

I watched my dearest friend devolve and there was nothing I could do to stop it. Just by her word choice and movements I knew she was contracting. Her vibrancy dulled. I was the only one who fully understood the depth of the change.

I started tormenting Todd and the manager. I followed them. I'd show up places they went and let them see me. At Dunkin' Donuts I would go in right along side them. At the gas stations I'd pull in right next to them. I'd let Mr. Wertz see me near Todd. One day they went to the supermarket. I went in, too. The manager was in one isle and I slid up to Todd in the next isle. As the manager turned the corner to come up the isle I leaned into Todd and whispered a vague reference then I walked away from Todd. The manager caught up to me and asked me, "What that fuck are you doing?"

"Shopping," I said. "I got a sick friend." I dropped my packages into his cart and left.

I messed with them for about four weeks. It was so easy. I watched them fall apart. I got little sleep. I'd follow them home. Todd freaked out every time he saw me. As soon as I got to know his pattern I'd wait in the dark for him in the parking lot. As they got into the car I'd slowly drive by on my motorcycle. A couple times I beat them back to their house and I'd pull out of the driveway as they pulled in.

Mr. Wertz caught me once. It was early and I hadn't got much sleep the night before. I had staked out my usual position in the parking lot of their work. I fell asleep. He came up to me and put his foot on my neck. He stepped down and said, "I could kill you anytime I wanted to, punk."

Todd grew nervous because the manager was so nervous and, because, he knew who I was and that I was one of the guys that beat him up. Each time, when Todd saw me, he just looked with a stupid vapid stare then he'd remember who I was. He'd scramble in the other direction.

It was time.

A week before Christmas I borrowed my father's car. I told him my motorcycle had a flat and it was getting cold outside. He took the bus to work anyway, so it didn't matter to him. As long as he had it on the weekends so he could go to the packie he let me use it. I got to Todd before dawn as he was walking to work. I pulled up alongside him and said, "Todd, I'm sorry I've been bothering you. Get in the car. I'll give you a lift to work. Maybe we can clear things up."

"No. I can't."

"Come on Todd. I said I'm sorry. I got a little pissed off because of what happened, but it doesn't matter now. I know you weren't the one who started it." He was hyperventilating as I talked to him and walked faster trying to get across the street. I kept cutting in front of him with the station wagon. He seemed to relax a little when I said I knew he wasn't the one behind it.

"Get in. We'll go down to the Dunkin' Donuts and I'll buy you a donut." He wavered.

"I'll be late for work."

"No you won't. We'll go to the one in the Landing. Come on. Get in."

He got in.

Why Todd walked to work and Wertz drove was a mystery to me, but I wanted him to see Todd and I together. I drove past their work place, but Wertz wasn't there yet.

I hoped Todd was as big a simpleton as he seemed to be. He picked out four donuts and a large coffee with cream and eight sugars. When we got back in the car I said, "Kelli told me what happened."

Todd didn't say a word. He looked forward, slurped his coffee, and ate a circle out of the center of a jelly donut.

It sickened me to say it, but I said it, "Hey come on Todd, I've seen Kelli naked. She's a pretty girl."

"Yah. She was." He shuddered.

"So what did you think? I mean touching her and all that."

"I'm not supposed to talk about it."

"Come on Todd. Be a guy. What'd you think?"

He blushed. "It felt nice touching her."

"That's it? It felt nice."

"Yah, but, it seemed to hurt her."

"What did?"

"What Mr. Wertz did. He can be mean sometimes, but only when a young person sasses back to him.

"I've got to go to work now."

"Okay Todd. Well, tell the boss that I'd like to know what he thought about seeing her naked, too."

Todd seemed thrilled at the idea of being a channel for some locker-room boasting. "Okay. Thanks for the donuts."

We pulled into the parking lot. I stopped the car right by the door so he would see Todd getting out. He saw. He stayed inside and simply unlocked the door to let Todd in.

I turned and left.

School was closed for Christmas break. That night my brothers and I went Christmas shopping. We tried to have a modicum of holiday spirit in the house. And I wanted to get Kelli something. Dennis, Jeff, and I went to the South Shore Plaza. Dad was home when we returned. He suggested we get a pizza. It was a nice evening with four of us. Dad went to bed early as always and Dennis and Jeff watched TV. I left for Kelli's house. Dennis waved as I went out the door. Jeff was absorbed in the Charlie Brown Christmas Special.

I walked toward Kelli's, but instead of following Commercial Street I walked onto High Street. When there were no cars, I slipped into the woods and crept up to Mr. Wertz and Todd's house. It was too familiar. My mouth went dry. My hands shook and I was overheating on that twenty-eight degree night. I could see them in the living room watching TV. I knew exactly where the cellar door was. It was locked. All the basement windows were locked too. I seemed to know that before I tested each window.

Mr. Wertz didn't want people peering into his property so he grew his shrubbery tall. I threw a rock though one of the cellar door windows. As they ran downstairs, I hustled up a tree and watched them. All the cellar lights came on. I saw them peer under the stairwell and into a tool room. Then they came outside with flashlights and searched the ground.

Todd was very agitated. I heard him say, "I'm sorry. I know I promised I wouldn't say anything, but he already knew all about it."

"Shut up Todd. Just be quiet." Mr. Wertz was straining to see or hear anything.

They went back in to the cellar, but they didn't go back upstairs. I climbed down out of the tree and snuck up close to the busted window. A peculiar smell came out of the broken window. I was sick to my stomach. I was trembling. I could feel my whole body tighten. My waist was seizing. The way the muscles convulsed it felt as though my hips and pelvis were gasping.

I peeked through the broken mullion. Todd was bending over to pick up what looked like a baby-lotion bottle. I didn't know what I was going to do next. As much as I wanted to, I couldn't kill them. Kelli had buried the event deep so even if I went to the police she wasn't going to come forward. I was impotent. As I stared Mr. Wertz stepped up behind Todd and swung a baseball bat at his head. Todd fell and Mr. Wertz hit him again and again and again. I wanted to look away, but I couldn't. I wanted to run, but I couldn't. It was as though something was holding me there making me watch this. I managed to shuffle my feet slowly backwards while he kept swinging the bat.

Over the years when I've thought of that murder, I am surprised at my own indifference. I felt very little about what I witnessed that night. I've gotten more upset over other crimes I've read about and seen. I feel nothing about Todd's murder. He was the first of two people I've seen killed. The second was a sailor in the Philippines when I was with the Navy. He died from knife wounds he took in fight over a hooker. That upset me greatly. I'm not insensitive. I'm trustworthy, patient, and empathic, but my lack of response to Todd's death must have also killed something deep in me at the same time.

After I gathered my wits I walked back into the woods. The night was beautiful. The moon shone very bright. The frozen earth did not give under my steps. It crunched. I didn't know these woods as well as the woods in my neighborhood. I just wanted to emerge from them far away from Mr. Wertz's house. I emerged near the police station. I could have called the police and the problem with Mr. Wertz might have been resolved, but somehow I knew it wasn't over, yet.

Todd never showed up for work again. Through Kelli, via her friend that still worked there, I heard that Mr. Wertz said Todd had left to see some family and it was unlikely he was coming back. The family, he said, was concerned that Todd wasn't being looked after adequately; what with his being slow and all.

I went to Kelli's' house. It was late. We watched some television and then I went home. We never stayed at each other's homes again.

The winter spun into spring. We went back to the river. She got accepted at UMASS. I took a student loan in anticipation of my first year of college.

Kelli followed through on her threat not to go to her prom. Her old boyfriend called her several times to ask her back out to the prom. She said no. Two other boys asked her to the prom also. She said no to them, too.

I kept trying to talk her into it. We argued about it. One day we walked the river to Bare Cove Park, on the Hingham side of the river. It was one of my favorite places; an abandoned Navy base rehabbed into a park. I always felt good and confident there. Her love for the area originated on the river and went toward land. Mine went from the land out to the river. I think she went with me to Bare Cove because she knew it meant a lot to me. So there, that day, I said, once again, "You should go."

"I'm not going."

"We can double date I'll make sure no situations arise."

"No."

"I'll take you."

She stopped walking on that one. She looked at me. It was a look I had never seen before. I couldn't describe it, but the words that followed matched her look, "That's sweet Marty, but you're a guy and I know what you'll be looking for and like I said, I don't want to deal with that. And I really don't want to have to deal with that from you."

That hurt and it made me mad. "I'm not like that and you know it."

"I know you're not and I'm sorry I said that, but leave it alone. I'm not going."

She turned away from me and, for the first time ever, didn't look back at me. She walked herself home. It felt like my mother had died all over again. I had to once again deal with the world all by myself.

Two weeks before prom night I told my prom date I wasn't going. She cried and got very upset. She wanted to know why. I couldn't tell it was because my dearest friend had been raped. It sucked the life out of her and, subsequently, me.

I couldn't explain anything to my date. The only thing I could say was, "I'm sorry, I'm sorry, I'm sorry."

It was one of the most difficult things I've ever done, standing there, breaking her heart, dashing her plans, and not being able to give her any reason. I think she probably still hates me. I called Kelli's old boyfriend and said, if he was still looking for date to call my now ex-girlfriend. He could use my tickets and take my tux. He called her, they went together, and had a good time.

I didn't tell Kelli I wasn't going to the prom, but she found out two days before the prom.

She was angry when she called, "I just heard you're not going to the prom. Is that true?"

"Yup."

"Don't be a martyr, Marty. I feel bad enough about everything already, I don't want to feel worse because you think you have to take care of me."

"That's not it. I know you can take care of yourself."

"Then what is it?" she yelled into the phone.

"We talked about this last fall. We were going to get a table together, I was going to get my father's car and the four of us were going to go together then go out for a breakfast then go up to Great Hill and have a champagne toast at dawn. Remember? My father would have given us a bottle. Do you remember us talking about this?"

"Yes."

"Well if you're not going to be there then I wouldn't have a good time, so I decided not to go."

"You're being foolish."

"No I'm not. We've talked about this, our lives are going to change in a couple months. I'm going to Boston and you're heading to UMASS. We're not going to see each other as much. We'll stay in touch, but it's not going to be the same. I'd rather spend the night watching TV with you than spending the night thinking about what you're doing. So I'm not going."

"You are so maddening." She hung up on me. She hardly ever hung up on me, but when she did I knew I won. She didn't hang up because she was mad, she hung up because she knew I was, if not right, at least unwavering.

Over the two nights before the prom my father and her parents tried to push us into going together. They didn't understand why we weren't going to the prom together in the first place. My father said, "Well if your date stood you up why don't you go with Kelli. You two are always together anyway."

I shrugged it off and said, "We're going to hang out together at her house."

"If you need some dough or if Kelli does to get a dress or whatever, I can give you some cash."

"Thanks, but that's not it, Dad. She just doesn't want to go."

"Okay, but if you or Kelli change your mind the offer stands."

"Thanks." I was surprised at the attention my father paid to this issue. Kelli told me her parents asked her the same question and made a similar offer. It was a milestone in our lives. Go together and enjoy yourselves, they said. We didn't. On that beautiful, warm late May Saturday night we were, however, together.

I went to her house mid-afternoon. We took our bikes and went for a ride. The town was empty. Normally, whenever we moved around town we'd always see someone one of us knew working somewhere; pumping gas, bagging groceries, waitressing, cutting grass, and so on. Someone would yell from their car as they drove past. That night there was nothing like that, there was however a very different aura through the town. It was a gentle, affirming, and enveloping feeling. It was as though Weymouth knew another cycle moved from its womb and it was giving a satisfied sigh.

We took our canoe paddled out to the harbor. As we passed some of the North Weymouth homes we caught glimpses of fathers taking pictures of their sons and daughters dressed up, pinning a corsage or bootineer on their date. We turned back down the river and watched the sunset. As much as I thought I had resigned myself to not going to the prom, I was irritated with her. I didn't understand why she wouldn't go. Why couldn't she believe that I would not allow a sexually threatening situation to arise? Why wouldn't she go with me? I believed what she said about not wanting to have to deal with the pressure, but I didn't understand how it made her feel. I didn't understand how she now viewed herself or men or her body. I only knew that she grew more mistrustful of men, her judgment, and me.

Over the years, six women I met have told me they had been raped. Five of the six were date rape situations. They said things got out of hand and the guy didn't stop when the girl asked him to stop. Two of those women said they felt that if they didn't have sex with the guy, it would have turned violent. The sixth woman had been grabbed as she walked home from work. She never defined it as rape because she said there was no penetration. It seemed to me however, that all the other activity still made it a rape. Three other women have told me their boyfriends took their virginity before they were willing to give it. That sounded like rape to me, too. One of them said since it was gone she decided to continue having sex with the guy, experimenting and practicing with him.

They all told me they grew mistrustful of men. They retreated from men for a while. However, none of them ever prosecuted the man. They all thought they had done something to bring it on. They all felt that what happened was wrong, but maybe that they behaved in a way that contributed to it happening. None of them seemed to have received the degree of repeated violence Kelli received.

Kelli and I paddled back down the river and stopped at our spot. We sat there and looked up at the sky. I saw a tear. By her manner I knew she was upset, but she wasn't talking. We were quite a pair. I was irritated and she was upset and teary.

She said, "I'm sorry you chose to spend the night with me."

"Kelli, how could I have spent tonight, of all nights, without you?"

We went back to her house, had bite to eat, and settled down in front of the TV. Her parents went to the plaza and to a movie. We had the place to ourselves for a few hours.

As we sat there I knew my purpose was to show her that not all men are cruel. I knew she knew that, but I felt she had to trust men and her body or else she would miss out. I rubbed her shoulders. Then I gave her a massage.

I told her to sit on the floor in front of me between my legs. I started rubbing her shoulders. She tensed up immediately. I kept gently rubbing, kneading, circling. I moved my hands up her neck and into her hair.

I had figured out, young, how to give a back rub better than most of my peers. Most of the back rubs I had received and have watched involved the fingertips being driven like nails into muscle. The skin grabbed and basically pinched in bulk. I used the pads of my fingers and moved the skin with my palm in more of a cupping motion than a bulking action.

I held her forehead with one hand and moved my fingers through her hair. I pulled her head back and set it against the couch. I moved my hands across her forehead down her cheeks across her lips and gently against the front of her neck. I felt her relax when I rubbed under her chin. I rolled her ears between my thumbs and forefinger. Then I moved laterally out to her shoulders, rubbing, kneading, and gently pressing. I had to make a decision, if I pushed my hands further and rubbed her back, her legs, her stomach, her feet, would it scare her? Would she be alarmed that I was going to do something to her? Would it help her or would it destroy our friendship? I wasn't going to fondle her or feel her up. That was the farthest thing from my mind. It was one of those rare moments of teenage wisdom. I wanted to be selfless.

She sat there. I moved my hands back in from her shoulders. I pushed my fingers under the button at the top of her blouse. She had her eyes closed. I rubbed the muscles at the top of her chest. I removed my hands and undid two buttons. She breathed normally. She took a leap of faith and trusted me.

I rubbed the muscles that helped shape and support her breasts. I gently, slowly moved my hands and fingers in a small circular motion. I didn't grab. I didn't wrench. I didn't jerk. She sat there between my legs facing away from me with her eyes closed. She was beautiful. From the light of the television, with Kelli in my arms I saw the beauty of women. I understood what it is men seek to cherish in women. It is the sum of beauty, vulnerability, and absolute trust. So many things add into that total; intelligence, humor, hair, eyes, body. So many things take away from that formula; nagging, weight, irritability, shrew-like behavior, controlling.

Kelli let herself trust, as she never had before and maybe never did since.

I slowly pulled my hands back and moved them back over to her shoulders and down her arms. I unbuttoned her blouse and took it off. She undid her bra and lay on the floor. I followed her to the floor. I sat beside her and continued rubbing her back; top to bottom with small circular motions. I ran my hands along her spine and out to the curve of her ribs. I sat gently on her and pushed my hands against her back as I moved her skin and muscle. Her breathing was very steady.

From the outside of her dungarees I rubbed her bottom and down her legs. Her breathing didn't change. I didn't feel her tense. I reached my hands underneath her hips to undo her pants. She lifted her hips up for me. I unhooked the button, pushed the zipper down, and slid her pants and panties off. I slowly and deliberately and innocently worked my hands, my palms, and my fingertips over her bottom and down her legs.

I rubbed her thighs, the back of her knees, her calves and her feet. Then I came up the anterior side of her body: Her shins, kneecaps, thighs, hips, abdomen, and chest. I got back to my starting point and realized she had opened her eyes and was watching me. Just about at her collarbone I looked at her and she looked at me. She reached up and covered my hands with hers. She settled her chin into the space of her hands and mine together at her neck. She pressed my hand against her lips and held it there for a minute. She faintly kissed my hand. She stood up, grabbed her clothes, and went into the bathroom. She changed then went in the kitchen and made us some popcorn. I settled back on to the couch. We fell asleep on the couch together. Her mother woke me up and told me to call my father if I was going to stay. I said no. I should go home.

School ended a month later. We paddled the river almost every day in June and July. We swam, trapped our lobster, dug the clams, and picked the berries. We went into Boston for Red Sox games. We took day trips to Cape Cod, or canoed to the closer Boston Harbor Islands and rode the ferries to the outer islands. One day we pushed the canoe really far out in the harbor, near the dangerous Hull Gut, and explored the abandoned buildings on Peddock's Island. A storm was moving up the coast and by the time we paddled back the waves were knocking us around pretty good. We swamped a couple times.

She left for UMASS Amherst in August. I was miserable for the three weeks until I started college. My surliness made Harold tell me not to come back until I was ready to work and be civil about it. I took Trailways out to see her the second weekend she was there. She was so busy with orientation and setting up study groups that I hardly had any time with her. When I got to school myself my attitude eased somewhat and gradually diluted.

Throughout college then out into the real world we stayed in touch through intimate letters. I knew she started dating again, student teaching scared and thrilled her. Her father got very sick and nearly died. In fact I had put in a special request chit for leave to go see him before he died. He recovered. After college she met someone she really liked and married him when she was twenty-four. By that time I had been married and divorced once and it looked as though my current marriage wasn't going anywhere. I was happy for her. At her wedding I kept a low profile. We sat and talked briefly at the reception in the lobby of the hotel. She seemed happy, sort of, but I don't think she was as happy as she was during the times we were together, particularly the time we enjoyed on the river. I took a picture of the river for her and had it framed and matted as a wedding gift.

Eventually, I had to start sending my letters to her through my father's address. Her husband, although not a physical abuser or nasty, was a controller. She thought it best that we correspond through another address.

One of my ex-wives believed that women who lose control of their lives, or at least are in situations in which they have lost the capability to effect their own happiness, are the ones who get bad cancers. I think that is true for both men and women.

Kelli died of breast cancer when she was thirty years old, leaving three boys and her husband.

I think about her a lot.

I went to her funeral. I spoke some words to eulogize her. My words were dry and dull. I couldn't convey the beauty and glory of my friend Kelli. I greeted some old friends there, and then I walked out on the marsh to our spot. I spoke to the river and thanked it for this place. I thanked the grass. I thanked the air and the water. I thanked God for her. I thanked God for making me a man Kelli trusted.

I wanted to cry, but I forced myself not to.

CHAPTER 15

▼

ELDRITCH STEPS

Weymouth's countenance had not changed, much. Except for an occasional house with a new cover of paint or another home jammed onto the land. It felt very familiar and slightly alien. The early fall sights were the same, leaves were turning color and falling; when a car drove by, the fallen leaves drafted off its bumper for a few feet. Fallen chestnuts nearly tripped me when I stepped on them. They rolled under my shoe like a lop-sided marble.

The air seemed to offer a balm. Everything, from the tops of trees to the leaves, rolled with the wind, unperturbed. Unlike a storm in which everything spun, irritated and chaotic, today everything moved with a purpose. Me too. I just didn't know it. I had been walking in a very mission-specific manner. Even in the unplanned moments at the cemetery and with Danny I was concerned only with what was in front of me. Only now did I start looking around and seeing.

On someone's lawn I dragged my foot over the dewy grass and created a perfect arcing swath through the moisture. A few hundred feet later on Broad Street, at a place where a short stonewall held back an elevated lawn, I reached down to touch the earth. The earth felt warm, but my hand had to pass through the cool dew first. Oddly, while my right hand was pressed to the earth my left hand followed suit. The way my hands were positioned and my fingers spread, it looked like I was preparing to play a keyboard. I wanted to press my cheek to the ground and taste the dew, but if I lapped the grass someone looking out a living-room window might find it odd enough behavior to call the police. Who cares, I thought. I lay my cheek against the grass. It was luxurious, but I didn't linger. I stepped on and let the dew dry into my skin.

It was still early. I had been moving since five o'clock. It seemed as though hours, possibly days, should have passed, but I still had plenty of time to spare before I was due at Harold's. I had moved less than a half-mile since Danny's departure.

A clue, that would help clarify why I was here, remained elusive.

I turned up Chard Street and passed by the high school. I came out in front of the town hall, city hall as it read now. I turned right onto Middle Street.

I planned to go right, past Legion Field and onto Commercial Street. I would be clear of Gilbert Road and the house. But I couldn't. My steps had become labored and my stride almost down to a shuffle. I stopped at the entrance to Legion Field, opposite Gilbert Road, and stared up the incline. So much happened within a half-mile radius of where I stood.

I didn't come to Weymouth to have a cathartic experience and break free of whatever controlled me, but at the beginning of Gilbert Road a powerful dubiety came over me.

Behind me, Legion Field; in front of me was what? The genesis of my denouement? I had to walk that road before I could go any further.

I turned right and stepped down the stairs into Legion Field, instead.

▼

CHAPTER 16

JACK HAMILTON, TONY CONIGLIARO, GLENN FULLER & MARTY ROBERTS

Baseball is the perfect equalizer. Everyone gets a hit. Everyone gets a homerun, eventually. Everyone gets to force an out, make a tag, squeeze a run-down, and steal. Everyone strikes out, fly's out, and is thrown out. You're batted in or you bat a run in. And you watch; you watch the sky and clouds, the balls go over the fence, someone dive for a catch, and someone run into a puddle for a catch. You watch yourself in the eyes of other males. In their eyes you see what you do well.

Legion Field had three distinct sections. The high school's football and track field was fenced off. On Saturday mornings it was opened. We usually hopped the fence during the National Anthem to avoid the twenty-five cent student admission. Opposite the football field were the swings, slide, basketball, and tennis courts. On the other end were two baseball diamonds, stands, and the low point in all of Legion Field, which always had water in it. It froze in winter and made a boring circular skating pond, although that boggy area was about to change, too. I had read that as part of the agreements Hingham forced on the Greenbush reconstruction effort was a tunnel through Hingham Square. Dirt from the excavation was to be hauled to Legion Field and the boggy part to be filled with the dirt.

Just behind the backstop off the southernmost baseball field was a small grassy area perfect for summer baseball. The distance from home to first base was not ninety feet. Probably sixty. First to second, maybe eighty, second to third a steep descending fifty, and an almost unstealable one hundred feet third base to home. The outfield had room for a center fielder only. To fill the entire outfield would have had all of us crashing into each other.

The older kids hit the ball over the fence into the high school field regularly. Whether or not over the adjoining field's backstop was foul changed game to game, because sometimes someone actually played left field beyond the backstop.

I played third base and left field. The games were neutral, honest as possible, easy, and grand. The older kids played fair baseball. Teams were divvied up evenly, a mix of the young boys and older ones. Bats and gloves were shared unhesitatingly. Kevin played first base in Farm League and had a first baseman's mitt. He shared it. A half a dozen ratty baseballs materialized from nice, average suburban homes. Old men walking to the town hall or waiting for the bus would stop and watch. Occasionally they'd offer bits of advice. Brothers and sisters, cousins, and visiting family came to the park and watched. Sometimes when the teams were uneven, and they often were, cousins and spectators played.

A perfect day for me was a train ride in the morning, good tips on collection day from my paper route, having enough money in my pocket to buy something when the Hood ice-cream truck passed though the neighborhood, an early supper of hot dogs, hamburgers, macaroni and cheese, and cole slaw outside on the picnic table, and enough light left for an evening baseball game.

There was no catcher that day. If the ball went past, the batter had to retrieve it. Everyone swung at the first pitch.

Six to two, fourth inning, David had walked to first, I was on deck. Brian made a base hit to center field. David made it to third base. Brian was on first and I was up.

That summer my hitting was cold. I was fielding okay, but my hits flew out nearly every time; easy, high pop-ups in the infield, can o' corn for the fielder. By that point in the summer no one expected anything of me. I wasn't being cheered on for anything. That day the infield had moved in on me, and the outfield slept.

It was supposed to be a slow pitch ball game, but the pitching got faster and faster with every pitch.

I stepped into the batter's box, which was nothing more than grass stamped down either side of a flat rock that served as home plate. Glenn threw the first pitch down fast, but it was way outside. Even the outfield saw that one was outside. I didn't swing. I walked over and tossed it back to Glenn. The next pitch was faster and inside. I whiffed. Strike one. I said, "Slow it down," and threw the ball back to Glenn.

The next pitch was faster and nearly plunked me in the head. I dropped to the dirt. That time I whipped the ball back to Glenn and it slapped into the pocket of his worn glove. I knew it stung his hand.

Glenn went into his stance. He acted as though there was a catcher giving him signals. He shook his head twice then nodded. He stood, scanned the bases and balked, but no one was certain enough to call him on it. He turned his attention to home plate, wound up, and fired the ball.

I saw it leave his hand, transit over the dirt surrounding the mound, and part the air. Because of that pitch I've known forever how it is when athletes are in the zone and say they can see the ball only or the shot or putt before it happens.

The stitches rotated in perfect sequence. The remnants of the Spaulding ink flashed in and out of sight as though it was in a strobe light.

I lifted my left foot for hitting power. The baseball drew closer. The thirty-six inch bat steadied then launched. Gravity disabled the ball and the bat moved toward the ball for the inevitable collision. In my mind's eye I saw the point in the right field, over Glenn's left shoulder, opposite Don in left center field where the ball was going. Frenzied, minute, imperceptible calculations and adjustments were made as the ball and bat sped toward each other.

It was a beautiful hit. The wood crashed into the leather in the afternoon sun amid the breeze, slight humidity, and perfect temperature. It was the sweetest sound I've ever heard. I let go of the bat with my right hand and completed the hitting arc with the tip of the bat touching the ground behind me. I watched the ball take-off. I knew I had an easy triple, probably a homerun, and maybe over the fence. I broke into the run for first base when the ball smashed into Glenn's left eye socket. My glory died on impact.

The perfect vision that gave me the perfect hit also enabled me to see the skin around his eye bulge out around the circumference of the ball. I saw the blood and muscle pool into the black eye he was going to have for days. All of my senses were acute during that sequence. I heard the bone crack and felt the earth hiccup when he fell to the ground.

The infield was already moving in toward him. I slowed my approach to first and turned toward Glenn. The outfield still didn't know what happened to the ball that was on its way to them.

We surrounded the mound. I felt sick to my stomach. People had been hit before, usually by an errant pitch or someone miss-throwing to base. The resulting whap and yelp were irrelevant to the game. But no one had ever been hit in the face by a hit before. There was blood coming out of Glenn's eye.

A few minutes earlier Glenn's mother had come down to pick him to take him to the Y for basketball practice. She had been watching the game and had seen him go down. She ran down on the field.

He was crying loud. I slunk into the background. No one said anything to me. No one said that what I did was bad or that my hit was not responsible for what happened to Glenn.

Glenn slowly stood up holding his hand over his eye. He didn't put his hand to his face. It was too sore. He was able to walk to the car then he was off to the hospital. I think walking jarred his face and made it worse.

Without saying a word everyone seemed to blame me for having the perfect hit of the summer which caused Glenn's eye damage.

Tony Conigliaro of the Boston Red Sox and Glenn Fuller of Academy Avenue both took a baseball in the eye that summer; one from a pitch, the other from a hit. Glenn was okay and came back to play with a severe black eye as did Tony Conigliaro. Glenn didn't pitch again and I didn't try to hit much of anything for the rest of that summer.

Summer wound down. There were a few more baseball games and school started right after Labor Day.

I wished someone had said it wasn't my fault; someone to say, those things happen.

No one did.

No one ever has.

CHAPTER 17

▼

SKATING ON THIN ICE

I left Legion Field and turned up Gilbert Road. My heart was pounding and it wasn't due to the small hill that took Gilbert Road up and off of Middle Street. There was a small group of boys riding their bikes in the road. They behaved no different than the kids I hung with years earlier. I wondered if the chasm between younger boys and older boys remained as wide.

The boys of my neighborhood were divided by a three-year age gap. My friends and I were the emerging group; therefore, we were tormented about everything and beat at all sports by the older boys. When they were in a group, they taunted and teased us at every chance.

A favorite maneuver was when one of the older boys would talk to one of us while another one of the older boys knelt down behind the kid. The talking one suddenly shoved the younger boy backward and he collapsed over the other boy. Treachery came into play regularly. If, at a pick-up football game, one of us got a strong run going, invariably we would be tripped, clipped, held, punched, slapped, and straight-armed.

Through all of this male indoctrination everyone understood that this was the way it was. There was no malicious intent, it was simply initiation. We were harassed, tormented, mocked, and teased in a benign way. We had already started to torment the boys who were younger than us.

One of the older boys hired me to help him cut Mrs. Brown's lawn and actually paid me what he said he would, a buck. During these truces, the older boys showed us where the railroad tracks were, where the town dump was, and the where the paths through the woods ended.

It was always easy to find someone from the neighborhood to hang out with.

There was only one person everyone avoided.

The oldest boy in the neighborhood lived near the end of Gilbert Road. Greg. He was six years older than me and three to four years older than the other older boys. Two times he had been held back in school. Greg seemed to know things that none of the older boys knew. He knew how to break into a house when the owner was on vacation. He could get alcohol. He hung out with girls none of us had ever seen before. Greg had an older brother, too, who had moved out of the house under questionable circumstances. There was a rumor of jail.

He had a white Honda motorcycle and a double garage, which was very unusual. He didn't have a jackknife like the rest of us. He had a real knife. It was very big and sharp, very sharp.

One time he dissected a toad with a slow, steady easy push of the blade through its head. It was sickening to watch its face split in two from the inside out as the knife went in. There was something dangerous about Greg. He did cruel things, and that made him interesting.

Usually, when anyone in the neighborhood got in a fight there was an assumption of fair fighting. The unspoken rules were, no hitting in the face, no spitting, and, when someone went down, the fighting stopped. Above all, no one intentionally ever hit someone in the nuts. At the end of the fight, the victor asked, "You okay?" and helped the other back up. The next day the fighters were tepid toward each other, but at the end of the next neighborhood adventure their friendship resumed and the animus forgotten.

Greg didn't obey the rules.

In a fight he kicked in the nuts, hit in the face, and kept on punching or kicking after his opponent fell. He loaded snowballs with rocks and threw them at people's heads. In a fight one time he picked up a Pussy Willow branch and whipped Jason in the face with it, and continued whipping him after he fell. As the blood seeped through Jason's shirt, Greg stared at what he had done and never asked if he was okay.

One day at Legion Field a small pigeon was flapping around under the bleachers. One wing had either been broken or had not properly developed. It was doomed to hunger, cold or a cat. We wanted to help it, but Greg said it wouldn't live and he was going to put it out of its misery. There was silent acquiescence. We all wanted to see something die, but none of us wanted to do it. We wanted to witness a killing and watch death.

The death was supposed to be merciful, like on TV when a horse was shot because of its broken leg, or like when Alex's dog had to be put to sleep because it was so old.

Greg spent fifteen minutes killing it. He took its wings and bent them back across its body. He plucked it down to the bare skin. I watched the bird's normally vapid eyes show pain. Greg took his pen to its eyes and popped them out. I said stop. The bird was suffering. Finally Greg twisted its head three hundred and sixty degrees.

Rumors were he did the same kind of thing to kittens, hamsters, and his gold fish were taken out of the tank, left to flap around, submerged again then brought out again, and left to die. If any of the suburban myths are true, Greg was the kind of boy to make them true. Easily. He could have been the originator of or copied the story of cats buried up to their necks and a lawnmower run over their heads.

One time Greg took my dog's leash and lashed her legs together. He picked her up by her legs and swung her around. I was furious. I lunged at Greg. He let Hunter drop and attempted to straight-arm me. I dropped below his palm and kicked him in the knee. Greg didn't flinch. I stood up. We stared at each other. I was the first one to fight back against Greg. Even the older kids hadn't dared to do that.

After that he stabbed Hunter with a small knife he had concealed in his hand.

My shortcut path to school cut through the edge of Greg's backyard. Sometimes I saw him in his room through the window. Other times Greg hung out the window and smoked. Always I heard hard acid rock music blasting out of his room.

One day as my friends and I were walking the path; I climbed a tree to get the cigarettes Mike had hidden up there. I wasn't into smoking, so I dropped them down and volunteered to be the lookout while Mike and Ed smoked. I saw into Greg's room. I saw a model train set and Greg beating off. Greg looked past the magazine and saw me. He lowered the magazine, looked at me, gave me the finger, and went back behind the magazine.

It never happened to me, but sometimes he supposedly shot BB's and pellets at people walking the path.

The year he hurt Hunter, when fall fell into winter, Greg exacted his retribution for my kicking him in the knee. I didn't flinch, but I paid that sadist's price.

In winter there were two naturally occurring places to skate near my neighborhood. One was the baseball field at Legion Field. The other was a small swampy area the bottom of Cornish Street. The swamp was more fun to skate. It was larger. There were tree stumps and trees growing up through the ice. The frozen water wrapped around the woods for a skating maze. It was great zipping around the woods. In places it was clear enough for a small hockey game.

Skating at Legion Fled was boring. You skated around in a circle with lots of people in the way. The frozen swamp was exclusive and intricate.

Thursday afternoon, January 11, I skated late at the swamp. Greg was there, too. The tension of our summer altercation seemed to have passed. I had gotten out of school early that day. My paper-route was done. I was killing time. My friends had left and I wanted to skate through the frozen woods some more. Greg and I skated through the woods together. Greg cut dangerously near me making me wipe out a couple times. He blocked my escape from the partially revealed stumps. I told him to play fair.

Greg had an elaborate racecar and train set up in his room. He asked if me wanted to see it. It was getting dark, but Greg lived only at the end of the street.

"Sure."

When we got to his house his mother wasn't home. The other times I saw her she seemed nice enough, but she wasn't like the other mothers; she wasn't chatty and fat. She let her hair fall straight down. She was almost gaunt. She was never home at night. Our parents spoke of her with whispering voices.

I walked with Greg through a dark kitchen, a pictureless living room, dark stairwell, and dark hallway up to Greg's room. Greg unlocked the door to his room and turned on the light. It was a very cool room, black-velvet posters, a blacklight, and a train set that intersected with a racetrack. There was enough light that I could see the path we had stomped in the snow on the shortcut trail out his window. I realized he could see anyone coming in either direction along the path. He had a full bed, a green dresser, a chair, and pictures of the dead and wounded from the World War 2 and Vietnam cut from magazines and taped to the wall; there was a partially open closet, and a locking bedroom door.

In all of my friends' homes, we seldom closed the doors to the rooms we were in, and we never locked the door. Even if we were looking at a girly magazine, there was some unspoken rule that the door was to be unlocked. I trusted my parents to knock.

In a split second, Greg locked the door turned, gabbed me by my throat, and lifted me off the ground. His fingernails cut into my skin.

He said, "You fat little prick. Who the fuck do you think you are, kicking me last summer."

My larynx was being crushed. The pain was phenomenal.

I couldn't speak. I struggled less and less as I got dizzy and weak.

Greg set me down on the bed and pulled his knife out of its sheath. He put the tip to my neck and pushed up and in, slightly. I felt the blood run down my neck. He said, "If you move, it'll go all the way in."

He reached for a sword he had. He pulled the knife away from my neck and replaced it with the sword. As he did he dragged the blade across my neck, making a very shallow incision. The blood ran down under my sweater and t-shirt toward my back. With the sword against my neck, he took the knife and cut through the seam of my dungarees. I felt the knife cut into my perineum. I didn't flinch. With my body, I tried to move myself in sync with any movement he made with either blade.

He said, "If you move again I'll shove it up your ass and cut your balls off from the inside."

I could feel the point of the knife and the blood running into my underwear. The longer I laid there the more I felt the warm liquid spreading out across my butt.

He stopped. He stepped back, admired his work, and cut me loose. "Get the fuck out of here. Go home. Don't ever cut through my backyard again." He turned on his stereo and put headphones over his ears. He gave me the finger as I left.

I walked the five minutes back to my house. When I got in the house I took my underwear off and threw them away. Even though I did my own laundry, I didn't want to explain the blood if anyone else saw it.

I never cried and I certainly never said a word about what happened.

How could I?

I hadn't fought back, therefore, I was a pussy.

What was wrong with me?

How could I face my friends?

CHAPTER 18

▼

EMOTIONAL PERISTALSIS

The best I could hope for that fucking sadist was, he died young and it was painful.

Why was I remembering the horrible stuff like Billy losing his legs, the sadist, and the puppy? My life in Weymouth wasn't one tragedy after another. I wished the thoughts that surfaced were more of the carefree, fun times.

Maybe regurgitating the painful stuff was necessary so it could then be digested properly, then excreted.

▼

CHAPTER 19

JANUARY 30

There is a geological marker in Weymouth logically called the Weymouth Formation. It appears in the Mill Cove area and again across Boston Harbor in Nahant; fossils from the Cambrian period rest in the stratum there. The Ponkapoag fault passes near Weymouth. Another geological feature lay in North Weymouth, a large easily visible esker. The moraine of the last glacier is scattered all around Weymouth.

Maybe it was a geological event that saved my twelve-year-old life. A variation on the mantle plume theory, possibly. Maybe a geyser or hot spring got close enough to the surface the coldest night of that year. Regardless, some kind of geologic phenomenon must have allowed enough heat to pass through an old crack or fault line or fissure in the ancient and idle strata of southeastern Massachusetts to keep me from freezing to death.

What else could explain it? What else could have made a mushroom shaped, narrow column of heat rise through the mantle under Weymouth, January 30 that year? Heat that thawed the frozen earth and warmed me enough all night long to keep me from freezing to death. At daybreak I woke up. Chilled, but I woke and when I woke I cared enough again to want to live.

I did not go to the Old North Cemetery, where my mother was buried, to kill myself that night, but I didn't care if I lived, either.

Everything changed six months after my mother died.

It was a month into the new school year. I came home from school one afternoon; it had been a great day. I aced a vocabulary quiz, band practice had gone
well, and I came in first in the quarter mile run the gym teacher had organized.
With school done for the day I was headed out to play kickball with the kids in
the neighborhood.

My mother was always home when I got home. Usually I'd run in the door,
drop my lunch box on the counter, throw my books on the kitchen table, open
the refrigerator, grab something to eat then I'd be out the door.

As I passed through I'd say, "Hi Mom."

"How was school?" she always asked.

"Good. What do we have for a snack?"

"Look and see for yourself."

"I'm going to Legion Field to play basketball. What's for supper?"

"Cube steak. Be home at five thirty."

"Bye."

"Be careful."

That's how it was day after day, month after month. The food for supper
changed and the activity I was dashing off to varied, but the ritual was the same,
but that day when I got home from school my father was there, too. They were
both sitting at the kitchen table, my mother drinking iced coffee, my father looking up at the ceiling, still wearing his tie and sport coat.

I slowed for a moment. I looked at my father and said, "Hi." Then I threw my
books down and went to the fridge.

My father spoke, "Marty. You can't go out and play right now. As soon as Jef-
frey gets home we all need to sit down and talk about something."

Two parallel thoughts instantly ran through my mind; first, I was in trouble
for something I had done, and, second, what were my friends going to do without me there to play. I quickly scanned my recent activity history. I came up with
nothing. I had been on a stretch of non-mischievousness. I thought I was safe
from punishment.

I asked, "Can I go down to Legion and when I see Jeff come up the street I'll
run right back here?"

"No."

My only choices were to go to the dining room, my room or the picnic table
to do my homework. Jeff would be home in twenty minutes. I went to my room.
I flipped through a magazine. Dennis, my other brother was already in his room.
I could hear his 8-track playing.

Downstairs my parents barely spoke. I heard the chair scrape across the kitchen floor when one of them stood, then water running into the kitchen sink.

When Jeff got home my father came upstairs, knocked on Dennis' door and told him to go down to the living room. Then he knocked on my door and said the same to me.

Whatever was going on was serious. He never came upstairs to get us. He always yelled from the bottom of the stairs for us to wake up, get to sleep, get moving or knock it off.

When we all got down to the living room he said, "Boys your mother has something to tell you."

With that, my mother announced she had cancer. She said she was dying.

My father stood and went to the sink for water.

Nothing changed anywhere in the house. The clock above the refrigerator ticked on in its off-center position. A car drove by. No one yelled out. Jeff looked at her. His head leaned forward and lowered at the same time. Dennis didn't move.

I did not fully understand what cancer was, but by the sudden crush of gravity in the room I knew it was bad. I knew what death was. Sort of. I understood what a heart attack was. The father of one of the kids' in school had one and died. I understood people died when they got older, in war, and in accidents. Sudden deaths were an easy concept to understand. I couldn't grasp the concept of dying a slow death.

Dennis asked, "How long do you have to live?"

"They're not sure, but they think I've got six months or so."

I asked, "Why can't you go to the hospital?"

"I've been going to the hospital and seeing doctors for about four months already."

Jeff asked, "What will happen to us?"

"You boys will be fine. Your father will take care of you."

I looked at my father at that moment. While we were talking he had been staring into the corner where the ceiling and wall met. My father would take care of us. I knew there would be food and a house. We'd get help with our homework, receive advice, and be offered guidance. That would suit Dennis and Jeff okay, but for me there would no longer be someone to talk to about the events of everyday. I also knew there would be a lot more hitting.

If there was trouble or a situation that my father could effect he was the go-to-guy. He was very able. Nothing was too big or difficult or unworthy of his mettle. He was calm, collected, modest, reasoned, and perceptive. All of that plus good judgment, honor, and respect. When there was trouble he was the guy who responded first. He knew first aid; blood, burns, broken limbs, deep gashes, and cuts were no problem for him. He knew exactly what to do.

Near our house was an intersection where there were a lot of car accidents. He was always the first one on-scene. When we heard the squealing tires stop and concurrent crunch my mother was on the phone to the police and he was out the door running toward the wreck. I watched him pull someone from a burning car one night.

He always came to my farm league games and my brothers' practices.

I didn't understand this one until much later in life, but when a colored couple moved into the neighborhood, he befriended them. Not because he felt he had to protect them, but because he had occasion to interact with the husband of that couple through church. Dad liked him. However, I heard him say over the fence to another neighbor, "Go to hell. You're a bigot. Stay away from me and my family and if you mess around with the Washingtons, you're messing around with me, too."

He was serious. He fought in Korea. He had been awarded the Silver Star and Purple Heart medals. He was in good shape. I knew from how he hit me and my brothers he was strong.

You could say he presented well.

My father, however, was not a man of great sensitivity, diplomacy or patience when he could not take an action against the problem, whatever it was, whether it was real or perceived. Forces that seemed beyond his control frustrated him to no end. That made him a volatile man.

His temper was always just under the surface. We never knew what would send him off. His reaction was not always with a spanking either. He seemed to start his tirades by almost pouting. Then the clues followed; the jutting, locking, and, ominous grinding of his jaw. A ferocious silence then the fury, but not always.

One morning we were at breakfast, I noticed he had missed rinsing some shaving cream off. It was in his ear. I mentioned it to him and he went off on me like I was ridiculing or mocking him somehow. After that event, which followed a long stream of similar events, I made sure I finished my breakfast as he started his or I started mine as he finished his. My brothers did the same thing. A minute or two cross over with Dad was usually safe. Although, rather than risk another explosion, usually we'd leave the house early and wait outside the school until the doors opened.

We never knew what would cause the explosion, where or when it was going to happen or even if the explosion was coming. Dennis could have done one thing one day and my father would have no reaction. Jeff could do the same the next day and he'd explode.

I left the lawn mower out in the yard one night. It rained overnight. The next morning Dad saw it from the kitchen window as he poured his coffee. I saw the jaw go into position. He clutched the edge of the countertop. He kept staring out the window. I braced myself. He turned to me and said, "Marty, you've got to take care of our stuff better." He got louder. "One night out in the rain isn't going to hurt it but if you keep leaving it outside and don't take care of it, it will get rusty and stop working properly." He was yelling now and hands were red. The Formica seemed to disappear into his hands. "Then when we need it, it might not work, then we'd have to get a new one. They are expensive." He suddenly let go of the counter. With very jerky motions he poured himself a cup of coffee.

He sent me out to put it away. After school I was to clean it up, change the spark plug and oil, and make sure it worked.

Two days later Dennis left a shovel out in the yard overnight. Dew covered it by morning. Dad saw it from the kitchen window. The jaw went into position. Then came the explosion. He was livid. He went outside and picked it up. He came back into the kitchen with it. He shook it at Dennis and said, "What the hell is wrong with you." He stepped into the kitchen and grabbed Dennis by the back of his shirt as he sat at the table. With the shovel in one hand and Dennis in the other he pulled Dennis up close to his face. Dennis' feet dangled like he had just been dropped through the gallows' trap door. His dangling feet knocked the chair he had been sitting in against the table and knocked over the milk pitcher and all the juice glasses.

Dad was right in his face and yelled like he was possessed, saying he was going to take Dennis' record player and leave it out in the yard overnight. Still holding him by the shirt he yelled at Mom, "You're raising a bunch of retards that can't pick up after themselves." His face was red, he was breathing heavy. He put Dennis' face into the shovel. He said, "Don't ever make this mistake again."

With that, he set the shovel down, returned to the breakfast table, spread the paper open, asked my mother if they were still going to go look for a new car that evening (he spotted an ad from Ricky Smith Pontiac). He finished his cereal and coffee, kissed her, told us to have a good day at school, and left for work.

Just another typical morning in the Roberts' house.

Mom was the barrier between him and us. She could reason with him and get him to calm down, most of the time. She'd help him see that whatever one of us had done was not that big a deal. If we forgot to wipe our feet before we went in the house and soiled the carpet, she'd get on us to remember to wipe our feet. If she saw his jaw lock she'd remind him that we were kids. We would forget things occasionally and because we did forget, things would get broken and soiled. It didn't mean we were disrespectful and destined to be social misfits.

Usually, if he was coming after us to hit us, she would scramble to get up and in his way. He never hit her or pushed her or even raised a hand to her no matter how angry he was at us, manically wanting to follow through on his threat to spank the living daylights out of us. He towered over her. He'd puff himself up as big as he could, lean over her and say something like, "You're spoiling them." Or, "If they don't learn how to behave at home they're never going to know how to behave in public." Or the classic, "I know I'm rough on them, but it's a tough world and they've got to be ready for it."

Trembling she held her ground. She'd respond with something like, "Their home should be a place where they don't have to be perfect. I'd rather have them be themselves around here, make mistakes and know that a mistake doesn't mean they're bad. I'd rather have that than have them bust out and hurt themselves or someone else when they leave home."

I asked her once why she stood in his way.

She said, "One time I didn't and he lost control on Dennis."

I asked, "What happened."

"It doesn't concern you. Your father is a good man. He works hard to keep us in this house and plenty of food in the 'fridge." She paused and looked at me. She looked like she was going to cry, but she said, "You know sometimes he loses his temper and we all have to be careful when he does. When you boys were younger you didn't know how to stay out of his way when he was mad." She stood taller, "Well, now we all know to be careful to not make him mad, and get out of the way when he is."

Then she continued, "I always try to slow him down when he is going after one of you. He is never not going to spank you kids, but he has never gotten as mad as he was that day with Dennis."

If Mom wasn't home, stepped aside or didn't stand up to stop him, we got hit. If she stepped aside we knew immediately that whatever we had done was out of line. That behavior was never repeated.

I know my mother frustrated him because she wasn't a demonstrative, affectionate woman. He wanted someone to buddy around with; a wife who liked the same things he did and sought to do those things with him. I think vibrancy from her would have soothed him, somewhat. He wanted someone who openly showed adoring feelings toward him.

He exasperated her because of his moodiness. His moods swung from anger to the absence of anger. If he had a sensitive feeling he was at a loss as to how to show it. But they had an okay marriage. It worked. They did things together. They lived their commitment and vows, until death they did not part. The family worked with some laughter and a lot of anger, successes and failures, and good judgment and bad until she died.

My mother asked, "Do you have any questions about my sickness or what I just said."

Slience.

She asked, "Can I hug you?"

We weren't a touchy, feely, hugging family. Jeff, Dennis, and I squirmed and shuffled our feet. My father said, "For Christ sake, hug your mother."

We moved toward her and circled her. She put her arms around us and pulled us in close to her. She said, "As things go along you're going to get upset and have questions. You can always talk to me about what you're feeling."

When she let go Dennis went back upstairs. Jeff turned the TV on, and I went to play baseball.

Fall slid into winter. Usually, over the winter, our house was cold. Dad set the thermostat at sixty-five for the evenings. He pushed it down to fifty-two when he went to bed for the overnight setting. We all slept with the windows open year round, even open a couple inches during winter. By morning it was frigid in our house. He pushed the thermostat up to sixty-two for the day and then in the evening up to sixty-five. We kept the house really warm that winter. Better than seventy-five degrees all winter long.

We all tried to help out in whatever ways we could that winter. By about February she couldn't stand up for very long. Dad was doing most of the cooking. We were doing most of the cleaning. She hardly dressed up at all that winter. She stayed in her robe most of the time.

She always loved the winter. The cold, ice, snow, and gray days never bothered her. Year round she went for walks everyday. She initiated our mid-winter picnics. Every year on January 30, or the weekend day that was closest to it, we had a picnic. Temperature, snow or gray sky didn't stop us. It was postponed only once when it rained.

If we needed to, we shoveled a path through the snow in the backyard and cleared an area for people to gather. We cleared the horseshoe court and set up the badminton net. We brushed the snow off the picnic table and lit the coal bri-quettes in the grill. We set up the stereo speakers to blast out into the backyard and set out lawn chairs. Cousins, friends, neighbors, aunts and uncles all came over. They thought it was unusual, maybe even bizarre, but they came year after year. It became ritual. Everyone enjoyed it. They brought warm foods instead of cold potato salads, and lots of hot chocolate instead of cold soda. The house stayed warm for infants and anyone who got cold. Dad made a furnace of sorts out of a fifty-five gallon drum and the grownups sat near the fire in the lawn chairs with warm alcoholic drinks while we ran around.

We didn't have the picnic the year she died. There was talk of it, but she was cold that winter.

One day I saw how skinny she had become when she went outside on an unusually warm day. We all loved those winter days when the snow was still on the ground, but the air temperature rose into the fifties. If the sun was bright and the winds from the south everything warmed up; a strange mixture of cool rising up off the snow as far as our knees and the warmth of the sun and air warming us down to our thighs. We'd hear water from under the melting snow and ice run-ning into the storm drains.

I wasn't feeling well that day and had stayed home from school. I watched when she went outside and stood in the backyard. She opened her robe and removed the scarf she kept wrapped around her head. She must have thought I was asleep. She never would have done that if she thought anyone might have seen her. Her skin was so white. Not the Caucasian lack of sun in New England winter white, but a bleached gray. Her hair had become wispy. I could see that around the house. There in the sun I saw how much of it was gone. The only color that remained on her body was on her scalp where she once had her dark hair. Now it was a yellowish patch barley giving shape to what was her hairline. Always, whenever anyone came over the house she put on a wig.

The last month or so someone was always with her. Well into the nights someone was there. Dad still had to work. He took care of her overnight, but he got tired and needed help. We still went to school everyday regardless of her con-dition.

Friends and relatives came over more and more often, usually with food. Our grandparents came by regularly. They helped as much as they could. On the days of her chemo they took us out for dinner or we spent the night at their house in Quincy.

Dennis stayed in his room a lot.

Jeff watched TV.

I stayed busy.

My father did not lose his temper once during those six months. He was patient and kind with everyone, his sons included. We did not get yelled at or hit at all during that time.

Almost anything we wanted to do was okay. The rules were; we had to pick up after ourselves, we did our own laundry, we did our homework with no stalling, and she wanted to see each of us alone for a couple minutes each day. It was usually small talk. How was school? How did your game go? Are there any pretty girls in your class? Do you have any questions about what is going on? Sometimes it was silence. Dennis refused to see her at one point, as she got sicker. I overheard her telling my father to leave him alone. If Dennis was upset, he was not to make it worse. He obeyed and a few days later Dennis was seeing her again.

She died the day after the jonquils came up in the back yard. It had been a warm week. The snow melted, the soil muddy. The jonquils were her favorite. She said she always looked forward to that flower most of all, even when she knew winter wasn't quite over. It meant spring was nearby.

By that time she was not strong enough to stand. My father usually lifted her and carried her to a chair near the window. A couple times Dennis and I carried her there. It was the brightest and warmest spot in the house. During the winter, with the sun in the southern sky, as it traveled its east to west path the whole back of the house was warm in the sun most of the day. She and my father had created a garden that could be seen from anywhere inside the back of the house, but most fully from that particular window.

For the last two weeks of her life she looked out into the backyard everyday. She wanted to see when the jonquils poked up through the dirt. She told us the day she saw the robins came back. The next day the flowers peeked out of the garden. The following day my father came to school and got us. She was dead.

He had already got Dennis out of class. Jeff's school was down the street. We picked up Jeff and drove home. The hearse had already been there and taken her away. Her mother had been there when she died. Grandma was crying when we got home.

She died when Grandpa had gone to the store. By the time he got back home Grandma had already called Dad at work. Grandpa started calling everyone else, Dad's parents, Mom's siblings, friends and so on. People filtered in and out of the house over the next week.

I wasn't a very good son during that week. I took every opportunity I had to be somewhere else; bicycling, swimming at the town pool, hopping a train, staying late at school. Jeff stayed home and was right in the middle of everything.

Dennis stayed in his room as much as he could. The only time I was around was when we all had to be around, the wake, church service, funeral, and memorial.

I was grateful to have my paper route. It gave me a daily opportunity to get away from all that. Other than that, Dad told me to stay close to home. I didn't and he didn't enforce his order. Dad almost lost it at one point on me. I ended up in Hingham one day. I rode my bike there after finishing my paper route and got a flat tire. I had to call for a ride home. I could sense his anger by the way the car approached me. Before I got in the car I could see it was all he could do to not go off on me. I think all the people, at all hours, all the time irritated him. But he held back. I was grounded from going anywhere other than school. Still, I broke the rules of my confinement as much as I dared.

I became a center of attention in school and, in a pathetic way, I didn't mind it. Teachers, other students, the principal all spoke to me and said how sorry they were. If I needed anything I was to ask and they would be glad to help in whatever way they could. I got away with being late to school, not having my homework complete, and lingering in the hall between classes.

At the wake I didn't want to stand there and greet people. Dad let me sit in the back of the viewing room. Dennis didn't mind standing there. Jeff stayed by Grandma most of the time. I didn't cry at all, there.

The closed casket on the catafalque in the church was the thing that upset me the most. The casket was open for the viewing. I could see her. She was still with me. The closed casket took her from me.

I sat next to Grandpa during the funeral service. I whispered to him, "I have to go to the bathroom."

He grabbed my hand and asked, "Are you okay?"

"I'm okay. I just gotta' go bad." He followed me a minute later and saw me heading out the door of the church. He caught up to me and we walked around the parking lot.

There had been a light snow the day before. He said, "I think your mother got her liking the snow and winter so much from me."

I looked at him. I wanted to hear more about her.

"Yup," he continued. "As a little girl she always was outside in the snow, sledding or skating. It was funny, she'd take a book outside with her sometimes and brush the snow off a chair and sit there and read."

"I really like the mid-winter picnics."

"Me too. When she first suggested it everyone thought she was crazy. 'Cept me," he winked at me. "But we all agreed to come. Everyone had such a good time that first year that by the second year everyone was hoping she'd do it again."

I looked at the snow. It had been pushed up into piles on the edges of the church parking lot. The dirty snow reminded me of her skin the day I saw her in the backyard. I started to cry and quickly stifled it. Grandpa put his arm around my shoulder said, "No one your age should have to face this. It's a hard thing to go through as an adult and worse for a kid. It's okay if you want to kick or run or scream or cry."

I wiped my arm across my eyes. "I'm fine."

He asked if I wanted go back inside.

"No." I didn't want to see the closed casket.

He nodded. We didn't go in. When he saw they were going to roll the casket out of the church and load it into the hearse he steered me away so I wouldn't see the coffin.

I don't remember anyone talking on the ride to the cemetery. I looked out the window of the limousine and watched the town roll by. We rolled through the red lights. I saw people look at the hearse as it passed. I noticed the sand the town put down on the roads during the winter had now collected along side the curb. The trees were barren. The snow that had lightly dusted everything made the ground below the trees in the woods light, but I was tired of all the heaviness. I just wanted everything as it was. I wanted to ride my bike. I wanted my mother to be home when I got home from school. I wanted the mid-winter picnic. I wanted my Dad to have one of his mood swings.

Danny and his mother were in a car way back in the motorcade.

The ground at the cemetery was still frozen so they put her in a tomb to be buried later. I didn't have to watch that either. I sat with Danny and his mother on a bench far away from the tomb. I heard everyone pray and the pastor say there would be another brief ceremony when she was interred. That was it. I rode with Danny back to my house.

All of our friends and relatives were there. Over the next few weeks' lots of people stopped by, but it ebbed. Within a month it was just the four of us under that roof. I don't think my mother's siblings particularly liked my father.

My father tried really hard over the next few months. There was cautious peace. At one point he said, "Boys. It's just us. I'm as sad as you are but we've been forced to get along without her." He cooked, we cleaned, and by the summer we had reestablished a rhythm for the house.

Then Dennis and Dad got into a fistfight in the living room one night.

Up until Mom's death, Dad wasn't a get-drunk drinker. He'd usually have a cocktail when he got home from work. That was it. While my mother was dying it became two cocktails. After she died it became three. Then he started drinking all evening long. At first it was funny. None of us had seen anyone drunk before except on TV. With a couple of drinks in him he was goofy, but harmless. When he was drinking all evening he became mean and aggressive.

It was late in the evening. Dennis had been talking to a girl he liked on the phone for a long time. I watched my father stew about it all night, the grinding jaw. Although things around the house had been good over the last couple of months, it was tenuous. Dennis had a tendency to be a smart-ass. He occasionally pushed my father's button intentionally. My father, in turn, lost his temper quickest with Dennis. When he got off the phone Dad said, "You're just like a girl with all your yammering." I think he was trying to take his annoyance and make it come across as teasing. It failed. So often with him it wasn't what was said but how it was said.

We all had experienced his concealed irritation and knew enough to let it slide. Dennis shrugged it off. Then Dad transitioned into someone we had never seen before, disrespectful of women. He said, "Are you screwing her yet?"

It made us all instantly uncomfortable. He never asked a question like that before.

Dennis half-heartedly responded, "No."

He came back at him. "Why not." It was more of a challenge than a question.

I said, "Dad, come on."

"Shut up you little faggot. Come on, Dennis, tell us what it's like. I don't remember, and by the way your brothers are going they're never going to know. Tell us about it."

"Dad. Come on. Stop"

Jeff kept watching the TV.

"What's your problem?"

Then he tried to transition. He must have realized what he was doing or where the conversation was going to end up.

Dennis said, "I'm going to bed."

"Take out the garbage."

"I'll get it in the morning."

"Take it out now."

Dennis went around his chair to go upstairs.

Dad stood up and got in his way. He raised his hand like he was going to hit him. Dennis grabbed it and stopped it. With his other hand, Dad punched him in the stomach. Dennis let go of his hand and Dad knocked him to the ground.

Dad stood over him and yelled, "You think you've got enough to take me on, you little pussy. Come on. Let me see what you've got."

Dennis tackled him. He got two shots off into Dad's face. Then Jeff and I jumped in. We pulled Dennis off him. Dad stood up and moved towards us. Jeff grabbed his arm. I stood in his way. He stopped. Everything changed then. The fight was over. The peace was gone. That family was done.

"You think you're old enough to take me? Then you're old enough to make it on your own. Get the hell out of this house."

"I'm gone."

Dennis grabbed his coat and left. As soon as the door closed, Dad threw Jeff into a bookcase. As he hit, a picture of my mother fell and the glass frame broke.

He grabbed me around the throat and said, "Stay the hell out of my way."

That was it. He went to bed. Jeff and I didn't talk about it. We cleaned up the glass and picked up the books.

Jeff said, "Maybe we should go and try to find Dennis."

I said, "No. He'll be all right.

We heard the light click off in Dad's room. He was snoring a couple minutes later. I went to bed a half hour or so later. Jeff fell asleep on the couch.

My thoughts were all over the place that night. I was so confused.

The next morning Dad said, "When you see Dennis at school, tell him to come home."

When I saw Dennis at school I told him what Dad said, then asked, "Where'd you spend night?"

"I walked around for a while then snuck back into the garage and slept in the car."

He added, "I knew it was too good to last."

"I wish Mom were still here," I said. "He would never have done that if she were here."

"I knew he would go off on one of us sooner or later."

"What are you going to do?"

"I don't know, but as soon as I graduate I'm moving out."

He came home that night. Dad never hit him again. Dennis graduated high school on a Saturday. He was living in his own place by Monday.

After that night Jeff kept a low profile. Within six months his low profile diminished into almost no profile around the house. The school called occasionally asking where he was. My father would yell at him for cutting school. He got arrested for being with a bunch of older boys in a stolen car. Another time Jeff got caught throwing bricks through a school window.

Some how Jeff was getting money. He took karate lessons. When my father attempted to smack him, Jeff dodged it, which only infuriated my father more. After a while he stopped trying to hit Jeff. Jeff went wild. It no longer mattered where he was or who he was with. My father kept the roof over Jeff's head and food on the table. I think Jeff has been stoned from that year on.

Dad left for work each morning. Every evening he prepared supper. He was a good cook. He shopped well. There was always plenty of food in the cupboard and refrigerator. The meals were not fancy, but they were always good. He told us one time how he had grown tired of the meals his mother prepared and learned how to cook. He told us how much Mom liked it when he cooked. I tried to be home for supper most nights, Jeff materialized for food, and Dennis came out of his room to eat. After supper Jeff left, Dennis went back to his room, and I did my thing. I stayed busy.

Whether I was reading, riding or running, I stayed out of his way. If he was coming after me, I ran. It was after supper, after he drank that things got bad. All the branches of Weymouth's library, Tuft's Library, became my refuge. I'd stay gone until nine o'clock. That's when he went to bed. If he had thrown a tantrum that evening by the next morning, for him, it was as though nothing happened. We all still avoided breakfast with him.

It wasn't every night chaos erupted. The problem was the unpredictability of his mood. We could go days with everything okay, enjoyable, then he'd go off. Sometimes he'd try and hit one of us. Sometimes it was the verbal fury. And sometimes it was nothing.

My friends envied us. They thought my brothers and I had so much freedom. It wasn't that great. We came and went as we pleased, but it wasn't freedom. It was the lack of Dad caring. Danny's mother cared. She extended her mothering to me. She told me to tell Dennis and Jeff that they could come by anytime, too. When I'd go over to his house she asked about my homework, what I was feeling, and offered a permanent place for me to stay. I never said anything to her about what was going on at home.

Whenever anyone came to visit us, like our grandparents, we put on an act that things were okay. They probably knew better, but there was nothing they could do. They didn't butt in. What went on in our house was our problem.

Summer passed into fall and fall into winter. I stopped calling my father Dad and I couldn't call him Pop. I just called him Barry. The morose atmosphere grew into indifference then into apathy. No one cared about anything. We all knew how to hide. Dad knew how to pass out.

On occasion Dad noticed our clothes were looking faded. He gave us some money and said go get some new clothes. He gave us a ride to the store or we caught the bus to the mall. It was the only family sibling moments we had. Christmas passed largely unnoticed. There were Christmas cards, Dad cooked some really good meals, and we exchanged a few after-thought gifts. We went to Grandma's for the day. Then returned to our own roost.

January 30 approached. An edge to all of us surfaced. The edginess overruled the apathy.

January 28, as we walked to school Jeff said, "I wish we could have the mid-winter picnic."

"Me too."

"I really liked that soup Mrs. Williams made."

"I wonder if Dad thinks about it."

"He doesn't think about anything."

"I think he is thinking about it. He's been more cranky lately."

"What did you like best about those picnics?"

"I used to like the idea that we didn't let the weather beat us, but now that no one comes over anymore, I liked everyone being at our house."

"Are you going to be home tonight?"

"I think so."

"See ya'"

"See ya'"

The weathermen said a storm was coming. The three different stations predicted three different outcomes. One said the storm was to pass out to sea with a little rain. Another said it would pass over, the snow changing to rain. The other said it would snow, rain, and then get very cold. He was right. The storm pounced on Southern New England later that day. A Nor'easter came. It dumped a foot of snow. The surf was way up. Even inside Boston Harbor the waves were big. TV showed pictures of the waves from the open ocean smashing against the coast on the North Shore. The surf on the South Shore, inside the somewhat protected bay, was huge, too. The storm ended the following day. Then the cold came down from Canada.

On the coast the ocean usually kept the temperature more moderate. It still got cold, but the nights below zero were few. The winter temperatures generally hung in the twenties and thirties. A few miles inland it got colder and stayed colder longer. That year we got a cold snap that lasted a week. It never warmed up above ten degrees.

January 30. My father drank that evening. Dennis stayed in his room. Jeff wasn't home and I got punched in the face.

I knew, like we all knew, how to avoid him. We got so we could read him and knew when we should get out of sight. It was only when we were less cautious, vulnerable, he was able to dump on us. I was feeling sad because it was January 30. I was watching the newscasters talk about the storm.

Dad sat beside me. He asked, "How was school today?"

"It was all right."

He nodded.

"I'm hoping they cancel school tomorrow, but they haven't said anything yet."

The news broke to a commercial. The commercial showed a young couple frolicking in the snow.

He said, "Well, it's the thirtieth."

"I know."

"Your mother really liked those parties."

"Did you like them?" I asked.

"I did."

"I miss them."

With that I saw his jaw set and begin to grind. I said, "What? What's wrong with my missing those picnics?"

Dad started saying how he put up with them because Mom liked them so much. Then he went sullen. His whole mood shifted on the spot. It was like he never enjoyed the picnics. I always thought he liked them as much as we did. And he just said he liked them. During the picnics he seemed to enjoy them. He laughed. He cracked jokes with his friends, cooked, and he started organizing the effort to prepare the festivities and the supplies for the picnics several days in advance.

He said, "Those picnics were a pain in the ass to put together."

I don't know why he said those things, but it was like he had to ruin my only remaining good memory because he was feeling bad about what life had handed him, so he had to make me feel bad, too.

I said, "Maybe if we had a picnic again things would be better around here."

Then he said, "Oh, what? Am I failing as a father because I didn't put that friggin' picnic together this year? No one would come if it we tried to do it anyway."

"I think people would come."

"What the hell do you know about people?"

"I know everyone who came really liked it." I fought back the tears that suddenly wanted to come out, but my voice cracked.

"Don't be a crybaby. I could care less about that picnic. I'm here to put a roof over your head and food on the table."

"You don't even care that she's dead. All you care about is getting drunk."

With that he punched me in the face.

I nearly tumbled backwards out of my chair. I got up. I left. I had a sweatshirt on and that was it. I grabbed his old Army coat as I left and started walking around town. The streets were clear of snow. The sidewalk plows were working into the night. I walked all the way out to Weymouth Landing. I tried to walk the tracks to Jackson Square, but the snow was deep and there hadn't been any trains through to pack it down. I walked the streets all the way back to Jackson Square. I thought about going to Danny's house, but I knew they would be in bed. It was eleven o'clock. I couldn't go to Kelli's house either. She was out of town with her family. I watched the bus leave East Weymouth heading back to Quincy. I could be on that bus in the morning and in Boston within an hour. I did not ever have to go home. I thought about running away. I had a couple hundred dollars in savings. I'd have to get my money the next morning. That was it, I decided I was going to run away. I had to find a place to spend the night. The next morning, after my father left for work, I'd go back into the house and get my passbook, some clothes, my sleeping bag, and some snacks. I'd be fine. I'd be gone.

I was so cold and miserable; no hat, no gloves, no scarf. It was getting colder, too. I was shivering. I saw steam come out of the vent behind the Laundromat and I went there to warm up. At midnight the owner came in. He said I had to leave. I thought about a friend of mine from school who said he spent a night in the Morgan Memorial clothing donation box one night. It was a long walk to get to the closest box. I kept walking. It got very quiet. The stillness of the cold sent everything indoors. Even a cat I saw huddled against the front window of Central Square pharmacy gave up some of its sense of self-preservation to stay warm. Normally it would have bolted as I approached. It tensed and watched me pass, but it was sucking up every molecule of heat the window passed.

At some point I stopped caring if I lived. It would be so much easier to not have to deal with all of this. I missed my mother. My father was so difficult.

I walked back towards Weymouth Heights, down King Oak Hill, and under the railroad bridge. I walked past Abigail Adams house and realized I was near my mother's grave. I went to see it. If I was leaving, and I was, I wanted to say bye to her.

I went up the hill to her grave and pushed the snow off the marker and sat down. I was freezing. I told her I couldn't stay here. I asked her how I should deal with Dad. Then I started crying. Shivering, crying, and miserable I leaned against the marker. My tears created momentary warm paths on my face, then they froze. I looked at my watch. It was two o'clock in the morning. In five or six hours the sun would be up. At nine the bank opened. By ten I'd be in Quincy, by eleven in Boston. By noon I'd never have to look at my father again.

I thought I should keep walking to stay warm. I said, "Bye Mom. I promise I'll be back someday."

There was a shortcut I knew back to the road. I turned into a little wooded area and moved down the hill. I slipped on the path and smacked my head into a boulder.

When I woke the sun was up. I was at the bottom of the slope down from the cemetery, hidden behind the trees and bare brush. I saw a school bus pass. Car traffic was heading the opposite way of the bus toward Quincy, the subway station, and Boston. The top half of my face was cold. The part of my body that was against the soil was warm. It was like when the blankets get kicked off the bed during the night. I stood up. My cold half was stiff and achy. The warm side was okay. A little cramped. I looked around and recalled where I was and what my plan was. There was no snow in a small jagged circle around where I had fallen. The ground was a little muddy.

I walked out from behind the trees and walked home. No one was there. It was warm. There was food in refrigerator, so I ate. I took a shower and laid on my bed for a minute and woke up early in the afternoon.

I stayed for supper and went to school the next day.

CHAPTER 20

▼

HAROLD, AGAIN

An hour after my diversion along Gilbert Road, I crossed the Tufts crossing. A few minutes later I turned up the hill to Harold's house. My plan was to visit with Harold ten minutes, at most, then walk a little bit more to Weymouth Landing, catch bus 221 to Quincy Center, then the Red Line south to Braintree, and start the actual Greenbush walk component of my expedition.

Harold's place looked terrible. It looked like the grass had not been cut since I left. The roof shingles bubbled up. The paint on the trim I worked so hard at was cracked and chipped again. I creaked the yard gate open precisely at ten o'clock and walked up to the door. The same nervous feeling I always had when I used to see him surfaced, too. I expected to see him open his door as I approached. I was on time. This time I had to wait for him.

He didn't open the door. I turned the knob that rang the manual doorbell. Like years earlier, its discordant noise burped my arrival. It half rang and half knocked flat against the bell that fell off and didn't reverberate.

Finally he opened the door. I'm six feet two inches tall, two hundred and thirty pounds, but in front of him, I felt pubescent again. I grew bigger than him my junior year in high school, but I didn't remember him being so small. However, I felt tiny in front of him.

He said, "Hello boy."

"Hello, Sir," I responded.

Silence.

More silence. I felt as though I was shriking, more.

"Well. Do you want to come in or do you want to stand there all day?" he said.

After all the time I spent working around his house, I still barely ever even had a peek into his house. Change. I mumbled, "Okay." I felt as though I wasn't supposed to look around his kitchen, but I did. He had a small kitchen area. Sun light came though the grimy windows. The big old box radio I had bought the tubes for was on. There was a potbelly stove, rocking chair, a stack of wood, a small electric stove, an icebox, and a card table that served as his kitchen table. There were stacks and stacks of newspapers going all the way up to the ceiling, and he had a still. I wondered if that was his big secret for locking his doors all the time I worked for him.

He seemed not to have aged much. He still moved sturdily and spoke strong, although he did hold onto a cane and I noticed a little limp. He lost no more hair or teeth since I last saw him. He still wore the same combinations of clothes. The only perceptible change was he seemed smaller. He looked good, as good as Harold could. If I end up as solid as Harold appeared to be when I get to be 75, I'll be okay. I was already losing my hair. I have to watch my blood pressure and avoid spicy foods.

Over the years my various wives and different bosses have told me that I need to create a less intense presence. They suggest I learn how to prattle so I can put people more at ease.

In a burst I said, "I discovered the news about Greenbush's reincarnation on line one night. Are you familiar with the Internet, Harold? I see the Weymouth Landing station is gone. It was still standing when I was last here. Did someone set it on fire or was it knocked down? It'll be cool when they finish restoring Greenbush." I stopped my nervous blathering.

He looked at me when I finished speaking. He might have been looking at me sooner, I wouldn't know, my eyes were darting around the room. I'd glance at him then at the floor then out the window then the ceiling. He reached for his pipe, smacked it against an old bowl on a stand, which rang like a bell, then packed it with tobacco. "It burned down one night." He set a match to the pipe; the flame dipped and rose with each raspy breath he drew. He put the match out by pinching the flame between his thumb and finger. As soon as he was satisfied the tobacco was burning appropriately he continued, "Not long after you left." He reached for a note pad and gave me the specific date and time. Then he stated how long it took for the fire department to arrive and how long it took to extinguish the flames. Last, he reported when the charred remains were knocked down, hauled away, and the foundation paved over.

I took a breath and tried to pull Harold into a conversation and asked, "So, what kind of activity have you seen on Greenbush over the years?"

He didn't respond at first. He was looking at me. Maybe he was trying to decide if I was still trustworthy. Maybe he was waiting for me to shut up so he could get a word in. Finally he said, "There's been nothing to see since the Bay Colony stopped running trains. They parked a few box cars on the siding here for a few months and there were some inspection cars over the tracks, but that was years ago."

I looked out the window and said, "It looks like your lawn needs mowing."

He said, "Go ahead. The mower is still in the shed. You can cut the grass while I finish packing."

Shit. I had commented on the lawn, now I felt as though I had to mow it. My timing was getting thrown off. Oh well, I reasoned. He's an old man. I can spend a little more time with him and cut his grass. It was like how I felt years ago when I first volunteered to cut the grass. It's the least I can do for a senior citizen. Charity.

I went and found the push mower. The wheels needed oil and the blades had to be sharpened before it would cut anything. I was, of course, going to have to cut the weeds down with the sy first then rake the lawn before the mower would be able to go anywhere on his lawn. As I searched for the sy in the shed I started thinking, screw this, I've got my plans and a schedule to keep, and a flight tomorrow afternoon back to San Francisco. I didn't have the time to be doing goodwill work for Harold. I stepped outside, sat on the stonewall, flipped open my cell phone, and called the airline. There was a later flight I could catch if I missed my scheduled flight. I looked around his yard. Fortunately it was small. Okay, I thought I'd donate an hour to the old man. I went back to the shed and found everything as I had left it years earlier. I reached for the oil can and whet stone.

Harold was out on his porch looking through his binoculars as a ship maneuvered up the Fore River to the oil tank farm in Braintree. He made a note on a pad of paper.

"Has anyone mowed your lawn since I left?" I yelled from the shed.

"Of course," he said, implying that I was foolish for thinking it hadn't, never mind the four feet high weeds I was facing. He continued, "The town gets sick of it and every so often one of those useless public works flunkies will mow it or else some do-gooder comes by and cuts it. I haven't seen anyone so far this year."

He grumbled about how the town's senior citizens coordinator got his name and that busybody sends someone down here a couple times a year to patch things up. He said the Boy Scouts tried to make his home a project one year. He never said what the upshot of that effort was. I'm sure he chased them off.

He spoke, "Are you going to cut the grass or what. We've got to get going."

"What do you mean we've got to get going?"

"You said in your note you're walking Greenbush. I'm walking it with you."

With that he turned and went back into his house. He closed the door and turned the lock. The click of the lock sliding into place sounded like an executioner's call.

There was no misstatement. Harold was coming with me. Did he mean he wanted to rent a car and have me drive him down the line or did he mean he planned to walk with me? He is older than God, I thought. He's going to die and I'll be responsible for his death. I thought two days was a generous allotment of time for me to cover East Weymouth and Greenbush on foot by myself. If he was coming with me, that meant I had to be here at least a year. I never knew exactly how old he was, but he had to be at least in his late seventies and he probably had not walked any further than the bank or the market for forty years. I'd be there at least another week explaining his heart attack and subsequent death on Greenbush to the police.

No, he wasn't coming with me. As I cut the weeds with the sy I grew more and more pissed off at the idea of Harold slowing me down and upsetting my plans. As I pushed the mower through the grass I thought about how I was going to tell him that I was going alone. It was my walk. I'd be glad to delay my flight a day and come back after I finished the walk. I could get the photographs processed in one hour. I'd be glad to show him the pictures. I'd get a second set made for him, 5x7's if he wanted. I'd even rent a car and drive him wherever he wanted to go on Greenbush.

Harold stepped back onto the porch with his cane, carrying a bindle. He was serious. He was going with me. He pointed to an area on the lawn and said, "You'll need to hand clip that grass." He inspected the work I had already done then said, "Do you want a glass of eggnog."

"Thank you. No."

"I'll be paying you ten dollars for your work here today."

I waved off his offer.

I clipped the patch of grass in a panic. I didn't want to hurt him, but I didn't want him going with me either. I feared the loss of the solitude and quality of my walk, and his heart attack. When I do things by myself I can spend an hour taking a picture of anything I want. I can get as dirty as I want. I can stop and thank God for a beautiful view if I'm so inclined. I can stop and go as I want, unfettered.

I stopped pushing the mower and went over to him, "Are you serious. You think you're coming with me."

"Yes."

"It's seventeen miles."

"I know. Actually it's seventeen point six two miles from Braintree station to Greenbush. It'll be about another three quarters of mile from where we start in the Braintree yard to the Braintree station. I figure it's about eighteen point four three miles all together. Maybe a little more, about a half mile if we go all the way to the North River."

Of course he had it all figured out.

I had to stop him. He wasn't coming with me. At first I tried to reason with him, "Harold, I'm sure you think you can do this, but I've got to be back on the plane to California tomorrow. I can't miss my flight. I'll be moving pretty quick."

He just stood there.

"I can't be responsible for you."

Silence.

I tried anger, "I don't have the time to be taking care of you. I've got to get back to work in a couple days. Besides, what kind of shape are you in to be doing this? You're not going with me."

He said, "I'm walking Greenbush."

"I'll come back and visit with you. I'll drive you down the line and have the photos processed in one hour and I'll get a set made for you." I finished with, "You're crazy if you think you're coming with me."

He stood there after I finished my tirade. He looked at me. I saw his age, disappointment, and a deep grief. He half stepped, half fell back away from me much like I did so many years earlier when he came out the front door at me on the broken porch. He asked, "Please, let me come?"

The only humble, polite thing Harold had said in sixty years and he said it to me.

"I'm getting old and sick. I was glad to get your letter saying you were going to walk Greenbush. It made me think. I want to see the line again.

"As a young man I knew the line beginning to end. I've walked it and ran it and took the trains back and forth. It has been years since I've even made it to the spot where my guard shack stood.

"I don't want to slow you down, but I'm going with or without you." He locked the door, turned, and moved so slowly across the lawn. In his gray pants, suspenders, flannel shirt, boots, and cap he closed the gate to his yard and waited. He asked, "Have you seen the forecast? It's supposed to rain."

I didn't respond at first. I stood there glaring at him. Finally I said, "No I hadn't heard that."

"You should get a rain slicker."

I closed my eyes, sighed, and tilted my head. I didn't speak to him. I finished clipping, put the mower away, and locked the door to his shed. I picked up my backpack, walked out of his yard, past him, and down the hill. When I got to the bottom of the hill I looked back and there he was. Halfway down the hill, using his cane to hold him back, his bindle slung across his back, and apprehensively stepping down the slope.

At the bottom of the hill I made a journal entry, "10:53 a.m., Harold's coming with me. Shit!"

He made it down the hill and walked past me in the direction of the Landing. I caught up to him and passed him, then let him pass me again. As we walked along Commercial Street I noticed his stride lengthened. He was moving okay, and then he took a puff on an inhaler.

I was so mad I could hardly see. I stopped walking again and called my girl friend She wasn't home. I left a message explaining how the plans had changed and that I would be in Weymouth a few more days. I turned and watched Harold as he limped up to me. When he was certainly in hearing range I raised my voice and said, "That old fart Harold I told you about is coming with me." After Harold walked past I continued my message. In my gloom I added, "I'll probably be here a month because he'll probably die. I'll have to explain the circumstance and make arrangements to bury him."

I clicked the phone off and stared at the back of his head. He kept moving beyond me. He got to the bus stop, stopped, squatted, and fell back onto the bench. He repositioned himself on the bench then looked around to see if the bus was coming. I moved closer. We only had to wait for a couple minutes for the bus to come by and pick us up. I stepped up alongside him to try and intimidate him. I pushed, shouldered, nudged, and checked him. He planted his cane firmly into the ground and against his waist and didn't falter. The bus slowed. He moved toward the opening door when I bumped him out of my way.

He turned to me and said, "Be a jerk. I'll do this by myself."

The bus stopped. He opened his change purse and stepped up into it first. I was right behind him. I was going to torment him from here to Quincy. I'd make it so he would turn around and not do this. I'd get a taxi to return him home. I waited my turn to board the bus. As he stepped up he let one of his rank farts go. I fell back.

He asked the driver, "How much to Quincy?"

"For senior citizens, it's ninety cents," the driver answered cheerily, "Where did you want to get off?"

"Why do you want to know?" Harold snapped.

The bus driver said, "So if you fall asleep I'll still make the stop and wake you up."

Harold didn't say anything and sat down. The driver gave me a look as I got on that said, "Great, another miserable old man."

Harold stared out the window as we rode up Quincy Avenue to the Quincy Center Red Line stop. I sat behind him and watched him. He took it all in. He twisted and turned to get a look at the closed Quincy shipyard as we went past. At every turn and stop light he twisted in his seat and studied the surroundings. I saw that he was equally afraid and excited. Each time the bus lurched or braked suddenly he grabbed at the hand holding rail. I couldn't forbid him to go, but I had to get him to come to his senses. I asked him, "How often did you get out of Weymouth?" my belligerence barely in check.

He paused. "Not often. I walk to the market once a week, but I don't own a car. I never even had a driver's license.

"The only time I leave my house is to go to the doctor. The senior citizens center sends a van for me and haul's me down there when I need to go."

When we passed through Quincy Square he asked, "What happened here?"

"I don't know what you mean?"

"Quincy Square used to be the place to go for shopping. I read that it was struggling and a lot of the stores had moved on but I never imagined it had changed so much."

"When was the last time you were in the Square?"

"I took the bus to buy some pants at Sears a few years ago."

I felt sad for him. I told him, "Sears in Quincy closed about the same time I left for the Navy. It moved to the Plaza in Braintree. How come you didn't know that? You get the paper and you have a radio."

He seemed startled that it had been so many years. "I had heard about it, but I figured when they said the store was closing I guessed it was to modernize the building, not to shut it down."

"How do you get your clothes and stuff if you don't shop? Weymouth's got stores, but there's no clothing stores in the Landing."

"I order through the Sears catalog and walk to the Post Office to pick up my packages. I have them ship it General Delivery to 02188."

I realized how deeply isolated he was in his little house outside Weymouth Landing. In spite of the megalopolis that stretched from Boston, Massachusetts to Richmond, Virginia, here was an old man all alone and completely out of it. How many other people were there like Harold among the millions of people in that corridor? If I wasn't so annoyed with the idea of him coming with me I might have been profoundly saddened.

At Quincy Center we got off the bus, then paid the fare to get on the subway. While we waited I asked him, "When was the last time you've gone beyond the Landing."

He snapped back. "Are you going to be asking me all kinds of personal questions the whole time?"

Up to that moment my feelings might have been shifting to feeling that I would take care of him and make sure he made it all the way to Greenbush, safely. I threw my hands up and said, "You old prick. You've upset all of my plans here. I'm willing to let you drag your sorry old ass with me, but it would be nice if you showed some civility."

"Oh, I am so privileged that you're letting me come along with you."

The subway roared into the station and covered my response. We boarded. I sat away from him. We got off at Braintree. He didn't know that he had to pay another token to get off at Braintree. He got stuck in the turnstile. When he tried to back out of the turnstile his bindle jammed and got caught on the arm. He started swinging his cane at the turnstile trying beat it into some measure of cooperation. Commuters passing through to board the inbound subway saw him struggling, cursing, twisting, and hitting the turnstile. He looked to me. I stood there and watched him grow more frightened, more panicked.

To hell with him, I walked out of the station and watched him through the window. He started to lose his strength. He leaned against the turnstile and lowered himself to the floor. One of the MBTA employees there walked over to him. He helped Harold up and let him pass through the handicap gate.

As Harold walked out of the station I turned and walked away. Harold followed me. I walked about ten steps in front of him as we moved toward the former South Braintree rail yard. Beyond the severe irritation at the interruption to my plans I was mad. Mad at myself for allowing him to come along. And I was extremely frustrated with his confused and fluctuating nature. One moment he was surly. The next moment he deserved empathy. He ruined my walk before I even took one step.

I walked beyond the cement of the Braintree subway station. The sidewalk curved away right toward the parking lot. To my left lay the railroad tracks and the beginning of my Greenbush walk. I stood on the sidewalk rubbing my forehead, getting ready to step on to the tracks when he caught up to me. We stood there in silence. I stepped onto the tracks and he spoke.

He said, "I haven't left Weymouth since 1972 when the New Haven reorganized into the Penn Central Railroad. I had to go into Boston to sign some documents to make sure my pension got to me." He paused for a moment then added, "Except for a couple of trips to Sears."

He moved and nearly stumbled as he stepped down onto the tracks. He started walking. I followed him onto Greenbush.

CHAPTER 21

▼

GREENBUSH, DAY ONE

I looked backwards as we headed down the line. The South Braintree railroad yard was the beginning of Greenbush and the end of the T's Red Line. The subway station itself was cement on cement. Not visually scarring, but not pleasing either. Its tracks and six hundred volt third rail are fenced. It's totally utilitarian. Every ten minutes or so another subway train leaves for Boston. It's all very predictable and reassuring and convenient.

The South Braintree railroad yard was almost completely void of railroad activity. At one time it was the major junction for all lines approaching Boston from the south. The Middleborough line, Plymouth Branch and Greenbush merged in Braintree. Plymouth and Middleborough entered the yard at one end and the mainline to Boston and Greenbush confluence at the other. Greenbush banked east, then eventually turned south. The Boston-bound mainline banked west and eventually north. At one time, hundreds of rail cars, engines, cabooses, and men scattered across hundreds of acres of tracks assembling, repairing, tracking, and operating trains to send and receive goods from all over the country. Now only three or four tracks remained intact for the commuter rail trains to pass over and three more tracks each holding a few freight cars to serve the token amount of industry that remained in the area. The dozens of other sets of tracks had been removed or aborted. A scrap metal yard and a large lumberyard bordered the rail yard at one time. I had photographed this place extensively years ago. I wished I hadn't burned all of those photographs. It was a fascinating place.

It became an uninteresting place. It was boring office buildings and a predictable retail area consisting of Circuit City, Subway, Home Depot, ad nauseam. The same pedestrian businesses I could find anywhere in the country, set on different geography.

There was a large debate about restoring Greenbush. Beyond the work needed to restore the rusted rails, decayed ties and switches buried in the briars and brush and weeds, was Greenbush worth it? Was the traffic relief worth the expense? Was the risk of recreating active grade crossings that had been idle for years a hazard to South Shore hamlets? Greenbush had been idle for nearly twenty years. Two generations had passed since passenger rail service moved over the tracks. One generation had passed since freight service passed over the tracks.

Over the previous eighty years, activity and the actual line itself had been steadily reduced, abandoned, and ultimately the tracks removed. First the tracks that ran beyond the North River through Marshfield and Duxbury to Kingston were pulled up. Then from Greenbush and the North River the abandonment crept back northward. Scituate and Cohasset had the tracks pulled up first, then Hingham lost its tracks below the Nantasket Junction. The last train to Nantasket Junction was in 1978. All activity below East Braintree ceased in 1985. All that remained in use were the first couple miles of Greenbush to East Braintree where an occasional train from the Fore River Railroad switched a few cars.

Was it worth it? I certainly thought so.

I heard Harold stumble and slipped out of my trance. I slowed down and let him catch-up.

We stayed off the tracks that were still in use. Harold moved slowly. At first the loose ballast rock made him stumble, then the vegetation that grew up between the rails snared his feet and he fell. I let my displeasure be known. I shook my head, sighed heavily, and went over to help him. He was pushing himself up with the help of his cane. When he stood he held his cane out like a sword as though he was going to try and hold me back. He said, "I don't need your help." He turned and walked down the line.

We walked the half-mile or so where the subway and railroad tracks paralleled each other to a highway underpass. In front of us a bridge passed the Southeast Expressway on top. On the other side of the underpass the polished tracks of the Red Line and the reestablished passenger train mainline banked off toward Quincy and Boston. The rusty Greenbush tracks disappeared straight ahead into brush.

As we got close enough to pass under the highway my eccentric stroll became dangerous. We approached an unanticipated hazard. The underpass we had to go through had very close side-to-side clearance. To get through to where the tracks to Boston split away from the Greenbush tracks, we had to beat the fast moving trains. A train could shoot through the underpass very fast and very unexpectedly. We could see the tracks behind us and pass through the tunnel with no problem from the northbound trains sneaking up on us. The problem was the southbound trains. Because of the embankment and the highway noise above us, noise from an approaching train was muffled, almost to the point of being muted. We wouldn't hear it until it was right on top of us. The pass was only about two hundred feet long.

I could make it through easy enough. I'd start running and if a southbound train suddenly appeared around the bend, hell bent into the underpass toward me, I could drop to the ground next to the bridge abutment and the train would probably pass over me with room to spare. But there was only a few seconds opportunity to safely make that maneuver. Harold would not be able to do it and if he tried he would probably break a hip. The engineer would undoubtedly see us and hit the brakes. The sudden stop and the engineer thinking he had hit someone would trigger the police and a hearse.

We both stopped outside the underpass and considered the danger. I told him to wait. I looked behind us. All clear. I ran ahead, about halfway through a southbound subway train came around the corner. It startled me. Although it was to the side and fenced off from the railroad tracks, I stumbled and fell. The motorman saw me. As I fell I saw him reaching for his radio microphone. I picked myself up and ran the rest of the way. I was certain the police would show up soon. Harold had to get through the pass quickly so we could disappear onto the Greenbush line and away from the cops.

At the other end of the bridge the passenger platform that once belonged to the old Braintree station remained. From there I could see the tracks for a mile as they came southbound from Boston. I could also see the tracks curve back into the Braintree yard, but only for a couple hundred feet beyond the underpass. I didn't have a clear view all the way down the tracks. I couldn't watch for any northbound trains. But as far as I could see the southbound tracks looked clear. I yelled at Harold, "Come on." He couldn't hear me. I moved so I saw him and waved him on. Limping, slipping, and sliding he scuttled his way under the bridge. He was about two thirds of the way through when a northbound train appeared behind him. He looked back. I waved my arms and yelled, "Run, Harold." He started to move faster. The engineer started blowing the horn. I heard air dumping into the emergency braking system. It came up on Harold fast. I saw the engine grow huge behind him. All the light behind the tunnel vanished. The engine's headlight put a glow around Harold. Harold moved as fast as he could. The train's strobe light flashed. The combined headlight and strobe light made Harold appear as though he was in a rock video. There couldn't been more than three of four feet between Harold's rear end and the train's front end. I thought he was going to die in front of me. Sparks flew off the tracks from where the wheels and track met. The engine slowed enough and Harold made it to the cement of the former Braintree station passenger platform. I stretched my arm out to Harold. He grabbed and I pulled. He made it. As Harold stepped up, I looked at the engineer as the train passed by. He gave me the finger and his mouth formed some words I'm sure I could have figured out. I heard the air release from the brakes and the engine accelerated.

The passenger platform of the old Braintree station formed a triangle. A switch there connected the Greenbush tracks directly to the Boston-bound tracks. The middle of this triangle was where the Braintree station used to be. Harold stood there panting and looked at the commuter rail train as it disappeared northbound. He turned to me and smiled. I waved him off. He said. "We won't have to deal with that anymore." Then he added, "I used to run out ahead of the trains all the time."

He looked around the platform and wondered when it had burned down. I told him around 1975. I had an aunt who lived nearby and I'd check it out when my family came over for a visit. He shook his head and said it was the only two-story station in the whole area. It was the gathering point for all the people who helped operate and maintain the line. Anyone who worked the line needed to come to South Braintree occasionally for supplies, meetings, training, and so on.

As we stood on the old passenger platform we heard a noise come from the switch that accessed the Greenbush tracks. We saw the switch open and from the bushes that obscured the Greenbush tracks a headlight appeared. Slowly a small freight train descended on us. It was a Fore River Railroad freight train. It passed by us with three boxcars, two gondola cars, and three tank cars. The engineer gave us a wave as the train crept into the Braintree yard. We stepped out onto the tracks and strained to watch it diminish into the yard. After it passed through the tunnel, we watched it switch off the mainline. We heard the switch behind us close and a minute later a southbound commuter rail train blew past us into the Braintree yard also. The wind and noise tugged at us. The engineer looked at us as he quickly moved past. The windows of cars were just a blur. Just as quickly, the train banked off out of sight and the place was silent again. Harold turned back and looked at me. His eyes were sparkling. He was shaking his cane, nearly skipping with excitement. I laughed at him. He looked like he was dancing a little jig.

We dallied a moment. I had spent so much time alongside these tracks and so much time anticipating this walk, I wondered what I would see. I stared down the tracks toward Greenbush. A small feeling, like an early spin on a carnival ride, before it builds up momentum and g-forces, rose in my belly.

Harold said, "It's seventeen point six two miles from here to Greenbush. Let's get going."

We stepped back on the Greenbush tracks and walked into the brush.

Harold announced, "It's only one point one four miles to East Braintree." He pulled out a note pad and stub of a pencil. He looked at his watch then made a mark on the paper.

The T kept vegetation on the main line trimmed back. On Greenbush the vegetation crept into the bed. It was passable because of the occasional Fore River Railroad and CSX trains that passed over it. The railroad kept the vegetation at bay but not under control. Harold pointed out an old siding that was buried in the weeds and brush. The rust on the rails was so thick it was black. There hadn't been a killing frost yet, so pretty purple flowers still pushed up between the rails. This part of Greenbush was cut through a little hill. On either side of the tracks were huge blocks of Quincy granite holding the hill back. We passed under another bridge. There I saw spray painted on the abutment, the old New Haven Railroad logo. I pulled out my camera and took a picture. Harold made a note on his pad.

We walked alongside one set of well-used tracks. Another set of tracks lay rusting in the weeds alongside us. There was no switch onto or off of those tracks. They just lay there rotting and rusting in the weeds. There was a lot of trash along the tracks. There was logic to some of the refuse scattered over the rail bed; rusted bicycle frames, tires, lawn clippings, even appliances, but some of it made no sense; those big plastic playhouses for kids, a barbell, a car hood.

The tracks opened out to a level point and we walked on. We passed by the gravel pit operation. An old siding still went to the gravel pit. A trestle still stood holding the tracks up. I commented to Harold how I had seen hopper cars back out on the trestle dump their loads and go back to where they came. Harold said there used to be so much industry all along the tracks, but even in his day he saw many of the light manufacturing plants close up.

We walked into the first of the pretty areas. A stream ran under a bridge we crossed. A little millpond fed the stream. The trees circling the pond were changing color. Ducks floated on the surface of the water. We took our first break there.

I said, "Harold you're moving a lot better than I thought you would."

"After I got your letter I decided I wanted to walk the tracks too. I'd gotten so I could walk five miles with little effort."

"Why do you want to do this?"

"I just want to see it again."

We started moving again toward East Braintree when we heard a whistle. A train was coming. The Fore River Railroad train was on its way back. We had to get off the small bridge and into a wide area so there was a little distance between the train and us. We stepped into the woods like we were a couple of kids. The engineer saw us hiding in the wood and waved at us again. We stepped out and waved back. We felt the earth move and the easy breeze of a slow moving train as it passed by us. It was an old engine with the same freight cars I saw earlier in the Braintree yard behind it. The train stopped. I got an uneasy feeling that he was going to reprimand us or tell us to get lost.

The engineer said, "Hello. What are you guys doing here?"

Harold answered, "I used to work as a crossing guard at Tufts and I wanted to see what was left of Greenbush before the reconstruction begins."

My God, Harold was pleasant.

He continued, "My young friend here is making sure I don't break my hip."

He nodded, "Well okay. We're supposed to call the cops when we see somebody suspicious on the tracks. I don't think I have to worry about you guys vandalizing the cars I'm dropping off."

"Step on up here," he said. "I'll give you a ride for a couple hundred yards to East Braintree."

We stepped up onto the engine. The rhythm of the engine increased, then, with an ever so slight jerk, it crept forward. The conductor nodded at us. The single track we were on expanded into two tracks. Then the double tracks grew into three tracks and created a small marshaling yard in East Braintree where the railroad trains stored some of its cars. Another half a dozen freight cars sat on the tracks there. My memory from when I was a teenager was pumping out images. I had seen the station before it burned down. There was a small siding next to it. Harold said all the stations had a siding close by so the railroad could park a car there for storage and maintenance. Buried into the trees were telephone poles.

Occasionally a piece of wire dangled from its cross arm and many of the glass insulators remained.

The train stopped at the edge of the old passenger platform and let us off.

The sum of that short ride, the bells at the crossing, the lights, the engine's horn, the particular air I breathed there, the color of the sky and trees, and the warmth of the sun made me stop being mad with Harold and my tarnished Greenbush walk. Screw the schedule.

Harold and I watched the slow train pull away. It switched itself to drop off its cars and pick up the others waiting there in East Braintree. It pulled forward again then banked off toward Quincy. We watched the train disappear into the brush, then we laughed. Harold slapped his thigh and I kept grinning.

We moved forward along the platform. Where the East Braintree station once stood we stopped. Harold pulled out his note pad, glanced at his watch, and made another entry.

We walked off the passenger platform at East Braintree and over a grade crossing. Immediately the path became difficult to maneuver. Bushes, brush, and trees took over the tracks. Up to here we walked on the tracks. Not any more. Thick, thick brush took over.

At the crossing it looked like a train tried to push its way toward Weymouth Landing recently. The flange on the train's wheels had pushed the dirt out of the bevel at the grade crossing. Branches and small trees had been knocked over. A thin trail of silver striped the top of the severely rusted rails. The broken branches ran into the dense brush a couple hundred feet and stopped in front of a collapsed signal tower.

That hint of train activity on those rails gave us a half an hour of speculation and strange excitement. Maybe the train crew was exploring a little. If the engineer had pushed the train on another hundred feet or so there was another switch buried in the woods where he could have changed direction and switched to another track back to East Braintree and Quincy. We talked about the engineer's motivation like we were Monday morning quarterbacking. Why did he go down the tracks? Why did the engineer stop where he did? Was it because the ties and rails were in such bad shape? Maybe he realized he couldn't make it to the switch? If he did make it there, maybe he realized he wouldn't be able to open it because of the undergrowth. If the train derailed there it would have been a big problem rerailing it. A small bridge lay just past the switch. Undoubtedly the bridge hadn't been inspected for years. Maybe that was what stopped the train. If the bridge collapsed, the engineer certainly didn't want to have to explain why his train fell onto the road. Harold and I talked about it all the way over the next point six two miles to the Weymouth Landing station.

At the very edge of the Weymouth Landing passenger platform Harold made an entry in his notepad again. The car dealer in Weymouth Landing had taken over the area where the station and bed used to be. They were storing their excess inventory there. At the end of the platform where we were to cross over Commercial Street, at the bottom of the hill where Harold's house was, an eight-foot chain link fence stopped us.

Harold said, "I forgot about the fence. I watched it being built."

I had failed to notice it earlier that morning when we walked to the bus stop. We studied it. Harold wasn't going to make it over the fence. I could, but someone might see me and wonder why a grown man was hopping the fence. Car storage lot ... thief? The cops could be called and I'd have a lot of explaining to do. We walked back a couple hundred yards to a stairway that dropped us down into the dealer's sales lot. We walked through the lot and back up onto Commercial Street. Moments later we were at the bottom of the road that lead up to Harold's house. It had taken us nearly four hours from when we left his house to get back to it. If I were by myself it might have taken two hours.

"If you want to call it quits, we're right here. I'll finish it and like I said earlier, I'll rent a car and drive you wherever you want to go."

"No. It's slow going, but we should go as far as we can today. The distance between stations is going to start pushing out. One point three nine miles to go to Weymouth Heights."

"Yeah. Fine. You hungry? Gotta' hit the bathroom or anything?"

"Nope. Let's go."

We shuffled back to the tracks and pressed into the woods at the old Rhines Lumber Company siding.

"Harold, are you really expecting to spend the night outdoors?"

"Yup." He paused for moment. Just like years earlier when he wanted to reveal the tiniest bit about himself, he had to make a decision to do that. "I've slept out of doors at various places along the tracks over the years. I don't expect trouble. Are you prepared to spend the night outdoors?"

My hotel reservation in Cohasset waited, but there was no way we were going to make Cohasset. "No not really. I hadn't planned on company. I have a hotel reservation in Cohasset for tonight."

He stopped walking and lingered a long time, then he spoke, "If you want a blanket you can go up to the house and get one. There's an extra one in a steamer trunk upstairs in the bedroom."

"I'll be all right."

"No you won't. You've been gone a long time. You forget what it's like. It'll be cold and damp." He gave me the key to his house, pulled a sandwich out of his pocket, and sat down on the old loading dock at the burned-out lumberyard to wait.

The key was nearly worn smooth; the teeth were all but gone from the use over the years. It was a morbid moment when I went into his house. After all the years of my working for him and the reluctance he held for me to go inside, there I was. It was as if he had died and I was the one to clean out his estate. I went in through his kitchen, then the dining room. He kept a cot in the dining room. I saw he did have a bathroom after all. I think they called it a water closet in his day. There was an old toilet in there with a tank six feet off the ground and a long chain to flush it. The hopper was small, the toilet paper roll hung on a piece of rope, no sink, no faucets, and tub. It was dirty in there. The linoleum curled away from the floor, it had disintegrated in places, and the wood floorboards rotted. It was the loudest flush I ever heard.

I passed through the parlor and pulled back the drape that concealed the stairs. Every step creaked as I went up. The dust was like snow. I left footprints as I walked. It was an inch thick. I opened the door to his bedroom and looked for an old steamer trunk.

Light came through the cracks in the blinds. It was grimy. I could see an old chest of drawers, a brass bed, a chair, and a nightstand next to the bed. There were three pictures in circular frames hanging from the wall. The first was one of Harold with who must have been his mother and father. Harold looked exactly like his father. The second was a shot of him at the Tufts Crossing standing next to the crossing gate. The third was a photo of him seated with a woman standing next to him. Her arm rested across his shoulders. He smiled wide, proud, and pleased. He was holding her hand where it draped down from his shoulder. She smiled as only a young woman newly in love does, deep, full, and with a satisfaction in her eyes that ran all the way to her heart.

Sometimes the fashions, haircuts, and look of women of previous generations don't make the women attractive to my eye. This was the case with the woman in the picture, but they were obviously very happy with each other. I wondered who she was. Did Harold have a girlfriend or maybe a wife at one time? I knew my chances of finding out anything from Harold were remote.

I went to the trunk and opened it. In the tray on the top there were frilly things, lace handkerchiefs, a bra and girdle, and a maroon woman's fancy hat. I unfolded an old nightie. I hoped they weren't things Harold wore on occasion. I wondered if they belonged to the woman in the picture. Was this a hope chest she had? I saw some brooches and another photograph. Harold and the same woman were at Nantasket Beach. I could see the roller coaster that belonged to Paragon Park in the background.

There was a ticket stub showing passage from Cohasset to Weymouth Landing and an envelope addressed to Harold, postmarked Los Angeles, but no letter inside. Last there was a postcard of the Statue of Liberty addressed to Betty Edwards in Cohasset from someone named Stella. There was nothing else. I pulled the tray out and searched through the bottom of the trunk. I saw a couple of dresses. I pushed deeper and pulled out a blanket. Four pair of women's shoes lay in the bottom of the trunk.

I closed the trunk and looked in the drawers. There were no more clues anywhere else in the room. When I went back downstairs I stopped at his desk. I looked at the pile of papers there and I saw a note pad with my name on it. It was the log of every time and every thing I did at his house when I was in high school; it showed the time I arrived, the work I did, the time I left, and what he paid me. I flipped through it. On the last page there was a recent entry noting my letter announcing my trip to walk Greenbush. The last entry noted the time I arrived at his house that morning, 9:59 am.

I left his house, locked the door, and met him back down the hill. He studied me as though he was looking for some kind of sign that I saw what was in his bedroom. I didn't say anything, and we resumed our walk.

There was no path alongside the tracks here. The tracks had been cut through some boulders. Saplings grew everywhere. Trees had fallen across the tracks. Vines and roots buried the tracks and ties. Our feet sank into the compost below the mossy cover. He reminded me again it was one point three nine miles to Weymouth Heights, then one point three three more miles to East Weymouth.

The sky was clouding. It looked like it might rain after all.

When we emerged from the overgrown cut and waited to walk over the Tufts crossing, some of the drivers gave us stares like, what were we doing there in the woods? Many of them probably didn't even know railroad tracks lay there.

When we crossed over to the other side of Commercial Street he pointed out exactly where his shack stood. A few old cinder blocks remained. That was it. He had another great view out to the bay and looked right up the ways at the shipyard. He asked, "Can we stop here for a moment?"

"Sure." I stacked the old cinder blocks into a seat for Harold, and I sat on the tracks.

He was quiet and looked around the area. He drew a series of deep breaths and let go one long sigh.

"Harold, if we make it to East Weymouth today, I'll spring for a cab and you can spend the night back at your house in your own bed. We'll pick up where we left off tomorrow morning."

He said, "No. I want to spend the night outside wherever it is that we decide to call it a day."

He bent over to look below the branches and leaves to see out across the bay. He straightened up and then looked around the area that was once his work place. I think he was melancholy in his stoic way. Four old cinder blocks were all that was left of his work life. The vegetation had long ago consumed any wood or lumps of coal. The trees grew up and closed in around the tracks. They had become so dense it was almost impossible to see the road. We were no more than fifty feet from Commercial Street.

I asked, "Harold have you ever been here since you stopped working. You live less than a half a mile from here."

"No. There's no reason to come here."

We started walking again and very quickly it became extremely difficult. Once we passed out of the wooded area that surrounded the area where his shanty once stood, we walked into a marshy area that emptied into the Fore River. Harold said this was the most difficult area on the line for the crews to keep maintained because the weeds grew so thick here. Every year they had to cut it back. I recalled riding my dirt bike alongside the tracks and everywhere along Greenbush, but here was never easy to get through.

The further we walked the more difficult it became. In places the weeds were over ten feet tall. Weeds and bramble completely obscured the rails and ties. Wild raspberry bushes, cat-o-nine tails, and indiscernible thorny bushes grew out of the swamp and drainage ditch. The choke the underbrush had on the rail bed here made us have to crawl on our stomachs at times and weave into the woods then back to the tracks. We paused under the Idlewell Road bridge and talked about getting off the tracks and walking the road to East Weymouth. We decided, no. If we did that we would be defeating the purpose of walking the entire length of Greenbush. Besides, there were no crossings until Weymouth Heights. If we did get off the tracks we would have to cut through someone's yard. We ducked and climbed and crawled and stumbled our way through.

Harold used his cane as a kind of machete. Every time he had to stoop or inch along on his belly I prayed he wouldn't break his hip or have a heart attack. The wet, mossy, moist soil that held the weeds and reeds in place soaked through my day-hiking boots. I had to stop to wring out my socks several times. His leather footwear kept him from the Weymouth equivalent of trench foot.

Finally, we reached the bridge at Weymouth Heights. I asked him where the Weymouth Heights station actually was. I had never been able to locate any remains. He pointed out where it had stood. Then I saw how the land had been shaped for the building and parking lot. It was easy to miss.

We crossed over Green Street and continued on behind King Oak Hill toward East Weymouth. The brush and briers and bramble and thistle were thicker and taller on this section of the tracks than they had been for the previous mile. The weeds and vegetation were woven as tight as fabric. It took all my strength leaning into the blades and vines to make an opening for our next step. Then I'd have to turn around and press my back against the jungle until it gave way. The vines snared my legs and tripped me repeatedly. I pushed my way through and stamped out a path for Harold. Harold fell several times. One time he fell and landed on his hip right on top of the rail. He fell so hard I thought he might have finally broken it. I went to help him and he waved me off with his cane. He got up and limped forward even slower. His limp left soon, but his pace was very slow.

It was the exact same place Billy lost his legs more than twenty years earlier.

We passed by an old siding and a rotted loading dock. I asked him, "Why was there a loading dock here? There's nothing in the area except for a gravel pit."

He said, "There were many small businesses along the line, but few of them could afford or had the need for their own dedicated switch and siding. The railroad built a number of those gang sidings and left freight cars at the various sidings for a business to unload."

We walked on through a small shallow swamp that had formed over the bed from a plugged drainage pipe. Finally the jungle opened a little and we crossed Unicorn Avenue into the East Weymouth area. I told him it was here I first became aware of Greenbush, train tracks, and trains.

"Some friends and I tailed some of the older kids in the neighborhood here. The Penn Central had left a New Haven boxcar on the siding at East Weymouth and they were climbing around it. We explored it ourselves the next day after school. Then we came back again and explored a little further down the tracks and discovered the abandoned East Weymouth station.

"Another time I cut school and saw a work train on the siding at East Weymouth. I watched it for hours while the crew replaced the most rotted ties and slowly moved on up the line."

He said, "Around the time you were growing up and exploring the tracks there was minimal maintenance to the line, because it still had a few customers. It had to be maintained to some degree."

He continued, "During World War II I made some extra money by working here at the East Weymouth siding. At the beginning of the war the Army sent an anti-aircraft gun to Weymouth on a flat car. They parked it at the East Weymouth siding and moved it up to the top of King Oak Hill. I rode the train down from Braintree and worked as an extra hand when the Army truck showed up at the siding to transport it up the hill."

"Why did the Army ship here? They could have just towed one up from Camp Edwards or wherever?"

"Because, at the beginning of the war there was a shortage of guns, men, and trucks. That particular gun had come from a militia unit in Iowa because all the artillery in Massachusetts was either being sent overseas or already in use.

"That gun and others were shipped in to protect Boston. The same thing happened down in Hull and all along the South Shore. The Army shipped in two anti aircraft guns and positioned them out at Point Allerton for the Coastal Artillery Corp. The tracks going out to Hull had been idle for years, but when the war started, Fort Revere was reactivated and the tracks going out there reconditioned. But, within a couple of years all the guns were removed and sent elsewhere. The tracks to Hull went idle again and soon after the war they were torn up."

We passed the dual two-track crossing in East Weymouth and he pointed out where coal was dumped. We stepped off the tracks and onto the passenger platform at East Weymouth.

"Do you know that the first electrified rail line in the country ran here from Hull to East Weymouth and, eventually, onto Braintree?"

"Yeah, I learned that somewhere. I think it was crazy to have an unprotected high voltage third rail running here."

"Did you know Greenbush had been double tracked most of the way for many years."

"I thought it was, but I could never tell for sure."

I told him I made it to the East Weymouth station only a few times before it burned down. But I remember every detail of it. The view of the river, the smell of urine, the busted glass, its colors, red on the outside and green inside. The first time I went there I heard the glass, shattered and strewn all over the floor, crunch under my feet. I knew I was trespassing, and every step I took toward the next thing I wanted to explore seemed to announce my arrival. The pipes were capped in the bathroom. I could see where the sink once hung. The toilet bowl was still there. No tank or seat, just the bowl. Pieces of a bench in the waiting room remained, busted-up, but recognizable. The stationmaster's office looked out the tracks. Through the broken mullion I saw the gentle etching of Greenbush over the landscape.

A train crept by one day as I explored the station. I stared at it. The scene remains in my head as clear as any photograph: a black Penn Central engine pulling a half a dozen box cars into the station from the south. It was autumn then, too. The Back River was at high tide. The leaves were changing in the background. The click of each spike against its plate under the rail was mellifluous. Everything harmonized with the slow throaty thrum of the engine's diesel engine slowly passing as I stared out the window.

Two or three weeks later I went there to explore further and the station had burned down. The charred studs poked up from the foundation. Some were only a few inches tall and others still stood eight feet tall. I was so angry. I had recently bought my first camera. I had shot one roll of film in the camera and I was saving my money to have that roll printed, then I was going to buy another roll and take pictures at the station. It was gone. Someone took it from me. In the brief period of time I explored the East Weymouth station it took on an almost majestic omnipotent presence in my imagination.

I said to Harold, "Maybe this is why you're an old, odd bachelor and I'm likely to be one, too."

"You mean because we're here traipsing along some train tracks rather than with a woman?"

"Exactly." I was surprised at his accuracy.

"It's a lot less complicated being here."

"Amen." I thought of the photo of the woman I saw in his house and wondered if his comment didn't have something to do with her.

We stopped and stood there surveying the remnants of the East Weymouth station and its place in the world. For me it was like a visit to a cemetery, sad, but I was glad for the effect. I could still see pavement markings for parking spots and curbstones. A flagpole, or maybe it was a telegraph pole, still stood. The rectangle of the station's foundation stood out. Grass and weeds and small trees growing up out of it now marked its area. We walked to the end of the passenger platform where the Herring Run disappeared into a tunnel under the tracks. I had been there earlier that day with Danny. The fog had been lifting off the river then. An even, moist light bathed the river, the station, the sky, and the marsh with a low-contrast gray light as the view down the river released itself to me. I could see the moisture of the fog weave itself across my field of vision and into the atmosphere.

Now, as the sun set behind us, I watched the light disappear off the Back River. Looking out over the river again where it bent past Great Esker Park on one side and the abandoned naval ammunition depot on the other, I suddenly felt connected to this place. I hadn't shivered, but I felt as though I had. I hadn't yelled or cried out, but I felt as though I had. I hadn't been running and hit the endorphin release, but I felt as though I had. I looked around to see if Harold had noticed my demeanor change. He was looking out over the river, busy with his own thoughts.

It was an unusual place with which to make a spiritual connection. I felt peace, warmth, and a desire to bath myself in the seasons of this place. I think if someone else looked at that area they might say it's pretty with the river winding its way through the marsh. It was easy to see the horizon; the trees and river funneled the point of view. But the view also held an electrical substation, the idle town incinerator and former dump were the foreground to the scene. An old warehouse foundation and slimy rocks lined the riverbed at low tide; rusted fence, telephone poles, a couple of crummy homes, the littering of old industry, and a smelly old ornery man beside me. But still it moved me. I wanted to move back to Weymouth. The feeling to want to move back passed quickly, but the connection to that place was made indelible. Or perhaps the feelings were removed from some internal vault and allowed to be, again.

Harold shuffled his feet and asked, "Do you want to stay here for the night? We could go down to the marsh and find a spot or I know a spot right where the woods and marsh met where we could set up for the night."

I thought back to Kelli and her house. I couldn't picture a place to set up a small camp here, and I knew about the marsh and the river in this area. I knew both sides of the river well all the way out to the harbor. He led me down a narrow path that I knew, then out beyond the substation. We walked a small trail and stepped into a wooded area up off the marsh grass. Trees circled the area, a small fire pit was set in the dirt, and a perfectly sheltered camping spot lay there. He threw out his bindle and settled in.

"How did you know about this place?" I asked.

He smirked and said, "Go ahead and start a fire, boy."

I gathered up some wood and brush and started a small fire. I said I was going to walk up to Jackson Square and get some food and water. I asked if he wanted anything. He said no and pulled another sandwich and a bottle of something out of his bag. He offered me a pull on the bottle. It burned like nothing else I've ever drunk. It was his home-brew whiskey. It was as awful as it was powerful. He pulled out a pipe, packed it, lit it, and settled back. He took another pull on his bottle and barely winked as it went down. I walked off to the Square and bought a sandwich and small bottle of cheap sweet alcohol, Watermelon Scnapps, for myself.

As I walked back to our camping spot I heard voices and the footsteps of several people crunching across the leaves. I ducked into the woods and moved forward to edge of our camping site. I saw several teenagers exiting our campsite. I didn't see Harold anywhere. The kids left and I went back to the site. His cane was there and his bedroll, but there was no sign of him. I called out his name and soon I heard some rustling in the woods. He limped back into sight. He was angry. I asked him what happened.

"Punks. I heard them coming and moved into the woods, but they saw me. They gathered around me and I fell."

He continued, "They kicked some dirt at me and picked up my bottle. Lightweights. They took a drink and spit it out, then poured the rest of it on the ground. One of them stomped on my bedroll and pissed into the fire.

"There was a time," he said, "When I would have beat the crap out of all of them." He cursed, "Now, I have to wear hose to keep my legs from aching and a diaper so I don't shit all over myself." He limped away and picked up his bedroll. He picked up his bottle then threw it away. It smashed against a rock somewhere on the river's edge. He disappeared into the marsh grass.

I left him alone. What would I say to him anyway? After about a half an hour I walked over to the river's edge and saw him sitting on a granite block set there to direct the river. I handed him my bottle, he pushed it away and turned his face from me.

A few minutes later he said, "I'm going to finish this walk."

I went back to the campsite, restarted the small fire and finished my sandwich.

He walked back to the camp and announced, "I'm going to walk into Jackson Square and buy a bottle of whiskey."

"I'll go for you." I offered him my bottle again.

He took a long pull on the bottle, draining almost half of it. "This is like candy."

"You don't have to drink it." I wasn't going to drink anymore. Not after his crusty old lips had infected the bottle top.

"No. Wait. Tomorrow's Sunday and the packie's closed."

"Why don't you finish that one and I'll go back and get myself another bottle."

"As long as you're going." He reached into his coat and pulled out a change purse. He counted out ten silver dollars. "Buy me something. Whiskey."

"My treat Harold."

"Take it, boy." He forced the coins into my palm.

I walked to the square and got two more bottles; cheap whiskey for him and more Watermelon Snapps for me. When I got back to the camp we drank.

Usually when I bought alcohol it lasted a long time. I wasn't much of a drinker, but having some booze seemed to fit with what I was doing and whom I was doing it with.

We finished all three bottles that evening. I had a very strong buzz going. Our small fire died and I fell asleep very easily, the stars and trees spinning and rotating in my head. It didn't seem to faze him at all.

CHAPTER 22

▼

GREENBUSH, DAY TWO

When I woke up the sun was just breaking out over the Back River. I was as sore as I have ever been. I had rolled off the blanket I took from Harold's house and slept on the ground near the fire pit. I had dirt and leaves pressed into my face, and I was cold. There was dew all over my clothes. When I got around to looking at Harold, he looked dead. He slept on his back. His mouth was open, but there was no snoring. He didn't stir or twitch when I called his name. I pulled myself up and went over to him. I kicked his feet and called his name. Then he moved. When he opened his eyes he reached for his cane and sat up. He said, "I'll be ready in a minute."

He belched. It was as though some noxious gas settled over the area. I already felt like I was going to throw up. His toxic release made the feeling stronger.

He rolled his bedding back together and stood up. He was ready to go. He looked at me and said, "You look like you're in a bad way."

"My head hurts. My back hurts and my ass is cold and sore." The fallen, withered leaves that scattered all over the ground had matted into my hair and buried deep inside my ear. I took my bedroll and we climbed back up the small hill to the tracks. I threw up.

When we stepped back on the tracks, Harold pulled out his note pad, made his entry. He said, "It's one point eight three miles to West Hingham." He put his notepad away and pulled out another sandwich from a hidden pocket in his jacket, and began to gnaw on it.

The estuary of the Back River slipped from view. At that moment, he was moving faster than I was. As we crossed into Hingham I pointed toward the park on the river's bank that used to be a Navy ammunition depot. I said, "I always liked going there. Did you ever have anything to do with the railroad operations inside the base?"

"No. I know it was a big operation with all the bunkers and warehouses there. Each one had its own siding. Plus the Annex the Navy built down in the Cohasset woods during World War II. The shipyard had its own railroad, too.

"Before the war there was an infrequent special Navy train going there and we left plenty of boxcars at the siding there. But during the war there were a lot more trains on the tracks."

It was easier walking now. Although there were saplings and small trees all over the place and branches from older tress darkened the path, it was easy to walk, and there was a path alongside the tracks. As we passed behind the cemetery the single track grew into the three tracks for switching into the base.

Then Harold said, "Hingham had the best whorehouses around."

I started giggling like a junior high school boy.

He continued, "Back then Hingham had two Navy bases, a shipyard, and a harbor that still supported some fishing boats." He pointed in the direction of one particular house and added, "Some of these old Hingham broads would be surprised to know where their husbands spent time, and some of these Hingham know-it-alls would be surprised to know what their mothers did for a living."

In all of my waning disdain for the South Shore, I never considered that. But it made sense. Suddenly I had images of The Best Little Whorehouse in Texas in my head. I knew that wasn't real. Whorehouses were seedy, sweaty, smelly, secreting places of body odors and sticky money.

I have been to two, one in the Philippines and again in San Diego, both times with the Navy. I never told anyone about it. The only ones who knew were my shipmates who went there with me.

"You seem surprised," Harold said.

"No, not really. I just had never thought about it before. I had heard a rumor once of whores working out of an old house outside Jackson Square, but at the time I didn't really know what a whore was.

"Now that I'm thinking about it, there was probably one in Colombian Square in South Weymouth, near the air base."

"There were plenty of them. If there was a place where men worked there was likely to be a whorehouse close by." He pointed toward Quincy and said, "Think about the Fore River Shipyard there. Before the Navy base in Squantum closed and moved to Weymouth there was a cathouse there, too." He swept his arm and said, "Weymouth had a lot of factories at one time. Braintree had the railroad yard. Whores weren't hard to find."

I had to know so I asked, "You ever go to one?"

"Of course. I didn't go there regularly like some joes, but I went there once in a while.

"I had a favorite, but she ended up marrying someone."

I couldn't believe what I was hearing. "Whoa Harold, TMI."

"What?"

"TMI, too much information."

By this time we had passed through West Hingham and he announced it was point seven three miles to Hingham. We walked the tracks through the backyards that butted up to the line and into Hingham Center. There we turned off the tracks into a convenience store for some water and aspirin, then the doughnut shop next door.

As we walked into the donut shop I heard the older woman behind the counter ask the other girl working there, "How was your date last night?"

Without even looking at the customer she said, "Two fifty-six for the donut and coffee." She took the bills and passed back change to a dozen customers without missing a syllable of the dating adventure. She looked like she was in need of a date herself. There was no wedding ring and I don't know how one could fit around the girth of her fingers. It looked like she had five short and wide sausages attached to her hand.

"It started like it was going to be wicked. We went to DeVito's in Braintree for dinner. He opened the car door for me. Asked me if I had a favorite station he could put on the radio. Hell, at the restaurant he pulled the friggin' chair out for me to sit down. I almost landed on my ass."

"Sounds like he was a gentleman."

"Yeah. That's what I thought. He ordered wine and I had like three screwdrivers. You know how much I like those." She rolled her eyes at the other woman and they both rolled their eyes. "I was getting a wicked buzz even before we were done with the appetizers."

I was interested in the story by now. There were still a half a dozen people in front of me.

"So what happened?"

"He saw his friggin' ex-wife. That's what happened. I didn't know it then though." We booked it out of there before she even saw us. We were driving around in his car and he was so nervous.

"I had a good buzz and, you know, whatever was going to be okay with me. He said he was going to take me home because he was so upset at seeing her, but we stopped at Great Hill and he wasn't even," there was no sound to her voice while she mouthed the word, hard. "Finally I said, just take me home."

"Do you think he was still married?"

"I wonder if he was even getting a divorce. Ya' know, he only came by here a few times before he asked me out."

It was my turn. I ordered coffee and two donuts, hardly California food. As I was leaving I heard her say, "I bet you're right. He was probably still friggin' married."

Back on the tracks I was finally moving okay and Harold had a decent stride. I swear he had a little twinkle in his eye. A couple hundred yards south of the Hingham station train stops were bolted to the tracks.

"One point zero seven miles to Nantasket Junction," Harold announced.

The tracks through Hingham passed by another old cemetery, the town square, and a small trestle where Greenbush crossed a stream emptying into Hingham Harbor. It was a beautiful morning. I could see boats out on the bay. There were pleasure boaters still pushing, trying to get one more weekend on the water before winter set in. Tomorrow commuter traffic would hurry them toward Boston. I wondered if they would ever see the things I saw on Greenbush. Even when the line reopened, would commuters take the time to look or would their vision be limited to newspapers, business proposals, and legal briefs? They wouldn't see, they'd be stuck in the commuter daze.

As we walked through the backyards of Hingham I smelled bacon and heard the bustle of Sunday mornings. It was almost too quaint; some families getting ready for church others were out raking leaves and doing lawn work. Here I was walking with Harold, hung over and talking about whorehouses. The previous day we ran into no one as we walked. That morning we encountered a few people; children who waved as we walked past and dogs barked at us. A couple of dogs challenged us. Harold didn't like dogs. He swung his cane at them and hit one that got too close.

All the way down the line the zoning and residential composition changed, from the old, small houses with little yards set close to the tracks in East Braintree to the slight wooded barrier between Greenbush and backyards in Weymouth to a greater barrier, larger yards, bigger, and grander houses in Hingham. Soon, I knew, we would be swinging away from the coast and disappearing further into the woods. There the houses would be set further away from the tracks. Greenbush was mostly out of sight through Cohasset and Scituate. More trees and more swamps, marshland, and little bridges to cross were coming. We would step into little villages, the tracks passing through the edge of each hamlet then more woods. I knew less about this part of Greenbush. My range growing up was principally the tracks as they passed through East Weymouth, expanding up toward East Braintree and about as far south as Hingham Center. Over the years I had made it all the way down to Greenbush and up all the way into the Braintree yard numerous times; walking or tucked away in a freight car or riding my motorcycle or bicycle. But the ends of the line were less familiar to me than the middle.

As the flowing sunlight dried the dew, the evaporating moisture released the odor of the woods. It was so reassuring. I stopped and drew in a couple deep, almost profound, breaths. The woods of the West didn't release rich odors after a storm. The irritating dust just stopped blowing around for a few hours. The foliage was not peaking, but where there was a stream buried in the woods the color of the leaves changed. There was less settlement to see. The very suburban texture of the South Shore crept back away from the tracks. The houses had carefully mown and raked lawns. Every once in a while we passed an old junky house with cars rusting in the yards and old washing machines pushed out-of-doors. But those were few and far between.

Once we passed the Hingham Lumber Company the walking became easier still. The small trees and bushes gave way to a wide-open bed. Although old, decrepit, and in need of substantial restoration work, the tracks and ties had been intact until here. Below the lumberyard the rails and ties were dismantled. The tracks were still there, but they were pulled off the ties and laying aside. I wondered why, and Harold had no theory. Less than a mile later, past the abbey, the tracks were gone and only the ties remained in place. Then, barely across the Cohasset town line, the ties curved west away into the woods toward the Navy ammo dump annex. The southbound bed before us was open. No tracks, no ballast stone, no ties. It was cleaned thoroughly when the railroad pulled out.

At the town line we passed another cemetery and a golf course. There were more streams and ponds. I thought someday it would be nice to come back here with a canoe and paddle around the small waterways.

Harold and I weren't talking much. At times it seemed to me that I was walking alone. I stopped and took pictures when I wanted. I sat on a stonewall, buried deep in the woods, and made my journal entry. Harold passed. When I finished writing I quickly caught up and passed him. I picked up a stake to take back as a memento and I found myself wondering what homes were going for here. I wondered if I would want to live here. It all felt good, the weather, the woods, the ocean, the architecture. I could probably get a transfer, if not, I could get a new job very easily.

Harold was slowing down. Once we left Hingham Center his pace slowed. It is awkward to pace to someone so slow. He shuffled along and we had better than seven miles to go. He didn't announce the mileage between Nantasket Junction and Whitney, but I did see him make notes on his notepad. He did call out the mileage from Whitney to Cohasset. Then as soon as we crossed the town line in Cohasset he sped up. The tenor of his motion changed, too.

We crossed into Cohasset. At the first grade crossing, without a word, he turned off the tracks and started east up a small hill toward the ocean. I asked, "Where are you going?" He didn't answer me. I fell in behind him.

His old clothes, cane, bindle, and grubby appearance contrasted mightily against the fallen leaves, expensive architecture, sculptured geography, and the carefully groomed homes on this street. At the top of the hill he stopped and pulled the medicine bottle out of his bag. He tossed whatever pill it was into his mouth and turned down one small street then another and stopped at the driveway to the first house on that street. We were in front of a beautiful large colonial home. The lawn, of course, was perfectly clean. In the yard I saw a garden, a gazebo, and topiary. I could see Cohasset Harbor in the distance beyond the backyard.

He went up the walkway to the front door. I caught up to him as he got there and asked what was he doing. He waved me off and rapped his cane against the door. A middle age woman pulled back a gauzy curtain and looked at us. She opened the door.

Harold asked, "Is Jack or Betty here?"

She tilted her head and said, "No. Jack has been dead for ten, no twelve years. Betty died not long after.

"Were you a friend of theirs?"

"I knew them years ago."

The woman relaxed and swung the door open to an almost welcoming position. She came out from behind, no longer shielding herself with it. "Who are you?" she asked again. She looked at me. I shrugged my shoulders as though I was saying, I'm with him, but I don't know what he's doing. It was a truthful gesture.

"Where are they buried?"

"At the town cemetery."

Harold stopped her in mid-sentence. "In the Robbins family section?"

"Yes, but please, tell me who you are."

"I'm Harold," he answered.

With that she swung the door almost shut and said, "If you don't leave right now I'll call the police." Then the door slammed shut.

He smacked his cane against the door, turned, and walked away.

I asked, "What the hell was that all about?"

He stopped and turned toward me. He shook his cane at me and said, "Stay away from me."

I turned his anger back on him and said, "No. What the hell is going on here?"

He snorted and moved down the driveway. At the end of the driveway instead of going down the hill back toward the tracks he turned the other way. He was moving as fast and as well as I had seen him go this whole time. Shortly he turned again and an old cemetery came into view. He turned and walked to a very specific headstone.

There were monuments of all sizes there; new, tall grave markers popped up in family plots among the small old ones. There was a memorial to the immigrants who died in shipwrecks off shore on the notorious rocks of Cohasset. Dozens of unidentifiable bodies lay in the mass grave there. The cemetery was neat, well maintained, and obviously divided between the families with money and big monuments and the individuals who didn't have money with little grave markers. The wealthy monuments on the knoll gave way to little markers pressed up against the stonewall and woods.

I was very confused, but I didn't want to intrude. I walked up behind him. He stood there very quiet. I stepped back and waited. We stayed there a long time, then Harold unfastened his pants and urinated all over the grave and monument.

"What are you doing?" I yelled. "Stop it." I had moved up beside him. The name engraved on the monument read Jack Robbins. Below it read Betty Robbins.

When he finished he spit on the grave. He turned away and walked out of the cemetery. I heard the gravel crunch under our feet as we walked away, and wind rustling the dying leaves, but the loudest sound of all was the morose silence from Harold. He walked back to the tracks and we walked on in silence through the remainder of Cohasset and into Scituate. I didn't crowd him as we walked. I stayed thirty or so paces behind him trying to figure what this was all about.

I tried to crack a conversation open by asking him about an old turntable I heard existed at Cohasset at one time, but I got no response.

We had to turn off the rail bed just before we got into the North Scituate village. It was the only place on the entire walk where the bridge that crossed a large brook was gone. We turned off the bed and into the village of North Scituate. I walked next to the rail-bed back a couple hundred yards to the brook, turned around, and walked the short distance back into the North Scituate village.

Harold did not walk back to the edge of the brook with me. He walked across the intersection in North Scituate without looking. A mini van crossing the intersection came very close to hitting Harold. The car swerved around him and hit the horn. I thought I saw the driver giving Harold the finger.

The station at North Scituate was one of the two original stations on Greenbush that still stood. The other one was in Hingham. In Hingham it had been converted into a sub shop. Here in North Scituate it had been converted into a Laundromat, store, and dry cleaners.

As I crossed the square I yelled to Harold, "I'm hungry. I'm going to find a sandwich. Do you want anything?"

He didn't answer.

I went into a convenience store for one of their pre-made sandwiches. When I came out of the store there was no sign of Harold. I walked to the rail bed behind the building. There was no sign of him. He couldn't have gone far at his pace. I looked around the square. I didn't see him anywhere around there either. I sat on bench in a little park that butted up against the bed to eat my food when I saw him emerge from a bar. He crossed over to the station, stepped back onto Greenbush, and started walking. I watched him walk away. His entire manner, his movements, his very breath seemed to expel a dark miserable aura that contrasted deeply with the rich beauty of the woods, the light, and the air that surrounded this place.

I was tired of his sullenness. Why did he have to be so damn difficult every time anything beyond the rhythm of his breathing happened? He disappeared around a bend where the line curved south away from the station toward its termination. I sat there for fifteen minutes. The walk thus far had not been as bad as I thought it would be when he announced his intentions to come with me the day before, but the sulk Harold was having at the moment was as powerful as it was maddening.

After the short train ride in Braintree and the night out near the marsh in Weymouth I felt a kinship with him. We were probably the only ones in years who walked the length of Greenbush because we wanted to. We both understood the nuances of the line. It was certainly unusual for two grown men to walk an abandoned railroad line simply because we liked it. It probably goes beyond quirkiness and slips into oddness.

I enjoyed my walk in spite of Harold. He slowed me down, but fortunately he hadn't been as antagonistic as I thought he would be. However, I was tired of his moodiness. His mood moved between irritation, acerbity, and meanness and I was tired of it.

I threw the sandwich wrapping and Coke can away. I caught up to him quickly, walked around him, turned, and blocked his progress. He raised his cane to hit me. I grabbed it. He stared at me. I asked him, "What hell is going on?"

"It's none of your damn business."

"It is my business when someone threatens to call the police on me. Is this all connected to the girl in the pictures at your house?"

No response.

"Was that her grave? Was she an old girlfriend or something?"

Silence. He lowered the cane a little.

"Whose grave did you just piss on?"

Through his cane I felt his resistance release. He lowered the cane a little and stepped back a half a step. I let go of the cane. He held it up like he would still swing it. I stared back at him. I asked, "Is this why you wanted to come with me?"

After all the years of hostility to most of mankind and his minimal tolerance for me he eased up on his anger for a moment.

"Yes. I wanted to see her and him again." His booming and domineering speech paused. When he spoke it was clipped. "Betty was my girl, but he kidnapped her and took off to California for a few years. Betty is the girl in the pictures at my house."

CHAPTER 23

▼

BETTY

"What happened?"

He moved around me and said, "He wore her down. He offered her money and travel and all kinds of things until she couldn't say no. That's what she told me when they moved back here."

"What happened?"

He was walking very slow. We passed a swamp and disappeared into the woods moving further away from North Scituate. He said, "Years ago I was going to marry her." He was barely moving now. I noticed the sweat on his forehead. He was breathing hard and moved his hand toward his left chest and shoulder. He rubbed his shoulder and arm, then he burped. Oh no, I thought, he's having a heart attack. He reached into his jacket and pulled out a medicine bottle. He took a pill and placed it under his tongue. I recognized it as nitro. He started walking again very slowly. He said, "Come on we've got a little less than four point two nine miles to the end of the line."

The bed curved into a wooded area then it opened onto a small pond. The bed had been built up with fill here. The open ocean horizon lay just beyond the trees on the east side of the pond. I could smell the ocean. The foliage was beautiful here. The pond made a cold spot for the trees so the color was spectacular. The sun was showing its afternoon arc.

Throughout the walk my stride had moved me in front of him most of the time. I would slow down and we'd be abreast for while then I'd creep forward again. Unless I stopped to take a picture or to pick up something to study for a moment, I was out in front of him most of the way. Now we walked parallel. I wanted to know what the story was with Betty. He would have to tell the story his way, at his pace, but I knew he would tell me. I looked at him and his affect was void of any feeling. It was time to get this walk done. That's when he said, "Betty would have been my wife. She would have been my wife if it hadn't been for Jack Robbins."

"What happened Harold? Who was that in the house we stopped at? Why was she going to call the police on you?"

"That was their family. They don't like it when I'm around. They probably thought I was dead because I haven't been around for years."

He stopped talking. I had to wait for him to resume. We walked in silence past the remains of the Egypt depot when Harold told me all about Betty, with the kind of detail only poets and painters notice.

"Betty worked for the railroad as a secretary for one of the building maintenance supervisors. Her father worked with the stationmaster in Cohasset. He pulled some strings and she got the job with the railroad. It was the tail end of the Depression so everyone was glad for any work they could get.

"Moe, the supervisor, did an annual inspection out on the line every year. He was an okay guy. He had an eye for the women though. Every year a different woman rode with him on his inspection trips. He was married, but I don't think that stopped him from putting the moves on other women. He was a handsome guy. Women responded to him.

"He'd look at each of the stations, guard shacks, water towers, and so on. He did this every spring and decided which buildings needed work and which ones could wait. On the ones that needed work he ordered it to be painted or shingled or have the rotted wood replaced or whatever. That year Betty traveled with him. Her job was to basically be a scribe.

"It was the spring so I knew he'd be by I was whittling on the little porch I had built in front of the shack when I saw them coming. Moe was a friendly guy so I looked forward to his visits. He always had jokes and stories to tell. She stepped out of the car first that spring. She was young. She was beautiful. The women he took with him on his inspections were always young and good looking, but Betty, she was the cat's meow.

"She stayed in the background and wrote down what he said. I could see her tense up when he stood next to her. At one point she flinched. I didn't see it, but he probably pinched her bottom. She laughed. He patted her on the shoulder and told her to make a note that the Tufts Crossing guard shanty was to get paint and new a new roof.

"She seemed full of herself, like she was better than everyone. We didn't speak other than being introduced. She just nodded at me. She took notes. As they were leaving, Moe decided I should get new flooring too. Then they left.

"After they left I told my relief I thought she was a dish. We speculated about what Moe and the women he traveled with were doing. I didn't give her another thought after that.

"I ran into her again a few weeks later at the Hingham station. I had spent the day there fishing with a friend. I was waiting for a northbound train to get back to Weymouth. She was pacing back and forth, from one end of the loading platform to the farthest other end. I remembered her. I looked at her and she seemed bothered. It was early evening. It had been a beautiful day, warm with enough breeze to keep the humidity and mosquitoes at bay and I had a basket full of fish on ice. I was sitting on the bench outside of the station. I said hello as she walked past me. She flinched again then stopped and looked at me. She studied my face for a moment, trying to remember where we had met. Then she said, 'Hello.' She was waiting for the southbound train to get back home to Cohasset. She asked if the work had been done to my shack yet. I said no, but I knew it would get done. I asked how things were going for her and she said, 'Fine. Thank you very much.' My train pulled into the station and I left.

"I found out later she was indeed upset that day. She had been to dinner in Hingham with the fellow she was engaged to, Jack Robbins. He had gotten drunk and was making eyes at every other girl in the restaurant. After dinner he said he wanted go into town. She said no, so he left her in Hingham and he went into Boston.

"We met again a few weeks later and we spent the night together.

"The regular crossing man at Spring Street in Cohasset had gotten drunk and slept through a couple of trains passing the crossing. I had gone to cover that crossing while the railroad found a replacement. It was around dusk and I saw her walking down the street. I was outside at the time sitting in front of the shanty when she crossed the grade. I thought she had been looking at me so I waved. She stopped and looked at me and again she seemed startled. She had to search through her memory to remember me. She was like a cat at that moment. You know how they look ready to run while they decide if they'll let you come up to them or not. Then she asked if she could step into the shack for a moment. That got my curiosity going. It was against regulations, but I let her in. She stood in the doorway and kept looking up and down the road. I asked her what was wrong. She said it was the fellow she was engaged to. He was drunk again. He was being mean. She spotted his car coming down the street and stepped back inside the shanty. She dropped down into a corner, out of sight of the window and door and begged me not to let him see her.

"I had to go out to pass a train through anyway. I closed the door behind me and started lowering the gates. Jack tried to go around the gate. I flagged him down then watched him through the car window.

"He was fidgeting. I watched him take a long drink out of a bottle. As soon as the train passed he sped over the crossing. He slowed at the stop sign at the top of the hill. He turned right, hesitated, then swung back left. His car disappeared down the street. A minute later he came back through the intersection. It was like he was prowling.

"Betty was crying when I opened the door to the shack. There wasn't a lot of room in the crossing shacks; a table, a cot, a couple chairs, and a stove. I stopped in the doorway and saw her hunched down. She had pressed herself as deeply as she could into a corner. When she saw it was just me she sat on the floor. She started to calm down. Then we heard his car coming down the road again. She stood up and said if he found her there he would hit her again. I told her I wouldn't let him near her. I grabbed a chair and my pipe and went outside. I closed the door, set the chair on the ground and had a smoke. I watched Jack hunt for her with his car.

"He had turned around and was coming back down the hill. Once he got to the crossing he slowed down and crept his car through the area. He saw me and yelled from the car window if I had seen anyone walking by here in the last couple minutes. I waved him off. Jack didn't move his car for a minute or so. I didn't look at him. I listened. I listened for him to set the brake or the door to open. I wasn't going to let him near Betty. Whatever he was doing to her it scared her bad. I heard him let up on the clutch and give it some gas. He drove away.

"When Jack had been gone a few minutes I went back in the shack. Betty was gone. She had gone out the back window of the shed. I saw where she had torn her clothes on a nail. There was blood on the sill and it had dripped down the wall. I went around to the rear of the shed and looked for her. At first I didn't see anything except the dark woods. I called out her name and said it was okay. He's gone. There was no answer. It was getting darker and I felt sorry for her. But there was nothing I could do. I settled back into the chair outside of the shed. Then I heard her whisper, asking me if he was gone. I said yes. It was safe. She came back out of the woods. I saw that she was bleeding pretty good from her thigh. I told her to come back in the shed for some iodine and a bandage for her cut. She was so nervous she couldn't even hold the bottle still. I had her sit down while I cleaned and bandaged the cut.

"I asked what was going on with that guy. She walked over to the cot and sat down. She asked me for a cigarette. I only had my pipe with me. I had seen some rolling paper in the shack. I rolled her a smoke with my pipe tobacco. She lit the cigarette and laid down on the cot.

"She was supposed to marry him. She said he was a good guy, but when he got drunk he got mean. He didn't like it that she worked around so many men. She said was going to stop working as soon they got married.

"She told me the story of what happened the evening I ran into her at the Hingham station then she asked me what I was doing there in Cohasset. I told her. I said I would be done with my shift soon and I'd be glad to walk her home.

"She didn't say anything. I lit the lantern for some light in there and she asked if I wouldn't mind keeping it dark. So in the dark I sat there and she lay on the cot smoking. Then she said her parents where glad she was marrying a college-educated man, an engineer. They told her she should feel lucky. And she did. Jack was a nice guy, but when he got drunk he grabbed her and picked fights with anyone he thought was looking at her. He accused her of flirting. She said he pushed her around once in while when he was drunk. He imagined all sorts of things about her and the men she worked with. Jack almost got her fired when he picked a fight with Moe. She didn't work with Moe anymore. Moe had transferred her after Jack went after him and she was glad for that. She looked at me then. I don't know what she was trying tell me about working with Moe. But I think maybe she had to do things with Moe that she didn't want to so she could keep her job. A lot of other girls did.

"She sat up and looked at me. She said couldn't go home yet. Jack certainly would go looking for her there. Her parents let him take her out at all hours. She asked if I would just walk with her for a bit.

"My relief was coming soon. In spite of the regulations, it wasn't unusual for women to be in the guard shacks, but they were usually whores, wives or sisters. I thought she should hide in the woods again until my relief showed and then I'd meet her a short way down the road.

"She said no. She didn't care. She just wanted to stay away from Jack and her house until he was sober again. We stepped out of the shack when my relief showed up. He recognized Betty and gave me a look.

"We walked the tracks back and turned down a path she knew and walked the long way to the harbor. We walked to the beach. I found out she wasn't so stuck on herself. She was twenty years old.

"As we walked she spent most of her time trying to talk herself into loving Jack. She listed off his all his good qualities, his being an engineer, coming from a good family, handsome, and so on. But when I asked her why she said yes when Jack proposed she said she never really said yes or no and he had never really asked. It just happened. He started calling her his fiancée.

"It was flattering she said when they first met. Jack saw her on the train one day and followed her. He learned who she was and started hanging around, but she already had a beau and she had to deal with Moe, but Jack had his mind made up. He started showing up at her house talking to her mother, listening to her father. He helped her father with some work around the house. They were the ones who told her to give up on her boyfriend and start dating Jack. She wanted to please her parents and broke it off with the other boy, but not really. She was being courted by both of them for a while, then they found out about each other. She said it was nice to have both those guys being sweet on her, but she was dumped by both of them. That was okay with her. She'd go to the movies with other fellows and would occasionally run into Jack. But after a while no one else was calling her. Eventually she realized he was following her. Ultimately she figured Jack had chased off the other suitors.

"One night Jack came up to her and asked if she would consider going out with him again. He was sorry and said he would never act like he did again. He knew he got mad when he drank. He promised he'd try and control it. She asked him why, why did he pursue her so much? He said he missed her. He said he thought he loved her. He was never as happy as he was when he was with her. She gave in and they started to go together again.

"According to Betty he was good. He didn't drink much and he was in a good mood most of the time. Pretty soon he started calling her his fiancée and she never said otherwise.

"Not too long after Jack announced their engagement to their families he started being curious again about where she was all the time and who she was with. He started to insist that she meet him every day for lunch and pick him up at the train station when he got home. He taught her how to drive and gave her the keys to his car. Her family loved him. He was so helpful. So charming.

"Then one night they had gone to dinner and a movie and he had a couple drinks. He kept pushing her and pushing her and grabbing at her. She kept telling him she wanted to wait until they were married. He grabbed her in the car and said come on, they were going to be married in a few months anyway. Betty said no. He slapped her across the face. He grabbed and pulled at her clothes. Then he suddenly stopped. He apologized. He said he would never do that again.

"Jack dropped her off at her house that night. She said she didn't want to see him for a while. She tried to tell her mother about it. She didn't believe Betty. She was charmed to no end by Jack. Her mother said, 'No one's perfect. Sometimes as a wife women had to put up with things they didn't agree with.'

"Betty tried to tell her girlfriends that Jack was mean and had hit her. They couldn't believe it. How could such a handsome and nice guy be like that? She tried to avoid him, but he kept pursuing her. He apologized. He said he went to church and talked with the minister about his drinking. He said all the right things. She started going with him again.

"While we walked that night she talked the whole way to the beach. When we got there we sat on the sand looked up at the stars. We sat there until the tide crested. Minot light flashed out it's 'I LOVE YOU' signal and soon enough the first hint of sunrise began over the ocean.

"We left the beach just about daybreak and walked to her house in silence. She stopped around the corner from her house. She leaned against me. She said thanks for letting me talk then walked down the road to her house by herself.

"I walked back toward the tracks and caught the first northbound train. I was irritated with Jack. She seemed like a nice girl. Why did he have to act like that?

"On her way home from work the next day she stopped at Weymouth and walked to my crossing. She said thank you to me again. I asked her what happened when she got home. She had been yelled at by her father and ignored by her mother. Jack caught up to her that morning in Cohasset and drove her to work. He was angry, but was holding it back as much as he could. It passed and he said he was sorry. He kept asking where she was all night. He wanted to know who she was with. She said she didn't tell him. She thought he would have come here and picked a fight with me.

"I told her just let him try.

"She kissed me on the cheek and walked herself back to the Weymouth Landing station to finish her ride home.

"Over the next few weeks she stopped a few times. I started looking forward to her stopping by. She usually brought me a piece of pie or something. We'd talk about how things were going.

"She wondered how often I got to Braintree, where she worked. She said if I did get there I should stop by and see her. So I did. I started going to Braintree more regularly. I had absolutely no other reason to go except to see her. Pretty soon I was going there almost every day. We'd take a walk at lunch or have a little picnic. One of the other women in the office scolded her at first for being so forward about being seen with me. I didn't know what Betty said, but that other woman stopped bothering her.

"Jack stopped by to see her too. I could tell the days Jack had been there. Her manner was different.

"One day she told me Jack was going to be out of town the next couple days. I asked her if she would like to go to Nantasket Beach and Paragon Park with me. We did. It was in the fall just before the park shut down for the season. We had the place to ourselves. We rode all the rides, ate cotton candy, and walked on the beach. She guessed my weight within two pounds. She wouldn't get on the scale and let me guess her weight. She laughed and held onto my arm the whole day. I've never walked so tall as I did that day.

"I paid to have a photograph taken of the two of us together. That evening we sat on the pier looking west back out over Hingham Harbor. With the sunset I kissed her. I said break it off with Jack. She looked at me and kissed me back.

"A week later she did. Up to then, she hadn't dated Jack, but she hadn't broke it off completely either. Finally, she broke it off completely. She said he was surprisingly subdued about it. He said he understood. There had been distance between them for a while. Her family however said she had to leave. She couldn't live there anymore. Betty had a friend who had her own apartment in Quincy, so she moved in there.

"I found out later that Jack never told anyone that the engagement was off. He was saying that they had some nervousness about getting married going on, but that everything would work out.

"For the next few weeks, unless I had to work, she came to my house every evening. Sometimes she came after work other times she borrowed her roommate's car. Other times it was the train. She always took the last train back to Quincy.

"One day when I had to work she and Donna spent the day at the beach. That night when she came over she gave me a picture of herself in a bathing suit with a sexy pose.

"I had never bothered to learn to drive. One night I decided it was about time I learned to drive and get a car. I said to her if we were going to be married and maybe have a family, I'd need one. The next afternoon she borrowed Donna's car and taught me how to drive. That was a disaster. Every hill we came to I stalled it. One time I had five cars backed up behind us when we started up the hill. I rolled back when I let the clutch out. The guy behind leaned on his horn. I rolled back into his car. I got out of the car to say I'm sorry. I forgot to set the brake, so when he tried to back his car up to go around me our car stayed right on the front of his car. It was like they were attached. Then he rolled back into the car behind him trying to get away from our car. It was a mess. Betty laughed so hard. She slid into the driver's seat and pulled our car away. The other cars went around us. When I walked up to get back in the car she'd pull it forward a few more feet then stop. I'd walk up again and she'd pull forward again. When I finally got in the car she was laughing so hard that tears were running down her face. I guess it was funny.

"That evening, back at my house, Jack called. He asked her to meet with him. He said he just wanted to lay it to rest. She agreed.

"When she hung up I said she had no business with him anymore. She said I was right, but if she didn't tell Jack to stop, to remind him that it was all over he would always bother us. She asked me to trust her and be patient while she talked to him. I told her that anything she wanted to say to Jack she could say it in front of me there at the house. She agreed. She called Jack back and he drove to the house. They stood out on the porch. I stood in the doorway. She told him that she didn't want him to call her anymore. She wanted him to stop telling people that they were still engaged. It was over.

"Jack never even looked at me. He didn't say anything. He stood there with a blank look on his face.

"When she was done Jack spoke. 'You love me Betty not him. You're confused. Think about it, who's going to give you a better life, me or some guy that only went as far as the eighth grade in school and directs traffic. His job will be gone in a few years. Then what will you do. Think about it Betty.' With that he drove away.

"That evening I left to go to work. Betty said she was going to stay a little longer and maybe take a nap on the couch. When I got back the next morning she was gone like usual. She left me a note saying that she loved me. She didn't care what Jack said, she knew who she wanted. She thanked me for being patient with her. She wrote that she trusted me. She said I gave her some comfort that no one else could. In the note she left she said that she wanted to get married as soon as we could. She said she was going to stay Friday night and after Friday she was never going to leave again. She was going to start moving some of her stuff to my house over the next couple days. She said she wanted to be married Saturday.

"I had no family to include in the wedding. I got no brothers or sisters. My parents were dead. I asked one of the guys I work with to stand up for me. He said he would. I cleaned the house and I cleared out some space in the bedroom. She came over with a trunk full of stuff. I carried it upstairs and she went back to get more.

"I worked nights so I usually took a nap in the middle of the day. I woke up later that afternoon when Donna knocked at my door. She wanted to know if I had seen Betty that day. I told her she had come by earlier, but she hadn't been back.

"Donna said, 'She hasn't been home and all her stuff is gone. All she left was note saying, 'Not to worry, I'm okay.'"

"I told her, 'I've got a trunk of hers upstairs.'

"We went upstairs and Donna looked through it. She said that wasn't it. Most of the stuff in the trunk Betty had been setting aside for a few weeks.

"Donna knew we were supposed to be getting married. Betty had told her, but she wasn't going to get all her stuff at once.

"That was it. She was gone." Harold stopped talking. The story was done. We were at the Scituate station, rather, what was left of it. Harold said, "One point one five miles to go."

"That's it, Harold? She fell off the face of the earth and a hundred years later you're pissing on her husband's grave. Come on. What happened?"

Nothing, again total silence from him until we crossed over a road, I heard him draw a breath like he was going to speak, but all he said was, "Used to come down to Scituate to go fishing. Used to be a wye here. They upgraded the whole Greenbush terminal just before they shut it down." He paused then added, "Never made any sense to me."

"How come you never went with anyone else?"

"Time just slipped away. Wasn't really ever interested in anyone else." He rubbed his chest again and winced. He popped another one of his nitro tablets. Then he pulled a bracelet out of his pocket. "This is from the day Betty and me went to Paragon Park. I won her a little doll at one of the games there. She loved it and said she wanted to win something for me. At the ring toss we stood there for an hour and she never got the ring on the bottle. Finally the barker said, 'look lady pick whatever you want.' She went through every prize there. When she found the one she wanted she told me to close my eyes. She put this bracelet on my wrist. Before it wore away it used to say, Forever Yours."

He turned it in his hands and added, "I felt funny about wearing it and took it off. But I've always had it with me."

The landscape in front of us was transitioning from forest to marshland. The bed before us still lay flat and even with the smooth path. I could smell the salt from the ocean in the air. It had gotten cooler.

We crossed the road at Greenbush. The terrain showed the remains of the small railyard there. Under some of the bushes lay some old ties and ballast stone littered the area. I could see where the land had been sculpted for the wye that had been there.

I asked, "Do you want to walk out as far as we can on the marsh?" He nodded.

The tracks below there had been pulled up years before service to Greenbush was abandoned. The trees were thick, but unlike the stretch through Weymouth, walkable. The bed curved out on the marsh. We saw a hunter waiting in the brush. At the first tributary we stopped, the rail bed behind us. It lay across the water before us, visible there too. The remains of bridge pilings lay in the mud in front of us; more marshland then the North River. Across the marsh the hills rose up in Marshfield. Trees resumed the landscape. To the east a berm and dunes broke low to a view of the ocean. The sky was blue; a late in the day and early in autumn brilliant cerulean blue. To the west trees filled in the area to the river and marsh and it disappeared into the New England woods. It was low tide. I could see mussels in the mud of the water. Cool wind danced the grass and I was glad. Glad I had made this walk. I didn't hate New England or Massachusetts or the South Shore or Weymouth anymore. I was glad Harold had come with me, too.

Harold looked around the area too. I said to him, "Most people would think we were kinda' odd to take a walk like this."

He shrugged.

We turned back to the road. At the Whistlestop coffee shop we found some-one willing to give us a ride back to Weymouth, for twenty-five dollars.

When we got to Harold's house he said, "Last night was the first time I've stayed away from home, overnight, in over fifty years except for the hospital, and I made sure I was out of there the next day." He walked through the house as though he was looking to see if everything was as he left it. It was.

"I got to get going." I shuffled toward the door. "Do you need anything before I leave?"

"I'll pay you for copies of your photographs."

"Don't worry about it. I'll cover it."

"No. I won't be beholding to any man." He handed me ten more silver dollars.

It was pointless for me to argue. "Okay. I'll mail them to you." I walked over to him and offered my hand.

He had poured himself a drink and was at his desk. He pulled out his note pad and marked the date and the time we returned. He looked at me and said, "Thanks boy."

I retracted my hand and made a stiff arm, flip-of-the-wrist wave and turned to the door. When I reached the door Harold said, "She came by here once, after she moved back from California. Said she was sorry. Said she loved me, but a girl had to do what a girl had to do." He turned back to his notepad and scratched his pencil on it. As I shut the door behind me I saw him sitting there, his head tipped slightly forward. The setting sunlight, diluted by the grimy window filled Harold's house with feeble light that dissolved to nothing quickly.

I walked to Weymouth Landing, took the bus back to Quincy, and the Red Line down to Braintree. I found a room at one of the motels off the freeway there. Early the next morning I was on my way back to California.

CHAPTER 24

▼

EDGEWATER 7-3620 CALLING

My life resumed exactly where I left it; work and another relationship malfunction carried on as though nothing had changed. But something had indeed changed. From the moment I landed back in California, Weymouth, Greenbush, and the South Shore pulled at me. Every night I looked through my Greenbush photo album. I subscribed to The Patriot Ledger online and registered with the construction company doing the restoration work to receive emails on the status of the Greenbush restoration project.

I mailed Harold the photos and sent him a Christmas card that year. Danny, too. But, in mid-January my annual card to Harold came back, undeliverable. I wasn't an obituary reader. If there was an announcement in the online Ledger, I missed it, but Harold being Harold meant there probably wasn't one anyway. Who would have cared enough to alert the newspaper? I tried to think about Harold and what I would have said at a funeral service, but I couldn't stay concentrated. I forgot all about him. The likely scenario would be, when I pulled out my Christmas card list next year I'd remember he's dead and I'd put a line through his name.

However, Harold's ghost caught up to me in February. I received a certified letter from the Probate Court in Norfolk County, Massachusetts. The letter said that Harold had died and my name was found on some recently written papers in his house. Since they found no indication of him having family and no other recent reference to anyone else in Harold's estate, would I be the executor. I called the number they provided and agreed.

A moment of profound sadness moved through me when I reread the line, Harold Asher had died. It passed quickly. I think I should have felt more. I'd go by his grave and pay my respects.

I wrote Danny and told him I'd be in Weymouth again. I promised we'd meet for a beer when I got there. We did and he had me over for dinner several times. I met his wife and kids. They were an energetic and talkative family. I could have been there every night if I hadn't sought some quiet time. The last two times I had dinner there, a woman his wife worked with was there, too. We were left alone several times throughout the evening, undoubtedly to get acquainted. She said she always wanted to visit California. I offered to be a tour guide for her. Before I knew it she was coming for a visit in April.

Harold wasn't family, so I couldn't use the family leave laws or bereavement time. I had to use two weeks vacation to wrap up Harold's affairs.

In the depths of February in New England it was undoubtedly going to be cold. When I left California to conclude Harold's affairs I took the heaviest coat I had. The only thing that survived my post-Navy purge was my pea coat. As I pulled it out of a box in my storage unit, I realized I used fire to try and obliterate the first half of my life for no good reason.

At times, after returning from my Greenbush walk, I regretted burning my photos of Weymouth and those of my friends. I rued torching the trinkets and cards that are the heartbeats of a life lived. It would be good, I felt, to have saved a note from Kelli or a letter from an old girlfriend. I would treasure a token from the house I grew up in. Damn my bitterness. I discovered nothing on my walk that warranted the level of hostility I felt towards all things Weymouth for all those years.

At first, when I returned to Weymouth, I didn't stay at Harold's. I rented a car and stayed in Braintree again. However, after the third night I cancelled my reservation and stayed at Harold's. The first night there I fired up his potbelly stove. The area ten feet around it stayed warm, the rest of the house was cold and drafty, like a barn. It smelled of wood flooring, dirt cellar, and a hundred years of cheap pipe tobacco embedded into the wood.

I needed to check in with work. When I went to plug in my laptop to go online to read my email I discovered Harold's phone was an old rotary dial wall-mount with the phone number on the center of the dial rotor. It read, EDGEWATER 7-3620. I wondered if the phone line could handle my G4 laptop. The first problem was connecting the computer. The phone had one of the old four-prong plugs, not a modern clip-in plug. I dismantled the old plug and cut the snap-in plug of my phone cord. I tried different combinations of the wires until I heard a dial-tone through my computer. I hoped the line wouldn't explode or cause my computer to implode. I had visions of crashing the entire phone system on the South Shore. However, it served my dial-up purpose, slowly.

The slow-speed connection hastened my fatigue. When I was done with work I found a couple of old blankets, curled up on the couch, and failed to fall asleep. Sometime around three in the morning I began going through Harold's stuff. It was as though I was in another lifetime as I went through his house.

First off I had to deal with all the newspapers he kept all those years. They were everywhere. His cellar, too, was packed with newspapers. The top of the pile began with the year 1947. I glanced at the headlines, then read the entire paper. The advertising was fascinating. It all seemed very contemporary, but packaged in a different way. Initially I was going to throw them all away, but by the time I was done I had read every paper in house, beginning in 1923 and ending the day before Harold died. I couldn't throw them away. I made arrangements to donate them to the library.

There was a box hidden behind one stack of papers. It was his memento box, an old wooden Cliquot Club soda case, lined with wax paper. In it were, two gold coins, three bullets, dozens of postcards from around the world; Paris, Miami, Rio de Janeiro, Rome, Hong Kong, Los Angeles, and so on, but none addressed to him. The notes on the back varied in their penmanship, gender, and subject. I found his baptism certificate, eighth grade diploma, a few sepia prints of seashore and mountains with people smiling at the camera, a few more pictures of Greenbush, a photo of himself in front of his crossing guard shack, a picture of me raking his lawn, and a photo of a boy and a girl. Written on the back was, "Me and Mary." Sister? Cousin? Mother? No, too young. Neighbor? Girlfriend? There would be no solution to the mystery girl.

The box held his railroad retirement entitlement papers, a copy of tax bills, the deed to the house, eight wallets, and two letters from Betty. The oldest note was wrapped around the photo of Betty in a bathing suit, smiling coyly with a sexy pose.

It read,

My darling Harold,

I have never been as happy as I am now with you. This mess with Jack is over. Thank you for being patient with me. I know this hasn't been easy for you. I'm sorry. But now it is done.

When I first met you I was so troubled by what was going on with Moe and Jack I didn't notice how handsome and how dashing you were. When we met again in Hingham that evening I felt your kindness, but again I was lost in my troubles. Then that night in Cohasset you were a perfect gentleman. You showed me that there are kind, honorable, decent men in the world. I thought about you all the next day. Because you showed me decency that night I decided to end the engagement. I just didn't know how or when I would do it. I'm sorry it took me as long as it did. But now you have made me the happiest woman alive. All day at work I think of you. I do so look forward to seeing you.

The things a woman wants are not like what men want nor are they what men think we want. Your comfort, your patience, and your sense of honor are what I see, they are what I need for the rest of my life, and what I love most of all in you.

Friday, when I come over I want to stay Friday night. Will you have me my darling? I want to stay Friday and never leave again. Can I stay and never have to leave again? My darling could we be married on Saturday?

I love you.

Friday begins forever.

Love,

Betty

The second letter was written in 1966.

Dear Harold,

It was good to see you earlier today. I wish we could have spoken longer, but I saw how hurt and angry you were. I'm sorry I didn't write you years ago, but right after Jack and I got to California we started a family, Jack Jr. and Stella.

I want you to know you will always have a very special place in my heart, but I made my life as Jack's wife.

I owe you an explanation. I won't upset you with all the detail, but when I went home after spending the day with you all those years ago, Jack was at my apartment. We talked and he promised and I cried, then in a whirl-wind we were on the train to Chicago then an aero-plane to Los Angeles. I wanted to call you or write, but time slipped away then it seemed foolish and maybe hurtful to contact you. I'm sorry. I hope you will forgive me.

We may be moving back to South Shore, Jack's looking to see if he can start his own business.

My best wishes for you always, Harold.

With warmest regards,

Betty

I didn't care for Betty after I read her letters. Her actions hit a little too close to my own heart.

Harold was an unmitigated broken-hearted hermit, and I was but a few years from the same destiny.

His old house creaked and groaned with every gust and step I took. The noises were sometimes eerie. The cellar however seemed free of settling sounds, but when I set Harold's keepsake box down and put the cover back on it a plangent sound groaned from the beams. It sounded like an old man stifling a cry, sniffing, then sighing, and the breath faltering during the exhale.

Every place I looked in his house there was something; old pens with the ink hard and dried up, phone books, his logs, tools, an old suit, twenty unopened packages of long underwear, fuses, matches, washers, jars of various nuts and bolts, more unopened boxes; a new (in 1966) television, typewriter, a cot, a fedora and a derby hat, never worn.

I sold as much of his stuff as I could to an antique shop, donated numerous things to Goodwill, and threw almost everything else away. I kept the photo of Harold in front of his guard shack, one of his old hats, and the bell he rang at Tufts Crossing.

I burned the letters from Betty.

Four days before I was to fly back to California the phone company sent a lineman out to the house to rework the phone line. He told me that Harold and the house next door shared the last party-line in Massachusetts. The phone to Harold's house would be turned off the day I left, but he had to drop a new line to the house and the house next to door to sever the party-line. A realtor would make arrangements to take care of the lawn and low-level upkeep while she tried to sell the place. She was not optimistic about it selling fast; there just so much that had to be done to fix it up and make it contemporary. Mass Electric would turn off the electricity the day I departed.

By the middle of the afternoon I was restless. It was cold, but I went for a walk anyway. I grabbed my pea coat, locked the door and started walking. I was out of my usual workout routine. If I spent some energy maybe I'd get over the restlessness. I thought.

CHAPTER 25

▼

BABY LOTION AND RUBBING ALCOHOL

During my first life in Weymouth, hitchhiking was popular. In the paper, then, there seemed to be a lot of stories about hitchhikers. They traveled around the country. I saw them in Weymouth, too, but the hitchhikers I read about had a mystique unlike the hitchhikers I saw around town. The open-road hitchhikers had an allure of blithe freedom, coming and going on the whim of generous drivers and truckers. They were intriguing.

Their hitchhiking seemed very different than the hitchhiking I did around the South Shore. Mine was very practical. I was too young for a car and too old to want my father shuttling me everywhere.

There were occasional stories in the news of hitchhikers killing or getting killed, but those stories were hundreds of miles away in places like New York, Florida, California, Texas, and Colorado. Drugs were involved. There was a hitchhiking risk to women, too, that I didn't understand. When I hitchhiked around Weymouth, it never felt like a risky thing to do nor did it feel particularly carefree or liberating.

Most of the hitchhikers I saw were kids like me, maybe a little older, looking to get around town. Once in while I saw someone with a beard, backpack, a bandanna tied around his head, and a leather vest with fringes. I'd wonder if he was one of the carefree hitchhikers I read about. Sometimes I'd watch him until he got a ride. He'd run up to the stopped car, open the door, talk to the driver, and get in. In a moment they'd be gone. A few times I saw the hitchhiker step back from the car and wave as it drove away. He'd throw his backpack on his back and continue walking, turning around to face every approaching car with his thumb skyward.

He was walking along Route Fifty-Three. I was riding my bike past him when he spoke, "Hey young brother, where can I get some nourishment in this groovy village you have here."

I stopped several yards beyond and said, "There's a Friendly's restaurant up the road a mile or so."

"Right on."

He seemed so cool, so laid back. I rode my bike alongside as he walked toward the restaurant. We talked. He was from Kansas heading toward New Hampshire. He wanted to commune with Mother Earth in the White Mountains. He had been on the road for two weeks. He had just left Cape Cod.

He had peace symbols sewn into his clothing everywhere; on his cowboy hat, as patches on the torn knees of his dungarees, and on his backpack. When he lowered his backpack I saw, embroidered into his dungaree coat, another peace symbol, the words, Vietnam, if you haven't been there, shut the fuck up, and another patch of a three-leaved plant.

He smelled.

As we moved past the Weymouth Shopping Plaza he noticed the undeveloped swath of land between the plaza and the Mass Electric building. He turned into the woods there. I followed him. Under the high-tension lines he quickly rolled up a joint and offered me a hit.

That was frightening. I had never seen a marijuana cigarette before, (that's what the principal at school called them), but from the posters and photos at school I knew what it was. It was a drug, and drugs were bad. Evil. People did crazy things when they were high. They killed or got killed.

I said, "No." and turned my bike to ride away.

"Relax man, it's Mary Jane. Refer, you know. It's cool."

I didn't want to appear uncool and let him know that I didn't know about things like refer. I was confused. I didn't want to stay, but I didn't push the pedal forward to leave either.

He said, "It's not one of those kind of drugs that make people get all freaked out. It just gives you a mellow buzz."

Still I didn't leave, but I stayed several feet away from him. He took a few puffs then put it away. He didn't seem crazy. The only change I noticed was that he seemed to sway as he walked.

When we got to the restaurant, he said thanks and gave me a cool handshake with a little Flip Wilson effect. Not the traditional grabbing palm shake, but the one where you interlocked thumbs and grabbed the outside of each others hand. He said, "Give me some skin."

I didn't know what he meant.

He showed me, and then said, "Peace brother. Life is beautiful."

The last time I hitchhiked was home from a Quincy bowling alley late one Saturday morning.

My father dropped me off earlier in the day. I knew I could walk home or catch a ride home with someone there or take the bus. I could hitchhike home, too. I ended up hitchhiking that Saturday because I didn't save enough money for bus fare.

I had walked about halfway home when, in front of the Stop & Shop, a car stopped. I hopped in, and greeted the driver.

"Where you going?"

"East Weymouth."

The driver said, "That' where I'm headed, too."

"Can you drop me off at Legion Field?"

"Sure. Be glad to." The light changed to green. "Where you coming from?"

"Bowling in Quincy."

"Hard to get around when you're a kid, huh."

"Yeah. My bike has a flat and my father's out doing errands."

"How far have you walked?"

"From the Square."

"Why didn't you take the bus?"

"I spent all my money. I've walked it before. It's not hard."

"Wow. I'm impressed. That's got to be four or five miles. I wish I was in good enough shape to walk that far. You look like you're in good shape. Are you an athlete in school?"

"Yeah. Baseball. This is an easy walk. I'm more than halfway home when I cross the Fore River Bridge."

"It keeps you in good shape. Your girlfriend must really like all your walking."

"I don't have a girlfriend."

"How come? A handsome, strong guy like you! Bet you just can't decide which one you want to go out with."

"There's a girl I like."

"Glad to hear that."

We drove past the turn down Evans Street. I said, "You could have turned there."

"I know, but I want to stop at the store up there. I'm helping a friend of mine move some stuff and he wanted me to pick-up a couple Cokes. Hang on one minute and I'll get you home. You want a Coke?"

"Sure. Thanks."

"Wait for me."

The driver got out of the car and hit the power lock. At once all the doors were sealed. He bought three Cokes, a bag of chips, and the clerk handed him one of the magazines they kept behind the counter. He came out of the store, pulled the bag completely over the magazine cover and unlocked his door. He looked around the parking lot, repositioned his package in his arm, and slid into the car.

"Here you go." He reached over and set the bag on the passenger side floor between my feet. The bag fell open and a Playboy cover posed on the floor. As he drew his hand back it brushed my leg.

"Oops. Sorry. Go ahead and grab a Coke."

I stared at the Playboy. I wondered what the guy was doing. Wasn't it illegal or something to have this magazine?

He must have seen me staring at the cover. "Go ahead you can look at it if you want. You've seen tit before, haven't you?"

"Oh yeah. Lots." I set the magazine in my lap and slowly opened it. As the pages unfurled near the centerfold I saw a woman standing there, holding a sheet across half her body. One of her breasts and half of her pubic hair showed. I held the magazine tight to my thighs so the driver wouldn't see the massive boner I suddenly had.

"You said you spent all your money when I picked you up."

I unfolded the centerfold by now, "Yes. I only had enough for three strings and a candy bar."

"Do you want to make some money? We need some help moving. We'll give you ten bucks and I'll drive you home right after that."

"Sure."

I stared at the model. The only centerfolds I had seen prior to that were tattered and battered ones we had found in the woods. This one was so clean and crisp and shiny. I held it up.

"Be careful with that. I could get in trouble if someone sees you looking at that."

I carefully folded the centerfold back together then flipped back through the other pictures preceding the centerfold. In one photo I saw her from behind, her bottom barely concealed by a sheer wrap. In another photo her hand was very high up on the inside of her thigh. In that photo I could just see the folds and crevasses of her vagina through her neat pubic hair.

"What's your name?"

"Marty."

"Tell you what, Marty. Since your enjoying that magazine so much, I'll give it to you if you help. And I'll still give you the ten bucks. Could you move the magazine please? I want to grab a Coke."

I moved the magazine out of his way. The erection I had pushed mightily against my dungarees. It hurt.

The driver concentrated on the road while he reached for his Coke. This time, the driver brushed his hands higher across my thigh on his way to the bag. The action rustled my dungarees. It distracted me for a moment, then I set the Playboy back on my lap and paged deeper into the magazine.

We drove down Commercial Street toward Jackson Square.

"Should we check in with your folks first to make sure it's okay that you work with me."

There seemed something indistinctly wrong about looking at the magazine, being able to keep the magazine, being with the guy who bought it, and going home to ask for permission to work with the guy who bought it. It seemed as though somehow I might get caught doing a nasty thing. But I didn't want to jeopardize losing the magazine or the money.

"No. It'll be okay. I just have to go right home afterwards."

"Won't they be looking for you?"

"No. Dad's probably still doing errands. I don't have a mother anymore."

"Do you have any brothers or sisters or uncles or anyone else who maybe I could hire if we need more help?"

"Yes. I've got two brothers, but they wouldn't be interested."

"Okay. Well, it'll be the three of us then. We're almost there." He drove out of Jackson Square on High Street toward Hingham and turned into one of the driveways there. We weren't too far from my friend Kelli's house.

The house was one of the boring old ones around that part of town, built in the twenties. It was an off-yellow color, had a gravel driveway, and the garage was separated from the house at the end of the driveway. The driver's car matched the house, boring, a Chevy, Nova, four door, off-yellow in color, too.

He stepped out of the car and turned to the steps leading up to the side door. I moved slowly getting out of the car waiting for my erection to subside. I moved slowly around the car to give it a chance to fully abate. The driver waited at the top of the stairs watching while I turned the corner around the car. He looked up and down the driveway. I looked around. The yard was secluded. Trees and bushes grown up all around each side of the lot and hedges hid everything but the driveway itself.

The tumblers on the lock made a very solid, metallic echo when he unlocked the door. It sounded almost as though there was too much wood surrounding the door and a peculiar sound of solid metal and steel. He turned and looked at me and said something about the boxes and how much of an aggravation it is to move. He swung the door open and held it for me. When I passed close to him at the doorway I noticed he smelled like a mixture of rubbing alcohol and baby lotion. He was pasty white with porkchop sideburns and thick black horn-rimmed glasses.

He locked the door behind him. "We are working in the cellar. I don't want anyone walking in here and taking my stuff. You've heard about the burglars in the area, haven't you?"

"Yeah sure." I hadn't heard anything about that. I knew what thievery and burglary were, but it hadn't happen to me or anyone I knew, so crime was still somewhat of a mystery.

"Let's go down cellar and get to work." He opened the door and let me go through first. "Bob. I've got some help."

There was no response. "Bob," he said again. "I wonder if he went out to get something to eat. Let's go ahead and we'll do the heavy stuff when he comes back."

The stairway was steep. I felt the driver right up against my back as we walked down the stairs. It was dark. At one point he was so close behind he almost knocked me off balance. At the bottom of the stairs the driver reached past me and pulled the string to turn on a single bare light bulb.

I turned and looked around. There were stacks of magazines, a chair, and a lamp next to the furnace oil tank. It had the musty smell of old cellars. A pall of rubbing alcohol and baby lotion hung in the air. Beside the oil tank I saw dozens of cap-less bottles of rubbing alcohol and baby lotion lying on the floor.

"What do we have to move?"

"All this stuff. Do you want to make more money?"

"Sure."

"Bob will give you twenty bucks if he can put his hands down your pants."

Something clutched me around my chest. It felt like the same thing I felt at my mother's funeral. I couldn't avoid the feeling. I couldn't break free of it either. It was like the wind was knocked out of me and instead of the reassuring breath that follows a few moments later, the feeling that came was like the terror of almost drowning, like the time I almost drowned in Whitman Pond.

We were wrestling in the pond. We were throwing each other into the water, after an hour of this I got winded. I was thrown in one more time. As I was swimming back to surface, someone swam up under me, grabbed me, and pulled me back down. I struggled for the surface, I could see the bottom of the ripples on the surface and he still held me back and pulled down. I screamed and took in a lungful of water. I kicked viciously at my friend holding me back. I knew he was only playing, but he didn't know I was dying. I struggled and struggled and struggled and finally, somehow, he figured out I was in trouble and let me go. I broke the surface coughing and gasping. I was exhausted. My other friends dragged me to shore and I collapsed. The friend who held me under the water came up to me to see if I was okay. I wanted to punch him, but I didn't have any strength.

Drowning, that's how I felt the whole time I was in the cellar.

There was something inherently wrong with what he was asking, but I didn't know exactly what it was. I shook my head. I said, "No. I want to go home now."

"Wait a minute." He was instantly angry. "I buy you a Coke, let you look at my magazine. I offer to give it to you and some money if you help my friend and me and now you say no? I think you owe me."

Abruptly he spoke gently, "Bob, he's willing to pay you. It won't hurt." He stepped toward me.

"No." I tried to go around him to move back to the stairs, but he was blocking me at the bottom of the stairs.

He turned his palms outward toward me. Then rested his hands on my shoulders. "There's nothing wrong with it, it feels good. You know. You've jerked off. It feels like that."

"No." I started sniffling. I wanted to cry. I wanted my father or brother or any one of my friends to open the door at the top of the stairs right then. It stayed closed and dark.

"Bob will be pissed off if you don't help us. Now he may not give you any money at all and still put his hands down your pants." The driver pushed his hands down on my shoulders. It made my knees buckle from the unexpected pressure. I tipped off balance.

"Let me go. I can be gone before he even comes home."

"Too late. I heard his car."

Then I started crying.

The driver slapped me across the face. "Don't you cry, you fucking baby." Gentle again, he added, "We're friends now, so I'll keep Bob from you. I'll give you the money and Bob won't touch you. But you can't say anything to anyone. Okay?"

"Thanks." This guy was my savior and would keep Bob away from me.

"Come over here and calm down." The driver took my hand and led me over to the oil tank. He told me to sit down in the chair and stroked my head. "You got a dog?"

"Yes. A collie."

"Tell me where you live so I can take you home."

"I live near town hall."

"Okay. We'll get going in a minute. I won't let Bob near you, but I want you to put your hands down my pants."

I pushed as far back into the chair as I could. "No. Please let me go home."

He hit me in the face again; two slaps and one pulled punch. "You do what I tell you or I will find your home near Legion Field and the town hall. I'll tell your father about you looking at my Playboy. I'll tell him how you were hitchhiking. And if you tell him or anyone anything about what happened here I'll kill your fucking dog."

The driver undid his belt and said, "Here's what you're going to do."

I don't know how long I was there. I remember hearing the train horn. It was moving down the tracks toward Hingham. That was unusual for the train to be running on Saturday. I heard the horn first as it crossed Green Street. I listened and I listened and I strained to listen and finally I heard it cross Unicorn Avenue. Then, five minutes later I heard the double-crossing whistle as it crossed the two crossings near the dump and the East Weymouth station. It was very close. If I could get out of the house I could run and hop it.

It was after dark when I got home. I never heard the train return from Hingham that day. I don't how I got to the Hidden Village in South Weymouth, either; nor do I remember anything else.

CHAPTER 26

▼

THE END

The weathermen were ecstatic; Southern New England and the South Shore in particular was ground zero for a very powerful, late season storm. In the course of 24 hours eastern Massachusetts was to experience sun, rain, sleet, snow, clearing in the evening, then biting cold sweeping down from Hudson Bay. I finished some work on the computer and emailed the info to work. I walked to the supermarket as the rain transitioned to sleet and home again as the sleet went to snow.

I think my restlessness that day was due to the fact that I had been thinking of Kelli and all that happened with her. Late in the evening I left my house, again, and went for another walk. I could see the line in the sky where the clouds ended and the stars shined. The cold front was already pushing the last of the cloud cover away. As soon as it left the temperature was to drop more than 25 degrees overnight.

The cold this night would not bother me. My pea coat would keep me warm. But something else bothered me. I hadn't walked by Kelli's house on my pilgrimage a few months earlier. I decided to walk to her house that night, but in Jackson Square, where I was supposed to turn left to go to her house, I went straight and directly to the house where I'd seen Kelli's old boss kill Todd. As awful as that was, something else about that place gnawed at me. I stepped into the yard. The bare shrubbery was high. In the summer much of the perimeter of the house would be concealed. In winter the bare branches still wove a tight cloak. My gut was churning and it wasn't because I was trespassing. There was a lump in my throat that almost choked me. And, in spite of how dry my mouth was, I was spitting. Nothing came out, but I couldn't stop.

A light was on upstairs and the flicker of a TV broke the dark of the downstairs windows. I pressed myself into the shade of brush. It was all too familiar. A light came on in the kitchen and an old man shuffled into view. It was Mr. Wertz, Kelli's horror, and the driver of the car the last time I hitchhiked, my horror. They were both the same person. At that moment I was overwhelmed with fear. It was like the front end of a hollow-point bullet hit me; rather than traveling a precise path, it widened and tore apart everything in its way, sending shock waves through my whole body. I wanted to run from there, get out of Weymouth, and go to something warm and familiar in California or anywhere. Then the back of the bullet followed, smooth and exact, but leaching toxins, I became furious. I wanted to level this whole part of Weymouth.

On the other side of the window Mr. Wertz popped a pill or two in his mouth and washed them down with a glass of water. Like 100 million other Americans at bedtime, he took his pills and toddled back to the TV room, an old man and his nighttime ablution ritual, an old man who raped one girl, did God knows what to one boy, and fucked up both their lives.

I moved around the garage and to the back of the house to the exact spot I stood years earlier when he bashed Todd's head in. This time I stepped forward and tried the cellar door. It was locked. I knew I could muscle the door open, but I didn't know what I was going to do once I got in. A terrible feeling of capitulation smothered me.

I wanted to talk to someone. I wanted to ask anyone, "What I should do now." But nothing came; nothing but the wind, a car packing the snow as it drove past, and the bitter cold that held no sound, but, strangely, amplified everything.

There were no clear thoughts. I moved through surrender, nausea, an incredible tightening of every muscle in my body, fear, fatigue, and impotence. Impotence that echoed in my head, saying, I was unmanly, unable, pathetic, and undeserving. I sat in the snow while all of this moved through me. I was very tired. I could have easily fallen asleep when I saw the light in the cellar come on. He had come downstairs and settled into the chair he kept in the cellar. I saw him open a box and pull out a handful of index cards. I also saw that one of the basement windows was covered with cardboard.

Maybe I could show some strength and do something, but I couldn't open the window while he sat there. I'd end up right in front of him. I was terrified being in the same state with him. I would be more so if I were within twenty feet of him. That cellar was a dungeon.

Why was I so weak around this guy? I wanted to and I could confront him, as long as he didn't come near me. I was half his age and he was undoubtedly in bad shape. There was no reason for me to fear any physical action from him. But I was scared to paralysis. I was taking breaths and reminding myself to exhale slowly. I'd look at him and feel apoplectic.

He went to pack his pipe and discovered he had no tobacco. He left the light on and went upstairs. I dug for every bit of fortitude I had, and imagined myself having more than I did. I put my arm though the cardboard, unlocked the window, climbed into that slaughterhouse, set the window and cardboard back like it was, and hid in the dark under the basement staircase.

The cellar smelled of rubbing alcohol and baby lotion, still. My legs started shaking, my mouth went more dry. I stifled my choking sounds. Under the staircase I recognized the brown shape and coloring of old photographic chemical bottles. I saw an enlarger and other darkroom supplies stowed under the stairs. The guy at one time had been a photo hobbyist.

I heard the door open and close and the dreadful click of the latch on the cellar door. He walked down the stairs with uncertainty. He'd place one foot on a step then, rather than the other going all the way to the next step, he set both feet on the same step again. All of a sudden I had an image in my head of knee or hip surgery on an elderly person. He was moving how someone with a sore or untrustworthy joint moved. He came into view and shuffled to the chair. He was old and nasty, pudgy and pasty. He didn't have a grandfatherly or avuncular manner. Just an old guy with white hair, gelled into place, thick plastic rim glasses, a turtleneck, a velour bathrobe, and one of those portable oxygen tanks with a hose running to his nose. He sat down, turned on a space-heater and picked up the box. What I thought, from outside of the window, were index cards were actually photographs.

Kelli had said they had taken a picture of her. It couldn't be. The old creep couldn't be strolling down memory lane by looking at pictures of his victims. He put one photograph down and reached for the baby lotion. He put the lotion in his hands then slid his hand under his robe.

I felt like I was going to throw up. I lowered myself to the floor and turned away. Eventually I turned my head back toward him. He had set the photo aside and was pouring rubbing alcohol over his hands. He pulled a couple more photos out of the box, studied them for a minute then put them back. He closed up the box and set it on a shelf near his workbench. He shuffled his way back upstairs. I heard the TV come on.

I left my hiding spot and made my way over to the box. By the power indicator light on a plug strip I looked into the box. There were ten photos and dozens of cut outs from magazines of mostly young boys and a few girls naked or involved in some sex act. I recognized Kelli, and then I saw myself.

It was more than I could handle. As upset as I was with tears running down my face I was rage-filled also. I didn't care if he found me there or not; in fact I wanted him in the cellar so I could kill. He must have heard my shuffling, the sound from the television cut out abruptly and I heard him hobble across the floor again. The cellar door opened and he said, "Who's there?"

I picked up a glass jar of nails and dropped it onto the cellar floor. The busting glass and tinkling nails got his attention.

"I'm going to call the police unless you get out here now."

He wasn't going to call the cops. The last thing he wanted was the police anywhere near his kiddie-porn. He clicked the light on and started down the stairs. I pushed myself into the space below the staircase again. He went over to his bench. I watched him examine the broken jar, and then he glanced toward where his box of photos was supposed to be. When he saw it wasn't there he raised a baseball bat into view. He scanned the basement and then he saw me. I was coming out of the dark to get a jump on him before he could hit me. He almost got a whack on me, but I tackled him into his chair.

"You sick bastard."

"Who are you? Get the hell out of my house."

"You photograph people you rape." I dumped the box out on the floor in front of him. "You download kiddie-porn or cut them out of some sick magazine. What kind of person are you?"

He didn't say anything.

I reached for the photo of Kelli and turned it so he could see her. "I think the Weymouth police department would love to know what you've got here." The image of Todd being beat with a baseball bat roared into me head. "I'm sure they'd like to know about Todd, too."

"You're that friend of that cunt who worked for me."

"Yes I am. Her name was Kelli."

"But I got a picture of you, too," he paused. "And you came back. Why?"

I didn't say anything. I started feeling helpless again.

"Take those pictures and leave. No one ever has to know. It would be something for that information to get out about you," he leaned forward in his chair. "But you came back. Was there something you wanted?"

I was pulling back into the dark spot under the stairwell. All the smells were making me sick and weak; the musty cellar, the baby lotion, the rubbing alcohol, his breath.

"Have you been curious all these years?" He reached out and stroked the outside of my thigh, "What is it you're curious about?"

He moved his hand around the inside of my thigh. In the briefest moment I saw Kelli in my head, out on the Back River crying. He was talking some shit about did I want to try something again. He'd show me exactly what do. I changed my stance a little. My legs weakened and moved apart slightly.

"That's a good boy." He guided me down until I was sitting on the floor, my legs crossed. He reached over and turned on his space heater. I couldn't fight him. What in the world was wrong with me that I was allowing this to happen, again? He tried to push my head toward his waist. The baby lotion and rubbing alcohol was pungent. I turned away. I couldn't stay and let that happen again, and I couldn't kill in cold blood. I couldn't do it.

"What's the matter? You know you liked it. Why else would you have come back after all these years? Come back here." He grabbed me and spun me around. He slapped me across the face and got off a full strength punch to my face.

I was able to turn away. His punch landed on my cheek instead of my nose.

He said, "You pussy. You were just a little fag then and now you're just a grown-up fag." He opened his robe and moved toward me, "Here's what you're going to do."

I leapt toward him and tackled him back into his chair. I straightened myself up and then I kicked him in the chest with everything I had. He shot back into his chair. The chair moved and almost tipped over. He was struggling very hard to breath; I think I knocked the wind out of him. I watched him struggle. He started to take short, raspy, wheezy breaths and then reached into a pocket and pulled out a little bottle, just like the one Harold had on our walk.

He dropped it. He struggled to sit up and lean over to pick it up, but it was too much exertion for him. He set back into his chair panting, his head resting against the soiled antimacassar.

I noticed the fabric on the side of his chair smoldering. He smelled it too. He tried again to sit up, but the activity and the lack of his oxygen were too much. "Help me. Please."

That's when the chair first broke into flame. He stared screaming and struggling to get up. I kicked him back again. I opened his box of photographs and took out one picture. I looked at. No one I recognized. I threw it at him. His screaming became maniacal. I held onto the photographs of Kelli and I. I poured the rest of the photos and pictures onto the fire. The old paper burst into flames immediately.

He had stopped screaming. I don't know if he was unconscious or in that moment before unconsciousness right after the pain stops. I didn't look at his face. I didn't care. I took the photo of Kelli and the one of me and dropped them into the fire. The heat started curling the photos immediately. A moment later they burst into flames.

They vanished.

The flames were spreading. I walked toward the cellar door. When I looked back the whole chair was engulfed. I saw his robe was all on fire. His hair was gone. So were his eyebrows. I knew when I opened the cellar door the flames would flash and the house would be engulfed very quickly. With the oxygen I was about to give the flames and all that old, dry, exposed wood framing in the cellar for fuel it would make this house fire spectacular. I paused long enough to hope the flames wouldn't reach the house next door.

When the door opened, the fire drew so much wind in it almost knocked me off my feet. Then it quickly stabilized and I heard a roar begin. A ball of heat pushed me out the door.

I walked down the driveway out into the street. I didn't even glance back.

By the time I was back in lower Jackson Square I could hear the siren from the fire trucks. I dropped behind the Square and onto the walkway next to the Herring Run. It was so quiet. Like always, the closer I got to Greenbush and the East Weymouth station sounds softened and wind rolled gentler. That night I had a feeling of peace. Maybe it was contentment. Maybe it was closure. With my footprints in the snow, in the cold, frigid air, and brilliant moon I walked into serendipity for a moment. When I climbed up the embankment to the passenger platform I could see the trail I left behind me. It was so peaceful there. When I titled my head up a little further I could see the glow of Mr. Wertz's burning house.

Greenbush surrounded me. The passenger platform of the former East Weymouth station supported me. The Back River flowed behind me. I could see the ice flows and snow drifts and in the middle of it the water cracked the ice and kept the river moving. I bowed me head and talked to God for the first time in years. I said, "Thank you." I turned to leave and added, "Forgive me."

I walked Greenbush all the way back to Harold's house.

According to the paper the next day the fire ended up being a three-alarm call-out. Fire trucks came from Hingham and Quincy to cover the Weymouth stations while the Weymouth firemen worked to keep the flames from spreading to the neighboring houses. The fire chief was quoted saying, "The house is a total loss. It appears as though a space-heater was knocked over and things got out of control."

Two days later I left Weymouth, again, for the last time. I thought.

A couple months later, back in California, I read online, when the demolition crew leveled the charred remains they discovered a skeleton behind a false wall in the cellar. Forensic teams were called in and a few days later they reported that the skeleton had been there at least twenty-five years. Weymouth police were going to search old missing person records and see if they could reconstruct the face to help ID the body. Reconstruction, however, might be a problem because it appeared as though there was significant impact damage to the skull.

No one new much about the man that lived there. A quiet guy, kept to himself.

In May I took a few days off from work. I told my coworkers I was resuming an old hobby. I was going take a drive and photograph old railroad stations. I headed toward the Dakotas, paying cash the whole way. I stopped in Canova, South Dakota hoping find an old railroad station I could photo. No luck. The depot there had been razed years ago. I did, however, mail a postcard I bought from a 24-hours postal vending machine in Salt Lake City, while wearing dish-washing gloves. I addressed it to the Detective Bureau, Weymouth Police Department: Weymouth, MA 02189.

It read, "To identify the body in the basement of the house that burned last January, follow the life of Todd. Sorry I don't know his last name. He dropped out of Weymouth North in 1976. I saw the owner of the house beat him to death with a baseball bat."

CHAPTER 27

▼

RE-BEGINING

In November the realtor called. "I'm sorry Mr. Roberts, I've had no luck selling the house. My husband's employer is transferring him to Arizona. I'm going to pass your name onto another agent who will continue trying to sell it. I'm sure we will find the right buyer soon."

"Go ahead and take it off the market. I'm going to head on back to Weymouth and I'll need a place to stay. I appreciate all your efforts."

"Well that's a surprise, Mr. Roberts. I'll take the sign down. Do you want me to take it off the MLS also?"

"You may as well do that, too."

"Okay. When you get back here stop by the agency and we'll get the key back to you."

I hung up then realized what I had just done and said. What in the world made me say that was my next thought. I sat on my balcony thinking about moving back to Weymouth. The more I thought about it, the more I thought, why not. I had nothing to lose in California and I had something to gain if I moved back.

The logistics wouldn't be too hard. I could transfer to the Boston office. There was a standing offer for me to work there. The company would move my stuff and I'd be allowed as much as four weeks time before I had to show up. Or I could quit all together. I could acquire Harold's house with some legal maneuvering and I had some money in savings. If I needed to I could pump gas and meet the monthly nut, taxes, and utility bills.

There was no great relief or soothing feeling. All I had to do was follow through. I emailed my boss and asked for a meeting the morning.

Weymouth, here I come.

I sold all of my belongings, including the Sentra (I needed something more substantial for those New England winters) and packed everything I wanted to bring back to Weymouth with me in the back of a new SUV. I barely filled half the rear compartment.

The phone company turned the phone back on. I asked if 337-3620 was available. It was. I scheduled the electricity and water to be turned back on, and a cord of wood and a couch delivered to the house the same day I arrived. I arrived January 20th and wondered what in the world have I done?

The next week was filled with self-doubting as I furnished the house with a bed, kitchen appliances, water heater, and space heaters. If I stayed I was going to have a hell of a lot work just to do bring the house up to code. Making it an attractive and livable place was going to take even more work.

I still couldn't answer the question, what did I hope to achieve by moving to Weymouth. The migration in the United States is away from New England and the Northeast toward the South, Southwest, and California. Why did I go the other way?

All of my nights during the first few weeks were restless. During the day I had projects I could do to make the place more livable. I walked the length of Greenbush again, had dinner with Danny's family often, and walked all over Weymouth, Braintree, Quincy, and Hingham. There was little physical change.

One night, January 29th, I was particularly restless. It was snowing. I stared out the living room window all evening. At 10:00 pm I turned the lights out and lay awake looking at a streetlight at the bottom of the hill and the triangle of light it threw down. I was mesmerized watching the large snowflakes float through the light then land on the road, already covered with snow. Traffic was almost non-existent. When a car did pass by, the snow swirled. Moments later, it resumed its steady, glorious decent. I half expected my mother to walk up behind me and say, "It's beautiful watching snow fall. Rain is vibrant, and the wind whooshing at night is exciting, but snow is peaceful." She'd pause, then tell me, "You can go out and play in it if you want. Just stay in the neighborhood." With her permission I left Harold's house at 1:27 am. I went down to the bottom of the hill and circled the triangle of light.

Out-of-doors the snowstorm wasn't frigid cold, unlike Harold's house that seemed to trap the cold. As I paced the outer perimeter of the light I was warm. Eventually I moved, exarch under the light.

Face skyward, watching the snow fall and feel it land on my face, melt, and release a tiny bit of moisture against my skin I let the thought finally come to me, I was home. I spoke it, "I am home." Once I said it out loud it was an easy acceptance. I walked onto Greenbush there and into the woods a little. I looked back at the snowy streetlight and walked back toward it.

I felt good. It felt right.

I walked to the 24-hour Dunkin' Donuts in Weymouth Landing for coffee and a couple o' fat pills at two o'clock in the morning. It was exactly what I needed.

The snowplow drivers were just leaving as I walked in. The waitress was pleasant enough. She babbled on about the snow and how she was getting tired of winter and ready for spring.

"You know what I'm going to do," she said.

Must have been a rhetorical question that I missed. Before I could say "What?" she said, "I'm gonna' catch a weekend special on one of the airlines down to Florida for some sun. I'm going to sit on the beach and have someone wait on me for a change and bring me Mai Tai's or maybe I'll drink that coconut flavored rum." She rolled her eyes up and around, furrowed her brow then nodded her head. "That's exactly what I'm going to do."

She redirected her attention toward me. "You want some more coffee, hun?"

"Sure. Thank you. What else are you going to do in Florida?"

"Nothing. Just what I said, drink rum and Cokes and taxi back and forth to the beach. I don't even think I'm going to get a motel room. Maybe I'll just sleep on the beach," she thought for minute then added, "And if that slug I live with doesn't want to come, I'm going without him."

As uninteresting as she seemed to be, I was fascinated by her and loved listening to her talk. She seemed content in her uniform, out-of-style glasses, maroon leggings, and her fantasy of getting away to Florida for a weekend. She had what I hope to gain, contentment. As I left I gave her $100 bill and said, "Here's a donation toward your weekend dash to Florida."

I went back to my house and lay back down on the couch around 3:30 and fell asleep, easily.

On the radio the next morning, the deejay's announced the school closures. Sure enough, Weymouth schools closed because of the snow. Just like thirty years earlier, it was a tremendous feeling of anticipation, then, relief when I heard school was out for the day.

It wasn't cold at all, just a beautiful eight inch deep blanket of clean, pure snow. I walked around East Weymouth again, all the way from Harold's to Jackson Square and out to the Back River again, photographing it all in black and white as I walked.

I quit my job and hired on as a consultant. I worked nights on the computer and days painting and fixing up the house and yard.

One day, in late spring, I was walking toward Hingham on High Street when a Weymouth police cruiser pulled up alongside me. There were two officers in the car, the one on the passenger side, a sergeant, got out, the other put the car in park and stayed in the car. The sergeant asked, "You walk all around town?" It was more of a statement than a question.

"Yes I do. It's good exercise."

"Are you new to the area?"

"Yes and no. I grew up here and graduated North in 1978, but I left and lived out West for a long time. I just moved back here."

"That's why I stopped. You look familiar. What's your name?"

I told him. We were about the same age. I didn't recognize him or his name.

The Sergeant said, "Your name is sort of familiar, but I can't quite place it." Then he added, "What brought you back here?"

"I'm not sure. It's home. I think I just missed it."

"Really. I bet things haven't changed much."

"There again, yes and no. Weymouth hasn't changed much, but I think I changed."

He went to get back in the car, turned around, and offered me a handshake, "Welcome back."

"Thanks."

The sergeant had stopped to talk to me in front of Wertz's former house. I asked, "What happened here?" gesturing to the cement truck and construction workers pouring a new foundation. "Someone tear a house down to build a new one?"

"There was a fire a year or so ago. A guy died in the fire and we found another body hidden in the foundation."

"No kidding?"

"His space heater tipped over."

"What's the story behind the other body?"

"That's a strange story, too. We got an anonymous note telling who he was. Best we've been able to figure out is the guy who died in the fire killed the other guy years ago."

The radio in the cruiser squawked, the sergeant listened to the call, then said, "Work beckons. Take care." He slid back into the car, the blue lights came on, and they drove off.

Spring's slide into summer in Weymouth left me lonely. Out West I had friends. A half a dozen I could call to serve whatever need I had; golf, tennis, Giants' baseball games, fishing, hiking, there was no shortage of people or things to do. My timing was not always terrific. All of them had kids and/or a wife. But with a little planning I could turn up someone to hang out with. At the moment, I had a dearth of friends in Weymouth. There was Danny, but, like my West coast friends, he too had familial duties. New Englanders are not any more reserved than anywhere else I've ever been in making an acquaintance. Maybe it was me that was reserved in making friends. I had many solo drives to the mountains and bike trips around the South Shore. My trips to the local bookstores yielded only books.

It was fall before I had the place in good enough shape to get through the winter without fear of an electrical fire or the roof collapsing. In October I fixed the porch, for the second time in my life.

Over the months I watched the construction company clear the trees and brush away, then the old ties and track from Greenbush. I knew it was big job, but the volume of material and scrap that passed by the small piece of Greenbush I could see, showed the work was much more involved than I thought it would be.

I rode my bicycle down to Nantasket Beach at least once a week. I checked on the progress of the Greenbush restoration project at various places on my ride. I got to know several of the construction crews. I stopped and asked them how it was going every week.

When the Army Corp of Engineers finally granted permission to cut the brush and clear the bed on the wetlands designated area near Idlewell, the fight to stop Greenbush was finally over.

I saw some peculiar heavy equipment move past my house. I went and asked one of the foreman what was going on.

He said, "The bed is so overgrown here it jammed our equipment. We had to get some bigger chippers in here."

"What's after that?"

"We'll be pulling up the last of the track and ties and cutting more brush. The plan is to get as much done to the grade and bed before winter sets in."

That was it. Greenbush as I knew it was nearly gone. Trains were expected to start rolling in two years. I thought about making one more walk down the tracks, but I wouldn't see anything I didn't already know. There were tunnels in Hingham and Braintree now, I could see the Braintree tunnel being dug from my house. They fixed some of the old bridges and put in a couple of new ones. If I walked it again, I'd probably get questioned as a trespasser, and even if I could get permission, they'd probably want to send an escort with me, have me sign a waiver, give me a visitor ID, and make me wear a hardhat. No. I'd keep Greenbush in my head and heart.

Christmas passed uneventfully. Danny had invited me to his house, but I stayed home. That was okay. My work was steady; life was good. Even my luck at finding a good parking spot was improving, and I was choosing the swifter lines in the grocery store.

I would have to work hard to unconvince myself that my life is fine as it is in Weymouth. It would have been nice to have a girlfriend. I thought about calling Jackie, but it seemed too pathetic. It was just as well that I was a single man and destined to stay that way. My track record with women was poor.

I was however, a regular at the Dunkin' Donuts in the Landing.

At one time Weymouth was something of a vacation/retreat place. Bostonians retreated to Wessegusett Beach in North Weymouth. Cottages sprang up around Weymouth's ponds. It had industry, a military presence, and an interesting character, but it has been years since anyone looked at Weymouth as anything other than a predictable, pleasant suburb. Its bland suburban face was all I saw, and hated, for years, but now the sum of its neat lawns, hormonal teenagers, soccer Moms, and commuting Dads, and the moraine, hillocks, winter storms, and summer days are the character of Weymouth I treasure. It's like the craggy face of an old man. There is a reason for each wrinkle and a story of every life lived embedded in the creases that are the face of Weymouth.

978-0-595-42338-5
0-595-42338-8

Printed in the United States
94132LV00006B/280-282/A